Politics and History in
WILLIAM GOLDING

Politics and History in WILLIAM GOLDING

THE WORLD TURNED UPSIDE DOWN

Paul Crawford

University of Missouri Press Columbia and London

University of Missouri Press, Columbia, Missouri 65201
Printed and bound in the United States of America

5 4 3 2 1 06 05 04 03 02

Cataloging-in-Publication data available from the Library of Congress
ISBN 0-8262-1416-9

♾™ This paper meets the requirements of the
American National Standard for Permanence of Paper
for Printed Library Materials, Z39.48, 1984.

Designer: Stephanie Foley
Jacket Designer: Susan Ferber
Typesetter: The Composing Room of Michigan, Inc.
Printer and Binder: The Maple-Vail Book Manufacturing Group
Typeface: Palatino

For ——————————
Rhiannon, Ruby, and Jamie

Contents

Acknowledgments

I wish to thank Andrzej Gąsiorek for his meticulous advice and for the encouragement he gave me during what became a most difficult time in my life. Yet this book would not have appeared in the first place without Derek Littlewood, who got me hooked on the fantastic and carnivalesque, or further back, Tim Boswell, whose lineage and fascination with literature deepened my own interest. For more specific advice, information, or discussion, I am grateful to Alan Sinfield, Tony Davies, R. A. Gekoski, David Maund, Brian Brown, Peter Nolan, and Faye Hammill. Thanks must also go to the British Academy for their financial support during the early stages of putting this book together.

Abbreviations

Page references in the text to William Golding's major works, including his final trilogy, are to the following Faber and Faber editions, using the abbreviations indicated. Original publication dates are given where appropriate.

DV	*Darkness Visible* (1980 edition). First published in 1979.
EE	*To the Ends of the Earth: A Sea Trilogy* (1992 edition). First published in 1991.
FF	*Free Fall* (1961 edition). First published in 1959.
HG	*The Hot Gates and Other Occasional Pieces* (1970 edition). First published in 1965.
IN	*The Inheritors* (1961 edition). First published in 1955.
LF	*Lord of the Flies* (1958 edition). First published in 1954.
MT	*A Moving Target* (1982 edition).
PM	*The Paper Men* (1985 edition). First published in 1984.
PN	*Pincher Martin* (1956 edition).
PY	*The Pyramid* (1969 edition). First published in 1967.
SP	*The Spire* (1965 edition). First published in 1964.

Politics and History in WILLIAM GOLDING

1

Introduction

The World Turned Upside Down

> The "reversible world" and the "world turned upside down" are phrases used to denote the way in which carnival inverts everyday customs, rules, and habits of the community. Hierarchies are inverted, kings become servants, boys become bishops, men dress as women and vice versa. The elements associated with the bottom part of the body (feet, knees, legs, buttocks, genitals, belly, anus) are given comic privilege over the spirit and the head. The "normal" rules of moral custom are overturned and license and indulgence become the rule: the body is granted a freedom in pleasure normally withheld from it, and obscenity of all kinds, from mild innuendo to orgiastic play and a robust revelling in mud, excrement, and all sorts of "filth," is sanctioned.
>
> —Allon White, "Hysteria and the End of Carnival: Festivity and Bourgeois Neurosis"

A PROPERLY HISTORICIZED AND POLITICIZED READING OF WILLIAM Golding's major novels is long overdue. It is overdue because a timelessness to Golding's fiction has been privileged in what Philip Redpath rather scathingly refers to as "repetitive," "derivative," and "conservative" criticism.[1] In applying categories of fable, myth, and allegory, much of this criticism has restricted itself to Golding's portrayal of the human condition sub specie aeternitatis.[2] Here we are alerted to Golding's pre-

1. Redpath, *William Golding: A Structural Reading of His Fiction*, 11, 204.

2. See Philip Drew's description of *Lord of the Flies* as a "timeless allegory" in "Second Reading" (11). Leighton Hodson maintains that although "current affairs" are "never far away from the words on the page," they should be considered "incidental to a more universal examination of human nature" (*William Golding*, 107–8). Although critics frequently touch on the contemporary relevance of Golding's novels, they

occupation with humankind's perennial battle between good and evil, its fallen nature and experience of pain, grief, and guilt. This critical focus, of course, is partly due to Golding's own reluctance to view himself as a politically engaged novelist or his novels as *littérature engagée.* His politics are often implicit rather than explicit in his fiction. Alongside responses by Maurice Cranston, D. J. Enright, Roy Fuller, Philip Larkin, John Osborne, Stephen Spender, John Wain, and Colin Wilson to *London Magazine*'s questions on commitment in May 1957, Golding contends that "current affairs are only expressions of the basic human condition where . . . [the novelist's] true business lies." This exclusion of topicality, or what Golding trivializes as "current affairs," goes hand in hand with a view of him as "politically conservative"—an appropriate tag perhaps if we view his fiction as *simply* perennial or universal—yet his work *does* engage with contemporary historical, political, and social issues in the act of diagnosing "the basic human condition." While Golding claims that historically specific "symptoms" are of less importance than an Aeschylean commitment to "looking for the root of the disease," his fiction retains what Gabriel Josipovici calls "immediate relevance" and betrays political engagement even when he might deny it. The remark of another respondent to *London Magazine*'s questions is illuminating here. Roy Fuller notes: "The 'timeless' work of art is, more than any other, a product of its time, and surely internal evidence will always 'place' it."[3] In other words, "timeless" literature is context-bound and "engagement" is inescapable.

Golding's privileging of "timelessness" at the outset of his writing career ought best to be seen as part of cold war ambivalence toward, and hence distancing from, the politically committed writing of the 1930s. As Robert Hewison notes in his book *In Anger,* increased disillusion and disenchantment with communism after the war meant that writers turned away from political commitment and retreated "back into the 'ivory tower' from which the conflicts of the 1930s had drawn them." Certainly, many of the prominent "Movement" writers during the 1950s, such as Kingsley Amis and John Wain, had maintained an ambivalent stance toward social critique. While attacking class, Movement writers preferred neutral, consensus politics or what Blake Morrison refers to as "Butskellism." As such, they "defined themselves in opposition to the 1930s gen-

---

rarely go further than the sort of remark that Virginia Tiger makes about *The Inheritors* being a "mythopoeia relevant to contemporary man" (*William Golding: The Dark Fields of Discovery,* 68).

3. Golding, "The Writer in His Age," 45; Josipovici, *The World and the Book,* 236; Fuller, "The Writer in His Age," 44.

eration both socially (lower-middle-class as against upper-middle-class) and politically (political neutralists as against political activists)." This renouncing of politics, Hewison reminds us, "is a political act, and the drift from the Left became a move to the Right." As such, in renouncing political commitment Golding leaves himself open to being labeled a "conservative" writer. Certainly, his failure to appreciate or foreground politically radical aspects of his early fiction suggests that such a label is entirely appropriate. Yet, however much Golding's political "side-taking" in his fiction dips below his own line of sight, or behind a smoke screen of universalism, it does not escape visibility in the texts themselves. As John Wain remarks, an author's political attitudes will "generally appear in his work, even if he himself is the last person to recognize them." Similarly, in *What Is Literature?* Jean-Paul Sartre dismisses the idealism behind "universal" and, indeed, "eternal" fictions: "Whether he wants to or not, and even if he has his eyes on eternal laurels, the writer is speaking to his contemporaries and brothers of his class and race." Without doubt, Golding is not the kind of "committed" writer who, according to Sartre, "knows that words are action" and "has given up the impossible dream of giving an impartial picture of Society and the human condition." Golding's "commitment" is far more diffident. He hangs on to the dream of giving an impartial "diagnosis" of the human condition while at the same time satirically engaging with contemporary "symptoms" of that condition. This divided or ambivalent form of "commitment" can be seen to be part of what W. L. Webb has described as the "combination of contradictions" at the heart of Golding's fiction that "has baffled many a thesis-hunter: that strange mixture of the practical and the mysterious, the bluff and the sensitive, comic and solemn—in fact, the whole English bundle of contradictions, raised to a high creative power."[4] It is a "combination of contradictions" that includes not simply Golding's ambivalent angle of approach to the historical referent but also his sexual politics, representations of class, and treatment of postmodernism.

James Gindin has shown that Golding's past had been intimately connected with socialist engagement, so we should not, perhaps, be at all surprised that he wrestles with contemporary issues and events and, indeed, takes a particular attitude or stance toward them in his fiction. Golding's father was a Labour Party activist, and his mother worked for woman suf-

4. Hewison, *In Anger: Culture in the Cold War, 1945–60,* 23; Morrison, *The Movement: English Poetry and Fiction of the 1950s,* 95, 92, 93; Hewison, *In Anger,* 23; Wain, "The Writer in His Age," 51; Sartre, *What Is Literature?* 49, 13; Webb, "Golding Goes Down the Sea Again," 12.

frage. At the age of twelve, Golding began to write a history of the trade unions, organizations that he later found to be totalitarian in their application of the "closed shop." He has even described himself as "*Bitterly* left of center" and a non-Marxist "socialist."[5] Yet for all his socialist grounding, Golding appears, at least at a public level, to separate fiction from politics:

> A writer is a citizen with a vote, access to his MP, access to the correspondence columns of magazines, newspapers and the BBC—a citizen with the right to speak in Hyde Park if he wants to or feels he ought. Surely that gives him enough opportunities for non-professional engagement in current affairs? I should think that the Marxist ideal of total engagement has been blown on, even in Russia. I am a citizen, a novelist and a schoolmaster. If my teaching of English grammar need not be aimed specifically at the prevention of capital punishment why should my novels be?[6]

Cold war expediency, a distaste for "committed" literature, a "conservative" and aesthetically driven view of literature, and a spirit of compromise or moderation that owed something to his place within the "Establishment" perhaps led Golding to take this position. He seems to consider Marxism, in a similar light to the Movement, as "a phase to be passed through in one's adolescence, and to be grown out of as one matures." Yet despite his preferred channels of political engagement such as his writing of a joint letter to the *Times* (London) protesting the British government's support of U.S. policy in Vietnam, Golding's fiction still interrogates contemporary issues such as totalitarianism, genocide, and the inequalities of the English class system. This engagement is particularly evident in his novels of the 1950s and 1960s when the shock waves of the Holocaust entered postwar literature and high expectations of better opportunities for everyone after the war spawned attacks on the English class system, especially during the so-called cultural revolution. Indeed, the themes of atrocity and particularly class are an ongoing concern right across Golding's fiction, although he does not engage quite so powerfully with these issues in his later novels, but chooses instead to attack class more lightheartedly and to "encrypt" the trauma of World War II in forms that re-

5. Gindin, *William Golding,* 2–3; Golding, "Writers and the Closed Shop (with Sixty-two Other British Writers and Intellectuals)," 1; Jack I. Biles, *Talk: Conversations with William Golding,* 49. For Golding's comments on his attempted history of the trade union movement, see *Moving Target,* 160.

6. Golding, "Writer in His Age," 45.

flect and engage with the historical, postindustrial phenomenon of postmodernism or what Fredric Jameson calls the "cultural logic of late capitalism." As Dominick LaCapra has observed, postmodernism "has developed in the wake of the Shoah, which it has often explicitly avoided, typically encrypted, and variably echoed in traumatized, melancholic, manically ludic, opaque, and at times mournfully elegiac discourses."[7] As such, postmodern literature continues, in a different historical period and in a more intensely skeptical way, the earlier modernist questioning of traditional foundations of Western culture after the trauma of World War I. But, as LaCapra suggests, postmodernism can be seen as an avoidance of direct engagement with the atrocities of World War II. LaCapra's insight echoes my own recognition of a deflation in Golding's satire that, as it becomes more Horatian, and hence more lighthearted or celebratory compared to Juvenalian or noncelebratory forms, shifts from its interrogation of Englishness in relation to contemporary totalitarianism and atrocity to echoing postmodern indeterminacy. The deflation that occurs in this movement from Juvenalian to Horatian forms results in the "encryption" of the darkness of the Holocaust, and any critical maneuvers dependent upon it, thus making it less visible. This deflation also extends to Golding's attack on the English class system. His earnest treatment of stratification in *The Pyramid* (1967) turns into an altogether lighter or comical ribbing in *To the Ends of the Earth: A Sea Trilogy* (1991), which comprises *Rites of Passage* (1980), *Close Quarters* (1987), and *Fire Down Below* (1989).

A rethinking of critical paradigms is required in order to interrogate the current practice of reading Golding. This needs to be synthetic in nature, utilizing the growing body of theory about the fantastic and the carnivalesque to intervene in a critical discourse that has consistently read Golding's novels as mythic and allegorical figurations of an essentialized human condition. The new reading offered in this book places Golding's fiction *firmly* in its contemporary context by establishing the satirical aspects of his novels. In Chapter 2, I provide a theorization of the combined carnivalesque and fantastic modes at the heart of Menippean satire, an ancient polemical form that, in its reference to the writing of the Greek

7. Morrison, *The Movement*, 93; Golding, "War in Vietnam (Letter to the Editor with John Le Carré, Paul Scofield, C. P. Snow)," 9; Jameson, *Postmodernism; or, The Cultural Logic of Late Capitalism;* LaCapra, *Representing the Holocaust: History, Theory, Trauma*, 222. Theodor W. Adorno views the Holocaust as bringing an end to affirmative dialectics and promoting skeptical "negative dialectics" or "thinking against itself" (*Negative Dialectics*, 365). For Jean-François Lyotard, the Holocaust heralds an equally skeptical "era," or what he calls "After Auschwitz," in which epistemological foundations and grand narratives are debunked (*The Differend: Phrases in Dispute*, 88).

Cynic Menippus, predates Quintilian's *satura.* It is these carnivalesque and fantastic modes that are at the hub of Golding's major novels and guide my overall analysis. Briefly, a noncelebratory or Juvenalian satire dominates *Lord of the Flies* (1954), *The Inheritors* (1955), *Pincher Martin* (1956), *Free Fall* (1959), *The Spire* (1964), and *The Pyramid.* In *Darkness Visible* (1979), *The Paper Men* (1984), and *To the Ends of the Earth,* the satire is more lighthearted or Horatian in tone. Of course, the definition of satire remains fluid. Brian A. Connery and Kirk Combe, in their excellent *Theorizing Satire,* establish the major element of satire as an attack on matter outside the text.[8] It is unlikely that arguments cited about what constitutes satire will end. They will surely rumble on, not least because satire is a plastic or versatile literary kind that inhabits a variety of genres and is difficult to define comprehensively. If anything, satire would probably best be seen as combining the fantastic and carnivalesque modes in transgeneric attacks upon historical targets.

In my investigation of the significance of National Socialism and the Holocaust to a reading of Golding's early novels, I am indebted to those critics who have placed the toes but not the whole foot on such historical ground. The most prominent among these are James Gindin and S. J. Boyd.[9] I am also indebted to those critics who have noted elements that I locate as being at the heart of the fantastic and carnivalesque, those who acknowledge Golding's attack on the English class system and literary criticism, and those who have drawn attention to his preoccupation with the status of language and literature in the so-called postmodern era. Where appropriate, I highlight the individual contributions of these critics in the main body of my text.

The fantastic is evident in the Beast in *Lord of the Flies,* Lok's half-formed perception and the strange materialization of the New People in *The Inheritors,* the double death of *Pincher Martin,* Sammy Mountjoy's mystical experiences in *Free Fall,* the ambiguous miracle of *The Spire,* the entombed village of Stilbourne in *The Pyramid,* the miraculous world of Matty who emerges from apocalyptic flames in *Darkness Visible,* the visions of Barclay in *The Paper Men,* and the mysterious object released from the bottom of the ship and Wheeler's "ghost" in *To the Ends of the Earth.* These are just the tip of a dark iceberg of the many fantastic motifs in Golding's corpus—a corpus dense with Gothic nightmare, doubles, and the diabolical. The

8. See Gay Sibley, "*Satura* from Quintilian to Joe Bob Briggs: A New Look at an Old Word," 59; and Connery and Combe, eds., *Theorizing Satire: Essays in Literary Criticism,* 1–15.

9. See Gindin, *William Golding;* and Boyd, *The Novels of William Golding.*

reversed world and upside-down motifs of the carnivalesque are equally prevalent throughout his novels. Violent Dionysianism and scatology dominate *Lord of the Flies* and *The Inheritors.* In *Pincher Martin,* the protagonist has his mouth and flies open, literally consuming the world. Inversions and cloacal fetor overflow in nearly all Golding's novels, not least *Free Fall, The Spire,* and *The Pyramid. Darkness Visible* is oxymoronic, turning upside down the established binary opposition of good and evil as readily as Harry Bummer's "crucifarce" of Matty. Antipodean symbolism pervades *To the Ends of the Earth,* with Colley as equatorial fool and victim of the fecal "badger-bag"—a bag into which Golding is ever keen to place the reader's head.

In his major novels, Golding deploys the various symbols, themes, and forms of the fantastic and carnivalesque in five main ways. These deployments move beyond a general or universal satirical function to undermine all human endeavors or actions. First, the modes attack an English national identity that constructs itself in opposition to Nazism.[10] This is achieved mainly in *Lord of the Flies, The Inheritors, Pincher Martin, Free Fall,* and *Darkness Visible.* Second, they expose the poisonous nature of the English class system. This is done progressively in *Lord of the Flies, The Spire, The Pyramid,* and *To the Ends of the Earth.* Third, the modes critique religious dogmatism and authority. This is most clearly effected in *The Spire,* but is also featured sporadically in both his early and his later fiction: *Lord of the Flies, Pincher Martin, Free Fall, Darkness Visible, Rites of Passage,* and *The Paper Men.* Fourth, they lambast the world of depthless, postmodern literature, literary criticism, and biography. This narrower attack is carried out in *The Paper Men.* Finally, they intensify a questioning of "truth-telling" in fiction that is so much part of the self-conscious and metafictional aspects of many of Golding's novels. In terms of the latter, the protean, distortive, and indeterminate nature of satire's world-turned-upside-down complements a growing modernist self-consciousness in *Pincher Martin, Free Fall,* and *The Spire* that develops into a more intense, postmodernist, metafictional focus in *Darkness Visible, The Paper Men,* and *To the Ends of the Earth.*

Postmodern metafiction, as many commentators have noted, not least

10. Golding's attack on an "English" construction of national identity in opposition to Nazism extends to his assault on the English class system. In general, he chooses to attack "England" and "Englishness" rather than "Britain" and "Britishness," though I feel that the former terms are, for Golding, metonymic of the latter. Certainly, at times, he uses the variant terms synonymously. I will maintain the "English" focus, unless the context demands otherwise.

Patricia Waugh, emerged in the late twentieth century out of a tradition of self-conscious literature stretching back to Laurence Sterne's *Tristram Shandy* (1759–1767), and even beyond this, as Robert Alter suggests, to ancient Greek writing. Because satire's combined fantastic and carnivalesque are given to dissolution and multivalence, it is an ideal host to various reformulations and literary marriages, not least in modern and postmodern literature. In terms of the latter, Brian McHale locates an "affinity between postmodernist fiction and the fantastic genre." Indeed, Patrick Parrinder suggests that the terms *fantasy* or *fantastic* may substitute for the term *postmodernism*. Furthermore, Linda Hutcheon and Christine Brooke-Rose argue, respectively, that fantastic inversions of real and unreal can be linked with postmodern literary playfulness and be seen as the forerunners or antecedents of postmodernist metafiction. Equally, the multivoiced and heterogeneous nature of the carnivalesque is a perfectly suited analogue to late-twentieth-century postmodernity that Terry Eagleton neatly summarizes as

> a style of thought which is suspicious of classical notions of truth, reason, identity and objectivity, of the idea of universal progress or emancipation, of single frameworks, grand narratives or ultimate grounds of explanation. Against these Enlightenment norms, it sees the world as contingent, ungrounded, diverse, unstable, indeterminate, a set of disunified cultures or interpretations which breed a degree of scepticism about the objectivity of truth, history and norms, the givenness of natures and the coherence of identities.

Some theorists, such as Daniel Bell, Jean-François Lyotard, and Fredric Jameson, have claimed that this "way of seeing . . . springs from an historic shift in the West to a new form of capitalism—to the ephemeral, decentralised world of technology, consumerism and the culture industry, in which the service, finance and information industries triumph over traditional manufacture and classical class politics yield ground to a diffuse range of 'identity politics.'" Eagleton defines postmodernism as "a style of culture which reflects something of this epochal change, in a depthless, decentred, ungrounded, self-reflective, playful, derivative, eclectic, pluralistic art which blurs the boundaries between 'high' and 'popular' culture, as well as between art and everyday experience."[11]

11. Waugh, *Metafiction: The Theory and Practice of Self- Conscious Fiction;* Alter, *Partial Magic: The Novel as a Self-Conscious Genre;* McHale, *Postmodernist Fiction,* 74. On postmodernism and the fantastic, see also Neil Cornwell, *The Literary Fantastic: From*

Satirical form can complement or be illustrative of both modernist and postmodernist indeterminacy without attacking a target as such, or to put it another way, the major modes of satire—the fantastic and the carnivalesque—can operate nonsatirically. Golding's postmodern turn is marked with the publication of *Darkness Visible* in the late 1970s when the phenomenon of "postmodernity" or "postmodernism" had begun to be widely debated and the terms found wide currency among a number of disciplines seeking to describe and periodize late-twentieth-century Western culture. In *Darkness Visible, The Paper Men,* and *To the Ends of the Earth,* as with his earlier modernist experimentalism in *Pincher Martin, Free Fall,* and *The Spire,* Golding employs the fantastic and carnivalesque modes nonsatirically as part of an epistemological commentary on the constructed, fragmented, and indeterminate nature of reality. However, this nonsatirical function does not exclude the satirical function of these modes within the same texts. Often, both functions operate together or are interwoven.

Fantastic and carnivalesque modes operate on the border between rationality and irrationality, reality and unreality. They turn established, familiar notions, patterns, or conceptions on their heads and share the same root in Menippean satire, the elements of which may be deployed not simply in celebratory genres, but in noncelebratory genres as well. It is the noncelebratory side of Menippean satire that dominates much of Golding's fiction, particularly his earliest works. He uses the liminality between what is real and unreal, normative and transgressive, to negotiate his dark moral and political viewpoint. To do this, his art owes much to the violent traditions and history of carnival practices themselves, and to a wide variety of fantastic and carnivalesque literature, ancient and modern, polemical and nonpolemical. It is likely that Golding read the ancient Latin writings of Lucian or Varro (see *HG,* 172–75).[12]

In the modern period, we know from his literary allusions that he was familiar with Rabelais, Shakespeare, Swift, Poe, Bierce, and Kafka, among others. Sometimes fantastic and carnivalesque modes in Golding's fiction operate separately, but mostly they combine in a stereoscopic fashion to

---

Gothic to Postmoderism, 34, 82, 143–45, 150–52, 154–55, 157, 160, 174, 183, 211, 240. Parrinder, *The Failure of Theory: Essays on Criticism and Contemporary Fiction,* 109; Hutcheon, *Narcissistic Narrative: The Metafictional Paradox,* 82–85; Brooke-Rose, *A Rhetoric of the Unreal: Studies in Narrative and Structure, Especially of the Fantastic,* 364–89; Eagleton, *The Illusions of Postmodernism,* vii.

12. See also the wide reference to Greek and Latin cultures in Golding's posthumous novel, *The Double Tongue.*

interrogate the borders between a variety of oppositions: good and evil, sacred and profane, rationality and irrationality, art and life. In his early novels, *Lord of the Flies, The Inheritors, Pincher Martin, Free Fall,* and *The Spire,* an antithesis between oppositions is broadly retained, although a synthesis between various oppositions emerges both obliquely and progressively.

Few critics have examined satire in Golding's novels, or indeed referred to Golding himself as a satirist.[13] Although there are scattered references to imagery, devices, and techniques central to satire, there has been no study that comprehensively examines Golding's use of the reversed or upside-down worlds of the fantastic and carnivalesque.

The majority of critical contributions on fantastic aspects of Golding's work are brief, undertheorized, isolated, or sporadic. Among the more formidable contributors, Bernard F. Dick identifies not simply fantastic and Gothic elements in *Pincher Martin* and Golding's radio play *Miss Pulkinhorn* (1960), respectively, but also the double in *The Inheritors, Darkness Visible, Rites of Passage,* and *The Paper Men.* Kevin McCarron's broad sensitivity to fantasy in Golding's fiction, where he examines the postmodernist "coincidence" of the rational and irrational in Golding's later fiction, is more substantial. Yet, McCarron hardly makes a detailed study of the various functions of the fantastic in Golding's later fiction and, more fundamentally, completely overlooks this mode in the early fiction. Nor does he appreciate the satirical interplay between the fantastic and carnivalesque in the early fiction and nonsatirical deployment of *both* these modes in relation to postmodernism in the later fiction.[14]

If critics have neglected to evaluate the fantastic comprehensively in relation to Golding's work, no less have they underestimated or underplayed the range and function of carnivalesque upside-down symbolism. Motifs central to this mode are generally described either too briefly, in isolation, or, with the exception of James Baker and Bernard Dick, outside any tradition as such. Baker identifies Golding's fiction within an antirationalist tradition stretching back to Greek literature, and his differ-

13. The most sustained references to Golding as a satirist are to be found outside Golding criticism per se in Leonard Feinberg, *Introduction to Satire,* 28, 45–46, 71, 201.

14. Dick, *William Golding* (1967), 53, 90; Dick, *William Golding* (1987), 43–44, 96–98, 100, 141, 137. See McCarron, *The Coincidence of Opposites: William Golding's Later Fiction,* 7–10. Glen Cavaliero makes similar broad links between the ludic nature of fantastic aspects of Golding's fiction and postmodernism (see *The Supernatural and English Fiction*). McCarron notes: "In *Darkness Visible,* the earlier fabular mode has been replaced by that of the fantastic, a shift in form which is paralleled by a shift in the thematic concerns of the later fiction" (*Coincidence of Opposites,* 10).

entiation between Greek and Roman images of Dionysus is compatible with a recognition of the dual classical root of carnival in all its noncelebratory and celebratory aspects. The Alexandrine and Roman Dionysus is described as jolly Bacchus, the "god of wine," a dominant image even to the present day. The Greek Dionysus, however, is a violent, dangerous, and altogether more threatening figure. Dick extends this focus on the conflict between rational and irrational worlds in classical sources in his examination of Apollonian and Dionysian aspects.[15] Yet this opposition is never subsumed under Menippean satire, one of the earliest polemical forms, and its fantastic and carnivalesque modes. Such a comprehensive and synthetic approach is beyond the early approaches of either Dick or Baker.

Whereas certain critics pay close attention to the influence of Greek classical literature on Golding's work, the synthetic potential of addressing the Greek and Roman roots of the carnivalesque and its related fantastic has been overlooked. Keeping in mind Golding's familiarity with Latin literature and the shared mythology between Greek and Roman cultures, many elements in his fiction may be subsumed under both Greek tragedy and Menippean satire. In addition, we know Golding to be indebted to Shakespeare—a writer whom Michael D. Bristol, among others, sees as dealing widely in the carnivalesque.[16] This more synthetic approach allows for the dualism of the carnivalesque that incorporates both tragedy and comic satire, the noncelebratory alongside the celebratory. It will also permit the inclusion of Greek, Latin, Christian, and secular influences on Golding's work.

Like Redpath, I regret that few Golding critics have moved out of the narrow waters of fable, source hunting, and religious interpretations and that more recent literary theory has been applied only sporadically to his work.[17] The new, partly synthetic reading offered here marks a departure from these more limited analyses. By unifying and radically extending the rather isolated, brief descriptions and analyses of elements related to the fantastic and carnivalesque made by previous critics, we can bring into view a complex satirical structure that has largely gone unnoticed. This structure is the means by which Golding interrogates contemporary issues such as English totalitarianism and class, and what Lyotard has

15. Baker, *William Golding: A Critical Study*, 8–17; Dick, *William Golding* (1967), 29. See also Friedrich Nietzsche, *The Birth of Tragedy: Out of the Spirit of Music*.

16. Bristol, *Carnival and Theater: Plebeian Culture and the Structure of Authority in Renaissance England*. See also Bristol, *Big-Time Shakespeare*.

17. See Redpath, *Structural Reading*, 216.

termed "the postmodern condition." To neglect this major aspect of Golding's fiction in favor of timeless approaches is to misread his work. His work may be universal, but it is not universally timeless. Let me set out in a little more detail this historicist reading of Golding's novels.

Golding's first published novels, *Lord of the Flies* and *The Inheritors,* are of a pair and make an oblique response to the sociopolitical context of World War II, and particularly to the Holocaust and its aftermath. Immanent form and external context are bridged by fantastic and carnivalesque modes. In these novels fantastic and carnivalesque modes are deployed to respond, albeit in an oblique way, to this cultural context. The effect of World War II events on Golding's writing has been noted by himself and his critics. *Lord of the Flies* and *The Inheritors* can be thought of as grief responses to the various atrocities carried out in this period of history, especially the extermination of six million Jews. What has not been considered, however, is how Golding uses fantastic and carnivalesque modes to establish a powerful evocation of the context of World War II atrocity, register profound grief traces in its aftermath, and attack an English national identity that constructs itself in opposition to Nazism.

In *Lord of the Flies* and *The Inheritors,* Golding uses the fantastic and carnivalesque to subvert postwar complacency of Allied "civilized" nations, particularly Britain, about the deeds of Nazism. In *Lord of the Flies,* he emphasizes first the origin of evil within English schoolboys by the natural explanation of apparently supernatural events, and second their exclusionary gestures toward outsiders or outcasts that are deeply rooted in the anti-Semitic history of carnival. *The Inheritors* responds in an oblique fashion to Nazi atrocities against the Jews. Like *Lord of the Flies,* it was published shortly after World War II. Although set in the distant past, and lacking the surface details specific to the war found in *Lord of the Flies,* it does powerfully suggest the context of contemporary genocide and its aftermath. It is also a rebuttal of the racially elitist views of H. G. Wells. Fantastic hesitation creates uncertainty as to what forces are behind the insidious extermination of Lok's Neanderthal tribe. The natural explanation that it is the New People, progenitors of Homo sapiens, who are "racially cleansing" the territory of "ogres" subverts the notion of evolutionary progress and the achievements of civilization, and powerfully evokes the Jewish Holocaust. The carnivalesque practices of the New People subvert civility and mark the exclusionary and orgiastic violence of an advanced race to those it considers inferior or alien. This is powerfully demonstrated by the eating of Liku.

In his questioning of World War II atrocities, Golding is among those writers who apply their imaginative powers to representing the recent nightmarish past. We should consider him as part of a wider movement of writers in the "tradition of atrocity."[18] Although he does so obliquely, Golding effects an integration between literature and cultural context. He deals with *both* present and perennial issues. This interpretation renegotiates previous critical paradigms that have, for the most part, centered on the timeless or perennial concerns of these novels via the classifications of fable, myth, and nonpolitical allegory. Yet it is not that these classifications are faulty—in fact, they are demonstrably relevant to an understanding of his fiction—but that they have too often been understood as being antithetical to any concerns such literature has with contemporary context. The approach so far has been to displace any recognition of the significance of cultural context to Golding's writing. Even the classification *allegory* has largely been deployed by Golding critics to examine universal concerns, such as the nature of good and evil, rather than cultural context. In effect, to the benefit of a traditional focus on a transcendent valuation of literature, a narrow antithesis between the universal and particular, or perennial and historical present, has been privileged. Yet, in *Lord of the Flies* and *The Inheritors,* for example, Golding raises both universal concerns about humankind's barbarity or inhumanity and instantiates a particular historical occurrence of such behavior in his reference to the Jewish Holocaust. Such an instantiation may be read as a tokenistic and ultimate devaluation of the unspeakable horrors of the Holocaust. It may be read as merely an intensifier of his universalism. Such views do not consider Golding's nascent satire, though. Although his satire is weakened and defused somewhat by the universal and fabular aspect to these novels, Golding is attempting, perhaps struggling even, to critique an English national identity that constructs itself in opposition to Nazism. In *Lord of the Flies,* and more obliquely in *The Inheritors,* he attempts to remind the English of their own fascist past—for example, with Mosley and his Blackshirts—and the need to be vigilant about a return to totalitarianism in the future. This message is strengthened in his next two novels, *Pincher Martin* and *Free Fall.*

The fantastic and carnivalesque modes of *Pincher Martin* and *Free Fall* continue to interrogate the social and political context of World War II atrocities, yet move toward a focus on individual ethics in the protagonists, Christopher Martin and Sammy Mountjoy, respectively. Fantastic and carnivalesque modes in *Pincher Martin* and *Free Fall* highlight a deeply felt ethical unease in postwar England. Like *Lord of the Flies* before

18. Lawrence L. Langer, *The Holocaust and the Literary Imagination,* 34.

them, yet more intensely, they maintain surface details of World War II, and can be thought of as part of a *Vergangenheitsbewältigung,* or "coming to terms with the past," of World War II atrocities. This *Vergangenheitsbewältigung* was perhaps less visible in Britain in the postwar years, but Golding was not the only writer "coming to terms with the past" of World War II atrocities or the emergence of totalitarianism. However, the tradition of atrocity literature is strongest outside of Britain. This may be due in part to the isolation of Britain from mainland Europe and its relative insulation or immunity from what David Rousset has labeled *l'univers concentrationnaire.* Across mainland Western and Eastern Europe, many writers have been placed in a tradition of atrocity writing: Gerd Hoffmann, Heinrich Böll, Günter Grass, Anthony Hecht, Paul Celan, Albert Camus, Elie Wiesel, Jakov Lind, André Schwarz-Bart, Ilse Aichinger, Jerzy Kosinski, Nelly Sachs, Peter Weiss, Wolfgang Barchert, Ernst Wiechert, Primo Levi, Herman Kasack, Pierre Gascar, Jorge Semprun, Jean Améry, Tadeusz Borowski, Ladislav Fuks, Josef Bor, Arnost Lustig, and Piotr Rawitz.[19] Yet British atrocity literature in the postwar period is rather thin on the ground, although George Orwell's disturbing accounts of totalitarianism in *Animal Farm* (1945) and *1984* (1949) suggest more might have followed from other British writers. But this was not the case. Al Alvarez's denunciation of English philistinism in "Beyond the Gentility Principle" signals this paucity. Blake Morrison argues that, despite some oblique references, Movement writers, such as Kingsley Amis, Robert Conquest, Donald Davie, D. J. Enright, Thom Gunn, Philip Larkin, and John Wain, tended to evade "war horror": "That the Movement felt obliged to avoid a direct treatment of recent history may be partly explained by their belief that the interpretations of history present in the work of their forerunners (both the Modernists and the generation of Auden and Spender) were so gravely amiss as to discourage any further attempt to be 'relevant' or '*engagé.*'"[20]

Apart from Golding, few British postwar writers were questioning British values and fantasies of moral superiority following the Nazi atrocities against the Jews.[21] In contradistinction to those modernist writers who supported fascism, held the masses in contempt, and were anti-Semitic, Golding marks himself as deeply anti-Hitlerian. He can be seen to offer a postwar antidote to the extreme modernist politics of those such

19. Rousset quoted in ibid., 16. On these and other atrocity writers, see ibid.; and A. Alvarez, *Beyond All This Fiddle,* 22–33.

20. A. Alvarez, "The New Poetry; or, Beyond the Gentility Principle," 21–32; Morrison, *The Movement,* 91.

21. Langer, *Literary Imagination,* 30.

as Wyndham Lewis who, at least for a time, provided a rather uncritical account of Hitlerism in *Hitler* (1931) and *Left Wings over Europe* (1936). Golding interrogates the antihumanitarianism that is the base of all forms of fascism, not least the English variety. The salvation from English philistinism that Alvarez finds in the poetry of Sylvia Plath and Ted Hughes might, however, be extended to Elizabeth Bowen's *Heat of the Day* (1949), Angus Wilson's *Hemlock and After* (1953) and *No Laughing Matter* (1967), and Kazuo Ishiguro's *Remains of the Day* (1989). Even William Cooper's *Scenes from Provincial Life* (1950) portrays the threat of England turning into a totalitarian state on account of English support for, and Chamberlain's appeasement of, Hitler in the Munich Settlement of 1938.

Among those writings that refer to the Holocaust but do not provide a sharp critique of "English" values there are Arnold Wesker's play *I'm Talking about Jerusalem* (1960), Doris Lessing's *Golden Notebook* (1962), Anthony Burgess's *Clockwork Orange* (1962), George Steiner's *Portage to San Cristobal of A. H.* (1981), D. M. Thomas's *White Hotel* (1981), and Martin Amis's *Einstein's Monsters* (1986) and *Time's Arrow* (1991). In more general terms, as David Craig notes, new-wave writers such as Alan Sillitoe, Brendan Behan, David Storey, and Colin MacInnes join Golding in a preoccupation with violence.[22] However, it is the critical stance Golding takes toward English and, indeed, Allied moral superiority in the face of Nazi atrocities against the Jews that I wish to highlight.

The interrogation of the border between material and spiritual worlds, and the ethical positions taken up by individual protagonists in *Pincher Martin* and *Free Fall*, is continued with Jocelin in *The Spire*. Yet this later novel, published five years after *Free Fall*, marks a shift in focus from a strong response in terms of sociopolitical context in *Lord of the Flies*, *The Inheritors*, *Pincher Martin*, and *Free Fall*—ground Golding appears to retrace in *Darkness Visible*—to a more internalized fiction that explores the impact of ethical-religious uncertainty on the individual Jocelin, and critiques religious dogmatism, without any reference to World War II. Yet the novel can also be viewed as metafiction—as a fiction about the difficulties and ambiguities of constructing fictional meaning. Furthermore, Golding snipes at the English class system as he did in *Lord of the Flies*. And this sniping is the chief aspect of *The Pyramid*, a novel in which Golding exposes the detrimental effects of social stratification in Britain.

In a later return to what may be thought of as grief about the atrocious events of World War II, Golding widely deploys the fantastic and the car-

22. See Craig, *The Real Foundations: Literature and Social Change*, 270–85.

nivalesque in *Darkness Visible* to respond anew to the horrific devastation of wartime London, the Holocaust, the Vietnam War, and the looming, ever present threat of nuclear war. What McCarron calls a "coincidence of opposites" in Golding's later fiction renegotiates various binarisms such as good and evil, or Augustanism and romanticism. This is effected by the carnivalesque in tandem with the fantastic mode, and is deeply concerned with mapping the entropic postmodern condition. *Darkness Visible* combines with more or less equal emphasis two of the major themes or concerns in his fiction: contemporary atrocity and postmodernism.

The growing focus on the postmodern condition is evident across Golding's fiction: *Pincher Martin, Free Fall, The Spire, Darkness Visible,* and *To the Ends of the Earth.* The uncertainty and ambiguity generated by fantastic and carnivalesque modes here are part of a relativism that suggests Golding's immersion in and attention to the contemporary critical debate on the status of culture and, in particular, literature. *Pincher Martin, Free Fall,* and *The Spire* function to question the status of fiction in a way rendered more explicit by Golding's later, more playful, tragicomic, and more obviously metafictional novels, *The Paper Men, Rites of Passage, Close Quarters,* and *Fire Down Below.* All of these later novels reflect a growing postmodernist outlook or vision in Golding's fiction and advance beyond earlier modernist self-consciousness.

The fantastic and carnivalesque in *To the Ends of the Earth* and *The Paper Men* function in a noticeably tragicomic and playful way. In *To the Ends of the Earth,* these modes enhance or complement a dominant metafictional questioning of the "truth" status of fiction, history, and reality. Indeed, Susana Onega describes the "sea trilogy" as a "historiographic metafiction," a term that Linda Hutcheon coined in her book *A Poetics of Postmodernism.* According to Hutcheon, this blending of metafiction and historiography is the only kind of fiction that fulfills the "poetics of postmodernism." It is a "trend," Onega argues, that "very richly and powerfully catches and expresses the deepest concerns of contemporary man."[23] Yet in *To the Ends of the Earth,* the carnivalesque, in isolation, also functions to attack English class elitism and reveals a propensity in the English subject for atrocity such as that witnessed in the Terror of the French Revolution. Here Golding's preoccupation with the English capacity for violence, so strong in his earlier fiction, is again visible but less formidable in this lighter, more comical work.

Across Golding's fiction we can witness, then, a broad sea change from

23. Onega, "British Historiographic Metafiction," 92–103; Hutcheon, *A Poetics of Postmodernism: History, Theory, Fiction,* 105–23; Onega, "British Historiographic Metafiction," 102.

a strong, noncelebratory satire against English totalitarianism and class in his early work of the 1950s and 1960s toward an increasingly lighthearted attack—that is, one that is more Horatian in tone—against totalitarianism, class, and the whole English literature industry during the 1980s and 1990s in which the prime focus was on the status of literature. In the 1970s Golding published only one major novel, *Darkness Visible.* This novel, coming as it did at the end of a dry decade, at least in terms of the publication of his novels, can be seen to stand as a kind of watershed between Golding's early major concerns with contemporary atrocity and his later preoccupation with the postmodern condition. As such, the novel tragicomically straddles both of these domains and marks a perceived deflation or ebbing toward a more celebratory, comical, and nonsatirical form of postmodern literature that appears to encrypt and hence submerge the Holocaust. A weakening of Golding's grief response to World War II events appears to be mirrored in the changing functions of carnivalesque and fantastic modes. Elsewhere, critics have overlooked these significant aspects of Golding's artistic development.

Mark Kinkead-Weekes and Ian Gregor see Golding's art as a progressive investigation of how to disengage myth from fable and site it in history. They locate a shift from a fabular mode toward a more equivocal and mysterious "vision of unified opposites." Dick argues that the onboard orgy of *Rites of Passage* is more in keeping with Euripides' play *Cyclops,* a satyr play not a tragedy, and thus is considered to transcend yet again Greek tragic form in Golding. This transcendence, however, is hardly the serious parody of Golding's earlier fiction. This differential, which goes unnoticed by Dick, is significant in terms of mapping the transition in Golding's noncelebratory to celebratory carnivalesque, which is linked to a change in contextual function. Leighton Hodson notes the transition between the "unrelenting all-or-nothing tragic tone" of Golding's early work and his later tragicomic mode, but misses the significance of this development in terms of the relationship between his novels and traumatic historical events. It is worth bearing in mind that Don Crompton finds little developmental change across Golding's fiction. For Crompton, Golding's later work remains "gloomy" and has "shifted little from the 'grief, sheer grief, grief, grief, grief' that in [Golding's] view constituted the theme of *Lord of the Flies.*"[24] Yet the majority view locates a shift to tragi-

24. Kinkead-Weekes and I. Gregor, *William Golding: A Critical Study,* 118. For a critique of Kinkead-Weekes and I. Gregor's methodology in mapping Golding's artistic development, see Redpath, *Structural Reading,* 205–6. Dick, *William Golding* (1987), 124; Hodson, *William Golding,* 106; Don Crompton, *A View from the Spire: William Golding's Later Novels,* 187.

a political allegory that refers to the atrocities of World War II, but particularly those inflicted upon the Jews. He further suggests that allegory in *Free Fall* "communicates the deterioration of society and the resultant alienation of modern humanity after World War II." However, outside this historicizing form of allegory, Dickson stresses the timelessness of his fiction generally. A similar privileging of mythic timelessness overrides even Lawrence Friedman's highly contextual approach to *Darkness Visible:* "Although that world is 1940 [*sic*] London, it is essentially timeless." If Friedman is quick to announce Golding's grief in response to World War II atrocities, he is arguably slow to demonstrate how, for example, *Lord of the Flies* and *The Inheritors* historicize the Jewish Holocaust. In terms of *Free Fall,* while he notes that "for the mass of men the wages of godlessness are Sammy [Mountjoy]'s crimes writ large in Nazi atrocities," he does not make enough of this connection. Although McCarron rightly sees Golding's work as both "indebted to literature itself as it is to 'reality,'" the history of Belsen or Auschwitz takes second place to intertextual issues.[27]

More general commentaries on postwar English society and literature have noted Golding's engagement with contemporary events. For example, Stuart Laing argues that "the reversal of texts of high bourgeois optimism" in Golding's early work, and his focus on the irrational, follows Golding's participation in and reflection on World War II. He refers to Golding's revelation of "history as nightmare." In his analysis, Laing also emphasizes the uncertain role of fictional language as central to much of Golding's corpus. This, he argues, is apparent in the work of other postwar writers such as Wilson, Lessing, Wain, Amis, and Murdoch. Alan Sinfield maintains that the reversal of imperialist ideology following World War II atrocities was invoked by reference to the "savage" quality of human nature. He contends: "The myth of universal savagery is the final, desperate throw of a humiliated and exhausted European humanism." Of course, Sinfield rightly draws attention to the contradictions inherent in a "savage" myth that is "informed by both an anxiety about and a continuing embroilment in imperialist ideology."[28]

27. Oldsey and Weintraub, *Art of Golding,* 43–45, 173; see Dick, *William Golding* (1967), 34–35; Hodson, *William Golding,* 107–8, 32, 1. For links between Golding's work and Nazism, see Stephen Medcalf, *William Golding,* 10, 13; and Arnold Johnston, *Of Earth and Darkness: The Novels of William Golding,* 20. Tiger, *Dark Fields,* 34, 35–36, 206, 211, 63; see Johnston, *Of Earth and Darkness,* 38, 45; Redpath, *Structural Reading,* 17; Subbarao, *William Golding: A Study,* 139; Gindin, *William Golding,* 4–5, 48–49; Boyd, *Novels of Golding,* 40, 41–42; Dickson, *The Modern Allegories of William Golding,* 24–25, 74; Friedman, *William Golding,* 123, 80; McCarron, *William Golding,* 4.

28. S. Laing, "Novels and the Novel," 241–43; Sinfield, *Literature, Politics, and Culture in Postwar Britain,* 141.

In making a historicist reading of William Golding's fiction in contrast to earlier more formalist readings, it might appear that I am advocating a simplistic opposition or divide between historicism and formalism—taking an either-or approach. This is not the case. Indeed, while there is a potential conflict between formalist and historicist readings—the one rooting texts in literary conventions or models, while the other roots texts in particular social and political contexts—this is not inevitable. We can reconcile or connect the two in a synthetic way. We know, for instance, that Golding was deeply read and interested in early literary models, such as Menippean satire, and that he was tremendously affected by various social traumas or upheavals, not least the Holocaust and the cold war. It is perfectly reasonable that in representing horrifying and disturbing events occurring during and after World War II that he would choose appropriate literary models to do this. In order to dramatize or express traumatic events such as the Holocaust, Golding appropriated literary models that would have been familiar to him: the fantastic and carnivalesque. Put another way, his fiction is rooted in an interplay between formal choices and historical contexts. The novels as a whole, then, derive not simply from how Golding deploys the various symbols, themes, and forms of the carnivalesque and fantastic or from the trauma of atrocities such as the Holocaust, and the pressures and possibilities of life in post-1945 Britain, but from the interanimation or reverberation of both of these influences.

To date, it has been the cold war that has remained to the fore as the likely context for Golding's writing. Of course, the cold war, and particularly the possibility of nuclear holocaust, hung over Golding's imagination, yet the role of the Jewish Holocaust in his fiction is equally important. At first this might seem surprising because although the Holocaust was the great twentieth-century trauma, most observers would agree that we tend to be more conscious of it today, whereas in the 1950s there was a lot of avoidance and cultural amnesia. How far Golding was immersed in this cultural amnesia is difficult to say. Of course, "cultural amnesia" is overstated, as journalistic material about the Holocaust was in the public domain, material that Golding no doubt saw and read. It is fair to say, though, at least from the literary perspective, that there was a paucity of literature in the postwar years that dealt head-on with the Holocaust. Golding challenged this amnesia, first in *Lord of the Flies,* where he seems influenced by his experience of the cruelty and sadism of schoolboys during his career as a teacher; then the reports of Belsen and Auschwitz, events that had happened some ten years before; and finally, his own intimate knowledge of the extermination of humans that he gained while in active service in World War II.

In 1940, Golding joined the Royal Navy and served as an ordinary seaman before becoming an officer by successfully demonstrating his understanding of explosives and propellants. He joined a research team working on explosives until he blew himself up. Following his recovery he transferred to commanding first a minesweeper and then a rocket-launching ship. In 1944 he took part in the invasion of mainland Europe.[29] Golding's naval experience is woven into the fiction, as are surface details particular to World War II. He gives a strong account of the influence of the war, and particularly the Holocaust, on his early writing in his essay "Fable":

> Before the second world war I believed in the perfectibility of social man. . . . [A]fter the war I did not because I was unable to. I had discovered what one man could do to another. I am not talking of one man killing another with a gun, or dropping a bomb on him or blowing him up or torpedoing him. I am thinking of the vileness beyond all words that went on, year after year, in the totalitarian states. It is bad enough to say that so many Jews were exterminated in this way and that, so many people liquidated—lovely, elegant word—but there were things done during that period from which I still have to avert my mind less I should be physically sick. They were not done by the headhunters of New Guinea, or by some primitive tribe in the Amazon. They were done, skilfully, coldly, by educated men, doctors, lawyers, by men with a tradition of civilization behind them, to beings of their own kind. (*HG*, 86–87)

However, it was probably the moral distancing of the Allies from the Nazis that produced sufficient bile for him to make successive fictional rejoinders. Golding admits as much:

> Ballantyne's island was a nineteenth-century island inhabited by English boys; mine was to be a twentieth-century island inhabited by English boys. I can say here in America what I should not like to say at home; which is that I condemn and detest my country's faults precisely because I am so proud of her many virtues. One of her faults is to believe that evil is somewhere else and inherent in another nation. My book was to say: you think that now the war is over and an evil thing destroyed, you are safe because you are naturally kind and decent. But I know why the thing rose in Germany. I know it could happen in any country. It could happen here. (*HG*, 89)

29. I am indebted here to Gindin's account of Golding's war service. More than any other critic, Gindin has emphasized the significance of Golding's wartime experience to his fiction (see *William Golding*, 4–5).

Perhaps Golding would not have written about that Holocaust at all had this other more insidious "atrocity" of moral denial not disturbed him. But there were other contextual aspects swirling in the background. Indeed, it is likely that the atrocities carried out by Allied forces, not least Dresden, further motivated Golding to overturn the high moral tone of the victors, as did the racial violence against West Indian immigrants after the war. And where better to start than with Nazifying "civilized" British boys? As Golding commented to Jack Biles:

> *Lord of the Flies* was simply what it seemed sensible for me to write after the war, when everybody was thanking God they weren't Nazis. And I'd seen enough and thought enough to realize that every single one of us could be Nazi; you take, for example, this bust-up in England over colored people—there were colored people in some suburban part of one of our cities; there really was a bust-up over this—and you take the South, of North America, where you have a regular bust-up over Negroes. And take anybody's history, what it comes to is this: that Nazi Germany was a particular kind of boil which burst in 1939 or 1940 or whenever it was. That was only the same kind of inflamed spot we all of us suffer from, and so I took English boys and said, "Look. This could be you." This is really what the book comes to.

Later in a similar interview, Golding stated: "I could listen to people talking about 'bloody Nazis,' people who I knew *were* Nazis. Do you see, they were in fact Nazis; only they didn't happen to live in the Nazi social system."[30]

As a discursive practice my own historicism seeks directly to challenge timeless readings of Golding that largely ignore the chilling context of racial hatred and genocide. If such a challenge is not made, we will be left with an impoverished and depoliticized understanding of his work. We will be guided by a hemiplegic and deeply unsatisfactory criticism. My privileging of a historical approach to Golding's fiction, emphasizing the relations between his novels and cultural contexts, is not, however, without its problems. Although my overall historicism partly seeks to redeem Golding's instantiation of the recalcitrant history of the Holocaust from the denial of universalism, I am fully aware that acts of retrieval in historical study are fraught with difficulty, an awareness shared by Golding in his later "historiographic metafiction," *To the Ends of the Earth.* The status of history has been problematized by skeptical approaches to historiography. Here, opposing voices can be heard. On the one hand, there are pessimists who see epistemological crisis and cultural diversity as ex-

30. Biles, *Talk,* 3–4, 35–36.

ploding the value of history. On the other hand, we have optimists such as Theodore K. Rabb who draws an upbeat parallel between the upheaval in historiography in the 1990s and scientific revolution in the seventeenth century: "[D]isputes should be heartening: signs of vitality and engagement, not disintegration."[31]

Although I agree with David Perkins that the practice of literary history has great epistemological difficulties, I am not as pessimistic as he is about the value of interpreting literature in relation to cultural contexts.[32] Equally, I reject the view that seeking the context of a given writer's work amid a surplus of possible contexts is irredeemably flawed.[33] Historicists, like realists, are not the naive practitioners they are often made out to be. They understand quite well (they have been told often enough) the limitations of their modes of knowledge.[34] After all, objective truth is simply a tantalus to literary history. It is, as Salman Rushdie argues, the "unattainable goal for which one must struggle in spite of the impossibility of success." This struggle is all about delivering the most plausible explanations and interpretations. My historicism cannot attain objective truth, but it does have the pragmatic value of *competing* against discourses that prefer to lose sight of history, especially history as disturbing and uncomfortable as the Holocaust. It is hoped that a redemption of Golding's instantiation of history from the silence of universalism, in the words of Paul Hamilton, will "make a difference" in the realm of discursive practice. The political power or powerlessness of any discourse in relation to others is another question. Yet all that any historicist reading can do, as Carolyn Porter puts it, is "inhabit a discursive field." This is a more humble position and one that does not, Joan Wallach Scott argues, "acknowledge defeat in the search for universal explanation; rather it suggests that universal explanation is not, never has been possible." The possible interaction of my discourse with the world cannot be absolutized. It remains one of many insolubles. The *hopefulness* of making redemptive strikes aligns his-

31. Rabb, "Whither History? Reflections on the Comparison between Historians and Scientists," 75.

32. See Perkins, *Is Literary History Possible?*

33. Such disparaging critiques of context are made by Dominick LaCapra and David Harlan. "Harlan," Gerald N. Izenberg says, "draws the more general inference from LaCapra's criticism. If all the intellectual, artistic, religious and cultural traditions that might have been relevant to a writer's subject, knowledge, form and style are part of his context, 'the relevant community of discourse may include all of western civilization. And more . . .'" ("Text, Context, and Psychology in Intellectual History," 54).

34. For a "defence" of realism, see Raymond Tallis, *In Defence of Realism;* and Andrzej Gąsiorek, *Post-War British Fiction: Realism and After.*

toricism with theology, as Walter Benjamin insists. It is potentially salvific or redemptory. Needless to say, redemption proves difficult. What is retrieved is always fragmented, not the whole body. However, to substantiate a body from the past, albeit dead in the Greenblattian sense, is to prefer one reconstruction over another. No body is available for recovery, or exhumation, but what is salvaged is a construct that performs as a "living" body into the future. This "living body" replaces the absence or silence insisted upon by arch-relativists of history. It is Benjaminian rather than Rankean: "The true picture of the past flits by. The past can be seized only as an image which flashes up at the instant when it can be recognized and is never seen again. . . . For every image of the past that is not recognized by the present as one of its own concerns threatens to disappear irretrievably."[35] This "living body" competes by discursive friction with those who value political quietism.

Cultural materialists and new historicists, and indeed those who do not choose to wear such defining hoods, have argued for a social nexus in which literature is both produced by and produces cultural meanings. In broadly sharing such an approach (which is by no means homogeneous), while refusing reductive and affiliatory labels, I aim to synthesize the pervasive antithesis between formalism and social poetics in the spirit of Mikhail Bakhtin and P. N. Medvedev's *Formal Method in Literary Scholarship.* In so doing, my work approaches contextualization by starting with literature and progressing, as Alan Sinfield says, "towards the conditions by which it functions as a social practice." This historicist enterprise should contribute to a fuller vision of Golding's art and its engagement with contemporary history. It is a process that is intimately connected with considering Golding primarily as a satirist, a writer who attacks historical targets. The fact that formalism has looked down its nose at satire as something merely extraliterary or even subliterary may explain why most commentators have shied away from this aspect of Golding's work. However, as Connery and Combe suggest, the tide has turned of late, and satire is once again on the agenda: "Having suffered at the hands of critics who wished to exclude history from literature, satire can only gain by the resurgence of historicism."[36]

35. Rushdie, *Imaginary Homelands: Essays and Criticism, 1981–1991,* 101; Hamilton, *Historicism,* 5, 6; Porter, "Are We Being Historical Yet?" 770 (see also Porter, "History and Literature: 'After the New Historicism'"); Scott, *Gender and the Politics of History,* 10; W. Benjamin, *Illuminations,* 247.

36. Sinfield, ed., *Society and Literature, 1945–1970,* 8; Connery and Combe, *Theorizing Satire,* 11.

A historicist criticism of Golding's satire that acknowledges its limitations and the problematical status of history should seek more than what Lyotard, in the Wittgensteinian sense of language play, has called "paralogy."[37] Academic paralogy between historicists and formalists—which ultimately must be considered powerless and narcissistic—is not all.[38] To my mind, the intervention of a discursive practice amid other discursive practices can resist—if only in a small way—amnesiac approaches that in making a justified critique of the narrativization of history disavow the value of interpretations of historical events based on accumulated probability. Such objectivity-aimed discourse suggests a reduced fictional distance between events and representation, contrary to "narrative," which implies a doubtful, fictional status. As Deborah Lipstadt rightly argues, though historical interpretation "cannot be purely objective," it is "built on a certain body of irrefutable evidence: slavery happened; so did the Black Plague and the Holocaust."[39]

I challenge both the earlier formalism and that which has crept into new historicism where pan-textualism has taken root. Historicist scholars are certainly motivated ideologically from the present toward past events to evince correspondence between text and context, but there is constraint operating in formal and extraliterary material. For example, on the one hand, Golding uses carnivalesque and fantastic elements to register violent exclusion of the Jew-like outsider in his early novels, *Lord of the Flies* and *The Inheritors.* On the other hand, the recalcitrance of the Jewish Holocaust and mass extermination stands beyond the narrativization of history. Both the use of this literary form and the context of mass extermination are chronologically contiguous. Furthermore, surface details in these texts point to Nazism and Jewish history; in addition, the author's grief and artistic concern regarding the atrocities of World War II have been well documented. All these connections add to the plausible and valid bridging between text and context—the interanimation of formal and extraliterary material in these works. This is what Golding's texts *do* among other things in the performative sense of J. L. Austin, John R. Searle, and H. P. Grice, as taken up by Quentin Skinner. Such an approach avoids Alan Liu's criticism of the frequently formalist strategy of new historicism: "A New Historicist paradigm holds up to view a historical context on one

37. See Don E. Wayne, "New Historicism," 798.

38. This does not mean that Lyotard is morally lacking. He has shown, as Stuart Sim insists, a commitment to the events of Auschwitz that "deflect[s] any charge of crude relativism" (*Jean-François Lyotard,* 140).

39. Lipstadt, *Denying the Holocaust: The Growing Assault on Truth and Memory,* 21.

side, a literary text on the other, and, in between, a connection of pure nothing."[40]

There are limits to the fictional distance that can open up between past events and narration of those events. Historical evidence can and should counter the gross gestures of those who *too readily* blur fiction with history, those radical textualists who too freely debunk positivist objectivism. Whereas it seems perfectly reasonable to discard monological accounts of history, as Golding does in *To the Ends of the Earth,* and applaud all that is dialogical, there are brute, evidentiary resources of the past that may help to shape our future understanding. Terry Eagleton has attacked the "hedonist withdrawal from history" of such radical textualists. Their approach, he argues, amounts to a "liquidation of history." Andrzej Gąsiorek notes the emphasis placed by Graham Swift, Julian Barnes, and Salman Rushdie on historical knowledge: "This knowledge is acquired in textual form, but that textuality points back to a recalcitrant historical referent that cannot be wished away." And specifically in terms of Barnes's *History of the World in 10$\frac{1}{2}$ Chapters* (1989): although the "God-eyed version" of truth is described as "a charming, impossible fake," the reader is urged to "believe that 43 per cent objective truth is better than 41 per cent" because the alternative is a "beguiling relativity" in which "we value one liar's version as much as another liar's."[41] The following study is a gesture toward this 43 percent objective truth, and should counter the greatly dehistoricized readings of Golding's work to date.

Golding does more than compel the reader to stand with one foot in this world and one in the other world of mystery and supernaturalism—a kind of limbo that in many ways reflects the divided influence of his more spiritually minded mother and the rationalist, scientific trajectory of his father. Through the liminal, and through his "double tongue," Golding forces the reader to confront contemporary history. In so doing, he maps the difficulty of coming to terms with twentieth-century life, dominated as it was by the ambivalence of human actions in its wartime atrocities, ethical-religious fallout, and postmodern productions. Ultimately, Golding appears to offer no solution to ambivalence and indeterminacy. In the end, the relativity of terminology applied to Golding's novels and the epistemology of fiction in all its metafictional and postmodern strife

40. See James Tully, ed., *Meaning and Context: Quentin Skinner and His Critics;* Liu, "The Power of Formalism: The New Historicism," 743.

41. Eagleton quoted in Derek Attridge, Geoff Bennington, and Robert Young, eds., *Post-Structuralism and the Question of History,* 4; Gąsiorek, *Post-War British Fiction,* 174, 192–93.

are conducive to interpretations of the fantastic and carnivalesque. The persistent border country evident in Golding's fiction, between rationality and irrationality, natural and supernatural, flesh and spirit, mouth and anus, responds to changing cultural contexts. The greater part of his satire maps a shift from the trauma of the Holocaust to the "encryption" of this trauma in postmodern literary form. Golding's literary postmodernism reflects upon, or rather engages with, postmodernism as historical and postindustrial. Weaving through his attack on an England that constructs itself in opposition to Nazism and its "Final Solution" is an attack on the perennial English disease of class. The exclusionary gestures and cruelty of its class system suggest that, given the right conditions, England has the wherewithal to flex totalitarian muscles and proceed atrocity's way.

2

Menippean Satire, the Fantastic, and the Carnivalesque

> The one thing we know about satire is that it promises to tell us what we do not want to know—what we may, in fact, resist knowing. . . . [S]atire tells of the descent of humanity below itself.
>
> —Brian A. Connery and Kirk Combe, eds., *Theorizing Satire: Essays in Literary Criticism*

GOLDING'S FICTION IS PARTLY SATIRICAL, DRAWING ON STRATEGIES for indirect attack or critique that originate in ancient literary forms, particularly Menippean satire. Central to Menippean satire are two modes: the fantastic and the carnivalesque. Menippean satire provides a generic root for both these modes that may be seen to operate in tandem in much of Golding's fiction. Although the fantastic is subsumed within Bakhtin's conception of the Menippean-based carnivalesque, I choose to separate these modes that have been subjected to a variety of analyses not least by Tzvetan Todorov and Mikhail Bakhtin, respectively.[1] A growing body of theoretical approaches develops out of their seminal writings and informs Golding's deployment of these modes, not least in terms of their historicizing role.

Interest in Menippean satire, and debate concerning this ancient form, has been revitalized by Mikhail Bakhtin and Northrop Frye, among others. Bakhtin "conceptually links" the *menippea* with the fantastic and carnivalesque.[2] Both his analysis in *Problems of Dostoevsky's Poetics* and that by Frye in *Anatomy of Criticism* are central to our understanding of this composite form. Indeed, Joel C. Relihan has called Bakhtin and Frye

1. See Todorov, *The Fantastic: A Structural Approach to a Literary Genre;* and Bakhtin, *Problems of Dostoevsky's Poetics.*
2. See Rosemary Jackson, *Fantasy: The Literature of Subversion,* 15–16.

"deans of the study of modern Menippean satire."[3] Frye uses the term *anatomy* for Menippean satire, a form that amounts to a variety of literary productions over many centuries, incorporating "dialogue, stylization of character, fantasy, intellectual satire . . ." He adopts this term from Burton's *Anatomy of Melancholy* (1621), arguing that it suitably voices "the intellectualized approach of this form." Drawing on the Menippean satire of Varro, Lucian, Petronius, and Apuleius, he identifies its fantastic and moral utopian framework. "Anatomy" is one of Frye's four fictional forms, the others being novel, confession, and romance. However, Relihan notes that the various elements of "anatomy" are both "separable" and capable of combining to "result in other related comic, or noncomic, genres."[4] Both comic and noncomic potentials, I suggest, are actualized in Golding's work.

Bakhtin locates various elements to the *menippea.* He finds a general elevation of comedy. Yet comic elements may vary considerably from a strong form in Varro to a diminished form in Boethius. There is an unrestrained fantastic, beyond legendary and historical forms, that is highly inventive in terms of plot and philosophy. The fantastic is used not as "truth" in itself, but as foil to a truth, discourse, or philosophical concept. This subordinated fantastic, acting in unity with an idea and consolidating it, often takes the form of an adventure story. The fantastic combines the symbolic and religio-mystical with the filth and depravity of slum naturalism. This organic structure, which includes philosophical dialogue, is central to the *menippea* and its subsequent manifestations in novelistic forms. It restricts itself to pared down, ultimate questions about life, which tend to be of a practical and ethical nature. The action moves between and takes place on thresholds of heaven, earth, and hell. An experimental fantasticality is found in unusual points of view, often from above (catascopia), something that is absent from ancient epic or tragedy. Abnormal "moral and psychic states" are represented—dreams, madness, split personality, suicidal ideation. Indeed, epic and tragic integrity is lost to a divided, unfinalizable, or split mind. This extends to notions of a dialogized self and the trope of the "double." Characteristic of the genre is disinhibited and transgressive behavior or language that violates social

3. Bakhtin, *Problems of Dostoevsky's Poetics,* 107–80; Frye, *Anatomy of Criticism,* 308–12; Relihan, *Ancient Menippean Satire,* 4. More potently, Todorov has called Bakhtin "the greatest theoretician of literature in the twentieth century" (*Mikhail Bakhtin: The Dialogical Principle,* ix).

4. Relihan, *Ancient Menippean Satire,* 5; Frye, *Anatomy of Criticism,* 311; Relihan, *Ancient Menippean Satire,* 5.

norms. Such eccentricity and scandal liberate human behavior patterns from normalization. There is a focus upon oxymoronic combinations, abrupt contrasts, and *mésalliance.* The *menippea* contains "elements of *social utopia*"; this often includes a journey to an unknown land. We find the use of inserted genres at various distances from the authorial point of view. According to Bakhtin, there are multiple tones and styles that effect a "new relationship to the word as the material of literature, a relationship characteristic for the entire dialogic line of development in artistic prose." The *menippea* is involved with current, topical issues, and this journalistic nature of the form is borne out by Bakhtin's acknowledgment of Lucian's satires as "an entire encyclopedia of his times . . . full of overt and hidden polemics . . . full of allusions to the great and small events of the epoch . . . seeking to unravel and evaluate the general spirit and direction of evolving contemporary life."[5]

F. Anne Payne, who bemoans the fact that Menippean satire has been largely ignored by literary criticism and history, makes some significant additions to Bakhtin's inventory. She notes the following: dialogue between two stereotyped characters from clearly different perspectives; endless questing by a character; illustration by fantastic symbolism of the joy and terror achieved by the freedom of human thought; the superability of communication over event; hope and energy surrounding the problem at hand; the lack of a figure of unquestionable divine authority; obscenity without pornography. In Payne's words, Menippean satire denies "the possibility of an unquestionable standard, answer, method, attitude which some people mean to force down other people's throats." Here we find resonance with the tradition of Pyrrhonic skepticism and irresolution generally.[6] This extends to a strategy of textual parody in Menippean satire that, in keeping with dialogism, rebuts the authority of definition: "We experience aesthetically both the complexity and chaotic uncertainty of things."[7] In terms of a definition of parody as serious and critical, rather than purely comic, such textual parody is central to Golding's in-

5. Bakhtin, *Problems of Dostoevsky's Poetics,* 114–18.

6. Payne, *Chaucer and Menippean Satire,* 11. Payne locates modern use of Menippean satire in the work of John Barth, Thomas Pynchon, Philip Roth, and Kurt Vonnegut. For an inclusion of Vonnegut and Barth in a tradition of "modern fabulation" that includes Golding, Murdoch, and Burgess, among others, see Robert Scholes, *The Fabulators,* 13. For links between Menippean satire and Pyrrhonism, see W. Scott Blanchard, *Scholar's Bedlam: Menippean Satire in the Renaissance,* 11.

7. Payne, *Chaucer and Menippean Satire,* 14–15. On Golding's strategy of obscurity, see Redpath, *Structural Reading,* 30–34; and Allon White, *The Uses of Obscurity: The Fiction of Early Modernism.*

tertextual approach that employs not the simple reaction to and overturning of a prior text, but the simultaneous evocation of two opposed points of view. Bakhtin defines this double voice of parody as

> directed both toward the referential object of speech, as in ordinary discourse, and toward *another's discourse,* toward *someone else's speech.* If we do not recognize the existence of this second context of someone else's speech and begin to perceive stylization or parody in the same way ordinary speech is perceived, that is, as speech directed only at its referential object, then we will not grasp these phenomena in their essence: stylization will be taken for style, parody simply for a poor work of art.[8]

In all, Menippean satire delivers a topsy-turvy world where monism and authoritarianism are rejected. Equally, the form is implicitly philosophical and historicizing. It is a genre that Bakhtin sees as combining heterogeneous elements in a deeply organic, integral, and interrogative form. The contrary viewpoint then, evident in Menippean satire, promotes the symbolic subversion of the stable, familiar world—the "real" world—and questions its cultural authority.

Although a renegotiation of Golding's work within the genre of Menippean satire is attractive, such an approach may hinder as much as aid our understanding. A totalizing application of this genre will inevitably drain both our appreciation of the widely mixed modes of Golding's writing and indeed the variable nature and scope of literary works in the spirit of this form. In fact, Menippean satire is an ideal host to various reformulations, not least in postmodern literature. To avoid forcing Golding's novels into a genre that has in essence lost its center and has been deployed in various forms, we need to examine his fiction in relation to the range and function of fantastic and carnivalesque modes, those substantive components of Menippean satire that function, often stereoscopically, to subvert familiar notions of reality.

The ancient Menippean root of the "world upside down" includes contrasts between natural and supernatural realms, journeys to the world above and the world below—the subterranean underworld or diabolic world. The literary fantastic, from Apuleius's *Golden Ass,* through a post-Renaissance lull, to reemergence in the eighteenth-century Gothic, incor-

8. Bakhtin, *Problems of Dostoevsky's Poetics,* 185. See also Bakhtin, *The Dialogic Imagination: Four Essays,* 76.

porates ghosts, devils, monsters, and suchlike.[9] Such supernaturalism and focus on subterranean, heavenly, or transcendent worlds is intimately related to carnival grotesque and Menippean satire. The fantastic is also part of the link between primitive or carnivalesque ritual practices and literature. This is emphasized in Tobin Siebers's study of the violent, persecutory, and victimizing aspects of fantastic superstition. Here Siebers pays particular attention to "exclusionary gestures" of the fantastic in its representations of the outsider, stranger, or alien—all those whom society dreads and brands with the *signum diaboli.* Consonant with René Girard's *Violence and the Sacred,* Siebers stresses the need for greater focus upon anthropological and "social relations" concerning the fantastic. He asserts: "As a literature that represents the logic of superstition and descends into every conceivable kind of violence, the Romantic fantastic seems a poor form of escapism, but it may be a means of examining and reinterpreting social formations."[10]

It is apparent that Golding's novels deal in spiritual terror. Yet, a full analysis of the terrors employed by the fantastic mode has not been accorded a proper emphasis. In the second half of the eighteenth century, a strong, concerted revival of this mode occurred. In England, the work of Walpole, Beckford, Lewis, Maturin, Radcliffe, and Shelley emerged. From the romantic period onward to Stoker, Hoffmann, James, Kafka, and in modern times Lessing, Murdoch, Spark, Golding, Carter, Morrison, Rushdie, and so on, the literary fantastic developed and consolidated itself even further. However, such a consolidation has not occurred without change. Theodore Ziólkowski has described a gradual "disenchantment" with the magical and supernatural between late-eighteenth-century Gothic and late-nineteenth-century forms. This disenchantment marks a shift away from the "marvellous" to the "fantastic" and finally the "uncanny" in a diachronic interpretation of Todorov's synchronic terms. Thus, by the end of the nineteenth century it is "internalization of motivation" that "underlies almost all portrayals of the supernatural."[11]

That said, the emergence of the literary Gothic darkness and terror displaced the mood of sanity and rationality born during the Enlightenment. It bespoke the cellarage of the mind, timeless fears, primordial beasts, atavistic horrors, and all manner of mythic or folkloric terror. Newly formed monsters appeared: Frankensteins, Jekylls and Hydes,

9. See Julia Briggs, *Night Visitors: The Rise and Fall of the English Ghost Story,* 25–51.

10. Siebers, *The Romantic Fantastic,* 13–56, 27, 42, 45.

11. Ziólkowski, *Disenchanted Images: A Literary Iconology,* 242. See also Siebers, *The Romantic Fantastic,* 46–47.

and Draculas. We find mad monks, exotica, and pornography. It is this pre-Freudian realm that is captured in Piranesi's *Carceri d'Invenzione* in the eighteenth century and reflected in the work of Golding. Golding dismissed Freudian readings of his work, claiming in an interview with Jack Biles that he had not read Freud, and that basically he had the faculty, just as much as Freud did, of looking into his own mind. What we find in Golding's work originates not so much from Freudian schematism, although he cannot claim immunity from Freud, as from images of the cellar of the mind or even dungeon of the mind. These images are more about the Gothic fantastic than they are about psychoanalysis per se.[12] In *The Gothic Flame,* Devendra P. Varma compares the vast size and complexity of Gothic novels with the menacing splendor of Gothic cathedrals. This kind of diabolical grandeur is evident in Golding's work, not least in *The Spire.*

Yet writing in the twentieth century, Golding had access to the variant scope of the fantastic mode, not just its close link with romantic, Gothic forms. Golding taps into a diversified world of ghosts, metamorphoses, doubles, and other motifs, which, as Ziółkowski insists, have been progressively disenchanted. In its most disenchanted twentieth-century form, Ziółkowski argues, fantastic "magic images" can be deemed "purely playful."[13] As we shall see, in Golding's later fiction, postmodernism accounts for this more playful, nonsatirical fantastic.

Golding's early fascination with the irrational, the supernatural, and the cellarage of the mind is registered in his autobiographical essay "The Ladder and the Tree" in *The Hot Gates* (*HG,* 166–75). He relates the early influence upon him of darkness, graves, cellars, and ghosts. This was enhanced by the proximity of a graveyard to his childhood home in Marlborough—so close that Golding feared that the feet of corpses passed under his garden wall. About his parents at this time, he notes:

> How could I talk to them about darkness and the irrational? They knew so much, had such certainties, were backing all the obvious winners. I floated in their world, holding on to a casual hand, sometimes sinking again in the dark. Then I found Edgar Allan Poe's *Tales of Mystery and Imagination.* I read them with a sort of shackled fascination and recognized their quality, knew they were reports, knew that he and I had been in the same place. (*HG,* 170)

12. See Biles, *Talk,* 18; and Peter Brooks, *The Melodramatic Imagination: Balzac, Henry James, Melodrama, and the Mode of Excess,* 19.
13. Ziółkowski, *Disenchanted Images,* 242.

This fascination with the mysterious and supernatural found a natural contradiction in Golding's misdirected choice to study science at Oxford, a choice he quickly revoked by transferring to English instead. His split mind about rational and irrational aspects to the world is reflected in his adoption of the fantastic as a major mode in his fiction. "Science," he maintains, "was busy clearing up the universe. There was no place in this exquisitely logical universe for the terrors of darkness. There was darkness, of course, but it was just darkness, the absence of light; had none of the looming terror which I knew night-long in my very bones . . . even in daylight now, the dead under the wall drew up the green coverlet of our grass and lay back with a heart-squeezing grin" (*HG,* 173).

The frisson of horror is the response at which the Gothic novel, or black novel, aims. David Punter in *The Literature of Terror* considers the Gothic tradition "a body of material which was once the object of general belief—legendary, ballads, folk memories—but had begun to fall into disrepute [yet] . . . became during the eighteenth century a source of ambiguity and resonance which invited relation to contemporary anxieties." This, like Mario Praz's description of the "Gothic" as the "inevitable product of the revolutionary shocks with which the whole of Europe resounded" and Marilyn Butler's view of its paralleling the era of revolution, suggests a strong historicizing force to the revitalized Gothic fantastic in the tradition of the social and topical issues raised by Menippean satire.[14]

Correspondent to the upheavals that provoked anxieties and the registering of them in literary form during eighteenth-century revolutionary Europe, Golding adopts the fantastic mode in the face of the tumult of World War II; his use of this mode coalesces as an integral part of the carnivalesque in a historicizing amplification. Golding responds to the specter of genocide and totalitarianism hanging over postwar Europe. His appropriation of the fantastic, contrary to those who claim this mode is escapist, historicizes contemporary events and maps out the violent superstition behind the exclusion and attempted extermination of a race. Ziólkowski can be invoked in support of this interpretation. He says that "whenever there is a revival of interest in the supernatural, we should look for the cultural factors that account for that revival." It is, he argues, "a culture's choice of its representative images" that reveals "a great deal about the central concerns of that culture."[15]

14. Punter, *The Literature of Terror: A History of Gothic Fictions from 1765 to the Present Day,* 422; Praz, "Introductory Essay," 14; M. Butler, *Romantics, Rebels, and Reactionaries: English Literature and Its Background, 1760–1830,* 156–57.

15. Ziólkowksi, *Disenchanted Images,* 242, 247.

Todorov's work is seminal to study of the supernatural in literature and promotes differentiation between marvelous, fantastic, and uncanny modes.[16] Other critics following Todorov have extended or qualified these structures, utilizing his findings as a means of launching their own revisions. Christine Brooke-Rose, for example, is critical of the arbitrariness of Todorov's categories; W. L. McLendon attacks his principle that the fantastic is incompatible with allegory; Jackson concentrates on the subversive function of the fantastic mode. Crucial to all such investigations of the fantastic in relation to other modes is the immediate recognition of its separation as a "literary construct" within the psychological pool of fantasy. Otherwise, the fantastic as a subject of inquiry becomes a "catchall" and impossibly wide term.

Todorov offers three defining principles of the fantastic. The first principle is that "the text must oblige the reader to consider the world of the characters as a world of living persons and to hesitate between a natural and a supernatural explanation of events described."[17] As such, the person perceiving or witnessing the uncanny event must choose between one of two conclusions: that there has been an illusion of the senses and the laws of the known world remain intact; or that the event actually took place, has become a part of reality, but that reality must now be governed by laws still unknown to us. This fantastic moment can last only so long as the character's or the reader's hesitation does. If the hesitation resolves itself in an explanation of events as illusory, then what was fantastic becomes explained as merely uncanny. If the hesitation ends with a supernatural explanation of events, then we are in the realm of the marvelous. Once the hesitation is broken, the fantastic ceases to be. Todorov adds subgenres to this initial uncanny-fantastic-marvelous continuum to emphasize the slippage from one category into another, and the relativity of the fantastic itself—the pure fantastic occupying the central position: uncanny; fantastic uncanny; fantastic; fantastic marvelous; marvelous.

His second principle is that the same hesitation felt by the reader can also be experienced by one of the characters in the narrative. However, Todorov indicates that this principle is not a vital aspect of the fantastic. His third principle, which along with his first amounts to the bare bones of his definition of the fantastic, is that "the reader must adopt a certain attitude towards the text, must reject any allegorical or poetic interpretation." At this point, it is worth reiterating that McLendon takes exception

16. See Todorov, *Fantastic.*
17. Ibid., 33.

to this principle, viewing it as absolute and one-dimensional. Certainly, Todorov does not seem to cater to the kind of mixed "semiallegory" or "modern fabulation" of Golding's novels.[18]

However, it is important to understand Todorov's point. If the reader interprets the text immediately and pervasively as purely allegorical or poetic rather than as realistic, the first of Todorov's principles would be compromised—the strange events would not be seen as an intrusion upon the stability of the "real" world, but merely as allegorical, poetic devices. Yet allegory in Golding's fiction is what Dickson has called "modern allegory," a more flexible form, couched in realism. Besides, much of what is allegorical in Golding is subtilized and does not lend itself to intrusion upon any first reading of the fantastic.

Alongside Todorov's core principles, the fantastic is further delineated by verbal, syntactic, and semantic aspects. The verbal aspect highlights the tendency of the fantastic to use figurative language literally, and the frequency of first-person narrative—that which is more appropriately ambiguous.[19] The syntactic aspect posits the irreversibility of the fantastic text, that is, we cannot have the explanation of what is taking place first. Included in this aspect is the movement of fantastic tales through initial equilibrium, disequilibrium, and resolution in a final equilibrium. Though this shift may apply, as Todorov insists, to all narrative, within the fantastic genre the supernatural alters the equilibrium more powerfully. However, it is the impact of resolution, not the impact of disequilibrium, that is central to Golding's subversion of human "civilization." This is particularly the case in *Lord of the Flies, The Inheritors,* and *Pincher Martin.*

Finally, within the semantic aspect, Todorov deals with themes of the self and other. Of "themes of the self," which resemble "psychosis," he says: "[T]he principle we have discovered may be designated as the fragility of the limit between matter and mind. This principle engenders several fundamental themes: a special causality; pan-determinism; multiplication of the personality; collapse of the limit between subject and object; the transformation of time and space." His "themes of the other" refer to "transformations of desire" that may include incest, homosexuality,

18. Ibid.; McLendon, "Compatibility of the Fantastic and Allegory: Potocki's Saragossa Manuscript," 146. See L. L. Dickson, "H. G. Wells Upside Down: Fantasy as Allegory in William Golding's *The Inheritors,*" 156; Dickson, *Modern Allegories,* 1–11; and Scholes, *The Fabulators,* 99–144.

19. For a much needed refutation of Todorov's emphasis on the centrality of first-person unreliable narration to the fantastic, see Ziółkowski, *Disenchanted Images,* 250–51.

sadism, cruelty, necrophilia, and death itself. These themes are assigned to the psychoanalytical world of "neurosis." Such general themes correspond with and complement many elements of the carnivalesque.[20] Indeed, the fantastic, as we have already noted in its Menippean root, is inextricably linked with carnivalesque logic. This is especially true in terms of the link between the fantastic theme of psychosis or madness and carnivalesque foolery.

In *The Literary Fantastic,* Neil Cornwell traces the post-Todorovian theorizing on the fantastic and the various terminologies that have been applied. Since Cornwell has already adequately accounted for post-Todorovian theorizing to date, I will omit retracing such a review, and limit the discussion to the simplified yet core common ground between the different theories. This common ground recognizes an interdependency between the real world and that which is unreal, created, or fictive. There is broad agreement on the hesitant, uncertain, and ambiguous nature of the fantastic. This fantastic hesitation operates between natural or supernatural explanations of events that have a supernatural quality. Finally, the fantastic is generally considered both to have an "autonomous role" in literary history and "given to the expression of—and perhaps at times making an impression upon—particular social and psychological tendencies."[21] It is this common ground that I wish to remain close to and thus avoid the kind of centrifugal debate that has been spawned by too anxious a focus upon justifying the fantastic as a genre. Thus, I prefer to use the transhistorical and transgeneric term *mode.*[22] I do not wish to add to the already excessive blurring of and competition between terminologies concerning the fantastic and fantasy. Whereas the transgressive nature of humankind is powerfully registered by Golding's use of the carnivalesque, this second and related component of the Menippean form, the fantastic, and at times its Gothic forms, is adopted to interrogate the boundary or threshold between the rational and irrational, between scientific and religious or mysterious realms. It is Golding's fantastic mode, prevalent in his fiction, that frequently magnifies transgressive features of human behavior established through topsy-turvy symbolism. The full and disturbing impact of the "topsy-turvy" is often brought about in Golding's fiction by fantastic hesitation. Yet although Golding utilizes the

20. Todorov, *Fantastic,* 120, 137. For an analysis of connections and distinctions between carnivalesque and fantastic elements, see D. Losse, "Rabelaisian Paradox: Where the Fantastic and the Carnivalesque Intersect."

21. See Cornwell, *Literary Fantastic,* 12–34, 24, 27.

22. This is also the strategy adopted by Jackson in *Fantasy,* 13–60.

"pure fantastic" to good effect, particularly in *The Spire* and *Darkness Visible,* it is the generation of what I call "uncanny shock" in his early fiction that deserves greater attention. In *Lord of the Flies, The Inheritors,* and *Pincher Martin,* hesitation is naturally explained or dis-covered in a powerful and shocking way. It is this "uncanny shock" factor that has been displaced in value by genre theories of the fantastic and by the search for structural clarity in muddied waters.[23]

The gradations and transformations between the categories of the marvelous, fantastic, and uncanny, I suggest, need to be retrieved from the kind of intensive theoretical schematism to which both Brooke-Rose and Cornwell subscribe in a desperate attempt for resolution.[24] Being aware of the ambiguities involved, there is a fruitful "common ground" approach to correspondences of the pure fantastic, but more significantly to the shift from the fantastic to the uncanny in Golding's novels.

Important to my approach in this book is Jackson's claim that "fantastic literature transforms the 'real' through . . . dis-covery. It does not introduce novelty, so much as uncover all that needs to remain hidden if the world is to be comfortably 'known.' Its uncanny effects reveal an obscure, occluded region which lies behind the homely *(heimlich)* and native *(heimisch).*" It is such an occluded region that the combined force of the carnivalesque and fantastic reveals behind the comfortable, homely notions of Western civilization in Golding's early novels. In less than tragic terms, this similar though qualitatively different combination effects the discovery of the pluralistic and fragmentary economy of postmodern culture in Golding's later work. Jackson has advanced the view that fantastic literature is a literature of subversion, that it subverts the "real" or interrogates "reality."[25] It effectively makes uncertain what is familiar. And this form of subversion relies essentially on a threshold status between a "realistic" and "fantasy" world. On this border, we become uncertain and hesitate between explanations.

23. As Cornwell notes, Freud's notion of the uncanny, *Das Unheimliche,* has been considered by Margaret Carter to be "much closer to Todorov's fantastic than to the latter's uncanny" (quoted in *Literary Fantastic,* 37). Indeed, as Brooke-Rose argues, the notion of "pure" uncanny where "there is little or no supernatural, but only the bizarre or horrific . . . opens out onto all narratives with strange or unusual events, and ultimately onto all realistic fiction" (*Rhetoric of the Unreal,* 310). More simplistically, the uncanny can be read as that which is merely weird or strange.

24. See, in particular, Cornwell, *Literary Fantastic,* 39; and Brooke-Rose, *Rhetoric of the Unreal,* 84.

25. Jackson, *Fantasy,* 65. For a useful discussion of the subversive nature of the fantastic, see Jacqueline Howard, *Reading Gothic Fiction: A Bakhtinian Approach.*

Some texts may be purely fantastical, such as James's *Turn of the Screw* (1898) and Kafka's *Metamorphosis* (1915), whereas others might simply incorporate a fantastic mode that resolves in natural or supernatural explanation. Fantastic hesitation that is maintained across a substantial part of any text but not sustained at its end can be called "durative" fantastic. This form of the mode is used in *Lord of the Flies, The Inheritors, Pincher Martin,* and *Free Fall.* Fantastic hesitation that is merely elemental or haphazard can be labeled "residual" fantastic. This is deployed mostly in the later novels, *The Pyramid, The Paper Men,* and *To the Ends of the Earth.* Yet the so-called pure fantastic does not need to exist throughout any given text. What is definitive about the pure fantastic is that a text *ends* on a purely fantastic note. The only Golding novels that *clearly* achieve this are *The Spire* and *Darkness Visible.* Although *Pincher Martin* can be thought of as a borderline case for a similar categorization, the fantastic resolves more heavily in favor of a natural explanation and therefore should be thought of as "durative." Thus, a realistic text may shift at some point into the pure fantastic on account that the hesitation that is engendered is not resolved at the end of the text. This may, therefore, apply to "durative" or "residual" fantastic forms, although none of Golding's novels fall into this category. When a text such as *The Spire* or *Darkness Visible* hesitates from beginning to end, it should be thought of as "total fantastic" rather than "pure fantastic," since, as I have indicated, the term *pure fantastic* can be applied to both "durative" and "residual" forms. Furthermore, texts that are read as "marvelous" (often a synonym for "fantasy") may follow realistic conventions and loop into a domain critics call "magic (-al, -o) realism." Amaryll Chanady distinguishes between magical realism and the fantastic in the following way: "Whereas there is always the suggestion of a rational explanation in the fantastic, a magico-realist text prevents the reader from even considering a rational solution."[26] None of Golding's novels fall into this category, although *Darkness Visible* comes closest. However, a proper appreciation and understanding of the impact value when fantastic hesitation breaks into natural explanation have not been undertaken. In essence, this oversight has been brought about by an erroneous hierarchical structure to genre approaches to the fantastic, with the "pure" fantastic obtaining unwarranted primacy. Or rather, it has been granted merit on superficial terms of "purity," as if that confers upon it

26. Chanady, *Magical Realism and the Fantastic: Resolved versus Unresolved Antinomy,* 106. Often magic realism is closely linked to Latin American works of literature. On this subject, see David K. Danow, *The Spirit of Carnival: Magic Realism and the Grotesque,* 65–101.

some kind of functional superiority. There needs to be a parity of attention to the fantastic mode regardless of its status as total, durative, or residual. In the hierarchical conception of the fantastic, the primacy of the "threshold of hesitation" that varies in magnitude, and the value of breaking that threshold rather than maintaining it, has been neglected.

In general, I support Jackson's view that the fantastic, like its related mode of the carnivalesque in all its various manifestations, "points to or suggests the basis upon which cultural order rests, for it opens up, for a brief moment, on to disorder, on to illegality, on to that which lies outside the law, that which is outside dominant value systems."[27] Both the fantastic and the carnivalesque modes interrogate the borders between realms of the rational and irrational, real and unreal. They function on thresholds or shadow lines that make each realm permeable to the other. It is this liminality that Golding uses to negotiate his moral viewpoint, which moves, or progresses, or even struggles between an early, pessimistic dialectic and a more optimistic dialogism. Let us now turn our attention more directly to the carnivalesque, the second major mode in my study.

Bakhtin argues that the "top and bottom, face and backside" of things are presented simultaneously in the carnival image that is "a *new mode of interrelationship between individuals,* counterposed to the all-powerful socio-hierarchical relationships of noncarnival life." It is a "gap in the fabric of society," and since "the dominant ideology seeks to author the social order as a unified text, fixed, complete, and forever, carnival is a threat."[28] In registering the transgressive proclivities of humanity, but particularly the English, Golding turns to carnival. This topsy-turvy mode has been investigated by Bakhtin whose approach has been seminal to an ever increasing body of critical works on the history and significance of carnival and folk culture motifs in understanding a wide variety of literary texts. We need not retrace the already comprehensive analyses of the history of such forms, but draw upon them in relation to Golding. In so doing, the wider terms of Bakhtin's theories of the polyphonic novel, heteroglossia, and dialogism set out in *Problems of Dostoevsky's Poetics* and *The Dialogic Imagination* can be advanced. Such a body of theory provides for an "indissoluble link" between "the linguistic variety of prose fiction" and "its cultural function as the continuous critique of all repressive, authoritarian, one-eyed ideologies."[29] It also provides us with a link to Golding's

27. Jackson, *Fantasy,* 2.

28. Bakhtin, *Problems of Dostoevsky's Poetics,* 126, 123; Michael Holquist and Katerina Clark, *Mikhail Bakhtin,* 301.

29. David Lodge, *After Bakhtin: Essays on Fiction and Criticism,* 22.

use of the "double tongue" of the carnivalesque alongside the fantastic mode in undermining complacent assumptions about the moral superiority of "civilized" England and the Allies in his early fiction and about the status of fictive reality in his later work.

Of particular significance is how Golding's early thresholdism or liminality corresponds with the historical threshold of World War II, and effects, albeit differently, a contemporary interrogation like that which Bakhtin attempts in *Rabelais and His World.* Bakhtin's poetics of Rabelais's liberatory carnivalesque forms and, indeed, those of Dostoyevsky allows him to encode opposition to Stalin's totalitarianism. As Michael Holquist notes: "*Rabelais and His World* is, of course, *about* the subversive openness of the Rabelaisian novel, but it is also a subversively open book itself." Thus, carnivalized literature, a domain that strengthened in relation to the weakening of carnival ritual following the Renaissance, becomes a literary mode that historicizes the contemporary and debunks monism, authoritarianism, and certainty. As Julia Kristeva asserts, carnivalesque discourse is a "social and political protest." The only certainty for Bakhtin is a paradoxical unity of disunity. This "encrypting" of thresholds of conflict is similar, of course, to how fantastic forms reflect contexts of revolution, tumult, or trauma. We should not be surprised by this as both the carnivalesque and the fantastic share the same root. In this respect Golding may be placed alongside both his contemporary Bakhtin and indeed Rabelais who, Holquist argues, "knew that they were living in an unusual period, a time when virtually everything taken for granted in less troubled ages lost its certainty, was plunged into contest and flux." As such, Golding joins them in having created a "special kind of open text . . . explored as a means for inscribing" himself into his times.[30]

Bakhtin's *Rabelais and His World* provides ready-made features of the carnivalesque that may be applied in terms of both their early contradistinction and their subsequent similarity to Golding's form of the "world upside down": laughter, language of the marketplace, popular-festive forms and images, banquet imagery, grotesque imagery of the body, material bodily lower stratum, text in context. Each of these major zones of the carnivalesque system will be addressed in readings of Golding's novels in the following chapters.

Carnival and carnivalized literature, then, have a long tradition of turn-

30. Holquist, prologue to *Rabelais and His World,* by Bakhtin, xvi; Kristeva, *Desire in Language: A Semiotic Approach to Literature and Art,* 65; Holquist, prologue to *Rabelais and His World,* by Bakhtin, xv.

ing the world upside down, of symbolically subverting the dominant, ruling hierarchies of social existence. In the world of carnival, the stable, ordered conformity of social life is shed and suspended. Rules are forgotten for a period of time. In their place comes an enactment of desires and drives that has been repressed. The symbolic subversion of carnival is echoed in Golding's early use of carnivalesque motifs to register the transgressive nature of the English—their destructive, violent, and racist sides.[31] Conversely, in his later fiction, an arguably more optimistic form establishes a regenerative harmonization of positive and negative aspects of human behavior in spite of postmodern fragmentation and entropy. In this way Golding is open to both noncelebratory and celebratory readings of the carnivalesque. Peter Stallybrass notes this dual aspect of carnivalesque: "But carnivalesque dirt, like carnivalesque laughter, is radically ambivalent, being both a means of derision and debasement and a cause for celebration."[32] The noncelebratory focus is largely absent from Bakhtin's formulations.

Recently, several critics have drawn attention to the rather superficial applications of Bakhtin's theorizing of the carnivalesque in the West where a narrow focus on its celebratory and liberational aspects has been maintained. Paul Allen Miller and Charles Platter argue that Bakhtin's "antinomian tendencies have often been the subject of a facile appropriation which has obscured aspects of this complex and multi-faceted theorist not lost on his fellow Russians." They also outline the diversification of critical opinion caused by Bakhtin's "focus on the middle ground": "In sum, there are as many Bakhtins as there are perspectives from which he can be read because there are no perspectives in today's theoretical debates for which Bakhtin's work does not propose both a critical challenge and a welcome opportunity."[33]

Caryl Emerson asks this question: "How does Bakhtin's enthusiasm for the subversive, mocking, trickster-ridden underside of Greek and Roman

31. For discussion of the contradictory nature of the carnivalesque as officially sanctioned "unofficial" festivity, see Bakhtin, *Rabelais and His World*, 89; Terry Eagleton, "Bakhtin, Schopenhauer, Kundera," 178–88; Umberto Eco, V. V. Ivanov, and Monica Rector, *Carnival!* 6; Simon Goldhill, *The Poet's Voice: Essays on Poetics and Greek Literature*, 183–85; and Linda Hutcheon, *A Theory of Parody: The Teachings of Twentieth-Century Art Forms*, 74–77. For a view of carnival as a more diffuse, symbolic subversion, see M. Keith Booker, *Techniques of Subversion in Modern Literature: Transgression, Abjection, and the Carnivalesque*, 244, 247.

32. Stallybrass, "'Drunk with the Cup of Liberty': Robin Hood, the Carnivalesque, and the Rhetoric of Violence in Early Modern England," 52.

33. P. A. Miller and Platter, "Introduction," 118, 120.

culture . . . measure up against his equally passionate advocacy of continuity, personal responsibility, the need for words and deeds to be attached to individual voices and bodies—in short, his classicist emphasis on sobriety and wholeness?" In investigating the answer, Emerson outlines the work of three Russian scholars, Elena Volkova, T. G. Mal'chukova, and V. E. Khalizev. Volkova emphasizes a dual Bakhtinian aesthetics comprising not simply celebratory carnivalesque but also a more serious and classical "tragic guilt" and "tearful aspect of the world." Mal'chukova counters views of Bakhtin as a relativist and democrat by arguing for his moral absolutism. Finally, Khalizev describes authoritative and relative approaches to experience as classical and nonclassical, as respectively promoting dogmatic rigidity and nihilism. He regrets the fashion for readings of Bakhtin along nonclassical lines to the exclusion of his early and, as Carl A. Rubino suggests, his late focus on ethical coherence. Importantly, Khalizev stresses the serious historicizing aspect of Bakhtin's nonclassicism. In other words, Bakhtin's relativity seriously undermines a monologic Stalinism. Thus he claims that "'anti-relativist refinements and stipulations' are the very bridge between Bakhtin's early published manuscripts and his later literary scholarship."[34]

This finding of the "serious word" in carnival in relation to Stalinist atrocities is pertinent to Golding's more overtly classical and tragic approach to the form in his early fiction.[35] As such, Golding faces head-on what Bakhtin did not: the violence of carnival. Gary Saul Morson and Caryl Emerson have pointed out that Bakhtin "did not seriously consider the philosophical—and much less the political—implications of carnival at its least 'reduced.'" They note that "Bakhtin ignores the dangers of carnivalistic violence and antinomian energy. In short, it is not carnival but the 'carnival symbolic' that inspires him, not real individual bodies in interaction but the potential for extending, transcending, and rendering immortal the collective body."[36] In contrast, Golding's early carnivalesque is distinctly more overt in historicizing the atrocious events of World War II on account of its more serious, negative, and hence more violent representation. The deflation of this "serious word" in Golding's later carnivalesque (except in *Darkness Visible*) maps the shift from an intense

34. Emerson, "Irreverent Bakhtin and the Imperturbable Classics," 126, 127 (see also Emerson, *The First Hundred Years of Mikhail Bakhtin*); see Rubino, "Opening Up the Classical Past: Bakhtin, Aristotle, Literature, Life," 147; Khalizev quoted in Emerson, "Irreverent Bakhtin," 132.

35. Emerson, "Irreverent Bakhtin," 131.

36. Morson and Emerson, *Mikhail Bakhtin: Creation of a Prosaics*, 470.

historicism concerning contemporary human tragedies to one that concerns the postmodern condition and the resultant, still ongoing quest for a moral imperative that goes beyond the seeming defeat of nontotalization. Like Bakhtin, Golding is "concerned with how humans make moral choices under conditions of uncertainty."[37] Again, the carnivalesque here is not simply positive, but can be relegated to the more obliquely negative form with which Bakhtin targets Stalinism. In this way, a "double-voiced" carnivalesque of varying historicizing force operates across Golding's corpus.[38] Hence, within the "double tongue" structure of Menippean satire, we find yet another "double tongue" of noncelebratory and celebratory carnivalesque. This seriocomical divide or doubleness, as we shall see, also extends to the development of the fantastic across Golding's fiction.

The word *carnival* is generally seen to derive from the Latin *carnem levare* (meaning "'the putting away or removal of flesh (as food),' the name being originally proper to the eve of Ash Wednesday").[39] The Italian form *carne vale* means "farewell to meat." As such it denotes festivities preceding the Lenten fast. However, other popular etymologies abound. Two of them are worth bearing in mind. First, it is claimed to come from the Latin *carrus navalis* for the ship or float carrying Dionysus in Greek festivities. Second, according to Allon White, it derives from the taking up of meat as food and sex.[40] The word *carnivalesque* is generally deployed as a broad term for carnival elements in a wide range of rituals and literatures, from ancient times to the present, and not restricted to pre-Lenten festivities alone.

It is important, then, to recognize that carnival and the carnivalesque are not reducible to any rigid or monolithic structure. The term *carnival* incorporates rituals, spectacles, and a variety of folk culture motifs: fairs, feasts, processions, marketplace amusements, comic shows, costumes, masks, funeral wakes, dancing, mummery, dwarfs, giants, monsters, circus animals, parodies, travesties, vulgar farce, and "billingsgate."[41] These

37. For attention to moral aspects of Bakhtin's córpus, see Rubino, "Classical Past," 145–54, 153.

38. Morson and Emerson, *Mikhail Bakhtin*, 470.

39. *The Compact Edition of the Oxford English Dictionary*, s.v. "carnival."

40. For an account of Perocchi's derivation of *carne vale* from *carnelevamen*, and regarding the Latin *carrus navalis*, see Monica Rector, "The Code and Message of Carnival: 'Escolas de Samba,'" 39. See Allon White, *Carnival, Hysteria, and Writing: Collected Essays and Autobiography*, 170. It is worth noting that the OED does not support White's assertion. See also Peter Burke, *Popular Culture in Early Modern Europe*, 185–87.

41. See Peter Stallybrass and Allon White, *The Politics and Poetics of Transgression*, 8. Billingsgate comprises a range of oaths, swearing, curses, slang, and scatological language. Basically, it is a genre of obscene or low folk humor.

rituals, spectacles, and the diaspora of "carnival" motifs or images into various cultural representations and literatures can be subsumed under the term *carnivalesque.* Bakhtin's carnival is a heterogeneous and excessive party time where the people become one by participating in turning the known, familiar world on its head. This is a process of "debasing" or "decrowning," of making "high" forms "low."[42] But, as I will discuss, this is not the only face of carnival. A Janus-like face operates in carnival, not simply in Bakhtin's terms of the simultaneous presence of official and unofficial aspects to this form, but also between celebratory and noncelebratory aspects of popular excess.[43]

Carnival as an event or ritual is multiform across history, and occurs in different cultures, with variable intensity, duration, and significance. As Monica Rector notes, its history stretches back to ancient times "when it was remarkable for merry dances, masks, and above all for striking licentiousness." But its ultimate origins are rooted in primitive cultic feasts and rituals not conducive to historical objectivity, yet tantalizing to folklorists and anthropologists alike. Its "evolution" may be noted in the worship of Isis, the Bacchanalia, Lupercalia, and Roman Saturnalia. As I noted earlier, the element of violence, for example, evident in carnival practice up to and including the Middle Ages declined somewhat with the Renaissance. Rector finds evidence for this decline in the fact that "the celebration of Carnival began to show an artistic touch, characterized by balls and parades and floats." Carnival themes and motifs are increasingly appropriated as literary forms. Thus, the site for carnival extends from social event to literary production. The utilization of the carnivalesque in literature is diverse. Indeed, whereas carnivalized literature is often interpreted as celebratory and distinctly utopian, Golding's carnivalesque evinces both this form and a pessimistic dystopian form. As such, the term *Menippean tragedy* may suit the more destructive aspects of his early work.[44] Violent, anti-Semitic, and racist elements to the carnivalesque are foregrounded in his early fiction, whereas a more optimistic, comic, or festive form is developed later. Therefore, Golding's carnivalesque cannot be read within the purely celebratory focus of Bakhtin's study in *Rabelais and His World.* Rather, Golding adopts both noncelebratory and celebratory forms of the carnivalesque across his fiction.

We know, not least from the writings of Stallybrass and White and oth-

42. See Bakhtin, *Problems of Dostoevsky's Poetics,* 124–26.

43. See Bakhtin, *Rabelais and His World,* 81.

44. Rector, "Code and Message," 38, 39. See Payne, *Chaucer and Menippean Satire,* 12.

ers, that the process of abjection in carnival incorporates the violent abuse and expulsion of minorities or "alien elements" such as the Jews.[45] This abuse extends to the eating of pig meat at carnival time as a sign of contempt and hatred for Jews who are blamed for the Lenten fast.[46] Indeed, the history of post-Christian carnivalesque rituals has often been the history of anti-Semitism, played out with various levels of aggression. For example, the famous carnival in Romans "included a race for Jews, offering a sadistic opportunity for throwing mud and stones at them as they passed," and the May Day festival of 1517 became a riot against outsiders. In terms of more recent history of carnival violence, Dominick LaCapra notes the sadistic "rituals of degradation" employed in camps such as Auschwitz.[47] Such a history of the abjection of pig flesh and racist or anti-Semitic practices was surely not lost on Golding in the light of the Holocaust. Indeed, *Lord of the Flies* is replete with violent carnival images of the pig and the "piggification" of humans, which is a carnivalesque reversal between human and beast.[48]

Thus, although carnival may be viewed as counteracting that which "seeks to absolutize a given condition of existence or a given social order" and makes "possible the discovery of new and as yet unseen things," it is also a site of violence against the weak and marginalized. According to Scott Wilson: "Carnival licenses transgression in the form of cross-dressing, topsey-turveydom [*sic*], inversion and so on; however, the carnivalesque

45. See Stallybrass and White, *Politics of Transgression*, 19. On abjection, see Booker, *Techniques of Subversion;* Julia Kristeva, *Powers of Horror: An Essay on Abjection;* and Judith Butler, *Gender Trouble: Feminism and the Subversion of Identity*, 133. For further reference to the negative or violent aspects of ritual and carnivalesque, see Bristol, *Carnival and Theater*, 51; Burke, *Popular Culture*, 177–204; Robert Darnton, *The Great Cat Massacre;* John Docker, *Postmodernism and Popular Culture*, 191–92; René Girard, *Violence and the Sacred;* Emmanuel Le Roy Ladurie, *Carnival in Romans: A People's Uprising at Romans, 1579–1580;* and Rubino, "Classical Past," 142–43. On the mob or crowd aspects to ritual, see Natalie Zemon Davis, *Society and Culture in Early Modern France: Eight Essays;* E. J. Hobsbawm, *Primitive Rebels: Studies in Archaic Forms of Social Movement in the 19th and 20th Centuries;* George Rudé, *The Crowd in History: A Study of Popular Disturbances in France and England, 1730–1848;* Stallybrass and White, *Politics of Transgression*, 53–70; Enid Welsford, *The Fool: His Social and Literary History*, 234; and Scott Wilson, *Cultural Materialism: Theory and Practice*, xii.

46. Stallybrass and White, *Politics of Transgression*, 54. See also Burke, *Popular Culture*, 187, 198, 200, 204; Docker, *Postmodernism and Popular Culture*, 191–92; and White, *Carnival, Hysteria, and Writing*, 118–19, 148, 170.

47. Docker, *Postmodernism and Popular Culture*, 191–92; LaCapra, *Representing the Holocaust*, 170, 222, 173. See also LaCapra, "Bakhtin, Marxism, and the Carnivalesque," 291–324; and Terence Des Pres, *The Survivor: An Anatomy of Life in the Death Camps*, 222–23.

48. See Burke, *Popular Culture*, 188–89.

suspension of social hierarchy and the law also unleashes very unpleasant forms of violence, lynchings, queer bashing and so on, forms of transgressive 'enjoyment' that bond one sort of racist or homophobic community."[49] This was not missed in Golding's oblique yet nevertheless powerful evocation of Nazi genocide in *Lord of the Flies* and *The Inheritors,* and to some degree in *Pincher Martin* and *Free Fall.*

The misrule of carnival can, therefore, be other than celebratory. It is precisely this aspect of misrule that is featured in the detailed examination of *Lord of the Flies* and *The Inheritors* that appears in the following chapter. The Greek Dionysianism that James Baker has seen as altogether more violent and dangerous pertains to this early carnivalesque in Golding's fiction, though a more celebratory Roman Dionysianism gradually intrudes. We may infer from this intrusion of a more celebratory form and the shift in the subject matter of Golding's later fiction from the Holocaust and totalitarianism to issues concerning class, metafiction, and postmodernism a lessening of the author's grief about World War II.[50] We can observe this shift in emphasis, for example, between the violent, "pig-killing" of Simon in *Lord of the Flies* and the more comical "crucifarce" of Matty in *Darkness Visible,* or between the orgiastic eating of Liku in *The Inheritors* and the clownish behavior of Barclay and Tucker in *The Paper Men.* Golding synthesizes these Greek and Roman roots alongside Christian and secular traditions of topsy-turvydom, marking a shift from a "not-so-jolly" to a "jolly" or, more accurately, "jollier" form. Sometimes the break between "not-so-jolly" and "jolly" is difficult to find. It is subtilized in a move from what may broadly be described as tragedy to tragicomedy. The carnivalesque or "world upside down" is incorporated both in his use of symbolism and in the form of intertextual revisionism of prior literary works. This literary mode is used in various ways in Golding's novels, often in tandem with the related mode of the fantastic.

In Golding's early works, he roots into the tradition of carnivalesque transgression to disturb us in a resonant fashion. It is a noncelebratory car-

49. Bakhtin, *Problems of Dostoevsky's Poetics,* 160, 166; S. Wilson, *Cultural Materialism,* xii.

50. In addition, we may note Girard's objection to assertions by critics such as Rudolf Otto who refer to the unique nature of Dionysian rites: "There is no aspect of the Dionysiac myth or ritual that does not find a distinct echo in many primitive societies" (*Violence and the Sacred,* 131). This widens Dionysian parallels in Golding's work. Furthermore, Girard is critical of the Nietzschean Dionysus: "Only the quixotic masochism of our own age, the result of a long immunity to the violence that threatens primitive societies, allows us to see anything attractive in the Dionysus of *The Bacchae*" (132).

nivalesque, ramified by specific textual details, that acts powerfully to establish English totalitarianism, the cruelty of the English class system, religious fanaticism, and general transgressive behavior as part of the human condition. This early carnivalesque is marked by a didactic, fabular, and pessimistic trajectory. Yet his later carnivalesque, a more celebratory kind, operates within a less didactic literary form. This shift toward a regenerative carnivalesque, away from an early degenerative, satiric parody, combines the replacement of a tragi-fantastic mode by a "residual" mock-fantastic one. Such a change is in line with the development of his work from fable and myth toward realistic fiction.[51] It is also, as I suggested earlier, evidence of a "double tongue" to the fantastic mode itself. This shift in form corresponds to a development across the Golding corpus from fiction that responds to the sociopolitical context of World War II to that which encrypts the trauma of the Holocaust and other atrocities by immersion in postmodernist forms. This unveils a pattern at the root of Golding's historicizing fiction: that noncelebratory carnivalesque and fantastic modes historicize specific events within a fabular and mythic structure and that a celebratory carnivalesque and weakened fantastic historicize a general cultural paradigm in his later more realistic fiction.

Even so, such a progression is not clear-cut. A series of lurches toward a jollier, more optimistic form take place in this development, which warrant the term *struggle* above "progression." Golding's fiction appears to be moving toward lighter, more comic, and less pessimistic forms in a middle phase to his work, when *Darkness Visible* erupts like a "relapse" or "aftershock" to what can be inferred as his grief response to events of World War II—a great historical threshold—before quieting once more through *The Paper Men,* and a last phase of tragicomic equipoise in *To the Ends of the Earth.* Both the satirical and the historicizing potential of carnivalized literature is not to be overlooked in its noncelebratory and celebratory manifestations, two styles of carnivalesque that might be appropriately discussed in negative-positive or pessimistic-optimistic terms.

51. For the notion of "vestigial" fantastic as marking a movement in fiction toward realism, see Cornwell, *Literary Fantastic,* xii.

3

Literature of Atrocity

Lord of the Flies and *The Inheritors*

> We are post-Auschwitz homo sapiens because the evidence, the photographs of the sea of bones and gold fillings, of children's shoes and hands leaving a black claw-mark on oven walls, have altered our sense of possible enactments.
>
> —George Steiner, *Language and Silence: Essays, 1958–1966*

> Never shall I forget that night, the first night in camp, which has turned my life into one long night. . . . Never shall I forget the little faces of the children, whose bodies I saw turned into wreaths of smoke beneath a silent blue sky. Never shall I forget those flames which consumed my faith forever.
>
> —Elie Wiesel, *Night*

IN MOVING BEYOND THE EARLIER CRITICAL RECOGNITION THAT Golding interrogates English "immunity" from totalitarian violence and the institutionalization of this brutality in its class structure, we need to show how this attack is achieved through the use of fantastic and carnivalesque modes, modes that amount to Juvenalian or noncelebratory satire in opposition to merely universal or ahistoricist readings. As such, the fantastic is a technique of "literature of atrocity," significant in terms of the Holocaust experience, and its theme of demonization joins the noncelebratory carnivalesque in foregrounding exclusionary gestures toward the Jews. Yet Golding's attack on English constructions of national identity in opposition to Nazism is obstructed by the fabular and hence indirect form of critique in both *Lord of the Flies* (1954) and *The Inheritors* (1955).

Contrary to those who claim the fantastic mode is escapist, Golding uses it in *Lord of the Flies* and *The Inheritors* to interrogate contemporary events and map out the violent superstition behind the exclusion and attempted extermination of the Jewish race that has been viewed historically as an outsider race.[1] In *Lord of the Flies,* fantastic hesitation breaks into the shocking natural explanation that the "Beast" is not an external, supernatural force of evil. The only "Beast" on the island is the fascist group of English adolescent males who kill or attempt to kill outsiders: Simon, Piggy, and Ralph. In their noncelebratory, violent, and fascistic carnivalesque behavior, we witness English schoolboys not only dressing but even acting like Nazis. Alan Sinfield, in his book *Society and Literature,* argues that "the British themselves (in spite of fighting against fascism in the war) were not immune from that very sickness [of regarding human beings as means rather than ends], diagnosed by the existentialists, which had given rise to fascist violence and totalitarianism. William Golding, in particular, challenged the notion that the British were, in some peculiar way, different or special." Sinfield asserts that "when Jack and Roger turn upon Piggy and Simon, they are, for Golding, simply making manifest the brutal and violent pattern of behaviour that underlies Britain's stratified and bullying social order." It is not insignificant that the boys who take up leadership roles, Ralph and Jack, appear to be from a privileged background, perhaps educated at public or boarding schools. In his essay "Schoolboys," Ian McEwan says: "As far as I was concerned, Golding's island was a thinly disguised boarding school." Certainly, as S. J. Boyd suggests, Golding's "deep bitterness at and hatred of the evils of class" are evident in *Lord of the Flies,* as in his later novels, *The Pyramid* and *Rites of Passage.* Boyd claims that there is a "middle-class ambience" to Ralph, who "is not slow to inform Piggy that his father is officer-class," and Jack, who has a "privileged choir-school background." He argues that Piggy himself is very much a "lower-class" outsider whose accent—a "mark of class"—is mocked. Indeed, Piggy's "main persecutor" is Jack who has strong notions of hierarchy because of his privileged education and previous status as head boy of his choir school. Sinfield's and Boyd's insights can be extended to reveal how Golding mixes his critique of the English class system with a critique of English fascism—a dual attack that is achieved through the deployment of fantastic and carnivalesque modes. If this is Golding's aim, we might wonder at the unfair nature of such a linkage, especially since being a member of the privileged classes does not necessarily make you right wing, as Auden, Spender, and Orwell can attest with their radicalism and Marxism during the 1920s and 1930s. In

1. For a useful summary of critical positions that support or oppose the notion of "escape" in the fantastic, see Siebers, *The Romantic Fantastic,* 43–45.

broad terms, however, Golding does seem to critique not just English complacency about being anti- or non-Nazi, but also the English class system that perpetuates so much division and exclusion of "outsiders." This suggests some link between Golding's work and what Blake Morrison calls the "token rebellion" against social privilege by "Movement" writers of the 1950s.[2]

In *The Inheritors,* the "shock tactic" of breaking fantastic hesitation brings a startling recognition that "civilized" human beings commit genocide against those they project as monstrous "ogres" or devils. The Cro-Magnon people, progenitors of Homo sapiens, exterminate a race that, Boyd argues, resembles the Jews. The fantastic tension between the real and unreal in all these novels is strongly evocative of the Holocaust experience and the kind of writing it provoked. This tension was not only a constituent of the Holocaust experience but also an aesthetic technique in "literature of atrocity" that portrayed horrors in a manner that went beyond documentary account.[3] *Lord of the Flies* and *The Inheritors* can be included in this tradition.

The carnivalesque in *Lord of the Flies* and *The Inheritors* is revealed in the suspension and shedding of the stable, ordered conformity of social life. Rules are forgotten for a period of time. In their place comes an enactment of desires and drives that have been repressed. But the carnivalesque behavior in these novels is presented as violently anti-Semitic. This noncelebratory aspect to carnival has been foregrounded by Peter Stallybrass and Allon White's argument that carnival "violently abuses and demonizes" outsiders such as the Jews, whose abjection is promoted by carnival practices such as the eating of pig flesh. The history of carnival's noncelebratory aspect was not lost on Golding in the light of the Jewish Holocaust. Indeed, *Lord of the Flies* is replete with violent carnival images of the pig. Thus, carnival is a site of violence against the weak, the marginalized. This was not missed in Golding's powerful evocation of English "Nazism."

2. Sinfield, *Society and Literature, 1945–1970,* 35–36; McEwan, "Schoolboys," 158; Boyd, *Novels of Golding,* 10–11; Morrison, *The Movement,* 77.

3. Boyd, *Novels of Golding,* 40–42. See Langer, *Literary Imagination,* 43–49. Langer asserts: "To establish an order of reality in which the unimaginable becomes imaginatively acceptable exceeds the capacities of an art devoted entirely to verisimilitude; some quality of the fantastic, whether stylistic or descriptive, becomes an essential ingredient of *l'univers concentrationnaire.* Indeed, those who recorded details painstakingly in an attempt to omit none of the horror may have been unwittingly guilty of ignoring precisely the chief source of that horror—existence in a middle realm between life and death with its ambiguous and inconsistent appeals to survival and extinction, which continuously undermined the logic of existence without offering any satisfactory alternative" (43).

The carnivalesque, topsy-turvy world is widely represented in the violent, noncelebratory Dionysianism and scatology of *Lord of the Flies* and *The Inheritors.* This use of the carnivalesque cannot be understood within Mikhail Bakhtin's purely celebratory focus in *Rabelais and His World.*

Although *Lord of the Flies* is a strong attack on notions of English moral superiority vis-à-vis Nazism, such a critique is hampered somewhat by its fabular form. It subtilizes historical reference to Nazi-like group fascism. This obfuscation of historical reference continues in *The Inheritors,* which more generally attacks the notion of "civilization" rather than English moral superiority. However, we might see Golding's attack upon H. G. Wells's racial elitism and the comparison evoked between such views and Nazism as a general warning that the English have no grounds for complacency about their moral distance from atrocities carried out in the Holocaust. In *The Inheritors,* the Holocaust is strongly evoked in the racial extermination of Neanderthal Man but is again hampered by Golding's use of fable. As I will demonstrate in the following chapter, this reference to contemporary atrocity and fascism is strengthened in *Pincher Martin* and *Free Fall,* novels that shift progressively from fabular to historical form and delineate more closely the totalitarian personality.

In *Lord of the Flies* particularly, and perhaps more tenuously in *The Inheritors,* Golding's *Vergangenheitsbewältigung,* or "coming to terms with the past," concludes that the English and Nazis are not so different as one might expect. It is this painful evocation of similitude that has been overlooked in earlier critical readings. Both novels should certainly be included in the wider European tradition of "literature of atrocity." That we know Golding himself to have been deeply involved in the war, on intimate terms with its horror, and exercised by expressions not just of Allied moral superiority to Nazis, but of racial violence that broke out in England after the war as well, is significant for a full understanding of his early novels.

In *A Moving Target,* Golding tells of the impact this loss of belief in the "perfectibility of social man" had on *Lord of the Flies:* "The years of my life that went into the book were not years of thinking but of feeling, years of wordless brooding that brought me not so much to an opinion as a stance. It was like lamenting the lost childhood of the world. The theme of *Lord of the Flies* is grief, sheer grief, grief, grief, grief" (*MT,* 163). Despite such commentary from Golding himself, the effect of the war and other social contexts such as racial violence on his writing has drawn scant attention from critics. This emphasis has tended to remain submerged.

Furthermore, there has been no consideration of how Golding, "punch drunk" on atrocity, uses fantastic and carnivalesque modes powerfully to register his grief about this context.[4] The following readings of *Lord of the Flies* and *The Inheritors* aim to redress this lack. These novels, which can be thought of as a pair, make an oblique response to the sociopolitical context of World War II and its aftermath. They provide an uneasy coexistence of the universal and historical.[5]

Lord of the Flies

In *Lord of the Flies,* fantastic and carnivalesque modes are used to subvert postwar English complacency about the deeds of Nazism, particularly the Holocaust. Although oblique, Golding effects an integration between literature and cultural context. This interpretation renegotiates previous critical paradigms that have, for the most part, centered on the timeless or perennial concerns of this novel about a group of English schoolboys, deserted on a South Pacific island following a nuclear third world war, and their descent into ritual savagery and violence.[6] As most critics attest, the characters replicate those in R. M. Ballantyne's *Coral Island* (1858), who in similar straits pull together and overcome external dangers from natives and pirates. Ballantyne's schoolboys exemplify cultural assumptions of imperial superiority and conversely the inferiority of the "fuzzy-wuzzies" or "savages," the indigenous race feared for its cannibalistic practices. For Ballantyne's boys, evil and degenerative nature is outside of them, and the suggestion is that imperial colonialism is

4. Oldsey and Weintraub, *Art of Golding,* 173. Oldsey and Weintraub consider the branding of Golding's vision "by acts of superior whites in places like Belsen and Hiroshima" as the core unifying thesis behind his early novels (45). Dick suggests that Golding's focus on the evil side of humankind in *Lord of the Flies* resembles media presentations of Nazi atrocities that do not tell the whole story (*William Golding* [1967], 34–35).

5. On the paradox of timeless novels that remain contemporary, see Oldsey and Weintraub, *Art of Golding,* 11, 43–45, 173; and Josipovici, *World and Book,* 236. Dickson, developing the work of Edwin Honig and Angus Fletcher, evaluates allegory along the lines of what Scholes has termed "modern fabulation," which "tends away from the representation of reality but returns toward actual life by way of ethically controlled fantasy" (see Dickson, *Modern Allegories,* 1; and Scholes, *The Fabulators,* 11–14).

6. According to Crompton: "The book originally began with a description of the atomic explosion [cut prior to publication] out of which the children escaped, an event recapitulated exactly but in miniature by the fire that is destroying the island at the end of the book" (*View from the Spire,* 96). This is ratified by Golding who told John Haffenden that the "picture of destruction" in the fire scene "was an Atomic one; the island had expanded to be the whole great globe" ("William Golding: An Interview," 10).

beneficent, that the savage can be "saved" by the civilized, Christian Western man. Such inherent and dominant racial elitism is extended in Ballantyne's *Gorilla Hunters* (1861), in which older versions of the same schoolboys, on a scientific expedition in Africa, hardly differentiate between the gorillas and the natives.

Golding subverts these notions of racial and cultural superiority, of scientific progress, notions casting long shadows over atrocities against the Jews carried out in World War II.[7] He draws a parallel between the violent history of English imperialist adolescent masculine culture and the extermination of the Jews. He broaches the grim fact that English colonial warfare against "inferior" races, modeled on hunting and pig sticking, was not a million miles away from the extermination of the Jews. Pig sticking, of course, was at the heart of R. S. S. Baden-Powell's scouting repertoire. Indeed, in 1924 he published *Pig Sticking or Hog Hunting*, a guide for scouts on that very art. Given the whole setting of *Lord of the Flies*, with its reference to Ballantyne and empire boys, Golding appears to have the imperial scouting ethic in his sights. John M. MacKenzie alerts us to the greater reach of such an ethic:

> Africans swiftly became the human substitute for the usual animal prey. Baden-Powell constantly stressed that the scouting and stalking techniques of the Hunt could immediately be transferred to human quarry in times of war. Hunting was also . . . a preparation for the violence and brutalities of war. By brutalising themselves in the blood of the chase, the military prepared themselves for an easy adjustment to human warfare, particularly in an age so strongly conditioned by social Darwinian ideas on race.[8]

Golding's critique is not directed exclusively at Nazi war criminality but at the postwar complacency of the English who too readily distanced themselves from what the Nazis did. He reminds them of their long infatuation with social Darwinism. Graham Dawson maps the trajectory of the "soldier hero," an "idealized," militaristic masculinity at the symbolic heart of English national identity and British imperialism. He argues that this "imagining of masculinities" in terms of warfare and adventure

7. S. Laing argues that "the reversal of texts of high bourgeois optimism" in Golding's early work, and focus on the irrational, follows Golding's participation in and reflection on World War II. He refers to Golding's revelation of "history as nightmare" ("Novels and the Novel," 241).

8. MacKenzie, "The Imperial Pioneer and Hunter and the British Masculine Stereotype in Late Victorian and Edwardian Times," 188.

pervades the national culture, swamps boyhood fantasies, and, in particular, promotes rigid gendering, xenophobia, and racial violence.[9] In *Lord of the Flies,* Golding's critique of British imperial, protofascist history is powerfully registered by the Nazification of English schoolboys: "Shorts, shirts, and different garments they carried in their hands: but each boy wore a square black cap with a silver badge in it. Their bodies, from throat to ankle, were hidden by black cloaks which bore a long silver cross on the left breast and each neck was finished off with a hambone frill" (*LF,* 20–21).

James Gindin insists that Golding's description of Jack's gang—who are English—"deliberately suggests the Nazis." Despite a preference for the universal aspects of Golding's fiction, Leighton Hodson suggests Piggy might represent the "democrat and intellectual," Jack "Hitler," and Roger a "potential concentration camp guard." L. L. Dickson identifies the novel as political allegory, referring to World War II atrocities, particularly those inflicted upon the Jews. Suzie Mackenzie refers to Jack's gang as a "fascist coup" and sees the opposition between democracy and totalitarianism as one of the novel's themes. The "black" garments and caps are, indeed, highly suggestive of the Nazi *Schutzstaffeln,* or SS—the "Black Angels" responsible for the Final Solution. Certainly, Golding's candid comments to John Haffenden suggest this: "I think it's broadly true to say that in *Lord of the Flies* I was saying, 'had I been in Germany I would have been at most a member of the SS, because I would have liked the uniform and so on.'" They also suggest Oswald Mosley's Blackshirts. The silver cross may obliquely bring to mind both the Iron Cross *(Eisernen Kreuz)* and the anti-Semitic swastika. The reference to "hambone" may suggest the skull and crossbones or Death's Head *(Totenkopf)* insignia of the SS. Certainly, the "black cap with a silver badge in it" resembles the black ski caps decorated with the skull and crossbones worn by Hitler's early group of bodyguards, the *Stabswache.* Like Hitler's *Stabswache,* which was made up of twelve bodyguards, Jack's gang or squad is small in number. Nazification of Jack's gang is further amplified by its delight in parades and pageantry, which together with "the unshackling of primitive instincts" and "the denial of reason" is all part of what psychoanalytical theories categorize under the "style and methods of fascism," according to Ernst Nolte.[10] This mingling of Nazism and Englishness is not to be over-

9. See Dawson, *Soldier Heroes: British Adventure, Empire, and the Imagining of Masculinities.*

10. Gindin, *William Golding,* 22; Hodson, *William Golding,* 32. See also Medcalf, *William Golding,* 10, 13. Dickson, *Modern Allegories,* 24–25. McCarron has written that

looked. Of course, it is the violence of Jack's gang that most powerfully suggests links between them and the Nazis.

The centrality of violence to fascism can be charted, for example, in the appeal that Georges Sorel's apparent valorization of direct violent action in *Reflections on Violence* had for fascist ideologues. Adolescent male aggression, like that of Baden-Powell's pig sticking, is central to Nazism and other versions of fascism or totalitarianism.[11] Silke Hesse contends that because adolescents are "unattached," "mobile," impressionable, physically strong, and easily "directed towards ideals and heroes" on account of unfocused sexuality, the adolescent gang is seen as "a most efficient tool in the hands of a dictator." She concludes: "Of course, Fascism cannot be exhaustively explained with reference to male adolescence. Yet most of the major theories of fascism emphasize the youthful nature of the movement and, even more, its masculinity, in terms both of participation and of traditionally masculine values." Hitler himself has been called "an eternal adolescent" by Saul Friedlander. We may see Jack's gang as an English version of the *Hitlerjugend,* or Hitler Youth, who grew into the jackboots of the SS, or, indeed, Mosley's New Party (NUPA) Youth Movement. Nicholas Mosley notes that Christopher Hobhouse, of Mosley's New Party, "said he saw the NUPA Youth Movement turning into something like the Nazi SS." Again, Robert Skidelsky argues that as with fascism in general, "the most striking thing about active blackshirts was their youth." In an early review, V. S. Pritchett links *Lord of the Flies* to "the modern political nightmare," and hoped that it was being read in Germany.[12] I would rather suggest that Golding hoped it was being read in Britain and other Allied nations.

---

the novel "would not have been written had Belsen and Auschwitz never existed, or indeed had Dresden never been bombed by the Allies" (*William Golding,* 4). Mackenzie, "Return of the Natives," 40; see Rupert Butler, *The Black Angels;* Haffenden, "William Golding: An Interview," 11; see E. W. W. Fowler, *Nazi Regalia,* 150; Nolte, *Three Faces of Fascism,* 39.

11. The significance of male youth to fascist movements has been noted by historians and theorists of totalitarianism. See Hannah Arendt, *The Origins of Totalitarianism,* 227, 366, 377, 399; Renzo de Felice, *Interpretations of Fascism,* 179; Nolte, *Three Faces of Fascism,* 618; Noel O'Sullivan, *Fascism,* 74–75; and Alice Yaeger Kaplan, *Reproductions of Banality: Fascism, Literature, and French Intellectual Life,* 22. For a detailed examination of the importance of young male gangs to fascism, see Silke Hesse, "Fascism and the Hypertrophy of Male Adolescence," 157–75. She writes: "I would suggest that, rather than patriarchy, the very different structure of a gang of adolescent youths is the model of Fascist society" (172).

12. Hesse, "Fascism and Male Adolescence," 172, 175; Saul Friedlander quoted in Gerhard Rempel, *Hitler's Children: The Hitler Youth and the SS,* 1; Mosley, *Rules of the Game: Sir Oswald and Lady Cynthia Mosley, 1896–1933,* 211; Skidelsky, *Oswald Mosley,* 317; Pritchett, "Secret Parables," 37.

For Golding, the dominant and prevalent cultural assumptions found in Ballantyne's stories support the projection of evil onto external objects or beings, such as savages, and in Nazi Germany's case the Jews.[13] But Golding maintains that the darkness or evil that humans fear, and consequently attempt to annihilate, is within the "civilized" English subject. Importantly, Golding appears to have a specific continuity in mind concerning an evil that is not overcome or displaced by English civilization, but is, in effect, a potential that comes hand in hand with it. He connects adolescent English schoolboys from privileged backgrounds, the imperial scouting ethos, and fascism. Thus, whereas in Germany fascism actually sprouted, while in England it did not, there is nonetheless the possibility that the English ethos could easily tip over into fascism (as it does on the island) since privileged education and scouting ideology have much in common with fascism. In order to rebut Ballantyne's projection of evil onto savages, and to draw attention to the ability of the English—with their schooling in fascistic behavior—to mirror Nazism, Golding uses the combined forces of fantastic and carnival modes.

In *Lord of the Flies,* the world of the island is apprehended from the viewpoint of the schoolboys. Initially, they appear to be all-around empire boys, characters in the island adventure tradition that stretches back to Daniel Defoe's *Robinson Crusoe* (1719), Robert Louis Stevenson's *Treasure Island* (1883), and Ballantyne's *Coral Island.* But their preoccupation with natural phenomena and survival rapidly changes to a preoccupation with the unknown and inexplicable. They face beasts and phantoms in a succession of apparently supernatural events. Uncertain and fearful, the boys are subjected to unexplained phenomena. Suspense and hesitation as to the nature of the "beast" follow, and their fear increases accordingly. Although at first it is only the "littluns" that appear affected by this fear, the circle widens until all the boys, including Ralph and Jack, believe in the "Beast." The term *beastie* (*LF,* 39) quickly matures into "beast" (*LF,* 40). Initially, Ralph and Jack hedge their bets by stating that even if there was a beast, they would hunt and kill it. The mysterious disappearance of the boy who had seen the "snake-thing" compounds with the fall of snake-like creepers from an exploding tree and adds fuel to fear. In their beach huts the "littluns" are plagued with nightmares. And in pace with the growing sense of strangeness, the island environment itself becomes equivocal and menacing: "Strange things happened at midday. The glittering sea rose up, moving apart in planes of blatant impossibility; the

13. Hitler described the Jews as bloodsucking vampires (see *Mein Kampf,* 296).

coral reef and the few, stunted palms that clung to the more elevated parts would float up into the sky, would quiver, be plucked apart, run like raindrops on a wire or be repeated as in an odd succession of mirrors. Sometimes land loomed where there was no land and flicked out like a bubble as the children watched" (*LF,* 63).

Yet this strange transformation of the natural fabric of the coral reef is rationally explained by Piggy as a mirage. But such is the general uncertainty now of what is real and unreal that the fall of darkness is unwelcome. The equivocal nature of familiar things is constantly in view: "If faces were different when lit from above or below—what was a face? What was anything?" (*LF,* 85). The "littluns" are constantly attacked for their fearfulness. Jack calls them "babies and sissies" (*LF,* 90). Piggy proclaims that if these fears continue, they'll be "talking about ghosts and such things next" (*LF,* 91).

But no sooner has Piggy subdued his own and everyone else's doubts by advancing a scientific approach to reality than Phil, another "littlun," speaks of seeing "something big and horrid" in the trees (*LF,* 93). Although Ralph insists that he was experiencing a nightmare, Phil maintains that he was fully awake at the time. Then Percival says he has seen the Beast and that "it comes out of the sea" (*LF,* 96). Thus, doubt and hesitation increase. Maurice says: "'I don't believe in the beast of course. As Piggy says, life's scientific, but we don't know, do we? Not certainly, I mean—'" (*LF,* 96). Then Simon amazes the older boys by admitting that "'maybe there is a beast'" (*LF,* 97). Here, Simon elliptically hints that the Beast might be them: "'We could be sort of . . .' Simon became inarticulate in his effort to express mankind's essential illness" (*LF,* 97). The boys even vote on the issue of whether ghosts inhabit the island. Only Piggy fails to lift his hand. Yet Piggy's claim that ghosts and suchlike do not make sense brings its own fearful counter: "'But s'pose they don't make sense? Not here, on this island? Supposing things are watching us and waiting?' Ralph shuddered violently and moved closer to Piggy, so that they bumped frighteningly" (*LF,* 101).

Schoolboy nerves are further jangled by what follows: "A thin wail out of the darkness chilled them and set them grabbing for each other. Then the wail rose, remote and unearthly, and turned to an inarticulate gibbering" (*LF,* 103). But this noise turns out to be Percival reliving his own personal nightmare. For the moment there is the relief of natural explanation. The Beast from Air we know to be a dead parachutist, shot down over the island while all but Sam and Eric are asleep. This figure is uncannily animate, moving in the wind:

> Here the breeze was fitful and allowed the strings of the parachute to tangle and festoon; and the figure sat, its helmeted head between its knees, held by a complication of lines. When the breeze blew the lines would strain taut and some accident of this pull lifted the head and chest upright so that the figure seemed to peer across the brow of the mountain. Then, each time the wind dropped, the lines would slacken and the figure bow forward again, sinking its head between its knees. (*LF*, 105)

Sam and Eric who are guarding the fire on the mountain hear the strange popping noise of the chute fabric in the wind. Here, hesitation between a supernatural and a natural explanation to the Beast from Air belongs only to the characters. They return and tell the others of the beast on the mountain. Despite a natural though uncanny explanation being available to us, we cannot fail to empathize with the subsequent fear and hesitation experienced by the characters: "Soon the darkness was full of claws, full of the awful unknown and menace" (*LF*, 108). However, the disturbing fact that the only beasts on the island are the boys themselves begins to gain ground: "Simon, walking in front of Ralph, felt a flicker of incredulity—a beast with claws that scratched, that sat on a mountain top, that left no tracks and yet was not fast enough to catch Samneric. Howsoever Simon thought of the beast, there rose before his inward sight the picture of a human at once heroic and sick" (*LF*, 113).

Our own hesitation and uncertainty as readers has begun to shift more clearly toward a natural yet uncanny explanation that the boys are their own monsters. But the breaking of this central hesitation, as to the nature of the Beast, does not exclude further peripheral uncertainty between natural and supernatural events. Apart from the fact that we participate vicariously in the hesitation of Ralph and Jack as they hunt down the figure on the mountain, a "great ape . . . sitting with its head between its knees" (*LF*, 136), the pig's head or "Lord of the Flies" remains on the border between reality and unreality. It is animated: "the Lord of the Flies hung on his stick and grinned" (*LF*, 152). It appears to be a focal point of something supernatural—Evil, the Devil, Satan. Here, peripheral uncertainty is maintained. We hesitate between formulating natural or supernatural explanations. There is a definite sense of the "Lord of the Flies" as a possessed object, and this possession is registered through the visionary viewpoint of Simon. Though Simon has repeatedly been described as mad, hesitation remains as to whether the strange conversation he has with the "Lord of the Flies" is a fit-induced psychosis or not; indeed, we hesitate to ascertain whether psychosis disallows vision. This threshold between Simon's sanity or insanity—a hazy world of split personality, psychosis, and dreams—magnifies fantastic uncertainty, as does, in a more marginal way, the "doubling" of the twins, Samneric. Simon's "madness" has its base in both Todorovian "themes of the self" and carnival foolery. Ironically, it is the death of the equivocal and mysteriously spiritual Simon that erodes fantastic hesitation. His "madness" may also mark the beginnings of Golding's perennial questioning of religious authority throughout his work, a critique most powerfully achieved in *The Spire.*

A final break of the core hesitation concerning the nature of the "Beast" occurs when in Simon's eagerness to explain the human nature of the phenomenon, he unwittingly becomes the "Beast" and is murdered. An exchange of beasts occurs. At this point, we become fully aware of the boys as beasts, in their vicious murder of Simon. This most poignant and telling delivery of an uncanny explanation breaks fantastic hesitation most completely. Then, by way of contrast, the harmless, dead Beast from Air exits the island, though, for the characters, its exit remains a supernatural phenomenon.

The shift, then, is from a predominant hesitation about the nature of the Beast to an uncanny explanation that the boys, and humans in general, project fear onto other groups, individuals, or objects. Even so, the uncanny resolution of who or what really is the Beast on the island remains somewhat equivocal. We are still unsure of a background supernatural activity or influence. The natural and the supernatural seem to coexist, a realm perhaps more akin to Todorov's "fantastic uncanny." Supernaturality is still registered, for example, in the description of Simon's body, which, like that of Lycaon in Homer's *Iliad,* is devoured by "sea monsters."[14]

The characters continue to fear an external beast, with Jack's gang having already tried to propitiate the Beast by making an offering of the pig's head, deciding to "keep on the right side of him" (*LF,* 177). Even rational, scientific Piggy ends up thinking strange sounds outside his hut are made by the Beast: "A voice whispered horribly outside. 'Piggy—Piggy—' 'It's come,' gasped Piggy. 'It's real'" (*LF,* 184). Of course, the sounds are those of Jack and members of his gang stealing the remains of Piggy's glasses. Again, the shift from character hesitation to uncanny natural explanation is effective. Notions of "beast" are transposed onto Jack's gang.

14. See *The Iliad* 21.135–40: "Lie there, Lycaon! let the fish surround / Thy bloated corse, and suck thy gory wound: / There no sad mother shall thy funerals weep, / But swift Scamander roll thee to the deep, / Whose every wave some wat'ry monster brings, / To feast unpunish'd on the fat of kings" (in Pope, "The Dunciad," 466).

With Piggy's murder, and the "pig hunt" of Ralph under way, clarification of the human nature of the Beast is intensified. The natural as opposed to supernatural interpretation of events is given its final and fullest exposition. Yet, even so, the uncanny does not completely override the supernatural. The pig's head remains strangely animated, as when the hunted Ralph strays upon it: "[T]he pig's skull grinned at him from the top of a stick. He walked slowly into the middle of the clearing and looked steadily at the skull that gleamed as white as ever the conch had done and seemed to jeer at him cynically. An inquisitive ant was busy in one of the eye sockets but otherwise the thing was lifeless. Or was it?" (*LF,* 204).

Effectively, the fantastic elements in *Lord of the Flies* operate in tandem with those of carnival: they combine to disturb us and subvert dominant cultural notions of the superiority of civilized English behavior. These are the kind of assumptions that buoyed the complacency of England, and indeed other Allied nations, namely, that the atrocities perpetrated by the Nazis were an exclusively German phenomenon. Within the fantastic framework, it is the break from potential supernatural explanation to the chilling and uncanny reality of natural explanation that disturbs us: that the Beast is human, Nazi-like, and English. We participate in the shock that this shift in perspective brings. Instead of externalizing and projecting evil onto objects, phantoms, and supernatural beasts, we confront the reality of human destructiveness. This is registered in both a universal or "perennial" frame and a specific "contemporary" frame, polemicizing the English capacity for Nazism, especially in the light of its exclusionary class system. Although the novel is set in the future, the surface detail, as discussed by earlier critics such as James Gindin, corresponds to World War II. In effect, the fantastic interrogates the postwar "reality" of Britain and its Allies. Yet it does not do so alone.

The shift from the fantastic to the uncanny amplifies carnivalesque elements in the text that symbolically subvert, turn upside down, the vision of civilized, ordered, English behavior. In combination, these elements are the structures through which *Lord of the Flies* disturbs. Yet such is the inherent irreversibility of the narrative structure—its dependence upon hesitation or suspense of explanation—that we cannot read *Lord of the Flies* and register the peculiar shock it delivers a second time.[15] Indeed, there is something particularly "evanescent" about the pure fantastic, not as a genre, but as an element.[16] Ultimately, the shock recognition of the

15. Todorov, *Fantastic,* 89.
16. Brooke-Rose, *Rhetoric of the Unreal,* 63.

negative, transgressive, "evil" side of not simply human behavior but the behavior of English boys is what is disturbing about *Lord of the Flies.* Such shock recognition is effected by the combination of fantastic and carnival elements. Because of the fantastic's evanescence, we need to recall our first reading when we reexamine *Lord of the Flies:* we must remember our initial shock. We find no relief in the novel's coda at the end of the book when the boys are "saved" by an English naval officer. Our unease shifts from the carnival square of the island to the wider adult world—a world at war for a third time, a world in which the theater of war greatly resembles, in its detail of a paramilitary fascist group, machine-gunning and, in its dead parachutist, the familiar Second World War. It is a world of continuing inhumanity. This open ending is typical of "the satirist's representation of evil as a present and continuing danger."[17] The naval officer marks the gap between ideal British behavior and reality: "'I should have thought that a pack of British boys—you're all British aren't you?—would have been able to put up a better show than that—I mean—'" (*LF,* 222). The substantiation of the children as British subjects is not superfluous to the novel's meaning. It is fundamental to this novel's ethical interrogation of England, Britain, and its Allies at a specific juncture in history.

One of the most powerful carnivalesque elements in *Lord of the Flies* is that of the pig, which Golding uses symbolically to subvert dominant racial assumptions, in particular toward the Jews, and, universally, toward those humans considered alien or foreign to any grouping. This has alarming relevance to the atrocities committed against the Jews in World War II, yet has been overlooked by Golding critics who have not interpreted Golding's merging of the pig hunt with the human hunt, and the racial significance of eating pig flesh at carnival time.

The pig symbol is developed in *Lord of the Flies* as the pig of carnival time. It is a major motif: as locus of projected evil; as food for the schoolboys; as propitiation to the Beast; but more than anything, as the meat the Jews do not eat. This link between pig flesh and the Jews is reinforced by Golding's choice of the novel's Hebraic title. "Lord of the Flies," or "Lord of Dung," as John Whitley renders it, comes from the Hebrew word *Beelzebub.* As I noted earlier, Peter Stallybrass and Allon White argue that the eating of pig meat during carnival time is an anti-Semitic practice. It is an act of contempt toward the Jews for bringing about the Lenten fast. White asserts: "Meat, especially, pig meat, was of course the symbolic centre of carnival (*carne levare* probably derives from the taking up of meat as both

17. Connery and Combe, *Theorizing Satire,* 5.

food and sex)." That the pig becomes human and the human being becomes pig in the frenzied, carnivalistic debauchery of Jack and his totalitarian regime is important. The shadowing of pig hunt and human hunt, ending with Simon's and Piggy's deaths, and almost with Ralph's, signifies the link between the pig symbol and the extermination of those considered alien or outsiders. The name "Piggy" does not merely imply obesity. It is the lower-class Piggy who is always on the periphery of the group of schoolboys, always mocked, never quite belonging. As Virginia Tiger points out, "Piggy is killed . . . because he is an alien, a pseudo-species."[18] Piggy is alien or foreign, and, as such, he is a focus for violence based on the sort of racial assumptions found in Ballantyne's writing, but it is important to clarify the precise nature of his outsider status. The character name "Piggy" does not, unlike that of Ralph and Jack, feature in Ballantyne's *Coral Island.* Piggy is Golding's creation—a creation that suggests a Jew-like figure: "There had grown tacitly among the biguns the opinion that Piggy was an outsider, not only by accent, which did not matter, but by fat, and ass-mar, and specs, and a certain disinclination for manual labour" (*LF,* 70). We find something of the Jewish intellectual in this description of the bespectacled Piggy, with his different accent and physical feebleness. The stereotype of Jewish feebleness has been a stock in trade of anti-Semites and peddlers of degeneration theories.[19] It is here that we witness the anti-Semitism of carnival. In essence, Golding utilizes the imperial tradition of pig sticking to suggest a continuum between English imperialism and fascism.

Jack's gang persecutes Jew-like Piggy and those it considers outsiders. As a carnival mob they break the normal rules of authority with a willful, transgressive violence that marks a shift from liberal democracy to fascism and anti-Semitism. We witness the demise of Ralph's parliament and the ascendancy of Jack's totalitarian, primitive regime based on savagery, hunting, and primal drives. There follows aggressive sexual debasement and frenzy in the killing of the carnival pig, mimicking anal rape by sticking the spear "'Right up her ass'" (*LF,* 150):

> [T]he sow staggered her way ahead of them, bleeding and mad, and the hunters followed, wedded to her in lust, excited by the long chase and the dropped blood. . . . [S]he squealed and bucked and the air was

18. Whitley, *Golding: "Lord of the Flies,"* 43; see Stallybrass and White, *Politics of Transgression,* 54; White, *Carnival, Hysteria, and Writing,* 170; Tiger, *Dark Fields,* 63.

19. See Sander Gilman, *Franz Kafka: The Jewish Patient.* See also Gilman, *The Jew's Body.*

> full of sweat and noise and blood and terror. Roger ran round the heap, prodding with his spear whenever pigflesh appeared. Jack was on top of the sow, stabbing downward with his knife. Roger found a lodgement for his point and began to push till he was leaning with his whole weight. The spear moved forward inch by inch and the terrified squealing became a high pitched scream. Then Jack found the throat and the hot blood spouted over his hands. The sow collapsed under them and they were heavy and fulfilled upon her. (*LF,* 149)[20]

The transgressive connotations of this act are amplified by Robert and Maurice's mimicry of the event. In effect, the whole scene is one of a carnivalesque focus on the lower body parts, particularly that "low" orifice, the anus. As Allon White points out: "Orifices, particularly the gaping mouth, emphasize the open, unfinished, receptive nature of the body at carnival, its daily proximity to flesh and to dung." We may further note scatological details of the "littluns'" toilet habits or Jack's orgasmic fart. Later we witness the "befouled bodies" (*LF,* 172) of Piggy and Ralph. The orifice as mouth or anus is found in several descriptions in *Lord of the Flies.* Arnold Johnston considers that Golding's Swiftian scatology strengthens an accusation that the contemporary world evades home truths about human nature such as the killing of six million Jews.[21] We have the foul breath from the mouth of the dead parachutist and the vast gaping mouth of the pig: "Simon found he was looking into a vast mouth. There was blackness within, a blackness that spread" (*LF,* 159). The theme of "lower body parts," symbolic of misrule, is replicated elsewhere in the novel, as in Ralph's derision of Piggy's asthma: "'Sucks to your ass-mar'" (*LF,* 156). Here, we find the connotations of anal damage or marring and "sucking ass." In the mock pig killing that follows, Robert ends up with a sore backside. The transgression of sodomy is further evidenced in the likely spear rape of Simon on the beach implied by the kind of elliptical references expected of sexual taboo. Although no explicit reference is made to such actions, we must bear in mind previous pig-killing ritual and play:

> "Don't you understand, Piggy? The things we did—"
> "He may still be—"
> "No."

20. Stallybrass and White note that the Latin etymology of pig, *porcus* or *porcellus,* refers to female genitalia and that in Attic comedy, prostitutes were called pig merchants (*Politics of Transgression,* 44–45).

21. White, *Carnival, Hysteria, and Writing,* 170; see Johnston, *Of Earth and Darkness,* 38, 45.

"P'raps he was only pretending—"
Piggy's voice tailed off at the sight of Ralph's face.
"You were outside. Outside the circle. You never really came in. Didn't you see what we—what they did?"
There was loathing, and at the same time a kind of feverish excitement in his voice.
"Didn't you see, Piggy?" (*LF*, 173)

We must read this transgressive violence in political terms. Golding is explicitly linking extreme violence with anti-Semitism and the kind of "sadomasochistic homosexuality" that Wilhelm Reich and Erich Fromm considered integral to fascism.[22] Of course, we might argue that Reich and Fromm's analysis is misplaced or erroneous, yet Golding adopts this kind of popularized image. As Roger Eatwell notes: "Images of fascism are part of our culture. For most people, the word 'fascism' conjures up visions of nihilistic violence, war and *Götterdämmerung*. 'Fascism' has a sexual side too: but it is the world of Germanic uniforms and discipline, of bondage and sado-masochism, rather than love."[23] Whether or not "sadomasochistic homosexuality" is a definitive aspect or style of fascism, Golding certainly appears to have drawn on such popularized theories and images, even though such an analysis is ultimately contradictory in terms of the Nazis' exclusionary acts toward homosexuals. Yet it makes sense in that what is feared is persecuted in others.

Jack's gang descends into a meat and sex society, rejecting the liberal democracy of the conch-invoked meetings. Their carnival is filled with dance, chanting, fire, "fun," and irresponsibility—of general festivity. Those routines that reflect responsible society, such as keeping a fire going on the mountain, are neglected. They wear masks and painted faces. They dress and present themselves as a choir, an oxymoronic combination in light of their actions. The rules are challenged, turned upside down—as we have noted, Jack cries "Bollocks" to the rules. They are the "painted fools" of carnival, part of a masquerade (*LF*, 197). Of course, such imagery may equally apply to the imperialist notion of descent into savagery, both carnival "painted fool" and "savage" being "low domains." Golding provides a dystopian representation of carnival that dwells on the pessimistic, violent, and racist seam that has had its place in the history of carnival crowd behavior. He makes a strong connection between this history and contemporary fascism. This aspect of the carnivalesque

22. See James A. Gregor, *Interpretations of Fascism*, 50, 55, 68, 74.
23. Eatwell, *Fascism: A History*, xix.

cannot be appreciated by those "critics who remain purely within the celebratory terms of Bakhtin's formulation," nor those who universalize transgression.[24]

Golding's dystopian representation incorporates noncelebratory carnival decrowning, where a king figure is parodied and derided as the played-out subversion of hierarchical society. This is evident in Jack's thrusting of a pig's decapitated head on a double-pointed spear, as propitiation to the Beast. Such an oxymoronic symbol, referred to in the title of the novel as "Lord of the Flies," reflects the enactment of misrule, the turning upside down of order and authority, of what is crowned. What is "lord" is lord only to flies—those insects of the scatological. This symbol is both fitting to the overall dark or dystopian misrule of carnival in *Lord of the Flies* and the etymological base of "Lord of the Flies" as meaning Beelzebub or Devil.

We may view Golding's use of carnival in *Lord of the Flies* as registering his deeply felt unease about the nature of English "civilization" in light of the events of World War II—of totalitarianism and genocide: a "civilization," among others, that is primed for the total wipeout of nuclear apocalypse. The misrule of carnival in contemporary history is presented as integral not simply to Nazis or other totalitarian regimes but also to England with its divisive and cruel class system. Golding lays bare an alternative view to civilized English behavior, one that counters accepted, familiar, erroneous complacencies. In the isolated focus, in the "carnival square" of Golding's island, carnival affirms that everything exists on the threshold or border of its opposite.[25] In effect, Golding explodes a Nazi-English or them-us opposition.

So, to summarize, noncelebratory or Juvenalian satire with its combined fantastic and carnivalesque in *Lord of the Flies* subverts the view that the "civilized" English are incapable of the kind of atrocities carried out by the Nazis during World War II. These modes are deployed in the novel as an attack on what Golding deems to be a complacent English democ-

24. Stallybrass and White, *Politics of Transgression,* 191, 19. For early examples of crowd violence in carnival, see Ladurie, *Carnival in Romans;* Buchanan Sharp, *In Contempt of All Authority: Rural Artisans and Riot in the West of England, 1586–1660;* and Charles Tilly, *Charivaris, Repertoires, and Politics.* It is important to note the relevance of crowds or masses to theories on fascism. For a summary of the work of Gustave le Bon, José Ortega y Gasset, Emil Lederer, Sigmund Neumann, Eric Hoffer, Hannah Arendt, and William Kornhauser on the phenomenon of crowds or masses, see J. Gregor, *Interpretations of Fascism,* 78–127. See also Eatwell, *Fascism,* 4–10.

25. On the carnival square, see Bakhtin, *Problems of Dostoevsky's Poetics,* 128–29, 168–69.

racy, and its masculinity and classist attitudes in particular, in relation to the rise of National Socialism.

The Inheritors

The Inheritors is Golding's second published novel and is in many ways thematically coextensive with *Lord of the Flies.* Like *Lord of the Flies,* it evokes a carnivalesque world with the violent actions of the Cro-Magnon people, the supposed progenitors of Homo sapiens, who annihilate the last of the Neanderthal race. As in his first novel, Golding explodes the myth of cultured, civilized humankind. From the distant "past" *(The Inheritors)* and "future" *(Lord of the Flies),* the two novels carry a similar message: humankind is damaged and flawed; it is predisposed toward violence to "outsiders" and transgression. Carnival, then, is not simply a ritual phenomenon or an immanent literary form; it is rooted in the consciousness of humans. It is through the use of carnivalesque elements that Golding symbolically subverts those assumptions that mark humankind as civilized and constructive, not simply in a universal or "perennial" sense, but also in the specific and powerful sense of the context of "present conditions"—those of World War II events.

In *The Inheritors,* as other critics have noted, Golding subverts certain cultural assumptions evident in H. G. Wells's *Outline of History* (1920) and "Grizzly Folk" (1927).[26] In these writings, Wells projects a view of Neanderthal Man as an inferior wild beast and Cro-Magnon Man, his evolutionary supplanter (now questioned), as superior, intelligent, and civilizing. But again, Golding is concerned to highlight the destructive quality that comes with intelligence. Furthermore, he portrays the Neanderthals as sensitive and gentle and bound to their kin by a collective consciousness. In his book *The Neandertal Enigma,* James Shreeve argues that "it is not the triumph of a superior race that drives the plots" of *The Inheritors* and Jean Auel's later work *The Clan of the Cave Bear* (1980), but "the loss of an alternative one."[27]

This representation of the Neanderthals is in contrast to the aggressive intelligence of the Cro-Magnon, a race of people critically flawed, as Ted Hughes suggests, by the premature birth of their offspring. Here, Hughes

26. See, for example, Hodson, *William Golding,* 39–42.

27. James Shreeve, *The Neandertal Enigma: Solving the Mystery of Modern Human Origins,* 6–7. Although Shreeve prefers to drop the *h* in *Neanderthal,* I keep the more familiar spelling.

refers to rather speculative anthropological theory that the skeleton of Cro-Magnon woman had a greatly reduced birthing canal resulting in premature births. Thus, before Cro-Magnon Man, hominids may well have had a longer gestation period. The suggestion is that Neanderthal Man's instinctive potential and collective consciousness, unlike Cro-Magnon, had time to fully develop. However, Hughes admits such a theory throws only oblique and speculative light upon the novel.[28]

The Inheritors responds more generally to World War II atrocities by attacking notions of Western rather than purely English "civilization." Lok and seven other Neanderthals, having survived the Great Fire, are on their way to higher ground for the duration of the summer. Ravaged by natural disasters on that journey, they fall foul of the Cro-Magnons, or New People, who kidnap and kill members of the tribe. The New People view their victims (in much the same way as H. G. Wells in *The Outline of History* or "The Grisly Folk") as devils or ogres. We witness both what Bernard Bergonzi calls "the original act of colonialist exploitation" by the West and an extermination or genocide that suggests the Jewish Holocaust. The production and publication of this novel, like *Lord of the Flies,* are contiguous to this "defining event of our time."[29] Although set in the distant past, and lacking the surface details specific to World War II found in *Lord of the Flies, The Inheritors* powerfully suggests the sociopolitical context of contemporary genocide.

Fantastic hesitation creates uncertainty as to what forces are behind the insidious extermination of Lok's Neanderthal tribe. Natural explanation that it is the New People, progenitors of Homo sapiens, who are "racially cleansing" the territory of "ogres" subverts the notion of evolutionary progress and evokes the Holocaust. Again, Golding links masculinity with violent extermination. The patriarchal New People wipe out the matriarchal Neanderthal tribe. S. J. Boyd is keen to link the New People's actions to Nazi genocide: "In this context we should remember how in our own century an attempt was made to exterminate the Jewish race, a race identified by Hitler, as so often before, as a threat to the progress of civilization and the all-round bogey men of history, the sort of role Wells gives

28. Hughes, "Baboons and Neanderthals: A Re-Reading of *The Inheritors,*" 162. See also *Pincher Martin,* where Golding describes man as follows: "He is a freak, an ejected foetus robbed of his natural development, thrown out in the world with a naked covering of parchment, with too little room for his teeth and a soft bulging skull like a bubble" (*PN,* 190).

29. Bergonzi, *The Situation of the Novel,* 179; John Banville, "Introduction: George Steiner's Fiction," viii.

to the Neanderthal men in the epigraph to the novel." Boyd finds Lok's tribe "reminiscent of the Jews" and locates Jewishness in Mal's account of their genealogy and Fa's mournful words that owe much to the Psalms or the Lamentations of Jeremiah: "'They have gone over us like a hollow log. They are like a winter'" (*IN*, 198). Here, Fa links the atrocities committed by the New People and the image of "a smear on the smoothed earth that had been a slug" (*IN*, 198). Again, Boyd says: "Though it deals with prehistory, *The Inheritors* shares with *Lord of the Flies* a post-nuclear colouring" in its evocation of the Holocaust. Jack's gang destroys its island world by fire. The New People resemble "'a fire in the forest'" (*IN*, 197).[30]

The Inheritors, then, reiterates the theme of racial extermination found in *Lord of the Flies.* The carnivalesque practices of the New People mark the exclusionary, orgiastic violence of an advanced race toward those it considers inferior or "alien." This is powerfully demonstrated in the death of the child Liku who is roasted and eaten by the New People. She becomes a trace presence in the smoky air. Here, Golding appears to gesture toward those furnaces of the Holocaust that consumed great numbers of children. We also witness the kind of disbelief the Jews felt concerning their fate in Lok's failure to comprehend the New People's destructive intentions.

Golding's use of the fantastic takes a sophisticated turn in *The Inheritors.* It is manifest in the limited, equivocal point of view of the protagonist focalizer, Lok. We look over the shoulder, as it were, of a limited, unformed consciousness and are barely allowed the comfort of omniscient narration. This equivocating process ensures that hesitation follows. Like Lok and his people, we build up uncertain, provisional pictures about events taking place:

> "I have a picture."
>
> He freed a hand and put it flat on his head as if confining the images that flickered there.
>
> "Mal is not old but clinging to his mother's back. There is more water not only here but along the trail where we came. A man is wise. He makes men take a tree that has fallen and—"
>
> His eyes deep in their hollows turned to the people imploring them to share a picture with him. He coughed again, softly. The old woman carefully lifted her burden.
>
> At last Ha spoke.
>
> "I do not see this picture." (*IN*, 15–16)

30. Boyd, *Novels of Golding,* 41–42, 40. See also Dick, *William Golding* (1967), 38, 44.

Through an uncertain terrain, Lok and his people make their way, struggling to piece concepts and ideas together, often given to elliptical, anthropomorphic, and protoreligious identification of objects. For example, a collection of icicles is viewed as an "'ice woman'" (*IN*, 27). Virginia Tiger notes: "Both Lok's primitive perspective and the omniscient authorial descriptions deliberately limit any formulation or deduction or interpretation of events . . . concealing familiar elements in anthropomorphic images. Thus the cliff is described as leaning out 'looking for its own feet in the water,' the island 'rearing' against the fall is a 'seated giant' . . ."[31]

We face constant equivocation of natural phenomena and explanation. It is difficult to ascertain exactly what Lok and the others see and experience. We constantly face the uncertainty of sharing pictures to explain events. Ha disappears mysteriously and Lok's people refer to the "other men." Who these "other men" are we do not know. Still everything remains difficult to decode. Lok goes in search of Ha and comes across a strange rock that changes shape:

> As he watched, one of the farther rocks began to change shape. At one side a small bump elongated then disappeared quickly. The top of the rock swelled, the hump fined off at the base and elongated again then halved its height. Then it was gone. . . . He screwed up his eyes and peered at the rock to see if it would change again. There was a single birch tree that overtopped the other trees on the island, and was now picked out against the moon-drenched sky. It was very thick at the base, unduly thick, and as Lok watched, impossibly thick. The blob of darkness seemed to coagulate round the stem like a drop of blood on a stick. It lengthened, thickened again, lengthened. It moved up the birch tree with slothlike deliberation, it hung in the air high above the island and the fall. It made no noise and at last hung motionless. Lok cried out at the top of his voice; but either the creature was deaf or the ponderous fall erased the words that he said. (*IN*, 79–80)

Only gradually do we focalize through Lok's limited consciousness and recognize that the mysterious "other" is early humankind, and suffer the uncanny realization that the strange disappearance of Ha and death of Mal are due to these "other men." Like Lok, we suddenly stand before intelligent, violent humankind—ourselves made unfamiliar. Indeed, both Lok and Fa can see the smoke on the island, evidence of the "other" presence. Lok moves close to the water in the hope of seeing the "new man or

31. Tiger, *Dark Fields*, 79.

the new people" (*IN*, 99). Our gradual shift from a supernatural explanation to events that are uncanny is stark as, in Lok's absence, actions unfold at the overhang. The "other" have crossed the water and plundered the tribe, killing the old woman and Nil, and kidnapping Liku and the newborn. Lok hears the strange sounds of the "other": "He could hear their speech and it made him laugh. The sounds made a picture in his head of interlacing shapes, thin and complex, voluble and silly, not like the long curve of a hawk's cry, but tangles like line weed on the beach after a storm, muddied as water. This laugh-sound advanced through the trees towards the river" (*IN*, 104).

We suddenly, like Lok, stand before intelligent, violent humankind—the New People. We half-recognize them as ourselves. Yet also like Lok, we fail to comprehend fully the events witnessed. As we do, our shock and disturbance are intense:

> The bushes twitched again. Lok steadied by the tree and gazed. A head and a chest faced him, half-hidden. There were white bone things behind the leaves and hair. The man had white bone things above his eyes and under the mouth so that his face was longer than a face should be. The man turned sideways in the bushes and looked at Lok along his shoulder. A stick rose upright and there was a lump of bone in the middle. Lok peered at the stick and the lump of bone and the small eyes in the bone things over the face. Suddenly Lok understood that the man was holding the stick out to him but neither he nor Lok could reach across the river. He would have laughed if it were not for the echo of the screaming in his head. The stick began to grow shorter at both ends. Then it shot out to full length again.
>
> The dead tree by Lok's ear acquired a voice.
>
> "Clop." (*IN*, 106)

When Lok pursues the kidnapped Liku and New One across the river by climbing into the trees, he is delivered into a topsy-turvy world where he sees "random flashes of the sun below and above" (*IN*, 107) and is literally turned upside down when the branches give way: "They swayed outwards and down so that his head was lower than his feet" (*IN*, 107). In this inverted world he sees his reflected "double" and experiences "Lok, upside down" (*IN*, 108). In a fantastic "dreamlike slowness," he spies the horrific remains of the murdered old woman floating up to the surface and disappearing (*IN*, 109).

Like Lok, our view of events is turned upside down. By gradual recognition of natural phenomena, over the shoulder of Lok's limited consciousness, we shift from a fantastic world, where there is hesitation between explanations, where things are half-apprehended, barely ordered, to an increasingly clear resolution that we have been viewing this world through the eyes of Neanderthal Man—that the "others" are indeed the original colonists, our own progenitors, Cro-Magnon Man, and that these New People, like ourselves, are powerful, intelligent, and violent. It is this shift that, again, is mutually amplified with the carnivalesque elements that follow, and in combination renders unease and shock recognition as to the destructive nature of this first example of human civilization, and indeed the irony of intellectual evolution when a full account of humankind's history of violence, war, and destruction is made.[32]

The novel, then, presents a topsy-turvy account of human nature and registers a symbolic subversion of dominant cultural assumptions of humankind as superior, as morally progressive, beneficent, cultured colonizer. The disturbing nature of this discovery is further amplified by a description of Lok as a beastlike creature from a perspective similar to that of Wells in "The Grisly Folk" or *The Outline of History.* It is a perspective we cannot but reject as limited and prejudiced:

> The red creature began to sniff round by the fire. Its weight was on the knuckles and it worked with its nose lowered almost to the ground. . . . It was a strange creature, smallish, and bowed. The legs and thighs were bent and there was a whole thatch of curls on the outside of the legs and arms. The back was high, and covered over the shoulders with curly hair. Its feet and hands were broad, and flat, the great toe projecting inwards to grip. The square hands swung down to the knees. (*IN,* 218–19)

Golding effects a decrowning of the sacred assumption that one race is superior to another, a view that has proved useful to imperial colonialism and those wishing to carry out genocide. This decrowning is powerfully wrought in the ironic title to the novel: *The Inheritors.* The notion of inheritance is made topsy-turvy by what Tiger describes as the "violence, rapaciousness, and corruption" of the New People. She continues: "From the point of view of innocence, the biological evolution is a moral devolution, as ironic as the Wells epigraph or the Beatitude referred to in the title that the 'meek shall inherit the world.'"[33]

32. Howard S. Babb locates "narrative mystification and shock" in *The Inheritors* (*The Novels of William Golding,* 47).
33. Tiger, *Dark Fields,* 72, 85.

Constantly thwarted by their stumbling intelligence, Lok and Fa search for Liku and the New One who have been kidnapped by the New People. From the summit of a dead tree they study the behavior of the Cro-Magnon people, who have formed a camp below. From this unusual, catascopic viewpoint or vantage point—a feature of Bakhtin's inventory of Menippean satire—they witness a "violent celebration of the body, dirt, eating, drinking, and sexuality."[34] Although Lok and Fa's position may resemble that of the Yahoos in Swift's *Gulliver's Travels* (1726), it is the New People below who perform the "lower body" rites of carnival.[35]

The New People gather around their fire, are caught up in stag mimicking and hunting, and are surrounded by darkness: "Their Promethean fire itself metamorphoses darkness, makes the island so impenetrably dark that the night sight of Lok and Fa is temporarily lost."[36] As with *Lord of the Flies, The Inheritors* incorporates the carnivalesque motif of transformative fire, hideous in its shadow casting: "The people drank and Lok could see how the bones of their throats moved in the firelight" (*IN,* 166).

In this carnivalesque firelight the New People are transformed: "They were shouting, laughing, singing, babbling in their bird speech, and the flames of their fire were leaping madly with them" (*IN,* 170). Furthermore, the New People "were like the fire, made of yellow and white, for they had thrown off their furs and wore nothing but the binding of skin round their waists and loins" (*IN,* 171). Thus, the New People descend into drunkenness with a fermented honey drink that smells like "decay" (*IN,* 160), and perform brutal, violent sex. The camp yields a stench of filth and sweat. Orifices are open. The fat woman's "head was back, throat curved, mouth open and laughing" (*IN,* 171).

The Bacchanalian orgy, as in *Lord of the Flies,* blurs meat eating and sex. We find Tuami's "mouth creeping, his fingers playing, moving up as though he were eating her flesh" (*IN,* 171). Again, we find a vantage point from the dead tree: "Lok peered through the leaves again for the meaning of the words and he was looking straight at the fat woman's mouth. She was coming towards the tree, holding on to Tuami, and she staggered and screeched with laughter so that he could see her teeth. They were not broad and useful for eating and grinding; they were small and two were longer than the others. They were teeth that remembered wolf" (*IN,* 173–74).

34. White, *Carnival, Hysteria, and Writing,* 170.

35. See Hughes, "Baboons and Neanderthals," 161, 163. Richard Nash notes the liminal status of the "wild man" and the utility of this figure to satire's "border work" in "stripping away the civilized veneer of social respectability to reveal a bestial nature at the core" ("Satyrs and Satire in Augustan England," 98).

36. Tiger, *Dark Fields,* 85.

The New People's sexual orgy is drunken, violent, and wild: "A man and a woman were fighting and kissing and screeching and another man was crawling round and round the fire like a moth with a burnt wing. Round and round he went, crawling, and the other people took no notice of him but went on with their noise" (*IN*, 172). It is fierce and vampirish and cannibalistic: "Tuami was not only lying with the fat woman but eating her as well for there was black blood running from the lobe of her ear" (*IN*, 175). And later: "Their fierce and wolflike battle was ended. They had fought it seemed against each other, consumed each other rather than lain together so that there was blood on the woman's face and the man's shoulder" (*IN*, 176). This meat and sex orgy is most shocking when we realize, over the shoulder of Lok's limited intelligence, that Liku has been cooked and eaten. Lok can smell her around the campsite, but cannot grasp that smell's significance. Her presence is carried in the smoke: "There was no smell of Liku unless a sort of generalized smell in his nostrils so faint as to be nothing" (*IN*, 182).

Later at the deserted camp, Lok comes across the stag's head that "watched Lok inscrutably. . . . The whole haunch of a stag, raw but comparatively bloodless, hung from the top of the stake and an opened stone of honey-drink stood by the staring head" (*IN*, 199). The stag's head is reminiscent of the pig's head in *Lord of the Flies.* The sense of decrowning here is similar. The irony of the novel's title, *The Inheritors,* is further established in a scene of parodic drunkenness, where Lok and Fa inherit the honey drink from the New People and as a result suffer a similar sexual and aggressive incontinence, followed swiftly by a hangover. The *mésalliance* of the "savage" inheriting savagery from the progenitors of humankind is powerfully subversive. As in *Lord of the Flies,* Golding's carnival is a "carnival of hate."[37] In both novels, a less celebratory and more dystopian carnivalesque powerfully creates a topsy-turvy world that critiques the arrogant and culturally elitist discourses found in the texts of Ballantyne and Wells. Golding's intertextual strategy rebuts the texts of these writers. In effect, the combined force of carnivalesque and fantastic elements may be viewed as the engine house to Golding's early art—his attack on racial elitism.

My analysis of the subversive function of carnivalesque and fantastic elements offers a more radical reading of *Lord of the Flies* and *The Inheritors* than has previously been attempted. These novels undermine notions of racial superiority. They interrogate human civilization in the wake

37. Milan Kundera, *The Unbearable Lightness of Being,* 26.

of World War II atrocities. Combined carnivalesque and fantastic elements amplify a shock recognition of humankind's transgressive nature. These elements are integral, pivotal structures through which these novels interrogate contemporary "reality," its ideologies and cultural assumptions. They supply the impact of reversal, of turning established ideologies and viewpoints on their heads.

It is important that these novels are not "ethnically cleansed" by timeless approaches to Golding's work. The violence and hatred that "civilized" cultures perpetrate against the "lower" domains, such as the Jews and homosexuals (of growing importance to Golding), define their "higher" forms of expression and organization. The foot on the Jewish head both raises and simultaneously exposes the "higher" cultural body as fueled by exploitation, cruelty, and even genocide. With Golding we are made painfully aware of a "not-so-jolly" relativity. We need to recognize how these texts "preserve the face of violence for the distant future," and add their symbolic friction, if we are optimistic, in the production of cultural knowledge.[38]

There is a clear parallel suggested between the Cro-Magnon Men's atrocities and those carried out by the Nazis. But in effect, Golding attacks the whole mask of Western "civilization" that covers a long history of racial violence. Golding exposes this racial violence in his satire. Such a process has been highlighted by Michael Seidel who, influenced by René Girard, argues that the satirist succeeds in "bringing violations to the surface" that otherwise would have been covered up by "civilization."[39]

Golding, then, is among those writers who concern themselves with contemporary history and its atrocities. As such, his early fiction warrants examination not simply in terms of its "perennial" status, its focus upon the human condition sub specie aeternitatis, but in terms of its "present" contemporary relevance as well. Whereas both frames or foci coexist in his work, critics have tended to avoid the latter. As a result, readings of Golding have lost a vitality that the novels themselves afford. The dominant critical focus on the fabular and mythic framing of Golding's fiction, on its timelessness, has robbed those dependent on critical guidance of a more energetic reading. It has delivered a hemiplegic Golding. It has performed a critical stroke that has enervated the fascinating political and historical side to his fiction. Here, I hope to have revivified this aspect of Golding's work and suggested that the current practice of reading his fic-

38. Ibid., 67.
39. Seidel, *Satiric Inheritance: Rabelais to Sterne,* 17 (see also 17–21).

tion needs to be changed. Golding should be considered part of a wider movement of writers in the tradition of atrocity writing.

His early novels attack the "civilized" English for divorcing themselves from the kind of violent, adolescent masculinity that has been so much a part of the phenomenon of fascism. The novels are rooted in the historical moment of their production. Golding, the noncelebratory satirist, exposes English Fascist Man in the aftermath of World War II and the Jewish Holocaust. This historicized and politicized reading of Golding's "literature of atrocity" brings a new, radical understanding of his fiction. The timelessness of his work is countered. We no longer suffer that old formalist exclusion of history from literature. We witness Golding's determination to "'chasten, chastise, reform, and warn'" the "civilized" English that the black cap not only fits, but they are as likely as anyone to wear it.[40]

The Holocaust, then, is central to Golding's early fiction, although he avoids spurious documentary and is skeptical about the possibility of rendering a detailed historical account. Of Belsen, Hiroshima, and other atrocities, he asserts: "These experiences are like the black holes in space. Nothing can get out to let us know what it was like inside. It was like what it was like and on the other hand it was like nothing else whatsoever. We stand before a gap in history. We have discovered a limit to literature" (*MT*, 102). He can offer, then, only a frail memorialization of such atrocity—pointing to it yet not able to describe it in any full way. There has been much debate about who has the right to represent the Holocaust, and indeed about the very notion of the possibility of speaking or writing about such an event. Early on in the debate about the dangers of aestheticizing the Holocaust, Theodor Adorno claimed that writing poetry after Auschwitz is barbaric. He later revised this notion in his *Negative Dialectics:* "Perennial suffering has as much right to expression as a tortured man has to scream; hence it may have been wrong to say that after Auschwitz you could no longer write poems."[41] But his early comment became the "best-known point of reference" for those attempting to negotiate the limits of representing the Holocaust or, rather, the appropriateness of silence as a response to it.[42] Silence was preferred by those, like George Steiner, Elie Wiesel, and Irving Howe, who considered that the aestheticization of the Holocaust, especially by "long-distance observers and second- or

40. Connery and Combe, *Theorizing Satire,* 5.

41. Adorno, *Negative Dialectics,* 362.

42. See Saul Friedlander, ed., *Probing the Limits of Representation: Nazism and "the Final Solution,"* 2. See also George Steiner, *Language and Silence: Essays, 1958–1966.*

third-generation writers," might erode the historical facts.[43] Yet there was a great deal at stake in all of this. Opting for silence appeared to strengthen the arguments of deniers that the Holocaust ever happened. The whole issue of countering the deniers and moving beyond the difficulties of presenting the "unrepresentable" or speaking the "unspeakable" was taken up in several publications by Jean-François Lyotard. What is fascinating about Lyotard's contribution is how the Holocaust is both implicated in the advent of postmodernism and subjected to this era's arch-relativism, especially in relation to historical knowledge.[44]

Lyotard argues that the Holocaust art "does not say the unsayable, but says that it cannot say it."[45] In essence, we cannot know or represent the Holocaust. Despite the fact that it is "unsayable" and that, for Lyotard, verification that Jews were exterminated by Nazis in gas chambers is impossible, he says that "the silence imposed on knowledge does not impose the silence of forgetting." He likens the fate of Holocaust witnesses to people who survive an earthquake that has destroyed all the instruments capable of measuring it. They would still have "the idea of a very great seismic force" or a "complex feeling" about what had happened. The Holocaust left too great a seismic shudder in the feelings and accounts of those who survived to allow that complex event to be wished away. We can trace this shudder in the writings of Golding so as to counter those who would wish away this aspect to his work, even though Golding was not literally a "survivor" of the Holocaust.

For Lyotard, but of course not for positivist historians such as Pierre Vidal-Naquet and Lucy Dawidowich, "competence" of historical knowledge is "impugned" by the fact that the instruments to "measure" the Holocaust have been destroyed. He argues that historians should focus on the "metareality" of the destruction of reality and the "feeling" that remains when testimony is not available. Lyotard, of course, examines the problems of obtaining a definitive history of what occurred in "Auschwitz" as a means of demonstrating "the impossibility of any single, integrated discourse about history and politics." According to Dominick LaCapra,

43. Yael S. Feldman, "Whose Story Is It Anyway? Ideology and Psychology in the Representation of the Shoah in Israel's Literature," 228.

44. On the whole issue of presenting the "unpresentable," see Lyotard, *The Postmodern Condition: A Report on Knowledge,* 71–82. Lipstadt argues that those intellectuals who have promoted "deconstructionist history" (e.g., Fish, Rorty, de Man) have prepared the soil for deniers or so-called revisionist historians such as David Irving and Robert Faurrison. She maintains: "The deniers are plying their trade at a time when much of history seems up for grabs and attacks on the western rationalist tradition have become commonplace" (*Denying the Holocaust,* 17).

45. Lyotard, *Heidegger and "the Jews,"* 47.

Lyotard enacts "a massive metalepsis [substitution] whereby the Shoah is transcoded into postmodernism." LaCapra himself situates the Holocaust as a "point of rupture" between modernism and postmodernism. Similarly, Golding's fiction shifts from early representations of the Holocaust that struggle to move out of fabular evasion and make a "frank encounter" with the subject matter to fiction that "encrypts" this trauma in postmodern concerns about the status of literature, language, and meaning.[46]

In *Lord of the Flies* and *The Inheritors,* it may be that Golding wished to avoid effecting any kind of representation of the Holocaust that might appear to be what Lawrence Langer calls an "unprincipled violation of a sacred shrine."[47] Or maybe Golding was aware of the difficulty of "presenting the unrepresentable." Hence, his reference is somewhat masked by a universal or fabular setting of these novels. He does, however, strengthen his reference to broad or popular conceptions of fascism and the totalitarian personality in *Pincher Martin, Free Fall,* and *Darkness Visible,* perhaps to compensate for making too oblique a reference in these early more fabular novels. Yet even so, as we shall see, the later novels only barely connect with the "Final Solution" as such.

In conclusion, then, Golding surely knew that his representations of the Holocaust, and indeed fascism, were necessarily limited and partial. Yet he obviously wanted to make some kind of intervention with what he perceived as complacency among the English in particular about their moral distance from Nazism. This focus on English complacency is evident in Nigel Williams's comment on Golding's view of *Lord of the Flies:* "He once said to me that one of the main aims of his book was to tell the story of the breakdown of English parliamentary democracy. 'Don't make them into little Americans, will you,' he added." Golding does not attempt to be comprehensive or detailed in his reference to the Holocaust as he needs only to suggest the conceptual territories of this genocide and fascism to effect his satire. Golding knew that, like himself, the postwar reader would have sufficient familiarity with German prison camps and the Holocaust through a plethora of accounts. Like Clamence in Albert Camus's *La Chute* (1956), Golding did not need to play the historian here: "We children of this half-century don't need a diagram to imagine such places."[48]

In terms of the Holocaust, Golding placed himself within what Langer

46. Lyotard, *Differend,* 56–58; Friedlander, *Probing the Limits,* 5; LaCapra, *Representing the Holocaust,* 98, 222; Lawrence L. Langer, *Admitting the Holocaust: Collected Essays,* 11.

47. Langer, *Admitting the Holocaust,* 76.

48. N. Williams, *William Golding's "Lord of the Flies,"* ix; Camus, *The Fall,* 92.

calls the "culture of dread" as opposed to the "culture of consolation." We cannot accuse Golding of any sentimental aestheticization of the Holocaust or the Nazi "Final Solution." We may accuse him of being a "long-distance" writer like Sylvia Plath, D. M. Thomas, and William Styron, but not a barbaric one. Indeed, as Berel Lang admits rather reluctantly, there is some justification in the "barbarism" of imaginative writing about the Holocaust, even "bad" or "false" contributions, "as a defence against still greater barbarism—against denial, for example, or against forgetfulness."[49] Golding's early fiction offers a defense against this barbarity of amnesia and denial. His later fiction moves away from what may be thought of as a grief response and encrypts the Holocaust in his reflection on "post-Auschwitz" life and meaning. Having instantiated the massive "seismic" force of the Holocaust in his early fiction, he traces its aftershocks or aftermath as they threaten comforting epistemologies and rationality itself with further collapse and fragmentation. Indeed, the arch-relativization of meaning we call postmodernism has spawned a concerted attack on the historicity of the Holocaust. The Holocaust is treated as merely textual, as something that can be deconstructed. Part of this effort involves the extreme claim by deniers of the Holocaust that the mass killing of Jews in World War II was a hoax. In this sense, we might consider the Holocaust as heavily influencing the postwar skepticism that eventually developed into what we broadly call postmodernism yet subsequently fell foul of its more hard-boiled deconstructive and antifoundationalist pronouncements. Or, in other words, the Holocaust intensified the climate for its denial.

49. Langer, *Admitting the Holocaust,* 9; Lang, "The Representations of Limits," 317.

4

Self-Consciousness and the Totalitarian Personality

Pincher Martin and *Free Fall*

> Many, though not all, of the important self conscious novels in the twentieth century are deeply concerned with a particular historical moment, with the nature of historical process, even with the future of Western civilization, as they deploy their elaborate systems of mirrors to reflect novel and novelist in the act of conjuring with reality.
>
> —Robert Alter, *Partial Magic: The Novel as a Self-Conscious Genre*

> These men look for ecstasy not in embraces, but in explosions, in the rumbling of bomber squadrons or in brains being shot to flames.
>
> —Klaus Theweleit, *Male Fantasies I: Women, Floods, Bodies, History*

FANTASTIC AND CARNIVALESQUE MODES IN *PINCHER MARTIN* (1956) AND *Free Fall* (1959) function to establish a reversed or upside down world that acts in a new, nonsatirical way to complement uncertainties surrounding metafictional questioning of representational truth, extend Golding's earlier attack upon English national identity that constructs itself in opposition to totalitarianism, and, in a minor and as yet sporadic way, interrogate religious authority. Golding strengthens his earlier critique of English "immunity" to brutality by representing individuals in historical time as opposed to social groups in universal or fabular time, and by instantiating *both* fascist and communist totalitarianisms. We begin by examining the nonsatirical function of the fantastic and carnivalesque in *Pincher Martin* and *Free Fall* because it problematizes the previous satirical deployment of these modes and, with the exception of *The Pyramid*, features increasingly in Golding's fiction from this point onward.

In *Pincher Martin* and *Free Fall*, Golding's nascent preoccupation with fictional "truth" and meaning is enhanced or complemented by the fantastic and carnivalesque modes because they relativize oppositions such as real-unreal, true-false, and high-low. This nonsatirical function of these modes makes the novels particularly difficult to comprehend and may relate to the critique of totalitarianism in three interesting and partly contradictory ways.[1] First, the pervasive uncertainty and dialogism between oppositions afforded by the modes may offer a general critique of one-eyed, totalitarian approaches to life, be they political, social, philosophical, or linguistic. Second, they may be part of Golding's "coming to terms" with epistemological ruins in the wake of the Holocaust and other atrocities such as mass civilian bombing. This is plausible when we keep in mind the strong focus on these themes in his early work, and to a lesser degree in his later work. From this perspective of recent massive trauma, Golding appears to diagnose that the center of human meaning is lost. Finally, in conjunction with metafictional aspects to these novels, they may suggest a partial retreat from authorial "engagement" with contemporary sociopolitical issues and a movement toward a late-modernist, literary experimentalism that is merely concerned with aesthetic form. Unlike works of the avant-garde portrayed by Peter Bürger in his *Theory of the Avant-Garde,* Golding's experimentalism does not wish to destroy art as an institution, but rather seeks to interrogate the borders of fictional form in the less engaged, classical aestheticism of "art as its own end." Golding's preservation of an "art as its own end" dictum complements his reluctance to be "committed" or "engaged" in his fiction. Or, put another way, his universalism and aestheticism threaten to neutralize his political engagement. As Bürger notes: "Where the author is successful in organizing the work around the engagement, another danger threatens the political tendency: neutralization through the institution that is art."[2] There appears to be an ambivalence in Golding's fiction that both upholds artistic autonomy and promotes political praxis.

Although sharing a lower-middle-class background and rise through the grammar school to an Oxbridge education with many of the "Movement" writers and "Angry Young Men" of the 1950s, Golding did not share their predominantly antimodernist, comic, and insular focus. As Robert Hewison argues, the "experimental" nature of *Pincher Martin* and *Free Fall* contrasts sharply with the "resolutely unexperimental" novels of

1. For acknowledgment of the difficulty of these novels, see Babb, *Novels of Golding,* 88; and Boyd, *Novels of Golding,* 52.
2. Bürger, *Theory of the Avant-Garde,* 89, 90.

the Movement. "Nothing could be less provincial," contends Arthur Marwick, "than the settings of [Golding's] . . . novels." With *Pincher Martin* and *Free Fall* finding company with what R. B. Kershner calls "late modernist exceptions" in British writing during the 1950s and 1960s, Golding joins a "brief list of successful experimentalists since Joyce," such as Muriel Spark, Iris Murdoch, Lawrence Durrell, Anthony Burgess, Joyce Cary, and John Fowles.[3] Although Golding is marked out as being more experimental than the Movement and Angry writers of the 1950s, *Lord of the Flies* did betray an Angry turn in its attack on class privilege, and this theme continues in *The Spire* and *The Pyramid.* Indeed, *The Spire,* like the much later *To the Ends of the Earth,* both explores metafiction and attacks class privilege.

As previous critics have noted, *Pincher Martin* and *Free Fall* are metafictional novels that self-consciously draw attention to the acts of reading and writing and the constructed nature of fiction.[4] We can diagnose a shift in *Pincher Martin* and *Free Fall* toward an increased awareness of the unsatisfactory nature of all forms of pattern making in Golding's novels. As such, his writing joins what Robert Alter, in his book *Partial Magic,* sees as a long tradition of self-conscious experimentation in novels stretching back to Cervantes, Fielding, Sterne, and Diderot, and indeed in other literature right back to ancient Greek writing. The self-conscious novel, he argues, "systematically flaunts its own condition of artifice and . . . by so doing probes into the problematic relationship between real-seeming artifice and reality."[5] Of course, this "probing" of the relationship between text and world is not just prominent in *Pincher Martin* and *Free Fall,* but also a major feature of *The Spire* and Golding's later and arguably more

3. Hewison, *In Anger,* 116; Marwick, *Culture in Britain since 1945,* 33 (see also W. L. Webb, "A Vision of England amid the Encircling Gloom," 16); Kershner, *The Twentieth-Century Novel: An Introduction,* 70, 8. Iris Murdoch's *Under the Net* (1954) problematizes any simple division between the "Movement" and experimentalism since this archetypally "Angry" text, as Kershner argues, "is sometimes claimed for postmodernism" (70). We know from Golding's comments to John Haffenden that Golding read and enjoyed the writing of Murdoch, Durrell, and Burgess ("William Golding: An Interview," 12).

4. See Josipovici, *World and Book,* 252–53; Redpath, *Structural Reading,* 16; Boyd, *Novels of Golding,* 82; and McCarron, *William Golding,* 16–17, 19, 23.

5. Alter, *Partial Magic,* x. In *Metafiction,* Waugh acknowledges the long tradition of self-conscious fiction, yet prefers to use the term *metafiction* in relation to more recent, that is, postmodern fiction. I prefer to use the term *metafiction* synonymously with self-conscious fiction regardless of historical context, although, like Alter, I do differentiate between self-consciousness in one literary historical period and another where doing so is appropriate.

playful and tragicomic works, *Darkness Visible, The Paper Men,* and *To the Ends of the Earth.* The latter are more intensely preoccupied with the status of language and literature as part of postmodernism—a much wider and complex postindustrial phenomenon that became the subject of critical accounts from the 1960s onward. I will discuss this periodized "postmodernism" in Chapter 6, when I begin my discussion of Golding's later fiction. Suffice it to say, at this stage, that self-consciousness about the "truth" of representations, the status of knowledge, and indeed reality in *Pincher Martin* and *Free Fall* predates the critical accounts of postmodernism and further intensifications of self-conscious experimentation that followed in the wake of a widening debate about the state of contemporary life. It is part of a long tradition of fictional experiment deployed variously across major literary movements, not least modernism, that seemed particularly suited to the questioning mood that followed the devastation of World War II.

At this stage of a developing self-consciousness, *Pincher Martin* and *Free Fall* place Golding among "modern novelists" who "for all their affirmation of artifice . . . retain a residue of belief in the large possibility of capturing reality in fiction, however much they may be troubled by a sense of things collapsing historically." Like modernist works, *Pincher Martin* and *Free Fall* do not provide "an unambiguous expression of the new [postmodern] novelistic self-consciousness but . . . provide a decisively important background for it." There is, as Alter finds, substantial continuity between "the teasing puzzles of fictionality vis-a-vis reality" employed by modernist writers and later efforts at baring the literary device that from the 1950s onward has "come to be more and more a basic procedure—at times, almost an obsession—of serious fiction in the West." He concludes: "The creators of self-conscious fiction in our time do not constitute a school or a movement, and the lines of influence among them, or to them from their common predecessors, often tend to waver and blur when closely examined." However, Alter argues that there is an "aridness" and "indiscriminate invention" to postmodern self-consciousness. These aspects, perhaps justifiably, are what have brought a sense of the "literature of exhaustion," a phrase coined by John Barth that suggested novelty had reached saturation point.[6]

Self-consciousness in *Pincher Martin* and *Free Fall* confronts an "arbitrariness" and "necessary falsification" of textual representations in the

6. Ibid., 153–54, 179, 218–19 (see also 225, 230); Barth, "The Literature of Exhaustion."

wake of the particular historical moment of World War II, when values and, indeed, meaning were questioned and deep uncertainty and a sense of instability dominated.[7] As Alter notes, such self-consciousness often betrays concern over the future of Western civilization. It also signals where Golding's imagination will later turn—away from directly interrogating the sociopolitical context of World War II toward examining the cultural and aesthetic impact of what has come to be known as postmodernism, and that, as Dominick LaCapra has suggested, may well encrypt Holocaust trauma in fragmented, opaque, self-conscious fictions. The sociopolitical context that may well have further ruptured the Enlightenment project and spawned a greater mood of indeterminacy is registered in the intrusion of self-consciousness into Golding's work that yields a less politically engaged second phase to his oeuvre.

Pincher Martin and *Free Fall* are set not in the future or distant past, as were *Lord of the Flies* and *The Inheritors,* respectively, but in the recent past of the interwar years, World War II and its aftermath. This is significant. It is as if Golding found the "timeless" spin of the earlier fabular mode counterproductive to his satirical attack on an English national identity that constructs itself in opposition to fascism. Whereas *Pincher Martin* can be read as a creation myth or allegory about human evil and *Free Fall* as a myth of the Fall, similar concerns with totalitarianism as found in *Lord of the Flies* and *The Inheritors* are located in these novels. In *Free Fall,* Golding extends historical inscription to include left as well as right totalitarianisms, and both novels strengthen the reference to such contemporary issues by focusing on individuals in historical time rather than social groups in fabular or universal time. In so doing, he asserts that both communist and fascist forms of totalitarianism attract a certain kind of personality that need not be German or Russian, but can be English as well. The nationality of these violent, hobnailed, misogynic, and sadistic protagonists in *Pincher Martin* and *Free Fall* is not arbitrary. It is central to the meaning of these novels. Here, Golding's *Vergangenheitsbewältigung* concludes that the English are not immune to right or left totalitarianisms. It is this painful evocation of similitude that has been generally overlooked in readings of his work. Golding attempts to drive home a much more direct questioning of "English" values and "English" fantasies of moral superiority than he was able to achieve in *Lord of the Flies* and *The Inheritors.* As in the earlier novels, such a critique is achieved through fantastic and carnivalesque modes.

7. Alter, *Partial Magic,* 239.

By interrogating the border between material and spiritual worlds in *Pincher Martin* and *Free Fall*, Golding stresses the hell-bound and torturous remit of right and left totalitarianisms while submitting Christopher Martin in *Pincher Martin* and Sammy Mountjoy in *Free Fall* to lavatorial exposure by a replete carnivalesque. The carnivalesque, topsy-turvy world is widely represented in the violent, noncelebratory Dionysianism, scatology, and excessive consumption of both novels. This consolidates the notion of noncelebratory carnival highlighted by theorists such as René Girard, Peter Stallybrass, and Allon White. As with *Lord of the Flies* and *The Inheritors*, this use of the carnivalesque cannot be understood within Bakhtin's reading of the celebratory nature of carnival. The violent and sordid aspects of carnival are mobilized to interrogate the complacent view that the extremes of right or left politics could never succeed on English soil. In Christopher Martin and Sammy Mountjoy, Golding brings center stage, as it were, English totalitarian personalities. Hannah Arendt refers to just such a "totalitarian personality or mentality" and the "mass man" driven by loneliness toward the terrorist activity of totalitarianism.[8] Psychoanalytical readings of the "totalitarian personality," often in terms of fascism, refer to various traits: authoritarianism, sadomasochism, aggression, lust, greed, selfishness, anti-Semitism, racism, and ethnocentrism. Much of this kind of personality is evident in Christopher Martin and Sammy Mountjoy. However, rather than anti-Semitism, we locate misogyny.

In his influential two-volume study *Male Fantasies*, Klaus Theweleit identifies misogyny as fundamental to the totalitarian personality. He exposes the misogynic nature of the interwar Freikorps, a group of brutal men or "soldier-males" who can be seen as progenitors of German National Socialists or Nazis, and who bear the traits vital to totalitarian regimes elsewhere.[9] In the novels and memoirs of these soldier-males, who are strongly bound to men and male organizations, Theweleit unearths a deep hatred of women and suggests that it is caused by a dread of engulfment or dissolution by fluid femininity. This hatred of women and femininity takes precedence over a similar feeling toward the Jews that is, perhaps, more truly a development of National Socialism. He locates the origins of fascist murder in masculine desires rather than in terms of authoritarianism, an outbreak of irrationalism, the result of economic pressures, or simply as a symptom of repressed homosexuality. In essence, he considers fascism to

8. Arendt, *The Origins of Totalitarianism*, 306, 317.

9. See Dawson's *Soldier Heroes* for a later, though related, study and critique of masculinity.

be already implicit in the sexist way some men relate to women in everyday life. This link between sexist male behavior and fascism is particularly strong in *Pincher Martin* and *Free Fall.* The Freikorpsmen's delight in fantasies of annihilating women or rendering them lifeless bears some comparison with Christopher Martin's sadistic and brutal approach to his relationships with women and Sammy Mountjoy's equally cruel indifference to them. This brutal disregard for women and femininity was something that I noted earlier as part of Golding's representation of the masculine nature of fascist violence in *Lord of the Flies*—a violence that targets femininity in the anal rape of the female pig and the arguably "effeminate" Simon, and the destruction of the weakling, Piggy—attacks on women's buttocks being particularly prevalent in soldier-male fantasies.[10] Golding appears to formulate an early feminist critique of totalitarianism as intimately related to the violent oppression of women. This was extended in the patriarchal oppression of matriarchy in *The Inheritors.*

Similar claims about the misogynic nature of fascism are made in Alice Yaeger Kaplan's *Reproductions of Banality* in which she rejects the view that fascism results from the bewitching powers of Hitler and Mussolini, or that it can be simply equated "with images of the established Nazi state, that is, with black shirts and swastikas and with political sadism." According to Kaplan, such views are only part of "fascism's appeal." Even theories of fascism as a totalitarianism overlook the desires that put authoritarian bureaucracies in power. Kaplan focuses on this "erotic" aspect of fascism, that is, people's "fixation" on or "attraction" to it. She builds upon Theweleit's view of men fleeing the mother "into a phallic military atmosphere." She argues that an emphasis on creative, maternal unity in the early stages of fascism is quickly replaced by actions that are "grotesquely paternal." Women are reduced to "reproductive machines" so that fascist men "feel eternal, just as reducing 'others' to inferior races allowed them to feel like a superior race."[11]

Curiously perhaps, given the subject matter of *Pincher Martin* and *Free Fall,* there has been no detailed analysis of the dual function of the fantastic and carnivalesque to advance both the uncertainty generated by self-consciousness and Golding's continuing critique of Englishness through an exploration of the "totalitarian personality" and misogyny. This oversight can be rectified by examining how this dual function operates in each novel in turn.

10. Theweleit, *Male Fantasies I: Women, Floods, Bodies, History,* 183, 191.
11. Kaplan, *Reproductions of Banality,* 13, 14, 23, 24, 23.

Pincher Martin

Golding's third published novel, *Pincher Martin,* owes much to the "double death" theme of Ambrose Bierce's short story "An Occurrence at Owl Creek Bridge" (1891) and Taffrail's *Pincher Martin, O.D.: A Story of the Inner Life of the Royal Navy* (1916), a tale about a sailor who almost drowns after his battleship is torpedoed during World War I.[12] Golding reworks the latter, changing the setting to World War II. In his version of Taffrail's tale, Christopher Martin appears to survive drowning by climbing onto a rock, but—we later realize—his "survival" is no more than a brief, Biercean colonization of the afterlife or, rather, the last flicker of personal consciousness during which he literally invents hell for himself. When his hallucinatory world of rock disintegrates, it shows itself to be modeled on one of his teeth—a fitting symbol of his selfish, greedy, and consumptive life that we learn about through a trail of flashbacks. It has been a life of consuming anything and everything that comes within reach of his grasping fingers, mouth, or penis.

The nonsatirical function of fantastic and carnivalesque modes in *Pincher Martin* complements or extends the mood of uncertainty and equivocation established in self-conscious aspects of this work and opposes a spectrum of totalitarian thinking or approaches, "encrypts" the trauma of World War II atrocity, and marks Golding's nonengagement in preference for "ivory tower" experimentalism. In this highly self-conscious novel, the revelation that "Pincher" Martin's rock world is merely his own imaginative construction is prepared for by several references to the "natural" environment in terms of written text. The "rock" has "edges like the cut pages of a book" (*PN,* 77), the air sucks up Christopher's voice like "blotting-paper" (*PN,* 80), he "writes" on the "rock" with seaweed and, rather ironically, views his experience as having the makings of a great story: "'And what a story! A week on a rock. Lectures—'" (*PN,* 88). It is in Christopher's final gasp of consciousness, toward the end of the novel, that metafictional commentary reaches a climax when we are made patently aware that it is not simply Christopher or his rock that is fabricated like "cardboard" or "a painted flat" (*PN,* 195), but that the "reality" we read is merely paper with black lines upon it, and, more disturbingly, that our own "realities" are no less constructions or fictions.

Christopher's annihilation is prefaced by an engraved image in the rock of the "black lightning" (*PN,* 91) that destroys him. The image fit-

12. Taffrail was the pseudonym for Henry Taprell Dorling.

tingly resembles "bookworm" (*PN,* 177) and reasserts the textual construction and indeed deconstruction of Christopher, his "rock," and Golding's novel itself. Ultimately, Christopher's reality breakdown is a recognition of textuality and its ultimate, illusory status: "'There was nothing in writing!'" (*PN,* 199). This whole final scene tears like paper: "The sea stopped moving, froze, became paper, painted paper that was torn by a black line" (*PN,* 200). In a frightening collapse of constructed reality, the sea is "erased like an error" and the "lines of absolute blackness" interrogate and dismantle the "rock" that "proved to be as insubstantial as the painted water" (*PN,* 201). The self-canceling potential of words is remorselessly exhibited as the last square of engraved rock is obliterated by "black lines" (*PN,* 201). Eventually, the "island of papery stuff" is removed to leave a pair of kitsch claws "outlined like a night sign against the absolute nothingness" (*PN,* 201). These claws may refer to T. S. Eliot's poem "The Love Song of J. Alfred Prufrock" (1917) that explored the fear of mortality among other things: "I should have been a pair of claws / Scuttling across the floors of silent seas." Philip Redpath suggests that they may be viewed as "reflections of the writer's hands resting on the table or clutching the pen as he writes. The difference between claws and hands emphasizes the fact that Martin is not a writer and not therefore in the authoritative position of the writer. Ultimately, Martin dies because he is a character in a novel."[13]

In writing *Pincher Martin,* Golding may well have been influenced by Virginia Woolf whose fiction, Alter argues, centrally concerns literature as the "means to a human coherence" that "can be set over against the awaiting abyss." There are rather striking similarities between the fear of mortality explored in *Pincher Martin,* Eliot's "Love Song of J. Alfred Prufrock," and Woolf's *Mrs. Dalloway* (1925), in which Clarissa Dalloway is "pursued by the fear of her own imminent mortality . . . and the specter of bleak obliteration is externalized in the suicide of Septimus Warren Smith, which calls to the heroine's mind an explicit image of the engulfing abyss as she imagines that 'It was her punishment to see sink and disappear here a man, there a woman, in this profound darkness.'"[14] The impact of the self-conscious twist at the end of *Pincher Martin,* which questions the gap between text and world and suggests that both imaginative art and the lives we construct are set rather precariously over chaos and loss of meaning, relies entirely on the fantastic and carnivalesque. Fundamentally, the

13. T. S. Eliot, *Collected Poems, 1909–1962,* 15; Redpath, *Structural Reading,* 152.
14. Alter, *Partial Magic,* 149–50.

shock breaking of fantastic hesitation into the natural explanation that Christopher Martin's "rock-life" was a last desperate, imaginative act complements the uncertainty produced by a fictional self-consciousness that asserts the difficult enterprise of communicating meaning or "truth" in fiction. The "durative" fantastic builds the tension for what is essentially the revelation of the all too collapsible nature of fictional constructions. The "shock factor" of breaking fantastic hesitation into a natural yet uncanny explanation makes the self-conscious twist deeper, more profound, even nightmarish.

Fantastic hesitation is carefully established across the novel as Christopher's dislocated and alien consciousness battles to make sense of an increasingly puzzling, transitional, and multidimensional "reality." The realism of his experience on the rock—enhanced by detailed descriptions of survival—overlays hints that he might be dead. Supernatural and natural explanations compete but do not resolve until the end of the novel when we learn that he had drowned, and that the seaboots he had kicked off at the beginning of the novel were still attached to his washed-up corpse. Reality breakdowns, such as Christopher's strange voice that does not carry forth but is absorbed by the air around him, are explained away as the result of physical or mental illness; lack of sleep, exposure to the sun, and overwork are all offered as possible explanations for his hallucinatory experiences. His dreamlike flashbacks blur with his rockbound "reality" in such a way that differentiation between these states proves difficult. Indeterminacy is strengthened by the "doubling" of various figures and objects, such as Christopher's nose, the "Dwarf" who is also the "Old Woman," the chain of his dog tag, his reflection in a mirror. The double motif is particularly prominent in flashbacks of Christopher's theatrical life of playing two parts: "'Didn't you see the rehearsal list, Chris? You're doubling—but of course—'" (*PN*, 118). As reality is "pinched," and spatial coherence deteriorates, he experiences transitory, Kafkaesque metamorphoses into a lobster. Christopher self-diagnoses this and other abnormal perceptions and transformations as caused by pyrexial delirium or seafood poisoning and gives himself an enema to clear his system. However, the solubility of what should be insoluble guano, the appearance of a "red" lobster, and the striking resemblance the "rock" bears to a rotten tooth that had once stood in his head compounds doubt about the status of his reality. Christopher looks to bedlamite madness as a last port in the "reality" storm of erasure, black lightning, and nothingness. Achieving his ultimate, predeath hallucination of God dressed as a sailor, he dissolves under the pressure of damnation into lobster claws—into the essential image of himself, "pincher" of people and life, but also, as Redpath suggests, an image of the writer who gave him "life."

At one level of functioning, then, the fantastic status of Christopher's Promethean existence creates a strong sense of indeterminacy or the questioning of oppositions such as real versus unreal and rational versus irrational that interrogates the "reality" of the fictional text itself. However, the uncertainty about the "reality" of his survival and hence the uncertainty of the fictional enterprise is not achieved solely through the use of the fantastic mode. A vertiginous carnivalesque enhances this by relativizing spatial oppositions such as high versus low or up versus down.

The second line of *Pincher Martin* signals the topsy-turvydom employed throughout the novel in which natural and supernatural explanations jostle for supremacy just as Christopher struggles to survive after his warship is sunk: "There was no up or down" (*PN*, 7). This spatial aspect is encapsulated not simply in Christopher's suspension in the sea, before climbing onto "Rockall," but also in the description of a glass figure in a jam jar "delicately balanced between opposing forces" (*PN*, 9). This jam-jar analogy condenses his plight, caught as he is between transcendence and materiality, survival and drowning, life and death. Christopher is constantly going up and down his "island," or the sea is rushing up or washing down, just as he had bobbed up and down in it. His world is frequently turned upside down: "My legs must be up in the air over the other wall" (*PN*, 41). His skull is invested with antipodean potential: "He would heave the globe of darkness in which he most lived off a hard, wooden surface, rotate it and lay the other hemisphere down" (*PN*, 68). From his "globe," Christopher's cosmos is topsy-turvy, with the repeated relativizing of the spatial position of the sun and sky, and various inversions and reversals such as viewing Nathaniel as if he were upside down like a "bat" in some bizarre "reversed world" (*PN*, 103). Again, the "black lightning" that will exterminate Christopher's clinging consciousness resembles "a tree upside down" (*PN*, 177), and the final stages of his reality breakdown occur with his creation of an inverted *theos* in a parody of the Genesis creation story: "'In his own image created he Him'" (*PN*, 196). As the truth of his fabrication dawns, a vertiginous topsy-turvydom is all that can follow: "The centre did not know if it had flung the body down or if it had turned the world over" (*PN*, 200).

Golding, then, powerfully juxtaposes fictional creativity and the fantastical, hallucinatory construction of a "rock" upon which Christopher Martin faces disorientating experiences to bring about a shock recognition of the uncertain relationship between, and indeed "realities" of, text and world. However, at this early stage in Golding's shift toward a more aestheticized, metafictional experimentation in his later work, which effectively deflates satire, *Pincher Martin* still engages politically and satirically with the "historical moment" in an interrogation of the English totalitarian personality.

In *Pincher Martin,* Golding seems to suggest that confidence in English resistance to the "third way" of fascist politics can be no more than tentative. Although Oswald Mosley's Blackshirts might have petered out at the thin end of European fascism, they were still part of that extreme wedge of politics that gained ascendancy in the interwar years and found its fullest expression in Italy and Germany. Indeed, as Andrew Hawkey indicates, fascism had particularly strong roots in Britain even before the creation of the British Union of Fascists (BUF). He refers to the anti-Semitism of Houston Stewart Chamberlain, the "crude racial assumptions" behind British imperialism, Herbert Spencer's concept of "the survival of the fittest," and a host of predecessors to the BUF in the Britons, the British Fascists, the Fascist League, and the Imperial Fascist League. The smaller groups, notably the Britons, the Imperial Fascist League, and another group called the Nordic League, were, according to Richard Thurlow, "closest to the nazis in their thought and inspiration" and proved to be seedbeds for a more militant, racial fascism in Britain.[15]

Alan Sinfield considers *Pincher Martin,* like *Lord of the Flies,* to be a further attack on notions of British immunity from fascist brutality and totalitarianism: "The mental processes of a drowning Royal Navy lieutenant, whose ship has been sunk by the Germans in the war, reveal *his* brutal and amoral personality." Building on this all too brief and undeveloped insight into *Pincher Martin,* the protagonist, Christopher Martin, can be seen as resembling the "soldier-male" totalitarian personality outlined by Theweleit. The novel, which is set in World War II, presents Christopher's appetitive, violent, and carnivalesque abuse of other people, particularly women, and determination to survive in a way that suggests the misogynistic legacy of the protofascist Freikorps and the kind of extreme survivalism-at-all-costs preached in Hitler's *Mein Kampf.* That we know Golding himself to have been in command of a minesweeper and rocket ship during the war, and on intimate terms with the greed of war, is significant for a full understanding of *Pincher Martin.* Golding's naval experience and knowledge are woven into the fiction, as are surface de-

15. Hawkey, introduction to *Revolution and Reason and Other Essays by Oswald Mosley,* xxi; Thurlow, *Fascism in Britain: A History, 1918–1985,* 62.

tails particular to World War II. In keeping with Paul Ricoeur's view of the synthetic status of history, this is a significant analogue to Christopher's destructive appetites.[16] Christopher had been a lieutenant on a "war-time destroyer" that formed part of a convoy protecting merchant shipping from U-boats (*PN,* 51). The detail Golding gives to the ship and its passage confirms and deepens the war setting, concretizing the historical analogue against which Christopher's English form of brutality and exploitation is set. We find a panoply of references to the war such as moonlit bombing raids on cities and blackout curtains.

The final breaking of the "durative" fantastic into a natural explanation that Christopher had been suffering a kind of hallucinatory damnation offers a suitable critique of his totalitarian personality. It provides a shock recognition of his self-made hell—a personalized, Gothic, rockbound "torture chamber" that is a fitting punishment for living a sadistic, totalitarian life. In a protracted witching hour, he is accompanied by a headless dwarf, a giant, an old woman, and reptilian, vampirish, batlike gulls. Death, maggots, corpses, coffins, phantoms, ghosts, and childhood fears of the cellar all loom large as do the ax and block, executions, and decapitations. Christopher is tormented by a needlelike pain in his skull, and has thoughts of racks, pincers, and even Poe's pit and pendulum. Apart from getting the near-death hallucination he deserves, the shock recognition that Christopher's "after-life" is merely a limited hallucination that finally burns out adds to Golding's incipient critique of religious authority, initiated subtly in the madness of the "saint" Simon in *Lord of the Flies* and taken up more forthrightly in *The Spire* and some of the later novels.

Not only does the topsy-turvy carnivalesque enhance the fantastic indeterminacy of Christopher's island experience, but it also establishes the violent consumption that marked his life. Frequent references to the carnivalesque "lower body" in the novel alert us to his extreme, cruel, appetitive nature, but also achieve two major effects through a heavily scatological focus. First, the intensely low-bound nature of Christopher's self-created hell undermines or critiques his life in general. In other words, his character is appropriately associated with stinking, low materiality as opposed to any higher moral achievement. Second, the soft, fluid intrusion of lower body functions—of the viscera as such—is part and parcel of a more feminine dimension, as Theweleit suggests, and increases a sense of the dissolution and hence destruction of the masculine hard-

16. Sinfield, *Society and Literature, 1945–1970,* 36; Ricoeur, *The Reality of the Historical Past.*

ness at the core of his personality. What is crucial to a true understanding of *Pincher Martin* is the way Golding juxtaposes an English subject's atrocious appetite, exterminatory drives, and will to survive at all costs with the kind of "soldier-male" personality of the Freikorpsman that Theweleit describes—a personality strongly linked to the later National Socialism.

Theweleit contrasts the erect, rigid phallic pose of the Freikorps with vulnerable femininity, the dissolving influence of Bolshevism, and the perceived threat to Germany of the subhuman *(untermensch).* The soldier-male wraps himself up, as it were, in a fiercely destructive, masculine rigidity: "The monumentalism of fascism would seem to be a safety mechanism against the bewildering multiplicity of the living. The more lifeless, regimented, and monumental reality appears to be, the more secure the men feel. The danger is being-alive itself." The soldier-male is presented as maintaining phallic strength via his weapons and containing an otherwise fluid mass of people in militaristic parades, holding back like a dam the inner softness that threatens to undermine his firm stand. He has "the hard, organized, phallic body devoid of all internal viscera that finds its apotheosis in the machine. This body-machine is the acknowledged 'utopia' of the fascist warrior."[17] It is this kind of protective, armored masculinity that lies at the heart of *Pincher Martin.* Christopher Martin's metamorphosis is into the "body-machine" of a lobster. But his hard, phallic body that is thrust into a crevice only temporarily fends off dissolution. His lobsteresque masculinity is eroded in a particularly mucosal and often feminine softness.

Furthermore, if we acknowledge the Kafkaesque parallel, Christopher's metamorphosis also suggests he becomes *ungeziefer* (vermin).[18] The Nazi-like English sailor, not the Jew, as in Franz Kafka's *Transformation* (*Metamorphosis* [1915]), is changed into a repulsive, exoskeletal creature. This topsy-turvy rendering of Kafka's motif suggests that once Christopher has become the exoskeletal "soldier-male" he has simultaneously become subhuman like the lobster and deserves extermination. As Christopher has eaten others, he too becomes edible—a lobster—subject to the annihilation of "black lightning." The tables are turned and he is consumed. Maybe, Golding hopes that totalitarian individuals like

17. Theweleit, *Male Fantasies I,* 218; Jessica Benjamin and Anson Rabinbach, foreword to *Male Fantasies II,* by Theweleit, xix.

18. Steiner points out that in a "stroke of tragic clairvoyance," Kafka's term *vermin* (*ungeziefer*) was applied by the Nazis to the Jews they exterminated (*Language and Silence,* 144). Here, Steiner considers Kafka's writings as foreshadowing the excesses of totalitarianism.

Christopher get some of their own medicine before oblivion. All the better that it is self-generated, as history has shown totalitarian regimes to be particularly imaginative torturers. However, as Golding demonstrates by his choice of protagonist, we must choose not to view totalitarianism as simply a German affair. It is also an English style of living. In a Kafkaesque twist, Golding reveals the homespun version of a hard "soldier-male" *ungeziefer.*

In making Christopher Martin the "nastiest type," Golding appears to draw on specific details in Taffrail's *Pincher Martin, O.D.*[19] Apart from the more obvious parallels in terms of the naval focus, the novel's title, and similarities in the drowning episode, particularly concerning flashbacks and the removal of heavy seaboots, Golding may well have based Christopher on Taffrail's "hard-headed" sublieutenant who convinces a captured German skipper that "[t]he brutal British are capable of anything" when he suggests throwing the prisoners into the sea and ramming any U-boat that tries to pick them up.[20] Certainly, the "brutal British" theme is at the heart of Golding's own version of the "inner life" of the Royal Navy. Indeed, the sublieutenant in Taffrail's tale appears to be the model for Golding's protagonist rather than the ordinary seaman or "O.D." It is Golding's deployment of noncelebratory carnivalesque that brings home Christopher's "nastiness" and Freikorpian brutality.

A ubiquitous carnivalesque "low" symbolism stresses not simply the "materiality" of Christopher's existence, and hence his mortal boundary, but the astonishing greed and sadism that marked his life. Such traits, as identified earlier, are central to the "totalitarian personality."[21] Within the wartime context, the protagonist's fascistic style of life, his base and consumptive nature, his masquerade are exposed. From the start, Christopher's mouth is wide open, a symbol that is repeated throughout the novel, evoking a carnivalesque orifice that consumes the world. Suitably, his life and hallucinogenic existence on the rock reveal his greed. The jam-jar motif and the image of him as the "one huge, successful maggot" (*PN,* 136) eating all the maggots that feed upon a fish inside a Chinese maggot box are part of this overall symbolism as are the many references to food and drink. Not only are pebbles on the "rock" potato-shaped or the "rock" itself converted into a "hot cross bun" (*PN,* 109), but Christopher refers to his mind as a "'loaf'" (*PN,* 59) and his battling conscious-

19. Hodson, *William Golding,* 70.
20. Taffrail [Henry Taprell Dorling], *Pincher Martin, O.D.,* 294.
21. See Anthony Storr, "Intimations of Mystery," 139–40.

ness as a "pudding" that "has boiled over" (*PN*, 191). The sea masticates, seaweed appears tonguelike, and the "rock" is thought to emerge from some geologic indigestion or "gripe of the earth's belly" (*PN*, 77). Eating or being eaten, therefore, appears to be the ground of Christopher's being.

Christopher's "clever" (*PN*, 10) mouth eats, sucks, vomits, bites anything it can: air, water, food, and people. Left slackly open at rest, this mouth is always prone to consume. Again and again we witness the activity of his greedy teeth upon which he bases the topography of his hallucinogenic island. He is literally all mouth, consuming as fiercely and cruelly, Golding seems to hint, as Holocaustic furnaces: "'I breathe this air into my own furnace. I kill and eat'" (*PN*, 115). As in references to "smoke" and the "camp" in *The Inheritors*, here we find vocabulary that Lawrence L. Langer, citing Norma Rosen, suggests cannot be registered "without some form of associative despair."[22] Helen, Sybil, Mary, and Nathaniel become victims of Christopher's snowballing appetites and lust. Mary, for example, with her "apple-breasts" (*PN*, 148), is cast as a tasty morsel that excites his digestive juices, whereas Christopher's murder victim, Nathaniel, becomes the ultimate meal: "Christ, how I hate you. I could eat you" (*PN*, 100).

The "gaping mouth" is also related to "the lower stratum; it is the open gate leading downward into the bodily underworld."[23] Christopher affords a direct link between oral and sexual consumption, the low, evil "underworld" and a fascist personality. He mixes various acts of consumption with the "punishment" that "fascists" dole out: "You could eat with your cock or with your fists, or with your voice. You could eat with hobnailed boots or buying and selling or marrying and begetting and cuckolding" (*PN*, 88). For example, after sexually "consuming" Sybil, Christopher disarms the cuckolded Alfred by twisting his wrist, grinning sadistically like the decapitated pig's head in *Lord of the Flies:* "Secure in his knowledge of the cosmic nature of eating he grinned down at him" (*PN*, 89). Victimization and mocking the cuckold, of course, have a long history in the carnivalesque rituals of shivaree or what is called "rough music."[24] It is a theme that Golding picks up more strongly in the fate of the cuckold Pangall in *The Spire*.

22. Langer, *Admitting the Holocaust*, 77. See also Rosen, "The Second Life of Holocaust Imagery."

23. Bakhtin, *Rabelais and His World*, 325.

24. See, for example, E. P. Thompson, "Rough Music: Le Charivari Anglais"; Darnton, *The Great Cat Massacre*, 81, 87, 95; and Burke, *Popular Culture*, 177–204.

The link between Christopher's cuckolding, "eating" people with his cock, and warfare dominates *Pincher Martin.* Even his struggle to come to terms with the red lobster is couched in terms that reflect his aggressive, colonizing nature: "'What piece have I lost in my game? I had an attack, I was doing well, and then—'" (*PN,* 172). His rational anticipation of the weather is similar: "'Since I can foretell the weather I can be armed against it'" (*PN,* 172–73). His misogynic subjection of Mary evokes not simply the colonization of war in its most brutal form but also social Darwinism, being "nothing but another step on which one must place the advancing foot" (*PN,* 149). This compounds an earlier example of his lifelong subjection of other people, when he places his feet on hallucinatory faces to climb out of a crevice in the "rock." Again, this trope of standing on the bodies of people, so reminiscent of mass Jewish graves, is used when Christopher accuses his "God" hallucination of making him a consumer of people: "'Yet suppose I climbed away from the cellar over the bodies of used and defeated people, broke them to make steps on the road away from you, why should you torture me? If I ate them, who gave me a mouth?'" (*PN,* 197). The essence of his oral consumption is revealed: "he opened his mouth and gasped in the air as though he were winning territory" (*PN,* 37).

Christopher's consumptive existence frequently melds food with sex or excreting. It is this panoply of consumptive metaphors that provides a "meat and sex" carnivalesque of Rabelaisian proportions in noncelebratory style. This focus on "lower domains" is further stressed in the feminization of the "island" by birthing and pudendal symbolism. His hallucinatory world is replete with crevices, tunnels, funnels, and suchlike, and Christopher is frequently inserting himself into them, groping, prying, or sucking at them. Penile penetration of the crevice is repeated over and over again: "'My flesh is perceptible inside—as though it were bruised everywhere to the bone. And big. Tumescent'" (*PN,* 129). The anemones he eats like sweets are "slumped like breasts when the milk has been drawn from them" (*PN,* 63), and we never hear the last of his mouth at the "tit of the lifebelt" (*PN,* 16). Christopher's past life and present hallucination are marked by ingestion and abjection. All orifices are used. His fabricated rock reflects this orificial focus.

The whole backdrop of Christopher's psychogenic world revolves around various acts of sexual consumption. Such imagery reflects the dense materiality of Christopher's life and his transgressive desires. As the maggot that ate smaller maggots, he was not averse to sexually consuming men, women, girls, or even boys: "Think about eating women, eating men, crunching up Alfred, that other girl, that boy, that crude and unsatisfactory experiment" (*PN*, 90). The consumptive aspect of his character is brilliantly summarized by the theater producer, Peter, whose wife is "eaten" by Christopher. Peter suggests that Christopher plays one of the seven deadly sins, greed: "'Chris-Greed. Greed-Chris. Know each other. . . . Let me make you two better acquainted. This painted bastard here takes anything he can lay his hands on. Not food, Chris, that's far too simple. He takes the best part, the best seat, the most money, the best notice, the best woman. He was born with his mouth and his flies open and both hands out to grab. He's a cosmic case of the bugger who gets his penny and someone else's bun'" (*PN*, 119–20). Christopher's sadistic, sexual consumption of others is particularly marked in how he frightens Mary into having sex with him by driving too fast and his violent, misogynic fantasies about her: "'Those nights of imagined copulation, when one thought not of love nor sensation nor comfort nor triumph, but of torture rather, the very rhythm of the body reinforced by hissed ejaculations—take that and that!'" (*PN*, 149).

The scatological nature of the rock world that Christopher invents for himself suitably undermines his prodigious, "soldier-male" consumption. He is granted the kind of stinking environment of slime, feces, and urine that reflects his "low," brutal life. This lavatorial focus is magnified by Christopher's anxieties about having not opened his bowels for days and his self-administration of an enema. The evacuation is suitably theatrical, and not without due reference to wartime violence. The result is "explosive . . . like the bursting of a dam, the smashing of all hindrance" (*PN*, 165). His temporary victory and restoration are described in military terms that reinforce again and again Christopher's colonizing personality: "'I knew I should suffer and I have. But I am winning'" (*PN*, 166). Christopher's lavatorial exposure continues till the end. His life, marked by eating others and shitting them out, has brought its just deserts—a self-made hell that, like his own fascistic life, stinks. The "scatophagy" of "insoluble muck" (*PN*, 192) in his mouth further decrowns him.[25] Amid "slime and circling scum" (*PN*, 199), Christopher rejects the notion of salvation: "'I shit on your heaven!'" (*PN*, 200).

Christopher's existence is a noncelebratory carnival of the grotesque body: consumption, transgression, and excretion. His life revolves around theater and foolery; he is the ultimate "painted bastard," on a masquerade through life, consuming people. His palate is demonstrably that of a

25. Bakhtin, *Rabelais and His World*, 330.

Nazi-like totalitarian "soldier-male." Although by the end of the novel, Christopher's fate is thought to have been painless since he didn't have time to kick off his boots, we know from what has gone before that along the narrow frontier of death, as Martin's brain flickered out like a candle, he had plenty of time to suffer a kind of damnation. That his creation was hell is emphasized throughout the novel by the many references to the Devil, damnation, and the underworld—a feature at the heart of Menippean satire's topsy-turvydom. But Golding does more than simply this. He sets Christopher's sadistic lifestyle against the historical analogue of fascist atrocities during World War II. The deployment of the fantastic and carnivalesque to advance the self-conscious uncertainty of the novel does not detract sufficiently from engagement with English totalitarianism. At this stage, we might see Golding's formal experimentalism as reflecting the upheaval of Enlightenment values with the advent of totalitarianisms and as promoting dialogism in opposition to authoritarian monologism. *Pincher Martin* is not a timeless novel. It is of the times. Golding combines the universal trope of consumption with the practices of National Socialism. Not to see this is to miss Golding's inscription of history.

Free Fall

Golding's more mainstream novel, *Free Fall,* is a review of the life of an English artist, Sammy Mountjoy. Narrated in the first person, it is a quest to find out where he lost his innocent freedom and began to live an inflexible, selfish life. As such, the novel is "structured as one chronologically disrupted flashback."[26] Sammy examines his squalid upbringing in the slums of Rotten Row, the extremes of left and right politics prior to World War II, and pinpoints educational influences that have shaped him, not least the viewpoints of two of his teachers or "parents not in the flesh" (*FF,* 250): kind, atheistic Nick Shales and cruel, religious Rowena Pringle. Shales and Pringle symbolize an ongoing, irresolvable tension in Sammy's life between rationality and irrationality, the body versus the soul—it is a tension that extends to his awareness of the limitations of art's representation of reality and all forms of pattern making or explanation. *Free Fall* ends with a sense of the irreconcilable status not just of materialist and religious interpretations of the world, but of other disjunctures such as text and reality as well: "Her world was real, both worlds are real. There

26. McCarron, *William Golding,* 20.

is no bridge" (*FF,* 253). At the core of Sammy's self-examination is his uncompromising pursuit and exploitation of Beatrice Ifor. His determination to possess her regardless of the price is the point at which Golding locates Sammy's loss of freedom and, indeed, his "fall." His recollection of being tortured by the Nazis during the war serves to critique his own torture and abandonment of Beatrice, which led to her incarceration in a mental asylum.

The novel is a parody of Dante's *La Vita Nuova* (c. 1290) and uses a "durative" fantastic and noncelebratory carnivalesque to investigate further the uncertain status of fictional writing and critique both right- and left-wing forms of English totalitarianism. As such, *La Vita Nuova* offers the themes for both these concerns. Of those critics who have noted the Dantean influence on *Free Fall,* Kevin McCarron's contribution is of particular interest here. First, he argues that "through its use of a prose commentary *La Vita Nuova* is as much a book about the act of writing poetry," and, similarly, *Free Fall* "is itself very much concerned with the act of writing." This metafictional concern, a loss of faith in the episteme of representation, intensified by the "world turned upside down" of fantastic and carnivalesque modes, may well add to a twofold sense of lost stability evoked in the novel, that is, between the idea of man's Fall as described in Genesis, from heaven to earth (from perfect accord with God to discord and the consciousness of imperfection and sin), and that of World War II "free fall," which implies that there can be no landing point, no stable ground anymore. As such, both metafiction and the complementary uncertainty evoked by the fantastic and carnivalesque act as forces of destabilization in the novel, adding to the sense that Sammy Mountjoy is in "free fall." Second, McCarron locates a shift in *Free Fall* from Golding's earlier subversive revisionism to using *La Vita Nuova* "to suggest that Mountjoy's desire for Beatrice Ifor is inferior to Dante's devotion to his Beatrice."[27] This turning upside down of Dantean devotion is at the heart of Golding's critique of Sammy's totalitarian personality. The cruel nature of his "devotion" to Beatrice Ifor parodies Dante's higher or more wholesome feelings for Beatrice dei Portinari.

In Sammy's quest to find out where and when he lost his freedom,

27. Ibid., 19. As McCarron indicates, in *La Vita Nuova,* Dante celebrates "the beauty and virtue" of "Beatrice dei Portinari, who married the Florentine banker Simone dei Bardi and died in 1290 at the age of 24." This literary analogue in *Free Fall,* unlike those in Golding's previous novels that demonstrate their "partiality, or even incorrectness," reveals how "the views central to the earlier literary model" are "superior" (18, 19).

Golding primarily invokes the heavenly and visionary as a contrast to his base, exploitative, and noncelebratory carnivalesque behavior that mirrors the brutal, misogynistic "soldier-male" personality identified by Theweleit. The instantiation of English totalitarian man in *Free Fall* is far less oblique or Beckettian in style than it was in *Pincher Martin.* Golding produces a much stronger and detailed historical reference to left and right extreme politics in an account of conflict between the Communist Party of Great Britain (CPGB) and the British Union of Fascists, the excesses of both being compared to Nazism. This suggests that Golding wishes to redress the balance, at least temporarily, between formal or aesthetic concerns and engagement with contemporary politics and history. The fantastic and carnivalesque in *Free Fall* do function to intensify self-conscious uncertainty in the novel, but this is not as pronounced as it is in *Pincher Martin.*

Metafiction in *Free Fall* draws attention to the uncertain, difficult, and nontotalizable nature of communication and the epistemological crisis this betokens. Self-consciousness may be more than pure, formal experimentation for its own sake. As in *Pincher Martin,* it can be seen as reflecting the loss of stable epistemological ground in the wake of totalitarian atrocities. Sammy is an artist who searches for an elusive "pattern" to his life (*FF,* 6), yet is all too aware of the limitations and selectivity of art, its failure to mirror reality, and the difficulty of communicating in anything but a partial, unsatisfactory way. In particular, a debate ensues concerning the "incoherence" generated by the many "modes of change, filter and translation" (*FF,* 8) that lie between the writer and reader and results in them sharing "nothing but . . . [a] sense of division" (*FF,* 10).

The opening reference in *Free Fall* to books that "burst with a white hosanna" and Sammy's sensibility for the "miraculous and pentecostal" (*FF,* 5) suggests that the pervasive uncertainty surrounding text and world in the novel is complemented by a fantastical suspension between spiritual and material worlds. Again, the world of text and fantastic uncertainty are neatly juxtaposed following Sammy's release from the terrifying "torture cell" at the POW camp, when the linguistic representation fails to capture the miraculous dimension of natural phenomena: "Huge tears were dropping from my face into dust; and this dust was a universe of brilliant and fantastic crystals, that miracles instantly supported in their being. . . . The paper wrappings of use and language dropped from me" (*FF,* 186). Despite the intrusion of a "miraculous dimension," we sense early on in the novel that Sammy's "suspension" between two worlds can be explained naturally by the mastoid-inducing blow that he receives in childhood from the church verger, or by the madness caused by torture and imprisonment in a POW camp. Hence, there is not the kind of "shock factor" of natural explanation witnessed in *Pincher Martin.* In effect, the "durative" fantastic is much weaker across *Free Fall* than it is in *Pincher Martin* or the earlier novels.

Materiality in the novel is interrogated by the fantastical and contrasting worlds of heaven and hell. Sammy's movement into wickedness, by his lustful subjugation of the heavenly Beatrice, is emphasized throughout the novel through subterranean imagery. Shales and Halde are cast as devils, and Sammy, like Christopher Martin, constructs his own "hell" after living a savage, "evil" life. In the POW camp, Sammy's fierce imagination turns a broom cupboard into a torture chamber. This self-generated "hell" is a fitting punishment for his "crimes" against Beatrice and affords a broad contrast between his cruelty and a heavenly and miraculous "fourth dimension" that remains "indescribable" (*FF,* 187). There, like his victim, Beatrice, he endures a hellish nightmare that further erodes his sanity.

At the end of the novel, Sammy's uncanny vision at the gatehouse of the mental asylum of the goat "with horns of fantastication and the yellow eyes of lust" (*FF,* 237) reminds him of his brutal treatment of Beatrice. Whether what Sammy sees is a vision or an ornament of some kind remains unclear. Hesitation on this point is exacted by a lack of any reference to an object and by Sammy's resultant state of mind: "I thought to myself that I seemed not to be on the pavement but standing a little above it" (*FF,* 237). What is certain is that he has come to "the house of the payoff" where he will examine his "own experiment" (*FF,* 237), the abject Beatrice, who is the victim of his consumptive lust and disregard. It is fitting that his own mind is cast in some doubt by the goat "vision" and levitation above the pavement. He has not come through unscathed.

The carnivalesque topsy-turvydom in the novel adds to the broad mood of uncertainty and indetermination advanced by metafictional elements and the fantastic mode. It alerts us to a chaotic relativity of moral values that may suggest the upheavals generated by contemporary totalitarianism. The war has turned British life upside down, so much so that a straight reversal of its effects seems impossible. This is true of Sammy's bombed town that "does not stand on its head for the head is gone" (*FF,* 36). Throughout *Free Fall,* topsy-turvydom dominates in the spatial disorientation Sammy experiences after the verger cuffs his ear, the "ups and downs" of his recovery from the resultant mastoid (*FF,* 70), and his "free fall" between "high" morality and "low" transgression. Although he might live on Paradise Hill, his damnable lust for Beatrice parodies the Dantean ideal. Even his art is a commitment to "stand the world of appearances on its head" (*FF,* 102). In Halde's torture "cell," the vertiginous quality of Sammy's world is reemphasized: "Up there is up and down there is down . . . Don't forget which is which or you will be seasick" (*FF,* 177).

Topsy-turvydom is further in evidence in *Free Fall*'s rather transgressive focus on what Jonathan Dollimore calls the "inversion and displacement of gender binaries," particularly through the motif of cross-dressing. Beatrice wears a suit with masculine lapels, Evie claims she can pee up a wall like a boy, while Sammy fantasizes about gender reversal: "Might I perhaps change into a girl, wear skirts and a hair-ribbon?" (*FF,* 32). Such fantasies reappear later in the novel: "What is it like in the bath and the lavatory and walking the pavement with shorter steps and high heels . . . ?" (*FF,* 104). Here Golding seems ahead of his time in viewing gender as performative, something argued for much later by Judith Butler in *Gender Trouble.* Butler states: "There is no gender identity behind the expressions of gender . . . identity is performatively constituted by the very 'expressions' that are said to be its results." Hence, "Gender is the repeated stylization of the body, a set of repeated acts within a highly rigid regulatory frame that congeal over time to produce the appearance of substance, of a natural sort of being."[28] This take on gender as performative is explored further in Golding's *Pyramid* and *To the Ends of the Earth.*

Golding's early and brief foray into the issue of gender as performative and the inversion of gender identity in *Free Fall* arise from his strong focus throughout his fiction on theatricality and representation of modernist and later postmodernist uncertainty, rather than from any desire to advance what Dollimore calls "sexual dissidence," that is, a resistance to "conceptions of self, desire, and transgression which figure in the language, ideologies, and cultures of domination." While Golding's representation of dissident sexualities, as with his instantiation of homosexuality, which I discuss later in this chapter, can be seen as an attempt to undermine the dominant, "brutally homophobic" side of English society, it is not wholly convincing.[29] Rather, Golding's deployment of gender boundaries and diverse sexualities to advance indeterminacy or achieve

28. Dollimore, *Sexual Dissidence: Augustine to Wilde, Freud to Foucault,* 288; J. Butler, *Gender Trouble,* 25, 33.

29. Dollimore, *Sexual Dissidence,* 21 (see also Alan Sinfield, *Cultural Politics: Queer Reading*); Eve Kosofsky Sedgwick, *Between Men: English Literature and Male Homosexual Desire,* 3.

satirical effect in *Free Fall* and later in *The Pyramid, Darkness Visible,* and *To the Ends of the Earth* problematizes and contradicts the more radical trajectory of "sexual dissidence."

The fantastic and carnivalesque in *Free Fall* supply an indeterminacy that magnifies the uncertain status of fictional or artistic representation already advanced through self-conscious or metafictional aspects of the novel. The more dominant function of these modes, however, is to critique English totalitarianism. In this difficult novel Golding consolidates his more oblique sketch of the English "totalitarian personality" in *Pincher Martin.* As such, *Free Fall* warrants examination in terms of "a second fall and expulsion, not from grace this time but from humanity itself."[30] This notion of a "second fall" offers a counter to critical focus on the universal motif of original sin in *Free Fall.* It demands history.

The relevance of *Free Fall* to contemporary experience has, of course, been noted elsewhere. *Free Fall* is a novel that James Gindin finds "representative of contemporary manifestations of evil," and Ian Gregor and Mark Kinkead-Weekes argue that it convinces us "of the centrality and urgency of [Golding's] mythical account to modern experience." James Baker argues that the novel, like *Lord of the Flies* and *Pincher Martin* before it, takes account of the "irrationality of men in conflict" that Golding witnessed firsthand. Virginia Tiger sees *Free Fall* as tackling "the moral wretchedness that he saw the twentieth century had re-ratified." L. L. Dickson argues that the topic of guilt and spiritual collapse enhanced by images of falling, excrement, and blackness in the novel "communicates the deterioration of society and the resultant alienation of modern humanity after World War II."[31] Yet despite such avowals of contemporary relevance, historical and social contexts are relegated to the background by these critics. To date, Golding critics have barely mapped out how he interrogates English moral superiority vis-à-vis totalitarianism. This aspect is central to our understanding of a novel that some critics have found disappointing.[32]

In *Free Fall,* Golding not only echoes George Orwell's grim view of Soviet communism in *Animal Farm* and *1984* but, like him, also knits the gap

30. Langer, *Literary Imagination,* 76.

31. Gindin, *William Golding,* 48–49; I. Gregor and Kinkead-Weekes, "Strange Case," 62; Baker, *William Golding,* xiii; Tiger, *Dark Fields,* 202; Dickson, *Modern Allegories,* 70, 74.

32. See Dick, *William Golding* (1967), 69; Josipovici, *World and Book,* 247; and Subbarao, *William Golding,* 68.

between various extremes of totalitarian excess and Englishness.[33] In *Free Fall,* Golding tries to show that both left and right political rhetorics may appeal to (or even conceal) English totalitarian personalities, along the lines suggested by Hannah Arendt and Klaus Theweleit. He reveals the equally totalitarian potential of the left, an "honest man" (*FF,* 99) being hard to find in either camp. Indeed, *Free Fall* can be contextualized in relation to cold war disenchantment or disillusion with communism during the 1950s—perhaps Golding had in his sights those Marxist intellectuals of the 1930s and 1940s who refused to see what was going on in the Soviet Union despite leaks that purges were being carried out there. As Brian Moynahan observes, during the 1930s, poets and writers such as W. H. Auden, Stephen Spender, Cecil Day Lewis, Walter Greenwood, and George Orwell had "leftist sympathies"—though Orwell, who fought for the Partido Obrera de Unificación Marxista in the Spanish Civil War, grew increasingly critical of Soviet communism. Oxford undergraduates sympathized with and visited the unemployed Welsh miners in the Rhondda valley, Victor Gollancz started his Left Book Club, Virginia Woolf wrote for the communist *Daily Worker,* and others such as Kim Philby, Guy Burgess, Donald Maclean, and Anthony Blunt "flirted with Soviet Communism."[34] In fact, many left-wingers at the time refused to leave the Communist Party until after Khrushchev's famous speech to the Twentieth Party Congress in February 1956 in which he denounced Stalin's brutal and despotic rule. Yet even after this revelation, some left-wingers stayed members of the Communist Party of Great Britain. Doris Lessing's *Golden Notebook* (1962) deals in part with the impact that revelation of Stalin's atrocities had upon CPGB membership. The CPGB declined further after the brutal activities of Soviet Russia in its quashing of the Hungarian uprising in November 1956. Leading figures such as John Saville, E. P. Thompson, and Christopher Hill, thousands of its ordinary mem-

33. Beyond its attack on totalitarian Russia, Ben Pimlott considers *1984* to be highly critical of "British state socialism" under the postwar Labour government and "the pretensions and illiberalism of Western left-wing intellectuals" (introduction to *1984,* by Orwell, ix). Similarly, Hewison argues that Orwell achieves "a strong contemporary reference in his projection of a future totalitarian Britain" that, like Nazi Germany and Soviet Russia, employs "state direction and propaganda." In this way, Hewison ventures that *Animal Farm* and *1984* should not be deemed merely cold war books that are simply critical of Soviet communism; they also highlight homegrown totalitarianism (*In Anger,* 27, 28).

34. Moynahan, *The British Century: A Photographic History of the Last Hundred Years,* 159, 162.

bers, and representatives from trade unions such as the National Union of Mineworkers resigned their affiliation with the party. Saville and Thompson eventually joined up with other British Marxists, such as Stuart Hall, to launch the *New Left Review,* which acted as a kind of beacon for Marxian analysis of culture. With "commitment" still very much the concern of the new left, it turned to cultural criticism in an attempt to expose social injustice.[35]

In *Free Fall,* there is the irony of an English communist, Sammy Mountjoy, behaving in a similarly totalitarian and transgressive way as the Blackshirted fascists he condemns. Fantastical, heavenly visions bring about a sharp, critical contrast to Sammy's cruel, carnivalesque, and indeed totalitarian personality—a personality that is particularly visible in one of several parallels between *Free Fall* and *La Vita Nuova* identified by McCarron. Whereas, at one point, Dante experiences poetic feelings for Beatrice when he sees her in the company of two other women, Sammy desires to exterminate college girls shortly before Beatrice Ifor similarly appears with two female companions: "I was in the gutter, sitting my bike [*sic*], willing them to die, be raped, bombed or otherwise obliterated" (*FF,* 82). Of course, *La Vita Nuova* is not the only prior text that Golding utilizes to formulate his critique of the English totalitarian personality.

According to Bernard Oldsey and Stanley Weintraub, *Free Fall* bears a striking resemblance to Albert Camus's existentialist book *La Chute* (*The Fall* [1956]). Like *La Chute, Free Fall* registers the absurdity of human life, and presents alongside *Pincher Martin* "a double vision of man's fall in modern times." *La Chute* focuses on the guilt that Jean-Baptiste Clamence feels about his brutal disregard for women. This guilt is evoked through images of Gothic torture and judgment, but also, and more important, through the juxtaposition of Clamence's cruelty toward women and Nazi atrocities. Although the influence of *La Chute* on *Free Fall* may amount to wishful thinking on the part of Oldsey and Weintraub, especially since it was published in translation only two years prior to the publication of *Free Fall,* and as Bernard Dick notes, "Golding acknowledges no debt to Existentialism," Clamence is a plausible model for Sammy Mountjoy's own brand of rigid, hard "soldier-male" masculinity. Clamence, for example, treats one of his many conquests "so brutally, in every respect" that he sees himself as her "gaoler." He faces up to the fact that he too has desired to dominate others like those who rush "to join the cruellest party," and that he too stands guilty of oppressing women despite considering "misogy-

35. See Hewison, *In Anger,* 162–63, 174, 175.

ny vulgar and stupid." Sammy's brutish lust for Beatrice Ifor symbolized in his "vision" of a goat at the mental asylum may owe something to Clamence's recognition of himself as a misogynic "billy goat for lust."[36] Indeed, like Christopher Martin's nickname, "Pincher," which intimates his acquisitional brief, Sammy's surname, Mountjoy, not only signals goatish lust, but also parodies Dante's ideal Mount of Joy.[37]

Sammy Mountjoy is consumptive like Christopher Martin, yet perhaps not as grotesquely voracious. Here, Sammy resembles Quentin in Angus Wilson's later novel *No Laughing Matter* (1967) who, though outwardly professing opposition to fascism through his socialist activities in the 1930s and, indeed, criticizing the totalitarianism of the Soviet Union, rather loses his high moral ground in a voracious and aggressive approach to women. Again, in Wilson's earlier novel *Hemlock and After* (1952), Bernard Sands is ironically portrayed as experiencing a "sadistic excitement" at seeing "hopeless terror" on the face of a fellow homosexual being arrested on the charge of importuning. As Andrzej Gąsiorek notes: "Bernard's moral collapse is instigated by his recognition that the evil which gave rise to fascism exists in himself."[38] Like Wilson, Golding links communist and fascist totalitarianisms and implies that both, at bottom, attract antifemale and sadistic personalities. Furthermore, Wilson and Golding stress that such personalities are to be found in England as much as elsewhere in Europe.

Sammy's youth is marked by membership in the Communist Party and opposition to the excesses of the Blackshirts, but he is guilty of his own variety of exploitation that reaches its height with the subjection of Beatrice, among others, to his lust. In *Free Fall,* Golding further strengthens the link between an immature or adolescent masculine sexuality and fascism. It is a hard, masculine brutality that Sammy hoped could be buried under the larger atrocities of the war: "Why bother about one savaged girl when girls are blown to pieces by the thousand?" (*FF,* 131–32). In this wartime context, as with Christopher Martin, Sammy's cruel, greedy, lustful personality is evidenced in noncelebratory carnivalesque.

Throughout the novel Sammy is seen as immersed in low, dirty sexual behavior where women become meat to his greedy palate. Devourment of their "sweet, cleft flesh" (*FF,* 123) is juxtaposed with his brutal disregard and abjection of women such as Beatrice and Taffy. Like *Pincher Mar-*

36. Oldsey and Weintraub, *Art of Golding,* 105, 121, 122; Camus, *The Fall,* 48, 42, 43, 71.

37. See Friedman, *William Golding,* 74.

38. A. Wilson, *Hemlock and After,* 107; Gąsiorek, *Post-War British Fiction,* 99.

tin, Free Fall is littered with Rabelaisian, though noncelebratory, eating metaphors. Again mouths are wide open to consume people. Sammy, like Christopher, keeps his mouth and flies open. If he isn't observing the lecherous or inviting mouths of others, his own is ever receptive. Even the freedom he has lost by his uncompromising lust for Beatrice is linked to a gustatory existence—it is like "the taste of potatoes" (*FF,* 5). Nearly every human character, relationship, or behavior in the novel is at some point linked to carnivalesque consumption, be it Father Watts-Watt's desire for "forbidden fruit" (*FF,* 76), Sammy and Sheila giving "each other a little furtive pleasure like handing round a bag of toffees" (*FF,* 91), or Miss Manning's sexy, "creamy" looks (*FF,* 227). Although Sammy's own brand of consumption does not bring the stark metamorphosis Christopher Martin endures, Golding still marks Sammy as another version of *ungeziefer.* We find several references to his insectlike movements, not least when he "flurried back" (*FF,* 169) to a safe corner of his cell at the POW camp.

The "low" provenance of Sammy's totalitarian, sexual consumption of others is conditioned, Golding seems to suggest, in the scatological and sordid worlds of Rotten Row and Father Watts-Watt. In other words, Sammy is raised in environments that focus on lower body functions and transgression. Reference to Sammy's early life in Rotten Row makes much of "alleys," "passages," and "forbidden" exits (*FF,* 18)—imagery typical of Golding's playful use of phenomena to suggest anality. Indeed, as in *Pincher Martin,* the reader never escapes the anus or feces, right from "Rabelaisian" aspects of communal toileting in the slums (*FF,* 20), and Sammy's "invasion" of homosexual Father Watts-Watt's privacy as he strains on the toilet, through to Miss Pringle's disgust at Sammy's search in the Bible for God's "backparts" (*FF,* 201). Although the homosexual desires of Father Watts-Watt extend reference to a low, transgressive world of which Sammy becomes brutally a part, Golding has Sammy show sympathy for the parson: "Why should he not want to stroke and caress and kiss the enchanting, the more-than-vellum warmth and roundness of childhood?" (*FF,* 163). In an explanation of this sympathy to John Carey, Golding commented: "I would not wish to be among the people who persecute a minority—and I have deliberately given homosexuals every benefit, as it were, that I can, as one might have done, you know, to Jews or Negroes."[39] Yet Golding's vaunted sympathy is not unproblematical. His alignment of pedophilia with homosexuality is not exactly extending "every bene-

39. Carey, ed., *William Golding, the Man and His Books: A Tribute on His 75th Birthday,* 184.

fit" to homosexuals. Golding's instantiation of homosexuality often ties such "low" transgression with the targets of his satirical attacks. In *Free Fall,* as in *Lord of the Flies, Pincher Martin,* and his later fiction, savagery or moral decline is evoked in images concerning anal sex, homosexuality, and pedophilia. These transgressions are, therefore, part of the machinery of Golding's satire or critique. His sympathy for homosexuals, in other words, does not sit happily with his satirical method. Furthermore, Golding's portrayal of Father Watts-Watt's homosexual desires may add to the incipient undermining of religious authority located in *Lord of the Flies* and *Pincher Martin.*

While the Dantean, heavenly fantastic contrasts with Sammy's "stagnant pool" of low appetites (*FF,* 9), Gothic imagery reminiscent of Poe's *Pit and the Pendulum* (1843) magnifies his "soldier-male" brutality by comparing his treatment of Beatrice with the torture he endures at the hands of the Gestapo psychologist Dr. Halde while a prisoner of war. Similarities between the cruel, barbarous world of Nazism and Sammy's English schooling and subsequently misogynist lifestyle are explored not least, perhaps, in having Halde speak "perfect" English (*FF,* 138). Sammy's life is joined at the hip to the wider excesses of fascism, or as Lawrence Friedman puts it: "the gravity of his offence is inferred from the prison camp episodes that implicitly compare Sammy's moral crimes to those perpetuated on a far vaster scale by Nazi Germany."[40] His torture at the hands of Dr. Halde is partly enhanced by his own Gothic imagination that has been stocked since childhood with nightmare fears of the dark, rats, and tortures. In this repertoire of Gothic images, Sammy's fear of rats mirrors Winston's similar fears in Orwell's *1984,* a work that *Free Fall* parallels to some degree since both novels can be interpreted as attacking English totalitarianism.

Sammy's experience of Nazi torture finds a parallel with his relationship to Beatrice that often amounted to that of the executioner and his victim. Influenced by Miss Pringle who knew how to torture children "like a man with a pendulum" (*FF,* 195), Sammy subjects Beatrice to the "rack" (*FF,* 117). In effect, Beatrice's decline can be seen as the "joint work" (*FF,* 251) of Sammy and Miss Pringle. This presentation of the religious Miss Pringle as a "child torturer" counters or complicates the overall attribution of totalitarian behavior to men alone and may well add further weight to Golding's critique of religious authority. Female brutality is something that Golding extends later in his portrayal of Sophy in *Dark-*

40. Friedman, *William Golding,* 79.

ness Visible. Unfortunately, he has nothing to say about this aspect of his work. This should not surprise us, however, since by his own admission, Golding claims to have been quite "unaware" of many levels to his work until people pointed them out to him.[41] What comes across in this treatment is a sense that the creation of "totalitarian man" is dependent upon education and the complicit nurturance of women like Miss Pringle.

Golding further explores the influence of the English education establishment in the development of Sammy Mountjoy's totalitarian personality. At his school, the removal of Minnie, the moronic child who unlike Sammy and the other children failed to "keep step" with the "marching music" (*FF,* 33), powerfully undermines English moral distancing from Nazi atrocities founded on categories of the subhuman. Here, Golding juxtaposes the fascistic "stepping" of overt nationalism with the exclusion of the handicapped. Again, Minnie's removal after pissing on the school inspector's shoes suggests the kind of fate that awaited the Jews arriving at concentration camps: "we watched them pass through the gate. . . . We never saw her again" (*FF,* 35). The whole incident was, Sammy notes, "the occasion when Minnie showed us the difference between a human being and an animal" (*FF,* 54). This conferring of a subhuman status upon "defective" individuals is reminiscent of Adolf Hitler's social Darwinist outlook and his orchestration of Nazi eugenics. It is only later, when Sammy reviews his own totalitarian trajectory, that he chooses to "break step" with the mesmerizing influence of "marching music" on his youth (*FF,* 33).

Throughout *Free Fall,* Golding links Minnie's social extermination and subhuman status with Beatrice's similarly abject fate at the hands of Sammy. In a defining moment of Sammy's "fall," the mad Beatrice urinates on his shoes when he visits her at the mental asylum. Just as his bullying of younger boys at school caused one of them to wet himself in class, so too has his brutal disregard for Beatrice left her an incontinent shadow of her former self—an abjection that follows a similar trajectory to that of Minnie. As Mikhail Bakhtin notes, "drenching in urine," like the "slinging of excrement," is a "traditional debasing" gesture.[42] Here, the debasement reflects Sammy's moral lack. Links between Sammy's early social grounding, his choice of moral "free fall," and his exploitation and cruelty to others are magnified in a pervasive scatology throughout the novel, not least in the stinking cell Halde assigns him. Excretory symbolism builds to stress, among other things, the abject result of Sammy's cruel disregard of

41. Haffenden, "William Golding: An Interview," 9.
42. Bakhtin, *Rabelais and His World,* 148.

Beatrice who is tarred with the same brush as Minnie. As with Minnie, Sammy views Beatrice as subhuman: "She watched me with doggie eyes, she put the lead in my hand. . . . 'Aren't you human then? Aren't you a person at all?'" (*FF*, 121). The image of nationalistic "stepping" that evokes "goose-stepping" is also widely used in mapping his sexual exploitation of Beatrice: "Step by step we descended the path of sexual exploitation" (*FF*, 123). This sexual "torture" of Beatrice corresponds to psychoanalytical explanations of sadomasochistic traits of "fascist man" that have been identified by a number of theorists, such as Wilhelm Reich and Erich Fromm.[43] Certainly, Sammy evinces the kind of authoritarianism that Theodor Adorno, Else Frankel-Brunswick, Daniel J. Levinson, and R. Nevitt Sanford aligned with totalitarian behavior and the "soldier-male" misogyny diagnosed by Klaus Theweleit.

The link between Nazism and Sammy's categorization of the "subhuman" Minnie and treatment of Beatrice is strengthened by the section in the novel that deals with his "torture" under Dr. Halde. Where once Sammy had captured Beatrice's sexual submission in "electric light-shades of Guernica" (*FF*, 124), he now suffers in the "electric furnace conditions" of Nazi interrogation (*FF*, 144), and flees a succession of mind terrors that send him "screaming as into a furnace" (*FF*, 185). All these descriptions bring the "associative despair" and recollection of the German bombing of the Basque town of Guernica and the Holocaust crematoria. Halde's "torture" reminds Sammy of the Nazi legacy of "violated bodies" (*FF*, 176) and of their "cleverness" in shattering "all the taboos of humanity" (*FF*, 182). His predicament brings back the memory of Minnie's social extermination: "What is your name? Muriel Millicent Mollie? Mary Mabel Margaret? Minnie Marcia Moron?" (*FF*, 180). He learns that his own capacity for torture outstrips what Halde might have done: "Nothing that Halde could do seemed half so terrible as what I knew myself" (*FF*, 190). Golding suggests that there is a connection here between Nazi extermination of the handicapped or "undesirables" alongside the Jews and the fates of Minnie and Beatrice.

The results of Sammy's exploitation of Beatrice are not so far removed from his "black pictures" of "Belsen" (*FF*, 77). His cruel disregard brings her to a Belsenesque end: incarceration in a mental hospital that resembles a "prison camp" (*FF*, 238). Here the circle between Nazi atrocity and Sammy's hard, masculine "totalitarian personality" is neatly closed. He admits to having "moved forward to the world of lads" (*FF*, 232). Sam-

43. Hesse, "Fascism and Male Adolescence," 170.

my's brutality toward his wife might appear swamped by the wider atrocities of war, but we are made to see that his crimes are related to Nazism's "brilliant crimes" (*FF*, 232), or, as Friedman puts it, Sammy's "crimes" are "writ large in Nazi atrocities."[44] That a British subject, and indeed an English communist apparently at odds with all that the Blackshirts stood for, stands guilty of fascistic living is significant. Golding, the "non-Marxist socialist" as he has called himself, remains critical of totalitarian behavior *tout court*, and seeks to expose the English totalitarian personality, whether on the right or left of politics. Through an examination of his behavior, Sammy learns that he had acted like a Blackshirt and that the "'male totem'" is "'jackbooted'" (*FF*, 250). Here, Golding brings Sammy to an awareness of the link between adolescent masculine sexuality, the "world of lads," and the brutal, militaristic, and authoritarian nature of totalitarianisms. It is an aggressive, misogynist sexuality that Sammy shares with Christopher Martin.

In *Free Fall*, then, Golding overlaps "fascism" and "communism" through the common notion of "totalitarianism." This kind of overlap, as Alice Yaeger Kaplan notes, has always presented considerable difficulty in terms of workable definitions that separate left and right extremists. Paul Wilkinson blends both kinds of extremists in his definition that they are "anti-liberal / democratic; they are in favour of violence not only as reluctant final resort, but as an integral part of their struggles; they are strongly authoritarian in leadership and elitist in decision-making."[45] In one sense, Golding seems to want to universalize the "totalitarian" spirit: "It seemed to me that man's capacity for greed, his innate cruelty and selfishness was being hidden behind a kind of pair of political pants" (*HG*, 87). In doing this, Golding might be accused of evading the specificity of Nazi atrocities by conflating them with atrocities perpetrated elsewhere, a tactic employed by the revisionist historian Ernst Nolte.[46] However, unlike Nolte, Golding is not attempting to clean up the image of Germany's past, by pointing the finger, for example, at atrocities perpetrated by Soviet communism. Nor is his instantiation of the totalitarian personality *simply* a foil to the universalism of human evil—that deeper pessimism about "human nature" that is featured strongly in *Lord of the Flies* and *The Inheritors*. There is a connection in Golding's work between the "perennial" and the "political"—even though Golding appears to privilege "di-

44. Friedman, *William Golding*, 80.
45. Kaplan, *Reproductions of Banality*, 14; Wilkinson, *The New Fascists*, 194.
46. See Dominick LaCapra, "Representing the Holocaust: Reflections on the Historian's Debate," 108–27.

agnosis" of the human condition sub specie aeternitatis over and above engagement with and reference to contemporary social, political, and historical phenomena. However, in spite of Golding's proclamations about the "eternal" focus of his fiction, *Free Fall* radically undermines any view of English immunity from twentieth-century totalitarianisms. This is an altogether more political and satirical aspect of his instantiation of the "totalitarian personality." Yet to deploy the fantastic here, one could argue that Golding hesitates between explanations of human behavior that are quasi-religious and political, that is, he juxtaposes the concepts of original sin, and the Fall, for example, with a debate about fascism and communism in English life. Perhaps this suggests Golding is torn between radical and conservative positions—that is, if you like, between Orwellian and Eliotian art. In a sense, then, he may be thought of as pulling his satirical punches by attempting to universalize the "totalitarian personality," yet frustrating any universalization through specific historical reference and political engagement.

To conclude, the beginnings of Golding's concern with the status of literature in *Free Fall,* as in *Pincher Martin,* are revealed in metafictional elements and are enhanced by fantastic and carnivalesque modes. Although less pronounced in *Free Fall,* this creation of a strong mood of indeterminacy and relativity reflects Golding's "coming to terms" with a loss of confidence about the meaning of anything after the inhumanity of World War II. Golding's early concerns with the status of fiction and indeterminacy in general are not unrelated to the Holocaust, which had exploded postwar confidence in stable or totalized meaning. This loss of the center of human meaning following such stark inhumanity converged with the complex phenomenon of postmodernism that gathered momentum during the 1960s and 1970s, that is, late capitalism, new consumerism, diverse and popular media, and burgeoning deconstructionist philosophies—all of which placed further strain on traditional aesthetic, philosophical, social, and political explanatory systems. It is this historical, postindustrial phenomenon that Golding reflects upon in his later fiction, along with a strengthening of his attack on the English class system.

In common with *Lord of the Flies* and *The Inheritors, Pincher Martin* and *Free Fall* shatter the differentiation of "civilized" people, but particularly the English, from totalitarianisms, be they fascist or communist. This shattering is effected by a noncelebratory use of satire. Golding locates totalitarian, violent, adolescent masculinity in English subjects in *Lord of the Flies, Pincher Martin,* and *Free Fall* and "civilized" Western humanity and, more obliquely, English "civilization" in *The Inheritors.* English moral superiority to the Nazis is attacked by fantastic and carnivalesque modes that deliver the shocking revelation that the English have a similar potential for fascist and, indeed, communist totalitarianism. Idealistic English and "civilized" behavior is turned on its head. Golding's desire for greater "immediate relevance" is tellingly revealed by the shift his writing takes from fable toward history. He strives to remove the drag that fable added to his attack on postwar English moral complacency in his earlier fiction. The general and universal nature of fable somewhat defused his satire. English totalitarian man is progressively targeted in *Pincher Martin* and *Free Fall.* The more oblique attack in *Pincher Martin* is driven home in the more detailed and specific account of left-right totalitarianism on English soil in *Free Fall.* Ultimately, both *Pincher Martin* and *Free Fall* should be treated as "post-Auschwitz" novels and their protagonists as examples of what Robert Brasillach refers to as *homo fasciens.*[47]

47. See Kaplan, *Reproductions of Banality,* 10.

5

Constructions of Fiction and Class

The Spire and *The Pyramid*

> We watched some young men climb the south-east edge of the Great Pyramid. When they reached the top they were fifty feet higher than the spire of Salisbury cathedral. When I blinked down at my feet, looking away from the too bright sky, the tiny black ants working there seemed as big as the men and as capable of building one of these objects.
>
> —William Golding, *A Moving Target*

> I think that the pyramidal structure of English society is present, and my awareness of it is indelibly imprinted in me, in my psyche, not merely in my intellect but very much in my emotional, almost physical being. I am enraged by it and I am unable to escape it entirely . . . it's fossilised in me.
>
> —William Golding, quoted in "Golding Goes Down the Sea Again," by W. L. Webb

THE HIGHLY PLASTIC OR VERSATILE FANTASTIC AND CARNIVALESQUE modes are deployed variously in *The Spire* (1964) and more narrowly in *The Pyramid* (1967). In *The Spire,* fantastic and carnivalesque modes function in four ways. First, the fantastic and carnivalesque interrogate human cruelty and sinfulness in general. This function is related to the overall universal aspect of satire's undermining of all human endeavors. While Jocelin considers his construction to be miraculous, natural explanations gradually strip away, indeed almost obliterate, the supernaturalism surrounding the project, and what is exposed or revealed is a stinking pit of human transgression and sinfulness that he has encouraged and partly orchestrated. Second, they are used nonsatirically to amplify uncertainty surrounding the whole issue of the "constructed" nature of fiction. In other words, they combine to intensify or act as an analogue to the uncertain status of fictional representation explored through the novel's metafiction. They magnify the tension between notions of construction and deconstruction, between fiction as both capable and, at the same time, incapable of communicating meaning. In this way, *The Spire* follows the experimental, self-conscious trajectory of *Pincher Martin* and *Free Fall* that is at the heart of Golding's later postmodernist fiction, *Darkness Visible, The Paper Men,* and *To the Ends of the Earth.* Third, the modes attack monological religious dogmatism and authoritarianism—more specifically the medieval Catholic Church. Here, Golding enacts a pseudo-Rabelaisian critique, using images that "have a certain undestroyable nonofficial nature" and that are "opposed to all that is finished, to all pomposity, to every ready-made solution in the sphere of thought and world outlook."[1] As part of this, the modes undermine the religious monomania of Jocelin who, believing he has been specially chosen by God, strives to build the largest cathedral spire in medieval England. Finally, carnivalesque squalor further undermines the influence of class in the building of the spire.

Although *The Spire,* like *Lord of the Flies* before it, snaps at the heels of class privilege, its attack is lightweight or marginal compared to *The Pyramid.* In *The Pyramid,* Golding draws on his wider interests in Egyptology to reflect the "constructed" social hierarchy of the English village of Stilbourne in terms of a pyramid—a structure that he sets out to attack or undermine by deploying fantastic and carnivalesque modes. A much weakened fantastic Gothic is deployed to suggest the deathly, corpselike state of the stillborn community, strangled by class hierarchy and prejudice, while the carnivalesque plays a core role in attacking the notion of class superiority and exposing the cruelty at the heart of social stratification. When *The Pyramid* was published in 1967, the English class system appeared to be under threat. Although the leftist utopian dream of a "classless" English society was no nearer to becoming reality than it is today, the falloff in manual work and the growth of the middle class after 1964, A. H. Halsey argues, turned the social "pyramid" into an "electric light bulb."[2] *The Pyramid* marks a turn again toward the contemporary, but, as I will suggest, this "turn" is not nearly so committed as it might first appear.

1. Bakhtin, *Rabelais and His World,* 3.
2. Halsey, *Change in British Society: From 1900 to the Present Day,* 56.

The Spire

The central action of *The Spire* is the construction of what appears to be an impossible structure—a four hundred–foot spire. On the basis of a vision, Jocelin, dean of the Cathedral Church of Our Lady, drives Roger Mason, the master builder, and his "army" of workers to complete the project despite the marshy foundations that threaten it. The foundations—or rather apparent lack of them—are revealed in the pit Mason digs at the crossways of the cathedral. This stinking pit is forever kept in mind as the spire is erected and serves to reinforce the seeming irrationality and impossibility of the spire's construction and its human costs. Blinkered by an addiction to the supernatural, Jocelin drives his spire higher and higher against a tide of physical limitations. Workmen are killed, while Roger Mason is driven to complete the building by sheer economics and his sexual desire for Goody Pangall. Goody's limping and impotent husband is sacrificed in a pagan ritual and buried beneath the crossways as the whole normal fabric of cathedral life is overturned so as to afford the spire's construction. As Jocelin approaches death, his belief in being chosen by God is shaken when he learns that he only rose to the post of dean by preference, just like the boy canon, Ivo, whose father donated timber to the cathedral. Jocelin is told by his aunt Alison, a former mistress of the king, that she had used her influence to gain his appointment. This realization is part of Jocelin's gradual movement from "complete blindness to illumination," a process that is familiar in Golding's early fiction and attributable to his study of Greek tragedy.[3] The fallen Jocelin seeks forgiveness for having "'lain'" like a "'blight'" (*SP,* 202) on the cathedral community and presenting a "'bogus sanctity'" (*SP,* 209), but his attempt to be reconciled with Roger only stirs the unfortunate builder to loathe himself further and attempt to kill himself. Jocelin's own life comes to its end with an uncomfortable, ineffable, apocalyptic, and indeed puzzling vision of a sapphire kingfisher and an apple tree in bloom that, as Howard Babb notes, offers only "riddle." It is a suitable ending to a novel that V. V. Subbarao argues "lends itself to multiple interpretations" or, according to L. L. Dickson, has a "multiplicity of meaning."[4]

The Spire, Golding suggests, makes up for Anthony Trollope's inatten-

3. See Hodson, *William Golding,* 89; Baker, *William Golding,* 72–75; Dick, *William Golding* (1967), 78; Subbarao, *William Golding,* 82; and Boyd, *Novels of Golding,* 86–96.

4. Babb, *Novels of Golding,* 162; Subbarao, *William Golding,* 82; Dickson, *Modern Allegories,* 89.

tion to the physical presence and meaning of Salisbury cathedral in his "Barsetshire" novels. The daring construction of its spire provided Golding, who "taught under it for about twenty years," with an ideal subject matter for his equivocal art: one that balances a variety of oppositions, not least the supernatural and natural, the "high" and the "low," text and world, and faith and reason.[5] Beyond Golding's amendment to a Trollopean lack and the historical source for his novel, a number of literary influences have been suggested by critics, not least Ibsen's *Master Builder* (1892), but as Kevin McCarron rightly argues, *The Spire* is "the first of his books to use no literary analogue." At least not in any obvious way. Even Bernard Oldsey and Stanley Weintraub, who claim that *The Spire* may owe something to Ibsen's theme of the dangers of idealism, are suitably skeptical in finding it "less literarily reactive than Golding's earlier novels."[6]

As elsewhere, Golding uses a historically crucial period "which allow[s] him to depict a destructive collision."[7] Here, it is between "low" medieval paganism and "high" Christianity and marks a distancing from his earlier concerns with contemporary conflict. Thus, although *The Spire* is a self-conscious novel like *Pincher Martin* and *Free Fall*, it achieves a fuller preservation of "art as its own end" because it does not engage with or concern an intensification or magnification of "epistemological ruins" in the aftermath of World War II. Experimentalism, in other words, wins out to engagement. In an interview with John Haffenden, Golding admitted to oscillating between writing about twentieth-century life and writing about other more distant historical periods. Interestingly, he puts the latter strategy down to cowardice: "When I'm feeling cowardly I rush off and write a novel which has provenance in some age with which I'm more familiar."[8] Following on from the more "engaged" novels, *Pincher Martin* and *Free Fall*, *The Spire* is a more internalized fiction that marks a retreat from contemporary issues. This "retirement" from the contemporary may well have something to do with the continuing mood of cold war politics in Britain. Certainly, Golding was caught up in a cold war swing to the right in the arts. It is something that Doris Lessing's semi-autobiographical protagonist, Martha Quest, refers to in *The Four-Gated City* (1969), a novel that Golding drew heavily upon in writing *Darkness Visible:*

5. See Biles, *Talk*, 99. See also Golding, *A Moving Target*, 9–19.
6. McCarron, *William Golding*, 22; Oldsey and Weintraub, *Art of Golding*, 140.
7. McCarron, *William Golding*, 24.
8. Haffenden, "William Golding: An Interview," 12.

> The "cold war" was spreading, had already spread, from politics, to the arts. Any attitude remotely associated with "communism" was suspect, indeed, dangerous. Few intellectuals had not been associated with the left, in some form of it, during the 'thirties and the 'forties. Precisely these intellectuals were now running, in one way and another, the arts. Tom, Dick and Harry, they were now peddling, for all they were worth, a point of view summed up by the slogan: The Ivory Tower. This was admirable, subtle, adult, good, and above all, artistic. Its opposite was crude, childish, bad, inartistic.[9]

The Spire marks a pronounced shift in focus from Golding being "punch drunk" on atrocity in his critique of English constructions of national identity in opposition to Nazism in *Lord of the Flies* and *The Inheritors* and his powerful instantiation of English totalitarian man in *Pincher Martin* and *Free Fall*—ground he appears to retrace in *Darkness Visible.* The novel's setting in the distant past and away from contemporary history marks his preference for the "conservative" universalism that muffled his critique in *The Inheritors.* What follows his grief about inhumanity at this point in history is a growing concern with the status of meaning in literature. For Golding, the aftershock of recent atrocity appears to have led him to an increased sensitivity to the loss or nontotalization of meaning and disablement of fictional integrity. It is possible that the building of the "spire" may represent in some metaphorical or mythical way the wider social reconstruction—physical and epistemological—that followed in postwar England. S. J. Boyd, rather ingeniously, contextualizes Jocelin's growth away from "childish certainty" in terms of "the era of the Second Vatican Council, which went some way towards an *aggiornamento* in the Catholic Church, a bringing into line with the modern world of somewhat ossified or petrified doctrine."[10] As such, Boyd finds these concerns in *The Spire* repeated, albeit more playfully, in David Lodge's novel *How Far Can You Go?* (1980). But such thoughts about *The Spire* can be only speculative on account of Golding's apparent determination to steer clear of the contemporary.

Despite critical awareness of the growing self-consciousness of Golding's fiction, there has been no study of how the fantastic and carnivalesque intensify the uncertain status of his fictional representations in *The Spire.* The combined fantastic and carnivalesque modes are deployed in a nonsatirical or nonconfrontational way to complement metafictional un-

9. Lessing, *The Four-Gated City,* 148.
10. Boyd, *Novels of Golding,* 104–5. The Italian *aggiornamento* means "readjustment."

certainty. Like *Pincher Martin* and *Free Fall, The Spire* "probes" the relationship between text and world, and its self-consciousness remains part of the reemergent experimentalism of the early twentieth century that followed what Robert Alter considers an "eclipse" of this tradition in the eighteenth century. It is not the kind of self-consciousness at full tilt that we find in the "arid," "indiscriminatively inventive," and labyrinthine fictions of postmodernism. Despite the threat of collapse, the spire is completed and suggests at this stage of Golding's writing that the pattern maker can overcome pluralism and in the modernist tradition create "form and substance where perhaps there would be nothing."[11]

The Spire is overtly an artistic construction driven to rise into position despite the impossibility of arriving at any totalized meaning. In a paradox, it rises as it falls; it communicates as it fails to communicate. As noted by previous critics, it draws attention to its fabricated, constructed status and its inability to yield certainties.[12] What is left certain is the uncertainty of artistic communication. According to Virginia Tiger, *The Spire* deals in paradox: "[T]he world it invokes is pluralistic, intermingling, complex, yet it places a wilful and unrelenting patternmaker as its central intelligence." As such, the whole building of the spire is paralleled with storytelling and with the completion of a pattern. For Jocelin, the various events and stages in the spire's erection are so many "disjunct sentences" of a "story, which though they left great gaps, still told enough" (*SP,* 156). The construction of Jocelin's spire, and coterminously the novel *The Spire,* is humorously linked with penile erection. Golding admitted to Jack Biles that he had mischievously suggested to his publishers that they call the book *An Erection at Barchester.* The spire is a huge "architectural metaphor," not least for Jocelin's repressed sexual feeling for the red-haired Goody Pangall, but also for fictional creativity, according to James Gindin.[13] Ever threatened by collapse, the spire emphasizes sexual, religious, and creative impotency. However, the meaning of Jocelin's "spire," like the novel itself, remains radically unclear. The novel ends with Jocelin's difficult, jumbled, deathbed words and Father Adam's attempts to interpret them:

> He looked up experimentally to see if at this late hour the witchcraft had left him; and there was a tangle of hair, blazing among the stars;

11. Alter, *Partial Magic,* 142, 153.

12. See Crompton, *View from the Spire,* 1–2; Josipovici, *World and Book,* 251, 255; Kinkead-Weekes and I. Gregor, *Critical Study,* 206, 240–41; and McCarron, *William Golding,* 23–24.

13. Tiger, *Dark Fields,* 167; Biles, *Talk,* 100; Gindin, *William Golding,* 49.

> and the great club of his spire lifted towards it. That's all, he thought, that's the explanation if I had time: and he made a word for Father Adam.
> "Berenice."
> The Smile became puzzled and anxious. Then it cleared.
> "Saint?" (*SP,* 221)

The opaque nature of Jocelin's allusion to Berenice yields interpretative difficulty for Father Adam and, indeed, the reader. It requires a certain amount of detective work in classical mythology to establish that Jocelin compares the red-haired Goody Pangall to the wife of Ptolemy Euergetes "whose hair, vowed by her to Venus, was said to have been stolen from the temple of the goddess, and afterwards taken to heaven and placed in a constellation."[14] In this sense, the spire can be viewed as the product of sublimation. Opacity continues to bedevil attempts at interpretation. As Jocelin's building liquefies into a glittering topsy-turvy "upward waterfall" (*SP,* 223) during his deathbed delirium, so too does the novel. The reader is led by the nose to share Jocelin's own doubts: "'Now—I know nothing at all'" (*SP,* 223). The end of the novel dramatizes the limitations of interpretation in presenting nonresolvable poetic imagery. Golding leaves us with Jocelin's fading, flimsy consciousness that attempts to redescribe the spire: "In the tide, flying like a bluebird, struggling, shouting, screaming to leave behind words of magic and incomprehension—*It's like the appletree!*" (*SP,* 223). James Gindin tries to break through the incomprehensibility of this simile: "He has always venerated the apple tree, the natural tree, aspiring in linear space and multiform simultaneously. The image of the tree keeps Jocelin suspended even in death. The spire is transformed into a symbol of natural man, and the apple tree suggests both the faith in aspiration and the inevitable fall from paradise." Yet, ultimately, even Gindin's plausible interpretation remains just that, an interpretation. As Stephen Medcalf sees it, the "apple tree" and "kingfisher" images are Golding's "final raid on poetry." Perhaps the halcyon or kingfisher hints at the afterlife as in Ovid's tale of Ceyx and Alcyone where the grieving Alcyone and Ceyx, her drowned husband, are reunited by being metamorphosed into seabirds.[15] But we cannot really unravel these images.

This pronounced hermeneutical difficulty is further established in the presentation of Father Adam's attempts to decode Jocelin's final mum-

14. *Compact Oxford English Dictionary,* s.v. "Ptolemy Euergetes."

15. Gindin, *William Golding,* 54; Medcalf, *William Golding,* 36; see Ovid, *Metamorphoses,* 262–71.

bling: "Father Adam, leaning down, could hear nothing. But he saw a tremor of the lips that might be interpreted as a cry of: *God! God! God!* So of the charity to which he had access, he laid the Host on the dead man's tongue" (*SP,* 223). Here Golding leaves the door open for a supernatural after-death vision of God, but it is stripped of comfort. The reader is left with rather ambivalent, incomprehensible, and unsatisfactory "visions." Golding seems to suggest that in literary art, the reality of production, as with the spire, is nothing like the vision: "'It's an ungainly, crumbling thing. Nothing like. Nothing like at all'" (*SP,* 193). The novel is completed but leans precariously toward utter collapse and loss of meaning. It struggles under the weight of metaphor and on the shifting ground of language. The "kingfisher" and "apple tree" emphasize human dependence on metaphors, and such communication is less than what we desire, but that it is all that we have. The leaning spire, like Jocelin's leaning spine, reveals the determination of art against the odds.

The self-conscious uncertainty of *The Spire* is magnified through the deployment of the fantastic. At the heart of the fantastic is the fact that the building of the spire seems to rise against the laws of physics. It is held up on "floating" pillars, and at every turn Jocelin, attended by an angel at his back, appears to tap into a spiritual will that defies gravity and natural explanation. From its inception as a diagram of prayer in the visionary experiences of Jocelin to its production as if by faith alone, the spire rises despite natural constraints. The reader's judgment of whether the construction of the spire is ultimately supernatural or natural is suspended. Throughout the novel Jocelin refers to his personal "constructive" angel who aids his work. Yet with a critical prescience, Golding eventually reveals this angel as "deconstructive," a cancer that deforms Jocelin's spine and brings chaos and death. This naturalization of the angel as cancer erodes the wider fantastic hesitation in a way that works metaphorically to suggest the threat that hangs not simply over the spire as a building, but over the novel itself and language in general.

From the start, Jocelin claims the cathedral is a miracle, built as it is without foundations and floating on a "'raft of brushwood'" (*SP,* 38). Yet for Roger, the possibility that the cathedral floats on a raft is not miraculous, but a warning that to build further on such poor foundations would be foolhardy. Throughout the construction of the spire, Jocelin's fantastic interpretation is juxtaposed with Roger's natural one. This conflict enhances and maintains hesitation between explanations. However hard the pragmatic pagan, Roger, argues for a rational, natural interpretation of events, he is unable to overcome Jocelin's belief in the miraculous. Jocelin mocks Roger, telling him that it would be easier to believe a miracle than that the church floated on a raft. Roger Mason doubts that the pillars can support anything more than the roof and insists that to build the spire upon them would be nothing short of madness. But the spire is Jocelin's Folly, a "holy fool" production that flies in the face of natural phenomena. Jocelin, buoyed by his faith, sets out to build what he calls "'Four hundred foot of dare!'" (*SP*, 44).[16] Quite simply, Roger watches for the pillars to sink, while Jocelin expects them to float.

Across the whole novel, the boundaries between real and unreal constantly mingle and blur as the progress of the spire's construction appears to contradict the laws of nature but, like Jocelin's spine, is subject to those laws. Uncertainty and mystery increase with strange reflections and the intrusion of "diabolical" and "angelic" forces or entities. Throughout the novel, Gothic images, the grotesque and madness, particularly in terms of Jocelin's visions, strengthen the overall fantastic mood of uncertainty. In the dark, shadowy world of the medieval cathedral, devils, ghosts, witchcraft, and nightmares frequently bubble up to the surface. The site of holiness is also a site of a struggle with the profane. Golding welds the two in an interrogation of the worldly nature of medieval Christianity that is not divorced from the "low" and popular. The pit at the cathedral crossways acts as a kind of symbolic portal to a murderous, torturous, subterranean world and, indeed, cellarage of the unconscious mind, particularly Jocelin's. The fantastic in *The Spire* can be defined as "total," that is, hesitation between natural and supernatural explanations is maintained across the text and the novel ends with irresolution between them. Of course, the "pure fantastic" at the end of the novel only just survives the barrage of natural explanations that erodes the sense of Jocelin's project having supernatural backing.

The carnivalesque functions in tandem with the fantastic to advance the mood of uncertainty as a complement to the novel's questioning of the status of representation. Everything is made topsy-turvy and relativized, not least in the oxymoronic vision of the spire's construction as a "final beginning" (*SP*, 13) or as an "upward waterfall" (*SP*, 233). Jocelin's project literally turns cathedral life upside down. The cathedral becomes a "pagan temple," complete with workers like "priests of some outlandish rite" (*SP*, 10). The "high" spire is contrasted with the "low" fires of Midsum-

16. Redpath indicates the spire "becomes a four-hundred foot pronoun, and with its completion Jocelin is also completed as an individual character" (*Structural Reading*, 131).

mer Night worship of the Devil and the dirty language, songs, and behavior of the workmen. "High" and "low," "up" and "down," are relativized, and the irony of the "holy" construction of the spire taking place against a background of filth and depravity is strongly maintained. As the spire rises, it sinks into the pit. Rachel suggests to her husband, Roger, that for the spire to stand, the depth of its foundations must equal its height. Jocelin's achievement must then need to be his folly. This carnival folly is revealed at several points, not least in the reference to the spire as a "dunce's cap" (*SP*, 159).

The turning upside down of cathedral life and spatial relativization deepens an uncertainty that complements the questioning mood promoted by self-conscious aspects of the novel. Also, the fantastic and carnivalesque undermine Jocelin's authoritarian faith that may afford parallels between the rigidities of medieval Catholicism attacked by Rabelais and pre–Vatican II Catholicism, the notion of humankind's transcendence from its material, evil, and sinful base, and the English class system.

The "miraculous" rise of the spire gives the visionary Jocelin the height from which to fall to earth. His religiously driven quest is undermined by the growing sense that the "miracles" surrounding the spire's erection, and the supernatural, angelic influence, can be explained naturally. Although a totally natural explanation of the fantastical spire is not secured by the end of the novel, this possibility and the savage low materiality that thrives during the building work critique Jocelin's monomaniacal faith. His spiritual achievement is undermined by his encouragement and connivance at lower body transgressions and carnivalesque violence, the topsy-turvy profanation of the religious or sacred "high" being most powerfully evoked in the phallicism of the spire that undermines Jocelin's desire for spiritual transcendence. In more general terms, the seething pit of human transgression that accompanies the building of the spire reinforces man's sinful, temporal nature and suggests that religion, Catholicism in particular, cannot rise above this and, hypocritically perhaps, uses it to its advantage. The carnivalesque, "savage low materiality" evokes Jocelin's efforts, and indeed religion's, as rotten to the core. Golding himself steered clear of affiliation with any particular religion while maintaining a Deistic view of creation. In his interview with Jack Biles, he recounts that despite the rationalist influence of his father that ensured, in religious terms, he "belonged to nothing," he still developed an ostensibly, if eclectic, Christian morality.[17] Certainly, Golding's critique of religious author-

17. Biles, *Talk*, 83–87.

ity both here and elsewhere in his fiction suggests that he had quite a strong aversion to the exclusionary nature and potential harm of religious dogma.

In *The Spire,* religious morality is set against the earthy, filthy, material, and natural limitations of the world of hard-bodied pagan workers; the high and low are welded together, just as order is welded to chaos, and pattern or design to collapse and deconstruction. The creative, penile spire is closely bound to that which is at its root, the abject anus. This proximity between transcendence and materiality is maintained throughout the novel. The carnivalesque life of the workers constantly threatens to erode Jocelin's vision. Their violent and mocking behavior, however, is tolerated by Jocelin as a means to an end.

The lower body drags Jocelin down from any spiritual height and reinforces sinful materiality. The model of the cathedral with its "springing, projecting, bursting, erupting" (*SP,* 8) phallic spire is featured widely in this process. It is used dramatically and not unlike a sex aid to suggest Jocelin's repressed desire for Goody: "He detached the spire with difficulty, because the wood was swollen, and held the thing devoutly, like a relic. He caressed it gently" (*SP,* 55). He even has a wet dream in which he lies down like the cruciform structure of the cathedral with Goody astride him: "Only Satan himself, rising out of the west, clad in nothing but blazing hair [Goody] stood over his nave and worked at the building, tormenting him so that he writhed on the marsh in the warm water, and cried out aloud. He woke in the darkness, full of loathing" (*SP,* 65).

Sexual transgression at every point contradicts the "high" spiritual atmosphere of the cathedral, from the possibly incestuous relationship of Roger and Rachel Mason who "were more like brother and sister than man and wife" (*SP,* 75) to Roger's cuckolding of Pangall with the connivance of Jocelin who thought the illicit affair might keep Roger at his work, and the suggestions that the workmen were performing "outrageous combinations of the sexes" (*SP,* 45). Carnivalesque and violent sexual transgression invades cathedral life through the crowd of pagan workers who bring the "noises of the market place" (*SP,* 9), "tavern talk" (*SP,* 26), and "jeer" (*SP,* 19) and ritually mock the weak and marginalized. Here, the impotent, cuckolded Pangall becomes a typical target for the carnival mob that has already murdered one man at the cathedral gate. In his portrayal of the mocked cuckold, Pangall, Golding extends his earlier interest in the victimization of the "weak" Piggy in *Lord of the Flies* and the similarly cuckolded Alfred in *Pincher Martin.* The pagan workers make a "game" of Pangall (*SP,* 16), lewdly referring to his wife, mimicking his limp, before becoming violent toward him. Violence toward the excluded and marginal, an aspect of noncelebratory, racialist, or exclusivist practices at the heart of carnival, threatens to erupt out of horseplay that, as Roger tells Jocelin, is a pagan way of "'keeping off bad luck'" (*SP*, 42). Jocelin's growing awareness of low materiality—that "renewing life of the world" as "a filthy thing, a rising tide of muck"—is rubber-stamped when he provides the workmen with the "alehouse joke" of him "hurrying out of a hole with his folly held in both hands" (*SP*, 58). As with Pangall, they jeer and laugh at him. The "filthy" carnivalesque of frank sexuality extends to Rachel's vulgar explanation to Jocelin of her laughter as a coitus interruptus in her sex life with Roger. Jocelin's thoughts about this seem to allude to the comical incident in Hardy's *Jude the Obscure* (1896) when Arabella throws a pig's pizzle at Jude:

> She stripped the business of living down to where horror and farce took over; particoloured Zany in red and yellow, striking out in the torture chamber with his pig's bladder on a stick.
>
> He spoke viciously to the model in his hands.
>
> "The impervious insolence of the woman!"
>
> Then Zany struck him in the groin with the pig's bladder so that he jerked out a laugh that ended in a shudder.
>
> He cried out loud.
>
> "Filth! Filth!" (*SP*, 59–60)

Yet the comical, celebratory aspect of carnival is a feint to the undertow of violence. The austerity of Lent is contrasted with the carnivalesque life of the workers who are described by the visiting commissioner as "'"Murderers, cutthroats, rowdies, brawlers, rapers, notorious fornicators, sodomites, atheists, or worse"'" (*SP*, 167). They begin by aping Pangall and casting an effigy of Jocelin's head into the pit, but end by subjecting Pangall to a mock, if not actual, rape before killing him in a ritual sacrifice and burying him under the pavement with a sliver of mistletoe in his heart. We have to rely here on Jocelin's patchy evidence for what occurs amid a "gust of laughter" and noise that "defiled the holy air" (*SP*, 89). This feature of "noise" is central to the "rough music" and clatter of shivaree, as Peter Stallybrass asserts: "The charivari (in England usually called the rough ride, rough music, or skimmington) was a noisy procession in which the victim, or an effigy of the victim, was paraded through the streets and ridiculed by the community."[18] Jocelin sees the mob conduct-

18. Stallybrass, "'Drunk with the Cup,'" 50. See also André Burguière, "The Charivari and Religious Repression in France during the Ancien Regime," 84–110.

ing their shivaree, "having" Pangall "at the broom's end": "In an apocalyptic glimpse of seeing, he caught how a man danced forward to Pangall, the model of the spire projecting obscenely from between his legs—then the swirl and noise and the animal bodies hurled Jocelin against stone, so that he could not see, but only heard how Pangall broke—He heard the long wolfhowl of the man's flight down the south aisle, heard the rising, the hunting noise of the pack that raced after him" (*SP*, 90). Nearby stands Goody, her disheveled appearance and torn clothes suggesting that she has been raped. But Pangall and his wife are not the only carnival victims. Later, Jocelin himself is beaten up by a crowd that had gathered outside the alehouse when they heard he was there visiting Roger. He is subjected to a "sea of imprecation and hate" and left for dead in "the filth of the gutter" (*SP*, 215). The mocking and violence shown toward Pangall and Jocelin revisit Golding's earlier concern with the vicious treatment of those whom the crowd, mob, or extreme political group consider outsiders. In *The Spire*, however, Golding instantiates this long history of carnivalesque crowd violence without reference to contemporary manifestations as in *Lord of the Flies* or *The Inheritors*.

Jocelin's "high" spirituality is undermined by the violent, transgressive, and "low" behavior of the pagan workers and their treatment of cuckolded Pangall in particular. It is this kind of behavior that Jocelin has invited, connived, and encouraged in order to ensure that the spire gets built. His own sexual desires for Goody weld him to the "low" life of the pagans. He had arranged the marriage of Goody to the impotent Pangall to keep her in his lustful sight. Because of this, Goody was driven to find sexual fulfillment with Roger, which sparked a chain of violence in the mocking and murder of the cuckolded Pangall and Goody's miscarriage and death at the hands of Rachel, Roger's jealous wife. All this sits uncomfortably with the aims and aspirations of cathedral life.

Carnivalesque scatology amplifies the depths to which Jocelin has fallen and which, the novel suggests, is an unacknowledged underside or "low" aspect of Catholicism. From the height of the spire, in an example of Menippean catascopia, Jocelin surveys the low, stinking masses with their alehouses and brothels—rather as Lok and Fa observed the New People from a treetop in *The Inheritors*. The foul, anal pit at the root of the penile spire is suggested time and time again. Virtually everything in the cathedral is brown and, after rain, reeks like a urinal. A stench of rotting corpses emanates from the pit, and the "noisome" (*SP*, 55) building sweats like a giant insanitary armpit: "Presently ropes began to hang down from the broken vault over the crossways, and stayed there, swinging, as if the building sweating now and damp inside as well as out, had begun to grow some sort of gigantic moss" (*SP,* 53). The spreading muck brought about by Jocelin's spire decrowns even the heraldic splendor of statues of crusaders who now "wore filthy chainmail, or dung-coloured plate armour" (*SP,* 72).

Golding does not miss the opportunity of presenting the English class system as sharing responsibility for the immoral dung heap that the building project both inspires and unveils. The erection of the spire has depended on the influence of Jocelin's disreputable, adulterous aunt whose social power buys her a prestigious burial site next to the high altar. The influence of class upon Jocelin's enterprise, therefore, is decidedly unwholesome. The poor, stinking foundations of the spire and general "cloacal stench" add their critique to what class privilege has produced.[19] While the carnivalesque sexual transgression and scatology undermine the "high" aims of Jocelin, the Catholic Church, and, indeed, the privileged classes, Golding also deploys a favorite carnivalesque motif to critique greedy, lustful, consumptive behavior: the "open mouth" or "gaping jaws."[20]

As Richard S. Cammarota notes, "the image of the mouth, suggesting acquisition and consumption, has a lively history in the novel."[21] The image of the mouth is important in *The Spire* because its suggestion of "acquisition and consumption" attacks the hypocritical "sanctity" of Jocelin. This deployment of the carnivalesque mouth is very much in keeping with Golding's earlier fiction. Jocelin's open, consuming mouth extends in a dehistoricized, universalizing way, the kind of greed at any cost that Golding considered a central aspect of totalitarian behavior. Jocelin's spiritual appetite consumes those around him. Across the novel, his open mouth is frequently described, not least in the gargoyle replicas of him that he sees as symbolizing his praise of God, but we see as registering his consumptive nature. Rather like "Pincher" Martin who is devoured by the "black lightning," Jocelin receives his own comeuppance for leading a selfish, grasping life by being consumed by cancer. His gargoylish, predatory eagle's beak, with mouth "open wide" (*SP,* 23), suggests his contradictory concupiscence as much as anything. The spire symbolizes a repressed sexual desire to consume Goody. It is an erection regardless of human cost. Rather fittingly, the "illumined" Jocelin, aware of the human costs of his appetite, requests to be sculpted for his tomb with "head fallen back, mouth open" (*SP,* 219).

19. Oldsey and Weintraub, *Art of Golding,* 167.
20. Bakhtin, *Rabelais and His World,* 26, 339.
21. Cammarota, "*The Spire:* A Symbolic Analysis," 174.

In *The Spire*, then, Golding uses fantastic and carnivalesque modes in several ways. He extends the earlier use of these modes in *Pincher Martin* and *Free Fall* to amplify the uncertainty surrounding the status of fictional representation. This appears to be an attempt to come to terms with the limits of art—its balancing of chaos and order. As Jocelin's vision is undermined by competing natural explanations of supernatural events and the recognition of the spire's dependence on the carnivalesque lower body, both moral certainties and artistic integrity are subverted. We are not allowed a totalized view. Golding attempts to bridge the gaps that have opened up in our confidence about human morality and meaning. Like Jocelin, the spire oscillates between integrity and collapse. The fantastic and carnivalesque modes interrogate singularities and expose the nontotalizable nature of human meaning. Like Rabelais's *Pantagruel* (1532) and *Gargantua* (1534), *The Spire* attacks the austere, monological authoritarianism of the medieval church through the relativity, uncertainty, and, as Mikhail Bakhtin has argued, dialogism of a fantastical topsy-turvydom. It is an attack on one-eyed religious fanaticism and dogmatism in the figure of Jocelin, as it is also an attack on English class privilege, and generally on the sinful and nontranscendent nature of humankind. Furthermore, if we are to accept S. J. Boyd's insights about contemporary relevance, *The Spire* may also be a kind of allegorical dramatization of the changes brought about by Vatican II. However, *The Spire* escapes from the strong engagement with contemporary history evidenced in Golding's previous fiction, and while a formidable array of carnivalesque and fantastic themes and motifs are deployed in the novel, the lack of a dominant satirical target means that the overall effect of these modes is more aimless and ultimately less interesting. In effect, *The Spire* is less relevant to this book's central concern with Golding and contemporary history. It is almost as if Golding stockpiles fantastic and carnivalesque modes in the novel without any clear sense of what he wants to achieve with them.

The Pyramid

In the wake of *The Spire*, *The Pyramid* is a "condition of England" novel that attacks the "social pyramid" structure of English society through the satirical deployment of fantastic and carnivalesque modes. It has often been considered a failure, or at least as Mark Kinkead-Weekes and Ian Gregor argue, as a "partial failure" that enables progress toward a more substantial and profound vision than that attained momentarily in *The Spire*. Howard Babb finds the social comedy "colorless" compared to

Golding's earlier fiction. S. J. Boyd sees it at "the dead centre" or occupying "a kind of no man's land between the first group of five novels and the late novels beginning with *Darkness Visible.*" He continues: "A pyramid might be a flattened spire and, though the settings of the two novels are similar in geographical terms, in moving from *The Spire* to *The Pyramid* we move forward some hundreds of years into a world that seems flattened out and deadly dull."[22] Certainly, these criticisms are valid. *The Pyramid* is a lackluster novel that suggests Golding's attempt at a more comical form is misguided. The greater emphasis on comedy and farce in this and his later fiction may be intimately connected with an escape from the pessimism resulting from engagement with issues concerning atrocity and totalitarianism. Something of this spirit of "retirement" showed itself in *The Spire,* not least in its jolly phallicism and experimentalism. The fictions that follow are more tragicomic and, with the exception of *Darkness Visible,* deal in a more lighthearted way with issues of class and postmodernism.

Set largely between the two world wars, *The Pyramid* steals something of the architecturalism of *The Spire* without the building as such. The "architectural metaphor" of the pyramid is reflected in what Don Crompton calls the novel's "triadic structure." It is really an amalgam of three novellas that appeared in earlier periodicals.[23] The novel comprises three separate episodes in Oliver's life in the village of Stilbourne. In the first episode, the adolescent Oliver, a lower-middle-class dispenser's son, discovers sex with the "inferior," working-class Evie Babbacombe whose class-bridging voluptuousness has already ensnared Bobby Ewan, a doctor's son who belongs to the upper-middle-class world that Oliver resents yet aspires to join. The second episode sees Oliver, on his return home from his first term at Oxford, participating in a farcical performance of the Stilbourne Operatic Society. Part of this snobbish set is Imogen, an ideal, upper-class woman whom Oliver worships yet who falls beyond his grasp. In the final episode, the mature Oliver returns to Stilbourne and reviews his relationship with his music teacher, Miss "Bounce" Dawlish, and the damaging effects of the narrow, repressive, and class-ridden world of the village.

22. Haffenden, "William Golding: An Interview," 9; Kinkead-Weekes and I. Gregor, *Critical Study,* 262; Babb, *Novels of Golding,* 203; Boyd, *Novels of Golding,* 106.

23. Crompton, *View from the Spire,* 57. See Gindin, *William Golding,* 55. Because these novellas were purposefully drawn into a novel form, I have included *The Pyramid* within my study of Golding's novels. However, this principle does not hold for *Scorpion God,* which is avowedly a collection of novellas.

Several critics have viewed *The Pyramid* as being concerned with the evils of the English class system. Virginia Tiger considers the novel's pre-occupation with "social class and spiritual entombment."[24] L. L. Dickson accurately diagnoses the novel as "social satire," and Kevin McCarron sees the social differences between Oliver and Bobby as symbolizing "perhaps the most bitterly disputed demarcation line within the English class system; the one between the upper and lower middle classes."[25] In *The Pyramid,* the hierarchy of the "social pyramid" dominates, an "invisible line" (*PY,* 114) standing between the various stratifications and restricting social movement up the "dreadful ladder" (*PY,* 103). It is a deeply stratified world. For example, Mrs. Babbacombe's social greetings are ignored by those like Lady Hamilton-Smythe who are "entirely out of her social sphere" (*PY,* 43). Evie's talents as a singer are never required by the Stilbourne Operatic Society—ironically abbreviated as S.O.S. Oliver's parents look down on the Babbacombes, just as they are condescended to by the entire household of the "superior" Dr. Ewan. In an imperialist spoof, Bobby Ewan makes Oliver his "'slave'" (*PY,* 23) who in turn enslaves Evie (*PY,* 91). Class differentiation is placed at the core of social relationships, interactions, and conflicts. This hierarchical view even extends to pugilism, with Bobby's superior fighting skills contrasting with the oafish approach of Oliver. Oliver certainly appears to know the class protocol that governs social life in Stilbourne: "I had seen Evie often enough . . . she came from the tumbledown cottages of Chandler's Close. But of course we had never spoken. Never met. Obviously" (*PY,* 13). He also understands that Bobby should not have taken Evie to a dance in his father's car.

Class sensitivity and the petty competition for ascendancy are neatly emphasized in the middle section of the novel with the antics of the Stilbourne Operatic Society. Oliver finds himself volunteered as a violinist for the production of *The King of Hearts* and has to compete with Mr. Claymore who, Boyd notes, "seems to have won his place both in life and in the play more by birth than talent." This sparks a kind of "class war."[26] Throughout the novel, the ambition to climb the "dreadful ladder" is portrayed as a "god without mercy" (*PY,* 159). Much of the novel's drama depends upon either attempts to move up the ladder or the anxiety of slipping down it. The latter is particularly true of those in the middle of the "social pyramid" like Oliver's parents, who fear contamination from be-

24. Tiger, *Dark Fields,* 214–15. See also Medcalf, *William Golding,* 37; Crompton, *View from the Spire,* 61; and Boyd, *Novels of Golding,* 116.
25. Dickson, *Modern Allegories,* 96; McCarron, *William Golding,* 30–31.
26. Boyd, *Novels of Golding,* 118.

low. Such anxiety is to the fore when Oliver agonizes about the consequences for his parents if he got "inferior" Evie pregnant: "To be related even if only by marriage to *Sergeant Babbacombe*! I saw their social world, so delicately poised and carefully maintained, so fiercely defended, crash into the gutter" (*PY,* 82). In a similar way, Bounce Dawlish brings ridicule on herself by taking in the socially "inferior" Henry.

By the end of the novel, Golding powerfully stresses that class hierarchy damages people and is, as James Gindin notes, part of the "sterility" of Stilbourne life evinced in other "provinces" such as love and music. Oliver may well have the trappings of a successful climb up the "dreadful ladder," driving as he does a car of "'superior description'" (*PY,* 159), but the sterile, empty, class-ridden world of Stilbourne has eroded his love for other people, not least Bounce Dawlish whom we see as another victim of Stilbourne narrowness, spiraling into mental decline after leading a sexually repressed life on account of her father's demands that she attain musical excellence. Successively, Oliver has not loved Imogen, Evie, Mr. De Tracy, or Miss Dawlish. He is, Boyd argues, "very much the victim of the system, seeing the world and himself in classist terms." Through being a victim he has "learned to victimise" instead of love. The novel itself is dedicated to Golding's son, David, perhaps as a kind of guide. In the epigraph to the novel, we sense Golding's desire to warn him about the dangers of all kinds of "sterility," particularly death-making class pettiness: "If thou be among people make for thyself love, the beginning and end of the heart." As Dickson writes: "From *Lord of the Flies* to *The Spire,* Golding has implied that a corrupt individual can eventually corrupt his society. In *The Pyramid,* however, a corrupt society impedes individual moral choice."[27] The issue of "class," of course, was very much on people's minds in the postwar years, and it is in this context that we can gain further insight into Golding's treatment of it in *The Pyramid.*

High expectations of better opportunities for everyone following World War II spawned attacks on the English class system during the 1940s, 1950s, and 1960s. Brian Moynahan argues that the 1945 Labour government effectively attempted the "euthanasia" of the rich with its imposition of a heavy "surtax" or supertax and increased death duties on those with large incomes. Although such an attempt at redistribution was required on account of the country's bankrupt economy and its commitment to higher employment, welfare services, and state ownership, there

27. Gindin, *William Golding,* 60; Boyd, *Novels of Golding,* 118–19; Dickson, *Modern Allegories,* 98.

was, Moynahan argues, "an air of triumphalism and social revenge" about it.[28]

Class war in literature extended into the 1950s and 1960s, when, as R. B. Kerschner notes, "postwar disillusionment" in England "took the form of protest against the remnants of the British class system through a group of writers termed by journalists the Angry Young Men."[29] The "Angries" phenomenon was the culmination of a new generation of postwar writing extending from Philip Larkin's *Jill* (1946) and William Cooper's *Scenes from Provincial Life* (1950) to "Movement" works such as John Wain's *Hurry on Down* (1953) and Kingsley Amis's *Lucky Jim* (1954), and reaching an Angry peak with John Osborne's *Look Back in Anger* (1956)—a landmark drama that encapsulates much of the postwar antagonism toward what may be termed "posh" lifestyles and attitudes.

Like Cooper's *Scenes from Provincial Life, The Pyramid* examines the "ordinary" life of the provincial lower middle classes—a generally overlooked seam of English society prior to the 1950s. He does this largely through Oliver and his lower-middle-class parents. The kind of destructive consequences of society's addiction to hierarchy revealed in Blackledge's suicide in Roy Fuller's *Image of a Society* (1956) is also reflected in *The Pyramid,* although not with such a tragic result. *The Pyramid* may also be compared to Angus Wilson's *Late Call* (1965) that attacks snobbery and provincial shallowness.

Leslie Fiedler argues that this "literary class war" that amounted to an attack upon elitist, upper-class, aristocratic "Bloomsbury" was "a conflict between two worlds: the class world of the past and the declassed world to come." However, the flattering of the upper-middle-class view of the world—witnessed in the extension of the "country house" tradition in the arts that continued after the war—only gradually succumbed to more frank material and the challenge to privileged, aristocratic elitism that came with the Movement and the Angry Young Men. In the growing conflict between literary generations, a debate ensued over the virtues of old versus new blood. Fiedler notes that for the most part the Angries were made up of aggressively class-conscious, provincial academics: "Like their authors, the protagonists of the new novels are teachers, and their conflicts are fought out in terms of teaching jobs won or lost." Generally, the protagonists "must possess two qualities: a fear of success and a talent for anger." Fiedler maps out the Angry Young Men movement as anti-

28. Moynahan, *British Century,* 207–9.
29. Kershner, *Twentieth-Century Novel,* 69–70.

intellectual, middlebrow philistinism: "In their hands, however, militant middlebrowism sometimes functions as a useful weapon in the fight against a quiet upper-class reign of terror based on a frozen high style and a rigidified good taste."[30]

However, according to Robert Hewison, not only were the new Movement novelists "resolutely unexperimental" and antimodernist, but this new writing does not show the kind of socialist commitment associated with the 1930s: "Commitment of any kind was considered dubious . . . Critical and political caution went hand in hand." Hewison notes that in the cold war climate there was "little formal commitment" in general, despite "considerable emotional support for the sort of criticisms of society that came from the Left." So whereas the Movement was readily identified as part of "a wider class-struggle," as Blake Morrison argues, this link was often exaggerated or overstated by those who looked to it as part of a working-class "revolution" despite attempts by the writers themselves to "discourage critics from thinking of their work as class-conscious and responsive to social change." As such, the Angry apogee of *Look Back in Anger* was more "important for beginning a revolution in style rather than for its limited political content. The change in style showed itself in all sorts of ways. . . . In fiction, working-class life began to be treated with . . . directness." This "directness" began with John Braine's *Room at the Top* (1957), which, as Stuart Laing indicates, "became the crucial linking text between the 'Movement' novels of the mid-1950s (with their recognisably educated and intelligent, if down-at-heel, heroes) and . . . working-class protagonists" such as those in Alan Sillitoe's *Saturday Night and Sunday Morning* (1958), David Storey's *This Sporting Life* (1960), and Stan Barstow's *Kind of Loving* (1960). Laing argues that despite the relative affluence of the working class in the late 1950s and early 1960s, the notion of a working class continued in these novels, and in various other media. Such representations, he notes, came "through the gradual downward slippage" of the postwar genre of "the young male hero on the make in the fluid social situation of a new Britain."[31] Working-class protagonists, in other words, began to replace lower-middle-class ones. Golding's attack on class in *The Pyramid* can be linked to both the earlier and the later phases of this genre.

The Pyramid follows the often comical plot and theme of upward social

30. Fiedler, "The Class War in British Literature," 409–28, 419, 415, 420, 418–19.
31. Hewison, *In Anger,* 119, 140; Morrison, *The Movement,* 58, 65, 68; Hewison, *In Anger,* 140, 157; Laing, *Representations of Working-Class Life, 1957–1964,* 62, 61.

mobility found in Movement novels—a theme that echoed postwar social mobility and *embourgeoisement.* As Morrison maintains: "With the passing of legislation like the Butler Education Act and promise of equal opportunity in the Welfare State, the issue of social mobility was a topical one, and to find the theme of moving and marrying upward in contemporary literature . . . seemed to reflect the possibility that the social hierarchy was less rigid than it had been before the war." The frictions between the lower middle and upper middle class, of course, which are featured in the work of the Movement and Angry Young Men, are at the core of *The Pyramid.* As Paul Barker notes: "The pyramid is society, and most of the people that William Golding writes about . . . are somewhere on the middle slopes of it, either edging upward, sliding a little, or very glad to be static."[32]

In the Movement novel, the working-class or lower-middle-class male protagonist enters an upper-middle-class milieu and, in conflict with rivals, either succeeds or fails to secure a relationship with a middle- or upper-middle-class woman, and finally, on the basis of this, either gains a better job or returns to his original social status.[33] In *The Pyramid,* an upwardly mobile protagonist, Oliver, is readily irritated, frustrated, and angry toward both the limited world of his lower-middle-class parents and his upper-middle-class "superiors," such as Bobby, the doctor's son. However, he does not betray Fielder's prerequisite "fear of success." Oliver gains a scholarship to study chemistry at Oxford and enters the upper-class milieu of the Stilbourne Operatic Society through his middle-class musical credentials. These details are somewhat autobiographical, reflecting as they do Golding's own personal history and musical abilities. Oxbridge-educated in science before changing to English, Golding could also play several instruments and was, no doubt, well aware of the significance of both his education and his musical accomplishment for class status. At the S.O.S., Oliver meets and desires the upper-class Imogen who is married to Norman Claymore and ultimately beyond his reach. Thus, from the sexual point of view, Oliver fails to move up a couple of ranks from lower-class Evie. This desire and failure have something in common with Larkin's *Jill* or Amis's *That Uncertain Feeling* (1955), as opposed to the protagonist's successful attainment of *classy* women in Amis's *Lucky Jim* or Wain's *Hurry on Down.* However, while sexual liaison offers one way of improvement, education (followed by the independence it brings) offers another route. Oliver takes the latter. Whereas for Lewis in *That Un-*

32. Morrison, *The Movement,* 67–68; Barker, "The Way Up and the Way Down."
33. See Morrison, *The Movement,* 66.

certain Feeling and Kemp in *Jill* failure to make the step up the sexual ladder sees them returning to their original status, the ending of *The Pyramid* portrays Oliver as having a higher status in his post-Oxbridge career in chemical research.

Yet unlike Movement novels such as *Lucky Jim, The Pyramid* does not have an academic setting. Nor does it really "bear the marks of industry" that Morrison notes in "Movement landscapes," although we do learn something of Oliver's work in producing new chemical agents. Furthermore, like John Braine, Alan Sillitoe, David Storey, and Stan Barstow before him, Golding also examines working-class life. This "downward slippage" largely revolves around an examination of Evie and her father, Sergeant Babbacombe. The novel, then, shares with Movement fiction a rather effete, comic realism that looks predominantly at the conflict between the lower-middle and upper-middle classes and later fiction that takes a grittier view of working-class life. Since much of *The Pyramid* has a "Movement sensibility," it could be included as a late entry to the Angry genre as such or a later reworking (quite self-consciously perhaps) of Movement themes.[34] By the time he published *The Pyramid*—his most abrasive attack upon class—Golding knew that the postwar reader would be familiar with issues of class conflict, in part through the writing and drama of the Angries and later works that represented the lives of the working class. As with the Holocaust, fascism, and totalitarianism, he did not need to play historian here. Golding's fullest attack on class in this novel reflects much of the postwar groundswell of resentment toward the privileged classes and the desire for a more classless and equitable society—even if such resentment, especially in the cold war, did not quite culminate in radical politics.

Unlike *The Spire* and the earlier novels, *The Pyramid* offers a more tragicomic and less reactive kind of fiction. It is also a more realistic novel and does not utilize fantastic hesitation as such, yet deploys a "residual" or limited range of Gothic images to amplify, among other things, the class-made deadness or entombment of Stilbourne. It portrays the inhabitants of the village as zombielike on account of their petty, provincial, class-ridden lives. We do not find the fantastic hesitation and "shock" breaking evident in *Lord of the Flies, The Inheritors,* and *Pincher Martin.* Nor does it contrast earthly and heavenly domains as in the "durative" fantastic of *Free Fall* or the "total" fantastic of *The Spire.* The world of *The Pyramid* is expressly secular and natural.

34. Ibid., 62, 8.

Throughout the novel, Golding evokes death, not least in the grotesque place-name Stilbourne. The name of the town suggests that the people walking its streets are the living dead, and we learn that the scourge that has made them this way is class. The symbolism of the pyramid is central in evoking the idea of Stilbourne as entombed. The text invites its readers to juxtapose their knowledge of the pyramids as tombs with the pyramidal English class structure. In fact, across the novel, Golding deploys Gothic symbolism to drive this home. It is Evie who starkly diagnoses the living death of Stilbourne when she returns from London and meets Oliver: "'There must be *someone*!" "What d'you mean Evie?" "Someone alive!'" (*PY,* 105). The point is missed by Oliver: "It was a frivolous remark, I thought, with the fair going on behind us" (*PY,* 105). But we do not miss the significance of this contradiction of the Stilbourne fair being a carnival of the dead. Neither does S. J. Boyd, who remarks: "In this environment Evie's wearing of the 'celebrated, the notorious cross' [*PY,* 69] about her neck seems almost a hint that she fears the vampiric attentions of these undead tomb-dwellers." And after all, Evie has every reason to fear them and their class-driven prejudices. "The inhabitants of Stilbourne," Boyd concludes, "are trapped in their nightmarish little world."[35] This nightmare world of ghosts, witches, and haunting pervades the novel. Without Evie's vivacity, Stilbourne is as flat as a grave.

In the Stilbourne Operatic Society's performance of *The King of Hearts*—which maps the class war between, among others, Oliver and Mr. Claymore—we find Imogen saying her line: "'It is a strange, a haunted place. It frightens me!'" (*PY,* 122). Oliver's violin playing is "ghostly" (*PY,* 127). Indeed, later in the novel, when Oliver's music lessons with Bounce Dawlish are recounted, his violin is put back in its "coffin" (*PY,* 168). Throughout the novel, music, and, as we shall see, love, is deadened by class. We learn, for example, that Bounce has climbed the musical ladder only because of the aggressive ambition of her father. The disharmony and living death of Bounce's life is amplified in the Gothic darkness of her surroundings in which daylight could "only penetrate halfway down the room" (*PY,* 167). The monstrous personification of the grand piano adds to the chilling gloom and doom: "an enormous piano that grinned savagely at the curtains as if it would gnaw them, given the chance" (*PY,* 167). The deathly world of music that Bounce lived in and Oliver tasted is neatly illustrated in the last section of the novel where Oliver stands at Bounce's grave: "For it was here, close and real, two yards away as ever,

35. Boyd, *Novels of Golding,* 120, 121.

that horrible, unused body, with the stained frills and Chinese face. This was a kind of psychic ear-test before which nothing survived but revulsion and horror, childishness and atavism, as if unnameable things were rising round me and blackening the sun" (*PY,* 213).

The Gothic, living death of Stilbourne is further intensified in the many references to insanity and hell. Mrs. Babbacombe, who greets those outside her class, is considered mad. Other Stilbournian oddballs are the eccentric old Mr. Dawlish, an anonymous "deformed halfwit" (*PY,* 118), and a "strange lady wearing many skirts and a vast hat full of dead leaves" (*PY,* 163). Then there is Bounce, with her attention-seeking and disinhibited behavior that leads to her removal to a mental hospital after she walks naked through the town: "Bounce pacing along the pavement with her massive bosom, thick stomach and rolling, ungainly haunches; Bounce wearing her calm smile, her hat and gloves and flat shoes—and wearing nothing else whatsoever" (*PY,* 207). In later life, Bounce is portrayed as an archetypal dotty or demented woman in a cat-infested house. Oliver himself has a history of cyclothymic mood swings and occasional violence, not least toward his piano.

Stilbournian madness is compounded with frequent and often casual references to damnation and the diabolical. This is particularly telling in Evie's tirade against the abuse she has suffered at the hands of men, not least Oliver: "'You wouldn't care if I was dead. Nobody'd care. That's all you want, just my damned body, not me. Nobody wants me, just my damned body. And I'm damned and you're damned with your cock and your cleverness and your chemistry—just my damned body—'" (*PY,* 88). These words seem to have connotations of necrophilia. Such imagery reappears later when Evie accuses Oliver of raping her. She appears dead and sexually edible: "She was corpselike in complexion, her eyes and mouth black as liquorice" (*PY,* 110). Appropriately, Oliver tells her to "'go to hell!'" (*PY,* 110). She begins to accuse Oliver of gossiping about her incestuous relationship with her father but he fails to grasp the meaning: "'What the devil d'you mean?'" (*PY,* 110). Finally, we have the irony of Bounce's epitaph, "Heaven is Music" (*PY,* 213), which is juxtaposed with Oliver's imagination of her corpse in the grave below and the facts of her hellish life on account of her father's demand for musical accomplishment—so much a part of class status.

Like the "residual" fantastic Gothic imagery that suggests the living death of class-ridden Stilbourne, the carnivalesque in *The Pyramid* further subverts the idyll of stable, pastoral English life. Its exuberance, although often dark and noncelebratory, contrasts with the "sterility" of this narrow society and undermines its "pyramid" by showing its proximity to dung and transgressive sexualities. The low, carnivalesque practices act as something of a class-leveler as they are not confined to the lower classes, but are evident in the lives of more privileged and "superior" individuals. They also highlight unwelcome and, indeed, cruel consequences of these divisions or stratifications. In other words, loveless, noncelebratory materiality—a carnival of the dead—is the product of this class-ridden, repressive society. Despite referring to crowds, the drunken "mob" (*PY*, 142), and "a *riot* of swings and roundabouts, and mystery rides and tunnels of love and chairoplanes, the only object of which was the sale of pleasure" (*PY*, 102; emphasis added), there is no sense that carnival may spill over into social revolution. Carnivalesque appetites are constrained and restricted to effete, arguably "dead" public festivals, or else suppressed so that they remain private, hidden aspects of the lives of Stilbournians rather than anything more dangerous or threatening to the status quo.

The sexual consumption of Evie figures centrally in Golding's presentation of a carnivalesque underside to the narrow, repressive life of Stilbourne. She is a kind of class leveler, an object of consumption for all regardless of their position on the "dreadful ladder." However, we get the distinct impression that class hierarchy is too robust to be disrupted or leveled by sexual "contamination" from the lower orders. Variously, Evie is referred to as edible as "plums" (*PY*, 14), "the ripest apple on the tree" (*PY*, 39), or a "ripe nut" (*PY*, 96). Consumption is amplified in the many references to open mouths. The image of consumption evokes the kind of greed, exploitation, and aggression portrayed in *Pincher Martin* and *Free Fall* and suggests that Stilbourne's class-ridden, "sterile" atmosphere produces superficial, loveless victims and victimizers. Oliver, for example, is delighted when Bobby Ewan is injured on his motorbike because it gives him an opportunity to steal his girlfriend, Evie. Oliver's reception of the news of Bobby's accident bears traces of the nastiness of "Pincher" Martin. Here, as Boyd suggests, consumption is stressed to the point of cannibalism: "'Badly?' 'They don't know yet. Took him to the hospital.' I helped myself to HP sauce" (*PY*, 58).[36] At the news that Bobby may be crippled for life, Oliver is described as "digesting this news" and feeling "a little of Stilbourne's excitement and appetite at the news of someone else's misfortune" (*PY*, 63). In effect, the resentment that class hierarchy promotes lies behind Oliver's delight in Bobby's misfortune.

Beneath the surface of an ordered hierarchical society is a seething,

36. Ibid.

stinking pit of unruly, low emotions and behavior. The "social pyramid" with its suggestion of superior versus inferior human culture and morality is leveled when the hidden life of Stilbourne from the top to the bottom is unveiled in a rainbow of transgression. Some of this transgression is lighthearted and playful. The more "Rabelaisian" (*PY,* 89) or carry-on kinds of "low" behavior include activity such as Oliver flicking up Evie's skirt and grabbing her knickers, or being incapable of getting his halberd "up" the "back passage" (*PY,* 152) of the Town Hall during the performance by Stilbourne Operatic Society. However, much of the sexual transgression in *The Pyramid* is of an altogether nastier or darker sort.

Evie lies at the center of a transgressive vortex that has seen her sexually abused by her father, spanked by Captain Wilmot who also delights in squeezing the bottoms of young boys, and used as a kind of sexual toilet by various Stilbournian men, not least Bobby Ewan, Dr. Jones, and Oliver, whose aggressive, selfish lovemaking appears to border on rape. At least, this is what Evie claims when she meets him later in the Crown pub. Golding's references to sex are more frank or explicit than they were in his earlier fiction. Indeed, his reference to Oliver scattering his semen around Evie's "pink petals" (*PY,* 72) borders on the pornographic. This may owe something to the more "permissive" approach to sexuality in the 1960s, a theme Golding takes up more fully in *Darkness Visible.* Equally, the wide homoerotic references in *The Pyramid* may reflect this context.

Although Golding's homoeroticism in his previous fiction serves to deepen a sense of depravity that is vital to his satire and in so doing buys into homophobic constructions of homosexuality as repugnant, he largely avoids this tactic in *The Pyramid,* with the exception of the disapproval shown toward Captain Wilmot. Rather, Golding seems to suggest that the intolerance of Stilbourne's "social pyramid" breeds intolerance toward the sexually "Other." Oliver, that loveless product of Stilbourne life, rejects with a roar of laughter the image of the cross-dressing Evelyn De Tracy in a "frilly" (*PY,* 149) ballerina costume. Oliver's mother says little about the two women who had lived together in Stilbourne despite being dead "for half a generation" (*PY,* 178) and the "manly" (*PY,* 186), pipe-smoking Bounce cuts a rather marginal figure. This continuing sense of what Judith Butler views as the performative nature of gender noted in the previous chapter extends or complements the wider sense of "construction" in terms of class that dominates *The Pyramid.* The balletic De Tracy and pipe-smoking Bounce advertise the constraint that is part of both the social and, indeed, the theatrical construction of gender and class. As such, this instantiation of marginal or subordinate sexualities may be viewed as purposefully undermining the dominant, "brutally homophobic" side of English society whose class structure promotes the intolerance of difference. Thus, on one level, *The Pyramid* like *Free Fall* may be thought of as promoting "sexual dissidence." Yet Golding's "dissidence," if we can call it that, rides on class prejudices and stereotypes. It may reflect both his apparent sympathy for so-called subordinate and marginal groups, including homosexuals, and a shallow presentation of them for comic effect. Furthermore, as Alan Sinfield argues, because "dominant structures," for example, homophobic patriarchy, have to be invoked in order to be opposed, any dissidence "can always, ipso facto, be discovered reinscribing that which it proposes to critique." Dissidence, he points out, circumvents Foucauldian entrapment because, unlike the notion of subversion, it is not disabled by the inevitable sense of containment should it not succeed.[37]

Despite Golding's attack on misogyny in previous novels, similar limitations and contradictions to those in Golding's representation of marginal sexualities can be found in his representation of women, notably in *Pincher Martin* and *Free Fall.* The working-class "slut" Evie, like the devil woman Goody and giggling, infertile Rachel in *The Spire* and the subordinate, almost willing victim Beatrice in *Free Fall,* falls well short of instantiating a strong, positive female character. This continues in his later fiction in an almost medieval representation of Sophy as a pervert, harlot, and source of contaminative sexuality. Golding's fiction betrays an inability to get beyond a world of men and male protagonists that appears somewhat dated now that a more rigorous analysis of gender presentation has grown over recent years.

Despite such objections and contradictions, particularly the sense of Golding being complicit with homophobia, he is genuinely, if problematically, antipathetic to social injustice. In *The Pyramid,* he attempts to portray and expose the "low" domains of class-ridden English life. A stench emanates from the class prejudices at the heart of Stilbournian Englishness. Boyd contends: "Oliver and Stilbourne stink. Inside the pyramid it is very stuffy, the atmosphere is stifling and fetid, and the very air that one breathes is class." Scatology pervades the novel, from Evie's farting to her father's mispronunciation of the Latin inscription on her cross and chain: "'Hamor vinshit Homniar'" (*PY,* 25). Here scatology mixes with the sadistic violence that lies behind the motto "Love beats everything" (*PY,* 37),

37. Sinfield, *Faultlines: Cultural Materialism and the Politics of Dissident Reading,* 47, 49.

and again touches on earlier themes surrounding the totalitarian personality of "soldier-males." The "low" nature of Sergeant Babbacombe who incestuously abused his daughter is emphasized in his job of collecting pennies from the public lavatories. Oliver's own dirt is foregrounded, like various other Stilbournian men, in willingly lying with Evie on the "brown earth" among "dry pellets of rabbit dung" (*PY*, 96). Yet all the shit and dirt at the heart of the lives of Stilbourne's men are viewed as contamination from the lower classes, and particularly the lower-class woman Evie. When Evie has an affair with Dr. Jones, she is ostracized, blamed, and forced to leave the village. Oliver contrasts the clean world represented by Imogen and his parents and the sordid world of bottom-spanked Evie: "All at once, I had a tremendous feeling of thereness and hereness, of separate worlds, they and Imogen, clean in that coloured picture; here, this object, on an earth that smelt of decay, with picked bones and natural cruelty—life's lavatory" (*PY*, 91). But, as Boyd points out: "It is not, however, Evie that stinks and is diseased, it is the mentality of Stilbourne." The hypocrisy of assigning shit and dirt to the lower classes is tellingly shown in the reactions of Oliver's father to his son's lovemaking. His father tells him: "'Young men don't—think. I—you don't know about that place, Chandler's—Yes. Well. There's—disease, you see. One's not suggesting that one's necessarily—been exposed to infection—but if one goes on like this—'" (*PY*, 100). Oliver feels tainted by the lavatorial world of Evie and Chandler's Close: "I stood, a heap of dung, yearning desperately for some sewer up which I might crawl and reach my parents, kneel, be forgiven, so that the days of our innocence might return again. I stood, watching him make up prescriptions for all the ailments of Stilbourne" (*PY*, 100). The suggestion here seems to be that the whole "social pyramid" of Stilbourne is afflicted with sexual ailments. Perhaps the final word on the stinking life of Stilbourne should go to Bounce. Sacrificed to the "sterility" of her father's ambitions, having lived in a house where nearly everything is fecal brown, she declines mentally and ends up walking naked through the streets of the village in a "final flouting of Stilbourne taboo."[38] Her nakedness interrogates the social masks that the Stilbournians hide behind in order to keep coming up smelling of roses.

The Pyramid, however, is hardly a call for revolution. The conservative survivalist Oliver both is immersed in class prejudice and preserves it, being afforded all the materialistic fruits through an Oxbridge education. With the partly light, comical ribbing of class prejudice, this all makes for

38. Boyd, *Novels of Golding*, 116, 115, 122.

an arguably nonradical text, rather in the same way that Blake Morrison saw Movement writers rejecting class privilege while still joining the "club," as it were: "Though conscious and at times resentful of class distinction and privilege, the work of the Movement never seriously challenges their right to exist. There is little sense that the social structure could be altered; the more common enquiry is whether individuals can succeed in 'fitting in.'"[39]

Perhaps we can see something of this ambivalence in Golding's "non-Marxist," socialist trajectory that appears at times to be carefully situated between left and right politics. For example, in the second epigraph to this chapter, Golding expresses his anger concerning the stratification of English society. But as with his protagonist, Oliver, who is irritated by class divisions yet climbs the social ladder, Golding hints at his own personal accommodation of class, rather than any radical action against it. As such, Golding might be seen in a similar predicament to the "scholarship boys" who made up the Movement, and whose background, Morrison argues, pressured them to "understate social difference": "The result is a literature resourceful in managing to play down class differences while at the same time making class one of its central concerns." For example, the Movement novels *Jill, Hurry on Down, Lucky Jim,* and *That Uncertain Feeling* "effect this compromise by confusing social status with sexual status. The pursued heroines—Jill, Veronica, Christine, Elizabeth—are attractive as well as being from a higher social rank." Similarly, Golding portrays Oliver in pursuit of the physically attractive and upper-middle-class Imogen, thus blurring "the distinction between beauty and breeding." This link between Imogen's higher class and sexual attractiveness or beauty appears to reinforce rather than critique class superiority. Again, like Amis, Golding's "attacks on upper-middle class culture co-exist with an almost embarrassing reverence for traditional upper-middle-class 'types.'" This is neatly shown in Oliver's "reverence" for De Tracy, the upper-middle class producer of Stilbourne Operatic Society's *King of Hearts.*[40] Certainly like the church structure in *The Spire,* the class structure in *The Pyramid* is adaptable to dissidence and can circumvent or absorb it.

It appears that Golding, published by Faber and Faber (who tended to favor Oxbridge writers), regularly contributing to the BBC's *Third Programme,* and finally receiving a knighthood, never really strayed from the

39. Morrison, *The Movement,* 73.
40. Ibid., 68, 69, 70, 77.

"Establishment." Despite attacking class divisions, he never suggests taking a more radical response than joining the "club" or, as he wrote in *The Hot Gates*, getting further than walking the "social tightrope":

> My father was a master at the local grammar school so that we were all the poorer for our respectability. In the dreadful English scheme of things at that time, a scheme which so accepted social snobbery as to elevate it to an instinct, we had our subtle place. . . . In fact, like everybody except the very high and the very low in those days, we walked a social tightrope, could not mix with the riotous children who made such a noise and played such wonderful games on the Green. (*HG*, 168)

In conclusion, Golding's deployment of the fantastic and carnivalesque served various functions in turning the constructions of the "spire" and "pyramid" upside down. First, in *The Spire*, these modes amplified the theme of metafictional uncertainty and extended the experimentalism of *Pincher Martin* and *Free Fall*. These modes lend themselves to an uncomfortable realization of the ambivalence of human constructions, not least that of fiction itself. The achievement of human construction is left teetering, prone to deconstruction, magnified by the unresolved "total" fantastic. This late-modernist experimentalism and self-consciousness find both continuities and discontinuities with Golding's later postmodernist fiction. The fantastic and carnivalesque also emphasize and attack human cruelty and sinfulness in general and the limited, rigid, and hypocritical faith not just of Jocelin, but of the medieval Catholic Church as well. Golding's Rabelaisian strategy here may allegorize the limitations and monologism of the Catholic Church prior to Vatican II that Boyd sees as bringing about a much needed *aggiornamento* (readjustment) of the church to modern times. Finally, the carnivalesque in *The Spire* suggests the long history of the unwholesome influence of class in English life that becomes the major theme for *The Pyramid*.

In *The Pyramid*, "residual" fantastic Gothic motifs are used in a different way, not to create hesitation between natural and supernatural explanation but to emphasize the living death of the English class system. This elitism is undermined by the carnivalesque—the pyramid is laid flat. The religious aspirations of the Egyptians are turned upside down in *The Pyramid*. Boyd writes:

> The Egyptians believe that the roof of the sky is held up by their religious observances and rituals. They are intensely religious, believing

> this earthly life to be a state of death compared to the true life of the next world. The people of Stilbourne have no such vision, are highly irreligious or, rather, they have a religion which is entirely man-made and which fills the flattened heavens with disharmony: that religion is the worship of class.

Unlike the Egyptians, the Stilbournians do not aspire to escape living death. Boyd goes on neatly to link the flattening of the pyramid with both materialism and weapons of war: "The Egyptian world is destined, we know, to produce those stupendous religious and funerary monuments, the Pyramids; the best Stilbourne can manage is Henry's horizontal tarmac spread and Oliver's contribution to creating the tools of germ warfare. It is hard to find positive or hopeful elements in the dull and stuffy world of *The Pyramid*."[41] We suspect that Golding's commitment to changing the "social pyramid" of class stratification achieves a similar diffusion of radicalism that Blake Morrison diagnosed in the fictional works of the Movement and Angries. However, Golding joins them—albeit late in the day—in "attacking" the English class system at a time when "class war" was still very much in the air.

41. Boyd, *Novels of Golding*, 122.

6

Postmodernity and Postmodernism

Darkness Visible and *The Paper Men*

> "Matty" was reborn. And after how many years of disuse? "Matty" now was rather amusing, outspoken, competently incompetent, free from convention, free to say what other people did not say: yet always conscious of, and making a burnt offering of, these qualities. . . . Exactly, so she understood, had the jester gained exemption with his bladder and his bells . . .
>
> —Doris Lessing, *The Four-Gated City*

> [W]e have become irritated clowns, drunk or drugged, perpetually bereft of love, artists and philosophers of the meaningless.
>
> —Christine Brooke-Rose, *A Rhetoric of the Unreal*

SATIRE'S CONSTITUENT MODES OF THE FANTASTIC AND CARNIVALESQUE in *Darkness Visible* (1979) and *The Paper Men* (1984) have several interwoven, previously uncharted functions, which go far beyond Kevin McCarron's identification of a "coincidence of opposites" generated by fantasy in Golding's later fiction. Sometimes the fantastic and carnivalesque are used stereoscopically, whereas at other times they operate independently. Fantastic "religious vision" and carnivalesque "moral depravity" in *Darkness Visible* combine to present what James Gindin calls "a blistering indictment of contemporary England."[1] Postwar English life is viewed as spiraling downward to produce dysfunctional, atomized totalitarian personalities. Independently, the fantastic strategically and powerfully evokes recent atrocity and attacks British nuclear testing and weaponry, and support for U.S. policies in Vietnam. In *The Paper Men*, the two modes combine to satirize the authority of an English literature in-

1. Gindin, *William Golding*, 70.

dustry that Golding crudely and simplistically presents as being overrun by depthless writers and critics. As part of this attack, the writer Wilf Barclay is presented as misogynistic, sadistic, and exoskeletal—characteristics that link his behavior with the "soldier-male" personality. In the presentation of the absurd, often farcical religious ministry of Matty and the clownish life of Barclay who has "visions" and suffers the "stigmata," Golding also appears to be adding to his perennial critique of religious authority. More formidably, a core function of the fantastic and carnivalesque in both *Darkness Visible* and *The Paper Men* is to complement or intensify an examination of postmodernity and postmodernism through their topsy-turvy relativism and uncertainty. Here I am indebted to a number of critics, not least Bernard Dick, James Gindin, Philip Redpath, and Kevin McCarron, who have alerted the reader to Golding's preoccupation with language and indeterminacy in these novels.

In intensifying the mood of postmodern uncertainty, the satirical form in *Darkness Visible* and *The Paper Men* does not function to attack any particular target. The versatility of satire's nonconfrontational promotion of dissolution and multivalency makes it well suited to various reformulations and literary combinations, not least in postmodern literature. The fantastic and carnivalesque advance the climate of problematization fostered by postmodernism with its increased skepticism about accepted values and greater willingness to question what has gone before, or what anything means. This use of these modes appears to be more playful, celebratory, Horatian, and, indeed, Bakhtinian in tone than in Golding's earlier fiction, but only marginally so.

Darkness Visible and *The Paper Men* examine in a dark, often farcical way the vertiginous, postmodern condition of England and the wider world—a condition that has gathered pace in the wake of World War II trauma. As Gerald Graff writes: "Romantic and modernist writing expressed a faith in the constitutive power of the imagination, a confidence in the ability of literature to impose order, value and meaning on the chaos and fragmentation of industrial society. This faith seemed to have lapsed after World War II. Literature increasingly adopted an ironic view of its traditional pretensions to truth, high seriousness, and the profundity of 'meaning.'" Having both continuities and discontinuities with modernism, postmodernism became closely associated with postwar life, as R. B. Kershner summarizes: "Most accounts of postmodernism locate a break in sensibility following World War II, and some critics point to the dropping of the atomic bomb in 1945 and the commencement of the 'nuclear age' as a defining moment." Both novels concern what Robert Hewison sees as a "dethronement of language and logic" that followed the "retreat into silence" advocated by George Steiner after World War II and picked up speed in the 1960s and 1970s, most notably, perhaps, in the fallout from the counterculture of the 1960s.[2]

Increasingly, during the 1950s, 1960s, and 1970s, a depthless, playful, and questioning mood invaded cultural, artistic, and social aspects of life from art, architecture, literature, and film to notions of subjective identity, the status of knowledge, and society's sense of itself. This skepticism was the culmination of a growing dissatisfaction with the ability of science, technology, and reason to improve the human condition. It doubted the modernist Enlightenment belief that the world will yield its secrets to scientific inquiry.[3] This postmodernism, Hans Bertens explains, incorporates several themes: "It refers, first of all, to a complex of anti-modernist artistic strategies which emerged in the 1950s and developed momentum in the course of the 1960s," became involved with the poststructuralist debate in the 1970s concerning "representations that do not represent," and grew more politicized in the 1980s as a "postmodernism" that "attempts to expose the politics that are at work in representations and to undo institutionalised hierarchies" by advocating "difference, pluriformity, and multiplicity." This advocacy of "difference" is at the hub of the feminism and multiculturalism that gained momentum in the 1980s and involved a strong interest in minority points of view and marginalized voices. "Postmodernism," Bertens continues, is a "perspective from which [the] world is seen" and has moved out from the field of humanities into all other disciplines of inquiry. Considering the sheer complexity of late-twentieth-century experience and its multifarious, multivalent nature, it appears contradictory to attempt to delimit the term *postmodernism* to a given formula. It cuts across so many different academic disciplines and approaches that it is often seen as a difficult and confusing concept. Its heterogeneous status defies simple explanation and clear historical periodization such that Robert B. Ray claims: "The best way to understand post-modernism is with a list." Indeed, there are no easy answers to the question, What is postmodernism? Despite this difficulty over definition, Bertens argues that a "crisis in representation" is the "common denominator" of a variety of "postmodernisms."[4]

2. Graff, *Literature against Itself: Literary Ideas in Modern Society,* 33; Kershner, *Twentieth-Century Novel,* 69; Hewison, *Too Much: Art and Society in the Sixties, 1960–1975,* 84–85.

3. See Robert Hollinger, *Postmodernism and the Social Sciences.*

4. Bertens, *The Idea of the Postmodern: A History,* 3, 7, 8, 9; Ray, "Postmodernism," 144; Bertens, *Idea of the Postmodern,* 11.

In the early twenty-first century we are confronted still with a painful form of intellectual vertigo or what Christine Brooke-Rose calls a "reality crisis." Poststructural theories of knowledge, identity, language, gender, and power have brought forth a new order of viewing the world, where certainty is broken down by ambiguity, totalities are fragmented, "truth" is plural, and difference is celebrated. This new order is one that is suspicious of what Jean-François Lyotard calls "grand narratives"—for example, that science and technology will automatically yield better ways of living (no longer tenable in the face of diminishing world resources, global warming, and pollution) and that the theories of Marxism and psychoanalysis can explain the human condition.[5] It is suspicious, in fact, of all stories that claim authority over our lives.

Thinkers such as Jacques Derrida have cast considerable doubt over any possibility of representing the world exhaustively and accurately. Other philosophers such as Jean Baudrillard have posited the view that our "reality" is now reduced to the controlling influence of "simulacra."[6] Most postmodernist philosophies are antifoundationalist—that is, they do not propose that our knowledge rests on a single version of reason.[7] Rather, they consider that truth is established interpersonally and that systems of logic or ideas about the world are often parochial and local.[8] Postmodernism prioritizes language as a major feature of social life and insists that meanings are not defined by their correspondence with an external reality but have to be seen and qualified within their social contexts. Because contexts are so variable, it is difficult to make any definite statements about the world in general. Broadly then, a postmodernist view emphasizes discourse or "language in use" as the thing that constitutes reality: "Language is now necessarily the central consideration in all attempts to know, act and live."[9] It views language as incapable of "fixing" or denoting these realities. In this sense, postmodernism concerns the primacy of language in "constructing" reality, narrative as a culturally creative act and the dialogical nature of life. Postmodernism also takes a different stance toward the modernist outlook that individuals are the authors of their own ideas, speech, or writing. It is acutely aware that what individuals say or write is not their own production, but reliant on prior speech and writing.

So far I have described postmodernism as if it were something radical-

5. Brooke-Rose, *Rhetoric of the Unreal,* 3; see Lyotard, *Postmodern Condition,* 31–41.
6. See Derrida, *Of Grammatology;* and Baudrillard, *Simulacra and Simulation.*
7. See Hollinger, *Postmodernism and Social Sciences.*
8. See Clifford Geertz, *Local Knowledge: Further Essays in the Interpretation of Culture.*
9. Charles Lemert, "The Uses of French Structuralisms in Sociology," 234.

ly new, but it may be seen as having continuity with modernity, as Paddy Scannell, Philip Schlesinger, and Colin Sparks contend: "Whether postmodernism represents a sharp break from modernity or simply a late stage in that historical development is the crux of the matter." Bertens argues that "the self-reflexivity inherent in the modern project has come to question modernity at large. In the last twenty years, modernity, as a grand socio-political project, has increasingly been called to account by itself; modernity has turned its critical rationality upon itself and has been forced to reluctantly admit to its costs." On the other hand, a discontinuity between modernism—that Enlightenment quest for rational explanations and knowledge—and postmodernism is often central to the definition of the latter: "Modernism acknowledged the fragmentary, transient, dislocated character of the social world but tried to overcome it, to retrieve a lost unity, whereas postmodernism is content to accept and celebrate a de-centred political, economic and cultural global environment. It rejects deep structures, any notion of an underlying, determining reality. It accepts a world of appearances, a surface reality without depth."[10] It is almost as if postmodernism is defined by what it lacks rather than what it contains.

The postmodern world is one that is subject to a "massive, pervasive intertext" of proliferating symbols and signs, as in Jonathan Raban's *Soft City* (1974).[11] At its broadest, postmodernism might be seen as the running together of previously discrete units of meaning, be they images, words, or concepts. It appears that one possible consequence of postmodernism—that reductive conceptualization of the proliferation of signs, of recuperated artifact, of mass media, of textuality, where bricolage and appropriation of commodities, trash even, dominates—is numbness, insentience, wash-over. The essence of postmodernism is the making of anything from anything else, a promiscuous montage and blurring of images. Terry Eagleton argues:

> There is perhaps, a degree of consensus that the typical post-modernist artefact is playful, self-ironizing and even schizoid; and that it reacts to the austere autonomy of high modernism by impudently embracing the language of commerce and the commodity. Its stance toward cultural tradition is one of irreverent pastiche, and its contrived

10. Scannell, Schlesinger, and Sparks, eds., *Culture and Power: A Media, Culture, and Society Reader,* 2; Bertens, *Idea of the Postmodern,* 247; Scannell, Schlesinger, and Sparks, *Culture and Power,* 3.

11. Ray, "Postmodernism," 119.

> depthlessness undermines all metaphysical solemnities, sometimes by a brutal aesthetics of squalor and shock.[12]

Metafiction predominates in the works of a broad spectrum of postmodernist writers, from Iris Murdoch, Muriel Spark, and John Fowles to Donald Barthelme, John Barth, and Christine Brooke-Rose. The deliberate merging of story, essay, fiction, criticism, and history is also typical of some postmodernist texts.[13]

In his book *The Modes of Modern Writing,* David Lodge provides a rather formalist yet useful summary of the techniques of postmodernist writing that, as he admits, derive greatly from previous prose fiction such as *Don Quixote* (1605–1615) and *Tristram Shandy* (1759–1767). According to Lodge, postmodernist fiction "continues the modernist critique of traditional mimetic art, and shares the modernist commitment to innovation, but pursues these aims by methods of its own." He argues that "the general idea of the world resisting the compulsive attempts of the human consciousness to interpret it, of the human predicament being in some sense 'absurd,' does underlie a good deal of postmodernist writing." Thus, unlike the modernists who "for all their experimentation, obliquity and complexity, oversimplified the world" and attempted to reconcile it with the "human mind," postmodern writing undermines faith in coherence and unity. *Darkness Visible* resembles postmodernist texts such as John Fowles's *Magus* (1977) and Thomas Pynchon's *Crying of Lot 49* (1979) that evoke an "endemic" kind of "uncertainty," and have plots that are "labyrinths without exits." *The Paper Men* also advances an "endemic" indeterminacy, although it is not as labyrinthine or as sprawling a novel as *Darkness Visible.* That said, both novels present the "human predicament" as absurd, radically avoid coherence and unity, critique mimetic art, and have problematical "mock" or "false" endings that, Lodge maintains, separate postmodernist writing from the traditional novel with its closed ending or the modernist novel with its open ending. Underlying *Darkness Visible* and *The Paper Men,* as with much postmodernist fiction according to Lodge, is the generation of contradiction often promoted by sexual ambivalence or hermaphroditism that "affronts the most binary system of all," plots that have various "permutations" or "narrative lines," the disruption of fictional continuity (particularly by metafictional elements), the excess of "presenting the reader with more details than he can synthesise into a

12. Eagleton, "Awakening from Modernity," 194.
13. See, for example, Roland Barthes, *S/Z;* and Julian Barnes, *Flaubert's Parrot.*

whole," thus affirming "the resistance of the world to interpretation," and the short-circuiting of the gap between text and the world "by combining in one work violently contrasting modes—the obviously fictive and the apparently factual; introducing the author and the question of authorship into the text; and exposing conventions in the act of using them."[14]

Darkness Visible

Darkness Visible marks a postmodern turn in Golding's fiction at a time when, as we have seen, postmodernity and postmodernism were widely debated in a variety of disciplines. Like Pynchon's *V* (1963) and *Gravity's Rainbow* (1973), *Darkness Visible* is a quest "for meaning in a man-centred world where the multiplicity of interpretive systems make it impossible to envisage a whole form of which the fragments would be parts." As such, it is an extremely difficult and, arguably, deeply unsatisfying novel that Redpath claims "almost defies any interpretative act and challenges the critic to make the best he can of it."[15]

Part of the difficulty of interpreting *Darkness Visible* is Golding's refusal to talk or write about it. In a letter to Don Crompton, he wrote: "The fact of the matter is that for a number of reasons *Darkness Visible* is the one of my books I have refused to talk about: and the more I have been pressed, the more stubborn my refusal has become." Why Golding remains silent is difficult to ascertain. Crompton puts Golding's taciturnity down to the obscure complexity of the novel that defies explanation and, as such, further examines the binary "subjects that trouble and fascinate" him: good-evil, saint-sinner, spiritual-material. Redpath considers obscurity as the "main product" of the novel and its interpretative difficulty as Golding's way of "getting his own back" on early critical indictments of his privileging of "intentional fallacy." Perhaps his silence is part of this strategy. However, I suspect that he kept silent partly because he was distressed by the self-conscious, malformed, and apocalyptic miscarriage of a novel that reflected postmodern fragmentation in its form and themes and because he felt that the pluralistic nature of contemporary life made it difficult to arrive at explanations. He told John Haffenden: "I can't locate myself in the twentieth century. It is literally a place in which a man cannot locate

14. Lodge, *The Modes of Modern Writing: Metaphor, Metonymy, and the Typology of Modern Literature,* 220, 225–26, 226, 229, 230, 231, 237, 239–40.
15. Brooke-Rose, *Rhetoric of the Unreal,* 367; Redpath, *Structural Reading,* 56.

himself."[16] In *Darkness Visible,* Golding appears to suggest that the origin of this inability to "locate" oneself lies with contemporary atrocities of conventional and nuclear mass bombing of civilian populations, the Holocaust, and, even later, the Vietnam War. Here, Golding uses the fantastic to emphasize the horror of such atrocity and critique English distancing from it. Together, the fantastic and carnivalesque in *Darkness Visible* proceed to register the uncertainty and moral relativism of postwar-postmodern life and attack English depravity, racial intolerance, and totalitarian personalities.

The story line of *Darkness Visible* is divided into three sections. Part 1 focuses on Matty, a fantastical child survivor of a firestorm during the London blitz who develops into a farcical prophet or Ranter-like figure. He is associated with "Good." In part 2, the central figure is Sophy who, in her descent into terrorism, sexual transgression, and violent racialism, represents "Evil." Gindin argues: "Like Matty, Sophy is an issue of the Second World War, but she is the product of its social dislocations rather than its physical terrors."[17] Part 3 brings Matty and Sophy together in apocalyptic style when Matty thwarts Sophy's plan to kidnap and ransom an Arab princeling. In so doing, Matty is destroyed in a second fire. The novel ends with the pederast Mr. Pedigree's vision of the dead yet transfigured Matty. This final section that stresses that "One is one and all alone and ever more shall be so" (*DV,* 225) suggests the unsplendid isolation of postmodern individuals in a world where rationality and knowledge is, as Sim Goodchild admits, as lethal as atomic weaponry: "'We're all mad, the whole damned race. We're wrapped in illusions, delusions, confusions about the penetrability of partitions, we're all mad and in solitary confinement.' 'We think we *know.*' 'Know? That's worse than an atom bomb, and always was'" (*DV,* 261).

Set between the war and the late 1970s, the novel portrays a decaying England in the grip of a visible, hellish darkness, befitting the Miltonian allusion of the title:

> A dungeon horrible, on all sides round
> As one great furnace flamed, yet from those flames
> No light, but rather darkness visible
> Served only to discover sights of woe,

16. Crompton, *View from the Spire,* 11, 94. See Golding's rebuffs in Webb, "Golding Goes Down," 12; and Haffenden, "William Golding: An Interview," 10. Redpath, *Structural Reading,* 19, 56; Haffenden, "William Golding: An Interview," 12.
17. Gindin, *William Golding,* 67.

> Regions of sorrow, doleful shades, where peace
> And rest can never dwell, hope never comes.
> (1.61–66)[18]

Both the allusion to Milton's "notorious oxymoron" and the novel's epigraph from the lines of Virgil's *Aeneid,* "Grant me to tell what I have heard! With your assent / May I reveal what lies deep in the gloom of the Underworld!" (6.266–67), together imply "a dire view of the contemporary scene."[19] It is an oxymoron that occurs in *menippea,* and extends the disruption of norms—a strategy that is at the heart of *Darkness Visible.* While *Paradise Lost* (1667) is generally regarded as Golding's source for this oxymoron, as McCarron suggests, there are other candidates, such as Alexander Pope's *Dunciad* (1743): "Of darkness visible so much be lent, / As half to show, half veil the deep intent" (4.3–4).[20] *The Dunciad* is a strong candidate because *Darkness Visible* and indeed *The Paper Men* both reflect the detrimental impact of new communication technologies and the resultant spirit of meaninglessness and entropy.[21] Apart from these sources for the overall oxymoron, Golding's "condition of England" novel is undoubtedly greatly influenced by Doris Lessing's dark, visionary work, *The Four-Gated City*—a link that has been missed by critics.

Like *The Four-Gated City,* the fifth and final novel in the "Children of Violence" sequence, *Darkness Visible* presents a vision of a socially turbulent, violent, apocalyptic postwar England and global scene and also opens with images of the London blitz. It is particularly disappointing that Lawrence S. Friedman avoids the centrality of historical context to an understanding of *Darkness Visible* when he remarks glibly, "Although that world is 1940 London, it is essentially timeless," since Golding has been and remains deeply concerned with contemporary atrocities.[22] Apart from the reference to the blitz, the opening scene also alludes to the Jewish Holocaust in its link between the Old Testament "burning bush" (*DV,* 10) and references to "the furnace" (*DV,* 10) and "open stove" (*DV,* 12) that cannot be read without the "associative despair" Norma Rosen speaks of.

18. Milton, *Paradise Lost,* 47.

19. Crompton, *View from the Spire,* 11; Virgil, *The Aeneid,* 292; Webb, "Vision of England," 16.

20. Pope, "The Dunciad," 514. Here, as Seidel notes, "Satiric knowledge is somewhat akin to taboo or illegal knowledge." In a sense, Golding mirrors Pope's request "that he be given just enough light to reveal what ought to have remained hidden" (*Satiric Inheritance,* 23).

21. See McCarron, *Coincidence of Opposites,* 17–19.

22. Friedman, *William Golding,* 123.

Furthermore, the image of the burnt child emerging out of the "shameful, inhuman light" (*DV,* 11) is reminiscent of the famous photograph of Kim Phuc, a Vietnamese girl badly burned during a napalm attack on her village by the United States Air Force.[23] Here, Golding reinforces in fiction his earlier opposition to U.S. policies in Vietnam that he conveyed in his letter to *Times* (London). Finally, the nightmarish intensity of the firestorm and its devastation also suggests the nuclear excesses of Hiroshima and Nagasaki, which bears on Golding's view of British nuclear armament later in the novel when the Aborigine, Harry Bummer, persecutes Matty because he believes he is signaling to British planes involved in nuclear testing in Australia.[24] Britain tested an atom bomb, for example, in the Monte Bello islands off the northwest coast of Australia in 1952. Yet, Golding's reference here seems to concern more than nuclear testing per se. He appears to be evoking the more chilling fact that some of the British testing was done on Aboriginal land not cleared of Aborigines—for example, at Maralinga in the 1950s.[25] Matty himself goes on to protest nuclear testing there but is advised that his protest would be better served in England. As in his early fiction, Golding is concerned to throw a critical light on British complicity in the history of atrocity, not least against the Aborigines. We need to bear in mind that Golding's writing reflects the climate of fear, ongoing debate, and protest about nuclear weapons during the cold war period, especially in the wake of Russia exploding its first hydrogen bomb in 1953, the Suez affair in 1956, and the Cuban missile crisis in 1962. It is also a theme at the heart of *The Four-Gated City.* The fantastical horror with which *Darkness Visible* opens provides the moral repulsion for attacking England's part in atrocities and its potential for greater ones despite the witness given by atrocity survivors.

Matty in *Darkness Visible* is undoubtedly based on "Matty" in Lessing's novel—a "clumsy, self-denigrating clown" role or "false self" that Martha Quest adopts to cope with feelings of alienation in an "increasingly violent and disintegrating world."[26] Indeed, *The Four-Gated City,* as with some of Lessing's other works—for example, *The Golden Notebook* (1962), *Landlocked* (1965), and *Briefing for a Descent into Hell* (1971)—calls to mind

23. See Frank Tuohy, "Baptism by Fire."

24. I am indebted here to Gindin's observations. He remarks: "[A]n Australian aboriginal, full of anger, jumps on Matty's groin when Matty draws an elaborate cross with pebbles. The aboriginal thinks Matty has arranged the pebbles as a marker to British planes to begin nuclear testing" (*William Golding,* 66).

25. See John Pilger, *Hidden Agendas,* 234; and Jan Roberts, *Massacres to Mining: The Colonisation of Aboriginal Australia,* 47.

26. Elizabeth Maslen, *Doris Lessing,* 25.

the reach of R. D. Laing's book *The Divided Self: A Study of Sanity and Madness* that presented the schizophrenic's estrangement from reality and vulnerability to disintegration and came to be applied to society as a whole.[27] This use of the split mind as emblematic of contemporary society also lies behind Theodore Roszak's *Making of a Counter-Culture: Reflections on the Technocratic Society and Its Youthful Opposition,* in which he portrays a dominating and socially controlling technocracy that has estranged individuals from their true nature. Golding replicates the fragmented, doubled, or schizoid world of *The Four-Gated City,* giving Lessing's "Matty" a second and more extensive rebirth as Matty Septimus Windrove. In his Gothic black coat, which is reminiscent of Martha's attire in *The Four-Gated City,* Matty literally becomes a "burnt offering" (*DV,* 238)—a theme Golding borrows from Lessing.

Like Lessing and her character Martha whose "viewpoint," Ruth Whittaker argues, is one "of exile" and provides an "un-English eye" that sees "gaps and inconsistencies of which the English are unaware," Matty is an outsider and alien figure who looks with fresh eyes upon English life, its depravity, permissiveness, and descent into chaos. In a similarly fantastical presentation, both Matty and Martha experience mystical visions and engage in extrasensory perception, telepathy, and collective consciousness. Both novels end on a similar, although rather attenuated, "note of optimism."[28] *Darkness Visible* offers the survival of a mysterious Arab princeling who will "bring the spiritual language into the world" (*DV,* 239) and the fantastical redemption of Pedigree. *The Four-Gated City* ends with the "rehabilitation" of Joseph Batts, the child that Martha befriended who survives nuclear apocalypse.

Although the apocalyptic burning of the school in *Darkness Visible* is only emblematic of the fuller nuclear apocalypse of *The Four-Gated City,* it shares with Lessing's novel a concern about the threat of nuclear warfare and protest against such weaponry. In fact, there are a great many other themes or concerns shared by the two texts, not least the representation of postwar dysfunctional families in the Coldridges and Stanhopes, pointless violence and anarchy, terrorism, images of darkness and hell, references to various contemporary atrocities, sadomasochistic lifestyles, the new immigration and racialism, sexual permissiveness, homosexuality, and economic decline. In its own unfolding apocalypse, *Darkness Visible* mirrors the "vitality, confusions and contradictions of the Sixties" that

27. See ibid., 23; and Ruth Whittaker, *Doris Lessing,* 57.
28. Whittaker, *Doris Lessing,* 59.

pervade *The Four-Gated City.*[29] Indeed, the dark view of England, and indeed the world, presented in *Darkness Visible* is not surprising when we consider the social tumult that took place in the intervening twelve years since Golding's last novel, *The Pyramid.* It was a period bedeviled by a chaotic swirl of new and challenging trends, appetites, and lifestyles.

The "cultural revolution" brought several destabilizing social developments that Arthur Marwick has summarized in terms of affluence, consumerism, a "vogue" for classlessness, a preoccupation with youth, a transformation of sexual attitudes, and a more frank and explicit "permissiveness." The period saw protests against U.S. policies in Vietnam, commercialism, multinational corporate power, the oppression of women and homosexuals, and nuclear weapons. In the 1970s, when *Darkness Visible* was written, Britain suffered a rapid decline in its economic status and the collapse of consensus politics that, as Robert Hewison notes, "provoked a crisis of identity that was national, regional and social." The oil price increases of 1973 caused a worldwide recession that led to high inflation and unemployment in Britain, which in turn brought substantial cuts in public expenditure, and severe industrial unrest and social upheaval. British confidence was further eroded by Welsh, Scottish, and Northern Irish nationalism and the IRA terrorist bombing of the mainland. In 1976, 1977, and 1978, a series of riots at Notting Hill Gate Carnivals again brought home the racialist tensions that had been brewing since the immigration of black and Asian workers from the late 1940s onward, which were fueled by Enoch Powell's "rivers of blood" speech in 1968. The emergence of a more complex, disturbing society is mirrored in *Darkness Visible.* In this vortex of a novel, Golding registers the uncertainties, fragmentation, lost center, centrifugation, depthlessness, and entropy of postmodern England. He has commented that "in the second half of the twentieth century, one has no surety, no safe solid plank on which to stand: one has to drag out of one's entrails some kind of validity."[30] His examination of the lack of stable ground that remains in postmodern England and, indeed, the world at large, is complemented by the deployment of fantastic and carnivalesque modes.

In *Darkness Visible*'s "total" fantastic, we hesitate between natural and supernatural explanations of events and between what David Lodge refers to as "the obviously fictive and the apparently factual." This com-

29. Ibid., 24.

30. Marwick, *Culture in Britain,* 68–69; Hewison, *Culture and Consensus: England, Art, and Politics since 1940,* 159–60, 70, 136; Haffenden, "William Golding: An Interview," 9.

mitment to the fantastic is in keeping with the novel's postmodernist themes and concerns. From the start of the novel, Matty's status is radically unclear in a way that seems to mirror or reflect postmodernist skepticism about identity. His survival during the blitz is "improbable" (*DV,* 16), and his uncertain background, language, visions, or hallucinations problematize the novel's realism and intensify the overlap between art and life, fantasy and reality. We are never quite sure whether Matty is mad, some kind of prophet, a supernatural creation, or, indeed, a figment of Pedigree's imagination: "'There've been times when I wondered if you actually existed when no one else was looking and listening if you see what I mean'" (*DV,* 264). As an orphan, his origins are unfathomable; his face remains "strange" (*DV,* 207) or foreign, and he is nameless until the nurses treating his burns name him. This namelessness parallels Martha Quest's sense of herself as "a taste or flavour of existence without a name."[31] Furthermore, just as Martha adopts various aliases and marital names that fragment her "identity," Matty is frequently misnamed, as when Pedigree, for example, calls him "'Matty Woodgrave'" (*DV,* 212).

Matty's orphan status is, of course, intimately connected with the figure of the double in literature that is heavily used in *Darkness Visible* and that itself strongly suggests the "divided self," and by extension the divided, uncertain, schizoid quality to society that seems so much a part of postindustrial or late-capitalist postmodern life and, as Terry Eagleton has noted, its artifactual productions. Karl Miller remarks: "Where the double is, the orphan is never far away." Together, Matty's orphan status and the pervasive use of the double motif add to the postmodern mood of uncertainty captured in *Darkness Visible.* As Miller notes: "The double stands at the start of that cultivation of uncertainty by which the literature of the modern world has come to be distinguished, and has yet to be expelled from it." This "cultivation of uncertainty" and "multiplicity" through the use of the double, Miller points out, has been deployed in the deconstructive strategies of theorists such as Jacques Derrida who "has claimed for literary texts an uncertainty that derives from their employment of words with a double or undecidable meaning—words like Plato's *Pharmakon,* which could mean either poison or cure." Thus, Miller sees deconstruction, so much at the core of postmodern philosophizing, as "an entertainment of duality."[32]

The double or duality pervades *Darkness Visible,* in what Kevin McCarron

31. Lessing, *The Four-Gated City,* 27.
32. K. Miller, *Doubles: Studies in Literary History,* 39, viii, 434, 22, 417.

refers to as the "coincidence of opposites" and what Bernard Dick calls a "yoking of opposites." This doubleness extends to the characters and the fictional form of the novel. Hesitation between supernatural and natural explanations, the copresence of the "high" and carnivalesque "low," "good" and "evil," and the perennial and the present ensure that nearly everything about or concerning Matty is split or divided. The doubleness and even greater division and fragmentation that he experiences in front of mirrors in Hanrahan's house resembles a similar double or mirror motif in *The Four-Gated City* when Martha and the schizophrenic Lynda discuss difficulties of self-recognition in mirror images. Matty has a "bicoloured" face, "split personality," and a "bicameral or double brain" and is caught between madness and rationality, the material and the spiritual. Even his sexuality is ambivalent or hermaphroditic, caught as it is between the "two scales" of love for Miss Aylen and Mr. Pedigree (*DV,* 49). There are various permutations of doubled or paired characters in *Darkness Visible,* such as Matty and Sophy, Sophy and Toni, Matty and Pedigree, Edwin and Edwina Bell, Edwin and Sim Goodchild, Mrs. Appleby and Mrs. Allenby. These pairings add to the theme of doubling where, as Dick notes, "everyone is halved because everyone is someone else's double."[33] The characters Edwin and Edwina Bell, who dress and even talk the same, perhaps owe something to Charles Dickens's treatment of the double in *The Mystery of Edwin Drood* (1870).[34] As Peter Ackroyd notices, this novel "is concerned with the nature of the divided life and the dual personality." In *Darkness Visible,* Edwin and Edwina are so alike that they have a "kind of transvestite appearance simply by reference to each other" (*DV,* 197). As noted earlier, Lodge maintains that this kind of hermaphroditic emblem, which was featured earlier in *Free Fall,* is often employed in postmodernist writing. Golding has surely been influenced by the vast number of writers on duality, not least Joseph Conrad in *The Secret Sharer* (1912). Philip Redpath compares Matty with Lumb in Ted Hughes's *Gaudete* (1977) since both may be seen as divided selves, existing in the spiritual domain, with a doppelgänger in the physical world. Whereas Redpath sees the targets of both Golding and Hughes as rationalism and reductionism, I consider this antirationalism to be integral to Golding's examination of postmodernism.[35]

Ultimately, the seriousness of Matty's spiritual mission, and, indeed,

33. Dick, *William Golding* (1987), 98, 100, 96.
34. See K. Miller, *Doubles,* 183.
35. Ackroyd, *Dickens,* 1051; see Redpath, *Structural Reading,* 165–69, 176–77.

religious authority in a broader sense, is deflated by the farcical miracles, visions, spiritual tasks, and preparations that he undergoes. He is visited by absurd spirits whom Redpath finds reminiscent of the ghosts of Quint and Miss Jessel in Henry James's *Turn of the Screw* (1898).[36] Indeed, Gothic imagery is featured widely in *Darkness Visible*, further interrogating the borders between reality and fantasy. There are Gothic curses, environments such as the almost Piranesian Frankley's where Matty works for a time, objects or contraptions such as "forgotten passageways" (*DV*, 40), murder, death, hell, devils, nightmares, deformity, incarceration, madness, and sadistic fantasies and actions. Such Gothicisms extend the quality of uncertainty or instability into the dark, "evil," or inhuman sphere. This "inhuman sphere" gravitates toward the sadistic Sophy who fantastically perceives auras, practices nightmare-inducing weirdness to break up her father's relationship with Winnie, fantasizes about incarcerating her, and displays, as we shall see later, a passion for bondagelike torture. Complete with preternatural eyes "in the back of her head" that "stared into a darkness that stretched away infinitely, a cone of black light" (*DV*, 134), Sophy achieves almost demonic status and intensifies the unstable postmodern "reality" represented in *Darkness Visible.*

Fantastic instability continues in part 3 with Edwin Bell's attempt to convert the rationalist Sim Goodchild to Matty's vague spiritual mission. Initially, Sim is not convinced by the trivial miracles that Edwin is keen to point out, such as Pedigree's ball appearing literally to pass through the feet of Matty, or his mysterious "disappearance" with Pedigree behind the park's toilets. Yet for all his skepticism, the more plausible explanations of phenomena are disrupted by his mystical experience during a seance with Matty and Edwin at Stanhope's stables when the "barrier" or "partition" between physical and spiritual worlds appears to break down (*DV*, 234). Phenomenological instability continues with the fantastical burning figure of Matty—the "burnt offering"—who saves the possibly Messianic Arab princeling, and in Matty's ghostly, transfigured, and equivocal appearance to Pedigree who dies at the end of the novel.

The carnivalesque in *Darkness Visible* both advances the fantastic's evocation of the uncertainties of the postmodern condition and reveals the low and often cruel aspects of postwar English life. John Docker suggests that the carnivalesque both influences and mirrors the "exuberance, range, excess, internationalism, and irrepressible vigour and inventiveness" of twentieth-century mass culture.[37] In terms of uncertainty, the in-

36. Redpath, *Structural Reading*, 49.
37. Docker, *Postmodernism and Popular Culture*, 185.

verted world of the carnivalesque alongside the fantastic reflects postmodern heterogeneity and relativity. This "inverted world" is signaled by the novel's epigraph from Virgil's *Aeneid* that suggests *Darkness Visible* presents a kind of journey into the underworld.[38] The underworld that is featured in Mikhail Bakhtin's *menippea* marks a journey into lower, diabolic appetites and behavior. Such imagery is perfectly suited for Golding's representation of a depraved, labyrinthine postmodern England.

Matty is a carnivalesque Holy Fool, outcast, "butt" or grotesque (*DV,* 22), literal-minded "clown" (*DV,* 100). His "highminded" religiosity contrasts with "lowmindedness" (*DV,* 23) and is severely mocked during his journey to the "other side of the world" (*DV,* 115) when Harry Bummer farcically "crucifies" him and attacks his genitalia. A similar attack on "low" genitalia occurs when Mrs. Appleby and Mrs. Allenby attempt to maim Pedigree—reflecting, perhaps, the upsurge of 1960s homophobia. The antipodean theme, which is repeated in Golding's *To the Ends of the Earth,* and a wide range of other topsy-turvy imagery are employed in the novel. For example, Matty sees "the moon on its head" (*DV,* 56), a photograph depicts Lieutenant Masterman "caught upside-down in mid-air" (*DV,* 168), and Sophy, waiting on the towpath for the kidnapped boy, looks out at "the downs up there all a-glimmer under" (*DV,* 249). This "world upside down" complements the portrayal of postwar fragmentation in *Darkness Visible.* However, its more prominent function is to reveal the dark, perverse underside of contemporary English life.

In contrast to the fantastical, religious visions of Matty—however contradictory they are at times—carnivalesque consumption and transgression, particularly of a sexual nature, mirror 1960s "permissiveness." This transgression is most strongly presented in the pedophilic appetites of Sophy and Pedigree, but even the more mainstream character Sim Goodchild is portrayed as having once lusted after the Stanhope children. Sophy and Pedigree gravitate toward a lavatorial world of obsessive sex. Here the juxtaposition of diverse sexualities and scatology makes visible a squalid, taboo-breaking, dirty side to green-fielded England with its mask of civilized mores. Only Matty offers a symbolic resistance to scatologized "permissiveness." Unlike Pedigree and Sophy, Matty battles against the lower body and its proximity to dung: "I do not use a toilet often since I have given up so much of my earthly living" (*DV,* 97). The promiscuous Sophy casually rids herself of virginity and begins uninhibited, self-abusive, self-hating, and violent sexual experiments, stabbing Roland with a suitably dirty knife in order to achieve orgasm. Her extreme

38. Dick, *William Golding* (1987), 98, 99.

appetite is registered in images of her open, consuming mouth and her sadistic appetite for boys whom she finds "edible" (*DV,* 176). Like Christopher Martin, she is "metamorphosed into pure mouth."[39] Watching a schoolboy, she muses: *"Lovely my pet! I could eat you!"* (*DV,* 176). She wallows in the "dirty excitement" of sex (*DV,* 130), and the functions of her sexual body are all brought low in scatological imagery, from her period "stink" (*DV,* 131) and postcoital douching of "the mess of blood and spunk" (*DV,* 138) to feeling "her own turd" (*DV,* 138) lying behind the wall of her vagina. Scatology deepens our sense of perverted sex when Sophy fantasizes about incarcerating the Arab princeling in a stinking barge and killing him while she holds his "tiny wet cock in her hand" (*DV,* 252).

Sophy's desire for *"outrage"* (*DV,* 167) and anarchy is intimately connected with the novel's "sombre playing on the notion of entropy, and a civilisation running down at a rate of knots." Robert Alter locates this concept of entropy in much postmodern U.S. fiction.[40] In a context of the decline of the English economy and the world of books, Sophy yearns for "endless running down" (*DV,* 156) into the "mystery and confusion" (*DV,* 172) signified by radio hiss. Speaking to her father, she sees her dysfunctional family with its nonconventional sexual relationships as the result of postwar entropy and fragmentation: "'You, Mummy, Toni, me—we're not the way people used to be. It's part of the whole running down.' 'Entropy.' 'You don't even care enough about us to hate us, do you?'" (*DV,* 185).

While Golding is a long way from Mary Whitehouse's agenda, he evinces the widely felt anxiety that 1960s liberalism undermined the family and marriage. His "indictment" of contemporary English life, particularly through a damning representation of selfish, sometimes sadistic sexuality, can perhaps be seen as somewhat reactionary. He seems to be among those who suffer what Jonathan Dollimore calls "a general anxiety and sometimes hysteria over 'permissiveness' and the alleged breakdown of law and order."[41] Again, Golding presents subordinate or marginal sexualities in a contradictory way. On the one hand, his inclusion of homoerotic, pedophilic, and sadistic desires in the novel, and particularly the sympathy extended to Pedigree by Matty, may advance "sexual dissidence," yet these aspects are used satirically to evoke postwar moral decline in England. We suspect that Golding had deep misgivings about the

39. Ibid., 106.
40. Webb, "Golding Goes Down," 12; Alter, *Partial Magic,* 143.
41. Dollimore, "The Challenge of Sexuality," 81.

unchecked forces of liberalization that during the 1970s appeared to reap political, economic, and social crises that, at times, had cataclysmic or apocalyptic status. His instantiation of the sexually permissive Sophy as a totalitarian personality is particularly damning of such liberalism.

In Sophy, Golding appears to widen his critique of the English totalitarian personality by extending "soldier-male" behavior to women, building upon the more cursory presentation of an English totalitarian woman in the child-torturing Miss Pringle in *Free Fall.* Sophy is represented as looking "monstrous," sporting a "Hitlerian moustache of shadow" and "cap" (*DV,* 243). Here she reminds us of Jack in *Lord of the Flies,* not least with the suggestion of the infamous cap of the SS. Like her inhuman or "not human" (*DV,* 261) sister, Toni, Sophy has an aggressive attitude toward immigrants. In *Darkness Visible,* Golding evokes not only the widespread racial tension and intolerance shown toward the new Commonwealth immigrants who came to Britain during the 1950s and 1960s, and the growth of neofascist movements after the war, in particular the National Front (formed in 1967), but also the involvement of women in such radical politics. Golding may have had in mind women such as Françoise Dior who was sentenced in 1968 for conspiring to burn down a synagogue. Richard Thurlow argues that the influx of Commonwealth immigrants helped to keep "fascism" alive and well in Britain, where the "migratory flow of labour" fueled "nativist resentment over fears of economic competition, housing shortages and cultural clashes" and led to violence in the Nottingham and Notting Hill riots of 1958 and racialist attacks in Birmingham, Liverpool, Deptford, and Camden Town. The National Front, along with other groups such as the British National Party, the Greater British Movement, and the National Socialist Movement, spearheaded these attacks and generated propaganda against immigrant populations. Immigrants increasingly faced the "sporadic terrorism" of militant fascists who viewed them as "swamping" the English culture. As we saw in chapter 3, Golding considered these racialist attacks as evidence that Nazism was not just a German phenomenon. He also seems to consider postmodern chaos and relativity as favorable to totalitarian or fascist politics and behavior. Indeed, more recently, Terry Eagleton has argued that postmodernism's "distaste for ideas of solidarity and disciplined organization" and "its lack of any adequate theory of political agency" could leave the doors open for future fascisms.[42]

42. Thurlow, *Fascism in Britain,* 270, 242, 243, 287, 289; Eagleton, *The Illusions of Postmodernism,* 134.

In his portrayal of fascist responses to the immigrant "swamping" of English life, Golding resumes his attack on an English national identity that constructs itself in opposition to Nazism. Throughout the novel there are frequent references to the multicultural status of Greenfield, that Thames-based microcosmic England, where new mosques replace traditional churches that appear to be in terminal decline and new immigrant businesses such as Subadar Singh's Gent's Best Suiting "invade" the high street. Indeed, a postwar decline in church attendance, and increasing secularization of English society alongside the establishment of typically non-English religions, may well have influenced Golding's perennial questioning of religious authority both in *Darkness Visible* and elsewhere across his fiction. Certainly, *Darkness Visible* evokes an uncomfortable diversity of competing religious perspectives and authorities. Both Matty and Sim Goodchild show discomfort with Islam and its apparent disruption of English Christian heritage and authority. In fact, Sim's discomfort is such that Edwin asks him: "'Has the Front been getting at you?'" (*DV*, 203). Although Sim finds the question obscene and wishes to distance himself from extreme racialist views, he does show intolerance and prejudice: "Get a Paki, a lad, he'd work. Have to keep an eye on him though. *Don't* think that! Race relations. All the same they swarm. With the best will in the world I must say they swarm" (*DV*, 218).

But this level of intolerance finds its base in more mainstream and conservative anxiety about the state of England and is nothing compared to the aggressive neofascism of Sophy and her twin sister, Toni. Although narrative point of view is complicated in the novel, whenever we seem to be viewing events from the perspective of the Stanhope twins, black and Asian men are deemed to be lascivious or threatening. When Sophy joins Gerry's gang she persuades them to hold-up "Paki shops" and enjoys the threats to shoot them or bomb their businesses. Like her sadistic "mock murder" of the Arab princeling (*DV*, 252), the burning of the school for the children of rich immigrants may be read in terms of neofascist racialist violence. As Thurlow notes, much neofascist violence in England by militant groups such as the National Socialist Movement involved firebomb attacks.[43]

The breakdown of consensus politics during the 1970s gave extremist groups such as the National Front the oxygen they needed to grow in membership and influence. Immigrants were persistently and increasingly framed as criminals or potential muggers, and subject to flagrant

43. See Thurlow, *Fascism in Britain*, 270.

misuse of the Vagrancy Act by police.[44] Golding hints at this when he describes how the black man who had followed Sophy home after a dance runs off at the sight of a police car. The black "mugger" became a media fixation, as Michael Brake has argued: "The mugger, according to the media, was part of 'un-British' youth, a product of black immigration, part of the menacing, 'dangerous classes' gathering in the gloom of the collapse of the British Empire." Robert Hewison has linked the growing right-wing extremism and racism of the 1970s with "the growing popularity of romanticised versions of pastoralism and 'heritage' as an embodiment of Englishness." In the 1970s, "[t]he idea that Britain's heritage—and therefore a significant element in national identity—was in danger proved a resonant theme." The threat to national identity and its heritage is certainly reflected in *Darkness Visible,* particularly in terms of both U.S. mass media and new Commonwealth immigration, but also in the beginnings of an awareness about the "heritage industry" as a right-wing response or buffer to the perceived loss of Englishness. The reference to the pub the Copper Kettle, with "its fake eighteenth-century furniture and fake horse-brasses" (*DV,* 168), seems to show this. It is a theme dealt with more forthrightly in other British fiction such as Angus Wilson's *No Laughing Matter* (1967) and Ian McEwan's film script *The Ploughman's Lunch* (1985). In Wilson's *No Laughing Matter,* Marcus comments: "Everyone said the English and Americans would want a French name, but I risked Plantagenet and it worked. All those old queens in wimples made such wonderful advertisements." According to Andrzej Gąsiorek, this "reads now as a prophetic comment on the way the heritage industry packages history." He argues: "Recycling images from a glorious history that is as fabricated as the Edwardian daydream with which the novel begins, Marcus self-consciously evokes a noble past solely in order to promote sales."[45] McEwan's screenplay *The Ploughman's Lunch* attacks the Thatcherite remotivation of past history and memory to suit its right-wing politics. It reveals British "infatuation" with lies, myths, and "manufactured images."[46] This is neatly headlined in Matthew's revelation of the spurious "heritage" of the "Ploughman's Lunch": "In fact it's the invention of an advertising campaign they ran in the early sixties to encourage

44. See Hewison, *Culture and Consensus,* 162–64; and Paul Gilroy, *There Ain't No Black in the Union Jack: The Cultural Politics of Race and Nation.*

45. Brake, *Comparative Youth Culture: The Sociology of Youth Cultures and Youth Subcultures in America, Britain, and Canada,* 69; Hewison, *Culture and Consensus,* 165, 92; A. Wilson, *No Laughing Matter,* 461–62; Gąsiorek, *Post-War British Fiction,* 107.

46. See Kiernan Ryan, *Ian McEwan,* 45.

people to eat in pubs. A completely successful fabrication of the past, the Ploughman's Lunch was."[47]

Golding, then, taps into a wide range of destabilizing social developments in postmodern England, not least those arising from cultural pluralism and extreme right-wing responses to what is seen as a threat to English "heritage." Yet perhaps the most "destabilizing" postwar development represented in *Darkness Visible* is the intense consumerism and mass communications of television, radio, magazines, and newspapers that, Robert Hewison maintains, "contributed to the notion that Britain was undergoing perpetual and perilous change, where former conceptions of authority and social value were being challenged."[48] Such cultural destabilization, influenced by U.S. mass media, brought hostility from the Frankfurt School, particularly from Max Horkheimer and Theodor W. Adorno, in *Dialectic of Enlightenment,* who viewed the "culture industry" as a dominating force, as did Herbert Marcuse in his book *One-Dimensional Man.*

In Britain, the influence of U.S. mass media was attacked by F. R. Leavis, Richard Hoggart, and Raymond Williams who feared that the "long front of culture . . . could fragment into a rootless pluralism."[49] Of course, as a former teacher Golding would have been acutely aware of the Leavisite-led backlash in schools against popular mass-media culture in the 1960s and 1970s, and certainly on the evidence of *Darkness Visible,* he appears to be anxious about the damage popular mass media may exert not just on the world of literature but on wider society as well. Perhaps he too suspects that popular writing, music, and film manipulate public opinion, keep people superficially happy, and prevent them seeking political change.[50] Guy Debord's *Society of the Spectacle,* like Jean Baudrillard's *Simulacra and Simulation,* highlights the way that the "spectacle" or hyperreality neutralizes political dissent. In *Darkness Visible,* the decline of books and print with the advent of the "culture industry" reflects contemporary concerns that new instantaneously transmitted, depthless, and dominative multimedia images would replace literature and serious art. Golding says that "just as bad money drives out good so inferior culture drives out superi-

47. McEwan, *A Move Abroad; or "Shall We Die?" and "The Ploughman's Lunch,"* 106–7.

48. Hewison, *Culture and Consensus,* 127.

49. Ibid., 157. See F. R. Leavis, *Two Cultures? The Significance of C. P. Snow;* Richard Hoggart, *The Uses of Literacy: Aspects of Working-Class Life with Special Reference to Publications and Entertainments;* and R. Williams, *Britain in the Sixties: Communications.*

50. See Max Horkheimer and Theodor W. Adorno, *Dialectic of Enlightenment,* 120–67.

or" (*HG,* 132). The deflation of serious art, of course, is not unique to the new entertainments. As *Darkness Visible* suggests in its evocation of *The Dunciad,* dullness and poor writing were perpetuated by the invention of printing. Here, Golding draws attention to the long-standing struggle between "inferior" and "superior" literature that finds its latest flash point with the arrival of the "culture industry."

While Golding may in some sense concur with Marshall McLuhan's attack upon the Gutenberg typography for promoting "detribalization," individualism, linearity, or uniformity and for closing down the "human voice," he does not see in the new age of electronic media the means of overcoming these difficulties by a new interdependence of a polyphonic or dialogical "global" tribe. In *Understanding Media,* McLuhan charted the effects of different media on human perception and social organization, and, drawing on Teilhard de Chardin's "noosphere" in *Phenomenon of Man,* endorsed the electronic media's potential for unifying the world as a "global village."[51] In *Darkness Visible,* the new mass-media postmodern world is not given a utopian spin. The novel presents an anxiety about it, rather than McLuhanist celebration of it. For Golding, it coheres into a more pessimistic network—a kind of "global hell."

In *Darkness Visible,* a totalitarian, popular mass media is linked to the unwelcome decline of the book and entropy in general. Golding mixes the confusion of Matty's perceptions with the whole production of media gone mad, creating a snapshot record of postwar life in England between the 1940s and 1970s. He maps the spread of radios, televisions, pop music, cinemas, and computers. Even Matty's spirits seem to present computer-generated texts "faster than newspapers being printed" (*DV,* 90). Sophy fritters away her time listening to white noise on her radio and watching television "indifferently" (*DV,* 141). England appears drugged by "great newspaper stories of hideous happenings that kept the whole country entranced for weeks at a time" (*DV,* 147). This is emphasized in the media coverage following the terrorist attack on the school, when the seance is shown or discussed "'every newstime, every special report, every radio programme'" (*DV,* 261). Mass media coverage is presented as unrelenting and regurgitated. Whereas the media revolution is portrayed as the advent of "inferior" culture, metafictional aspects of the novel reveal that language itself, and the printed word or book, may be inherently or severely limited.

51. McLuhan, *The Gutenberg Galaxy: The Making of Typographic Man,* 250; McLuhan, *Understanding Media,* passim.

Paradoxically, Golding attacks postmodernism and postmodernity by using postmodern techniques such as metafiction that achieve an awkward, deeply unsatisfying narrative. The dense, labyrinthine, farcical novel *Darkness Visible* not only represents postmodern England as descending further and further into apocalyptic chaos but also achieves through its formal failure the status of being a literary symptom of such a collapse. Thus, Golding does not employ postmodern techniques in a chic, fashionable way in the novel, but rather reveals how their excess can lead to an unfortunate logjam of competing interpretations and narratological collapse rather than any balanced scrutiny of epistemological difficulties.

In *Darkness Visible,* postmodernity is envisioned as noncelebratory, dark, and chaotic. It is as if Golding's literary art has been unavoidably infected by postmodern arch-relativism to the point that he delivers, at a formal level, a deformed novel that he does not want to talk about. As such, *Darkness Visible* can be seen as a kind of "frontier" novel or apprentice piece that allowed him to indulge in postmodern techniques to the point of failure before accommodating them in more comical, playful, and ultimately less disruptive ways in his later narratives. In *The Paper Men,* Golding is still hostile, caricatural, and apocalyptic in his representation of postmodernity, but as with *To the Ends of the Earth,* we sense greater accommodation of its ludic possibilities. In these later works, Golding seems to loosen his left-wing humanist hostility to postmodernity and engage in a less pessimistic deployment of "playful" postmodern techniques.

The metafictional aspects of *Darkness Visible* are related to the late-modernist experimentalism of *Pincher Martin, Free Fall,* and *The Spire,* yet are now part of a later evocation of postmodern indeterminacy. Books with their "whole store of frozen speech" and "physical reduplication of that endless cackle of men" (*DV,* 47), bookshops, and booksellers dominate the novel. From the outset, language, communication, and interpretative difficulty are central themes in this pervasively self-conscious novel as they are in postmodernist fiction generally. Matty, for whom spoken words had been "awful passages of pain" (*DV,* 18) on account of his burn injuries, grows beyond a literalist approach to the Bible to a preference for the "wordless communication" that he had always suspected as being superior to the "dissociated traffic" (*DV,* 18) of language or what Edwin scatologically refers to as "'logorrhoea'" (*DV,* 204). Throughout the novel, the frail authority of the printed word is highlighted. Ironically, in his mission to "'get rid of language'" (*DV,* 199), Matty approaches those most dependent on it for their livelihoods: Edwin Bell and Sim Goodchild. Whereas Sim finds this onslaught on language silly and misguided, Edwin champions what seems to be a desire to turn upside down the modern world of signs gone mad: "'Precisely at that point you are invited to make a huge sacrifice that would stand our world on their—on its—head—the deliberate turning away from the recorded word, printed, radioed, televized, taped, disced—'" (*DV,* 200). Paradoxically, roles are reversed toward the end of the novel when Edwin insists on writing a book that gets to the "'truth'" about events surrounding Matty and the kidnap attempt, while Sim scoffs at the possibility of achieving "'History'": "'No one will *ever* know what happened. There's too much of it, too many people, a sprawling series of events that break apart under their own weight'" (*DV,* 258).

This comment summarizes the overall form of *Darkness Visible* as a difficult, complex, fragmented text, not least in its confused narration. The novel mirrors concern with the "power and complexity of language" and Bakhtinian multivoicedness that Elizabeth Maslen locates in Doris Lessing's work. According to Bernard Dick, *Darkness Visible* shows preoccupations with language similar to those in the work of Iris Murdoch, Tom Stoppard, and John Barth. Furthermore, its "multiplicity of meaning" or "polysemous structure" spawns a weakened "narrative foundation" and can be thought of as "a meditation on moral relativism." It is a "moral relativism" that we might, like Zygmunt Bauman, consider to be at the heart of postmodernism. Certainly, Kevin McCarron has picked up on this postmodern relativism or "denial of distinctions," or what he later calls the "coincidence of opposites."[52]

The grim facts of Britain's social, political, and economic decline became painfully obvious in the so-called winter of discontent of 1978–1979, just prior to the publication of *Darkness Visible.* Britain, like other Western democracies, appeared to be suffering from a changing, fragmented world economic order, increasingly driven by multinational companies, and fused with new consumerism and mass media, rather than old-style capitalist production. Daniel Bell's postindustrial society appeared to offer as yet newly unfolding, and therefore unsettling, social and economic structures. Golding, of course, stands among a diverse body of writers such as John Fowles, Donald Barthelme, John Barth, Robert Coover, Thomas Pynchon, Richard Brautigan, William Burroughs, and Christine Brooke-Rose, all of whom were influenced in varying degrees by the pervasive mood of uncertainty as postindustrial elided into the postmodern. In the late 1960s to middle 1970s, some fiction, such as Angela Carter's *Magic Toyshop*

52. Maslen, *Doris Lessing,* 1–2; Dick, *William Golding* (1987), 97–98, 109; see Bauman, *Life in Fragments: Essays in Postmodern Morality;* McCarron, *William Golding,* 43.

(1968), Martin Amis's *Dead Babies* (1975), and Ian McEwan's short stories in *First Love, Last Rites* (1975), reflected the "fantasy, eroticism and personal violence released by the counter-culture."[53] Like these, *Darkness Visible* taps into the frank, explicit "squalor and shock" that seemed so much part of the counterculture and the unfolding of postmodernity.

To summarize then, the fantastic and carnivalesque in *Darkness Visible* have various functions. A major function of these modes is to complement an examination of postmodernism through its nonconfrontational creation of "world upside down." The combination of this versatile, darkly playful fantastic and carnivalesque also attacks contemporary English life. Core targets of this attack are English totalitarian personalities, focusing here on female representatives such as Sophy and Toni who immerse themselves in carnivalesque exclusion of the "Other," violence, sexual consumption, and greed. On its own, the fantastic also registers the horror of recent atrocities, and attacks Britain's acquiescence in U.S. policies in Vietnam and its willingness to test and stockpile nuclear warheads. The novel marks a strong return to fiction dealing with contemporary life. Unlike *The Spire*, which marked a "cowardly" escape from the contemporary, and *The Pyramid*, in which the twentieth-century setting is little more than a backdrop, Golding chooses, in *Darkness Visible*, to "pull up [his] . . . socks and write about life as it is at the moment."[54] In taking a critical and hostile angle of view on postmodernity and postmodern depthlessness, he chooses deliberately to employ postmodern techniques to run his own novel into the ground, as it were—to construct a failing work. As such, *Darkness Visible* becomes a visible sign of Golding's struggle to write fiction in an age that so radically calls into question the significance of fiction and its truth-telling powers. It marks his own "rite of passage" as a writer into the more playful and overtly tragicomic fiction of *The Paper Men* and *To the Ends of the Earth*. However, even here, as we shall see, comedy is for Golding only ever a facade that lies over deep epistemological concern and anxiety in the late twentieth century.

The Paper Men

In *The Paper Men*, published five years after *Darkness Visible*, reference to contemporary atrocity is less pronounced and includes only brief, isolated references to D day, Churchillian "fighting on the beaches," the

53. Hewison, *Too Much*, 256.
54. Haffenden, "William Golding: An Interview," 12.

Holocaust, "the soughing of shells" (*PM,* 87), nuclear explosion, and Tucker wearing a "swastika the right way round" (*PM,* 177), all of which, perhaps, emphasize the destructiveness that rippled out from World War II into cultural life. But *The Paper Men* seems a long way from Golding's revisiting of contemporary atrocity in *Darkness Visible.* Despite this, the portrayal of English totalitarian personalities continues with Lucinda, who resembles Sophy, and whom Barclay considers to be "very nearly the last relic of the BUF" (*PM,* 51), a fascist organization that drew substantial numbers of women into its ranks.[55] If only in a token way, Golding again appears to moderate his heretofore wholehearted linking of the "totalitarian personality" with "soldier-male" masculinity. However, the representation of English totalitarian woman in Lucinda is overshadowed by the novel's central character, Wilf Barclay, whose misogyny, cruelty, greed, and "exoskeletal" nature replicate to some extent the "soldier-male" personality of "Pincher" Martin and Sammy Mountjoy. That said, the dominant function of satire in *The Paper Men* is something quite new to Golding's fiction. Rather than attacking contemporary manifestations of English Nazism in relation to new immigration as *Darkness Visible* does, the fantastic and carnivalesque modes in *The Paper Men* achieve a blunderbuss satire against "paper men," who are depthlessly part of literary production and criticism in postmodern America and England. Their presentation as "totalitarian" types aids this attack, and perhaps suggests Golding has concerns that the "culture industry" and postmodern uncertainty are favorable to right-wing or fascist desires. The modes also continue to complement an examination of the themes and concerns of postmodernism as they do in *Darkness Visible* and the later amalgam of novels, *To the Ends of the Earth.* However, increasingly in *The Paper Men* and the "sea trilogy," unlike his tortured work, *Darkness Visible,* Golding appears to deploy postmodern techniques in a more comical, lighthearted, and genuinely ludic fashion.

The Paper Men achieves a parodic version of Goethe's *Faust* (1808–1832), in which Rick L. Tucker, an American assistant professor of English literature, desperately pursues the clownish novelist Wilfred Barclay in an attempt to become his official biographer.[56] Backed by Halliday, a mysterious, devilish businessman, Tucker tempts Barclay to give up his "life"

55. Thurlow estimates that middle-class women accounted for 20 percent or more of the membership of the BUF (*Fascism in Britain,* 143–44).

56. In the end, however, as Gindin notes, "the application of Faustian metaphor or drama quickly breaks down, for it is impossible, in any meaningful way, to distinguish tempter from victim, Devil from man, corrupted from corruptible" (*William Golding,* 82).

to him. But Barclay goes on the run from the would-be biographer. As Barclay dodges across Europe, a slave to drink and his own grubby passions, he appears more and more grotesque. He plays victim to Tucker's relentless pursuit, but Barclay's ego cannot fail to enjoy all the attention. In the blur of alcoholism, he enters a mad, fantastical state that culminates in a stroke-induced vision of a red-eyed Christ or Pluto figure. At his wife's funeral, he presents his Christlike stigmata to the vicar only to be thought of in terms of one of the crucified thieves. When Barclay eventually decides to burn all his papers and deny Tucker the sought-after biography by writing it himself, Tucker shoots him dead. Tucker literally brings about a Barthesian "death of the author," but the farcical author, Wilfred Barclay, is the kind of writer that we feel deserves such annihilation.[57] The "death of the author" theme runs throughout the text, with Barclay, at one point, dreaming that Tucker is pursuing him in a hearse and the suggestion that one day his image would join those of dead belletrists hanging on the wall of the Random Club.

Don Crompton accurately maintains that *The Paper Men* "might be read as a passionate repudiation of a system that wants to elevate writers to a kind of priesthood, to find in their flawed gospels and the oracles of their interviews keys to the universe, or instructions for us all to live by" and of the "whole Eng. Lit. industry, wastefully devoted to discussions of ludicrous or insignificant aspects of literature." However, he does not indicate exactly *how* Golding achieves this attack by deploying fantastic and carnivalesque modes. More broadly, Golding's attack on literary criticism raised the hackles of some, like Bernard Dick, who rather defensively calls *The Paper Men* "misdirected revenge." Yet Kevin McCarron contests any simple notion of *The Paper Men* as a "vicious attack on literary criticism and critics." He says: "Paradoxically, and ingeniously . . . Golding actually agrees with several of the most contentious theories advanced by post-war literary criticism, particularly the notion that there is no significant difference between 'creative' writing and 'critical' writing; there is only a discourse that, in its entirety, can be called 'literary' and that the author's traditional and previously unquestioned authority over the critic is finished." As McCarron argues, *The Paper Men* "celebrates the death of the author."[58]

57. See Roland Barthes, *Image Music Text,* 142–48. The "death of the author" scene appears to reverse Golding's earlier championing of authorial intention when the critic is described as being "on the receiving end" of the author's "shooting." See Biles, *Talk,* 53.

58. Crompton, *View from the Spire,* 164, 169; Dick, *William Golding* (1987), 133; McCarron, *William Golding,* 45–46.

In *The Paper Men,* Golding appears to be reacting in a crude way to the media image of what was happening with English literature in the early 1980s, when, as Peter Widdowson notes, there was a "crisis" about "what should constitute an "'English' syllabus."[59] This crisis first showed its face at Oxford in 1980 and then most publicly with the Colin MacCabe affair at Cambridge in 1981 that sparked heated and, at times, hysterical debate about what had happened to English literature.[60] At the heart of this "crisis" was a "growing debate amongst radical critics about the value of 'Literature'; about the principles by which we evaluate different literary productions; and, indeed, about the validity of the category 'Literature' itself." The "Cambridge English debate" reiterated "the centrality of the 'canon' and the need ultimately to dispense with the distractions of history and theory in order to return to the unproblematic *reality* of the 'literary works themselves.'" In light of this, Widdowson predicted an uphill struggle between progressive, theoretical approaches and "establishment" or "conventional" criticism that propounds "common-sense" notions of literary "value."[61]

The Paper Men keeps company with other English fiction satirizing the world of academe and literary criticism, such as Malcolm Bradbury's *History Man* and David Lodge's *Changing Places* and *Small World. The History Man* is a possible intertext for *The Paper Men,* not simply on account of its similar title, but in its satirical attack upon new radical academics who challenge liberal humanist traditions, and in its tragicomic view of contemporary history. Furthermore, both *The History Man* and *The Paper Men* are not merely antagonistic toward this new wave of theoretical enthusiasm but also question liberal humanist values and the authority of the creative writer. Bradbury declares that apart from the portrait of Howard Kirk, a Marxist sociology professor, as a loathsome character, he also "had it in for everybody else as well . . . including myself as novelist."[62] *The Paper Men,* however, engages more clearly with the threat posed to the authority of the creative writer by new, radical literary criticism that, as Bryan Appleyard notes, took center stage from the early 1960s onward: "The artist appeared to be losing the initiative. The ambitions and pretensions of the critical theorists suggested that analysis was taking over

59. Widdowson, "Introduction: The Crisis in English Studies," 1.
60. See Alan Jenkins, "The Cambridge Debate, Continued"; R. Williams, "Cambridge English, Past and Present," in *Writing in Society,* 177–91; and R. Williams, "Crisis in English Studies," in *Writing in Society,* 192–211.
61. Widdowson, "Introduction," 2, 4, 6–7.
62. John Haffenden, *Novelists in Interview,* 36.

the task of art. Beneath the hard gaze of structuralism, to be an artist was of no more significance than to be a writer of advertising copy or a railway worker."[63]

Golding has frequently shown, if not a distaste for literary criticism, then a wariness about any conclusions it may draw. This is particularly so in terms of the newer radical and theoretical criticism that came with structuralism and Marxism. Golding was quite familiar, of course, with the world of the university and, at times, took delight in making gibes against literary critical approaches, not least structuralism: "I was a structuralist at the age of seven, which is about the right age for it" (*MT,* 160). This disdain of critics, particularly those engaged in structuralism, is reflected in *The Paper Men,* where Tucker's conference paper on Barclay's use of relative clauses is presented as deceitful and jaw-breakingly dull, and a female acquaintance is dismissed as a "structuralist to boot" (*PM,* 19). Barclay again seems to reflect something of Golding's antagonism toward critics when he celebrates the fact that despite "being an ignorant sod with little Latin and less Greek, adept in several broken languages and far more deeply read in bad books than good ones, I have a knack. Academics had to admit that in the last analysis I was what they were about" (*PM,* 21).

Barclay, and we suspect Golding, views the critical process of understanding "wholeness by tearing it into separate pieces" (*PM,* 25) and source hunting as both limited and comparable to "'Vivisection'" (*PM,* 45). The title of Tucker's project, "Wilfred Barclay, a Source Book" (*PM,* 101), may well be a gibe at one of the earliest critical books on Golding, Nelson's *William Golding's "Lord of the Flies": A Source Book.* In his essay "Gradus ad Parnassum," Golding is scathing about the academic influence on the literary world, particularly through creative writing courses and writer-in-residence schemes (*HG,* 152–53). In *A Moving Target,* he illustrates how his work has become "the raw material of an academic light industry," and, though flattered, he has found critical inquiries overstated, tiresome, or burdensome, especially from postgraduates "in search of a thesis" (*MT,* 169).

Golding, then, was never entirely comfortable with the critical process, although he did make some adjustments to it in reversing his early rejection of the Laurentian dictum "Never trust the artist, trust the tale," and giving some ground to the interpretations of critics and readers coming

63. Appleyard, *The Pleasures of Peace: Art and Imagination in Post-War Britain,* 234.

"fresh" to his "brainchildren."[64] This might explain the contradiction or mixed message that McCarron alerted us to in that Golding both satirizes literary criticism and incorporates its theory in *The Paper Men*.

Apart from its function of attacking the authority of the English literature industry, the world upside down of the fantastic and carnivalesque amplifies the postmodern mood of uncertainty and relativity that pervades *The Paper Men* and is central to what McCarron suggests is the novel's "cunningly buried commentary on the crumbling role of fictional authority."[65] Here, Golding is surely using this topsy-turvydom to suggest that literary criticism has reversed the values that he thinks should count in all literary endeavors, that is, elitist conceptions of the "great tradition" or canon of English literature and the commonsense "value" of literature that reveals universal or eternal aspects of human living. This view of literature was, of course, subject to radical attacks from the 1960s onward, particularly with the development of cultural and communication studies that began to examine popular fiction, television, film, and so on.[66] In *The Paper Men*, an antipathy to those critics who attack fictional authority fits in with Golding's critique of *social* values in *Darkness Visible*.

Golding self-consciously blurs the boundary between autobiography and fiction and "creative" writing and biography or criticism, and so adopts a postmodern ludic or playful strategy in *The Paper Men*. James Gindin argues that with no statement of redemption and "not even a statement of some semi-resolution through the process of fiction itself," certainty of meaning evaporates in *The Paper Men* and all that is revealed is the "self-questioning novelist." Philip Redpath claims that it is a novel that resembles Samuel Beckett's *Malone Dies* (1956) in providing an "account of its own incompletion." Golding's novel is in turn Barclay's autobiography, which relates the thwarted attempts of Tucker to write an official biography and ends with the Barthesian "death of the author," killed off not simply by Tucker, but by the writer Golding, who himself senses his own "death" in the postmodern world where the autonomous author is exposed as a myth, a fiction. We are left to ponder how much Barclay, like some doppelgänger, speaks for Golding in the same way that a loveless character in one of Barclay's novels appears to speak for Barclay. In

64. See Frank Kermode and William Golding, "The Meaning of It All"; and Golding, *The Hot Gates and Other Occasional Pieces*, 100. On this reversal, see Biles, *Talk*, 53–55.

65. McCarron, *William Golding*, 46.

66. See Widdowson, "Introduction," 2–3.

fact, there are many similarities between Barclay and Golding. Both, for example, have white beards, write intertextual fictions, and are "moving targets" trying to avoid "critical small-shot" (*MT,* 170). Equally, as we shall see, they are both antagonistic toward literary criticism and frustrate academic pursuit of their "lives" by burning their papers or what Barclay calls "'the paperweight of a whole life!'" (*PM,* 190). Yet Golding is not writing his autobiography through Barclay, so much as problematizing it and, as Don Crompton puts it, setting "traps for critical heffalumps": "Barclay resembles his creator only in his most public, that is to say his most superficial aspects." The novel is not, Gindin suggests, "undigested autobiography," but a metacritical discourse about autobiography.[67]

The Paper Men reveals a deep skepticism about the "truth-telling" ability of autobiography and biography—a skepticism that continues in the "sea trilogy." Golding problematizes the notion of autobiography and biography being true to the life, not least through Barclay's amnesia that opens like a black hole in his autobiography and a selectivity that may or may not unearth such details as him having "dockyard" sex with Lucinda (*PM,* 56). Golding himself was reluctant to write an autobiography as such or commission someone to write his biography. For him, autobiography was not just a flawed project but selfish or egocentric—what his character Johnny calls "'literary masturbation'" (*PM,* 113). Golding's skepticism about autobiography and biography mirrors the approach of many postmodernist thinkers, such as Paul de Man, who highlight life writing as fiction, and propose the contentious view that its interest is "not that it reveals reliable self-knowledge—it does not—but that it demonstrates in a striking way the impossibility of closure and of totalization of all textual systems made up of tropological substitutions." That is, where a figurative medium like language is used, there is an inevitable inability to characterize something completely and exhaustively in terms of what de Man calls a totalization. James Olney, mirroring the ideas of Jacques Derrida, Michel Foucault, Roland Barthes, and Jacques Lacan, states that the autobiographical text "takes on a life of its own, and the self that was not really in existence in the beginning is in the end merely a matter of text and has nothing whatever to do with an authorising author. The self then, is a fiction and so is the life."[68]

67. Gindin, *William Golding,* 87–88; Redpath, *Structural Reading,* 190; Crompton, *View from the Spire,* 158–59; Gindin, *William Golding,* 81. Biles chided Golding for burning his papers, calling it "a practice bound to grieve any scholar" (*Talk,* 22).

68. de Man, *The Rhetoric of Romanticism,* 71; Olney, "Autobiography and the Cultural Movement: A Thematic, Historical, and Bibliographical Introduction," 22.

What autobiography achieves is the construction of an individual's "face" that "deprives and disfigures to the precise extent that it restores." Thus, life writing or biography can be treated as fiction. As R. Elbaz states: "[T]hrough the processes of mediation (by linguistic reality) and suspension (due to the text's lack of finality and completion), autobiography can only be a fiction. Indeed autobiography is fiction and fiction is autobiography: both are narrative arrangements of reality." Susan Sontag notes that Barthes's autobiography, *Roland Barthes by Roland Barthes,* is "a book of his resistance to his ideas, the dismantling of his own authority" or what Philip Thody has called an "anti-biography." For Barthes, says Sontag, "who *speaks* is not who *writes,* and who *writes* is not who *is.*"[69] In *The Paper Men,* which may be seen as a kind of "anti-biography," Golding appears to mirror this breakdown in the authority of autobiography and biography. The title itself may suggest the "paper" rather than real flesh-and-blood status of biographical subjects. A similar Barthesian skepticism about biography can be found in Julian Barnes's *Flaubert's Parrot* (1984).

Like *Darkness Visible* before it, *The Paper Men* is metafictional, intertextual, playful, and labyrinthine, although not as dense or "sprawling" a narrative. The novel draws attention to its status as artifact, and all manner of paperwork litters the text: letters, notes, fan mail, billets-doux, journals, novels, biography, and literary criticism. There are numerous references to other writers, particularly playwrights and poets, and to writing and other media such as television, photography, and cinema. The multi-voicedness of language is stressed, as are problems with communication as in poststroke dysphasia, and natural phenomena and events are seen for their value to fictional representation. We are made sensitive to "the contrivances of paper, manipulations of plot, delineation of character, denouements and resolutions" in opposition to a "real world" (*PM,* 114–15). Fiction and "reality" blur as Barclay persistently compares "real life" to fictional narratives and characterization. For example, Tucker's "'strangled'" cry is the only one he has "experienced outside fiction" (*PM,* 11), and when he wonders how long the silence between Mary Lou and himself might last, he comments: "How long? In a novel I'd watch a clock on the wall" (*PM,* 66). Throughout, the novel problematizes authorship, self-consciously blurring biography and fiction and, as S. J. Boyd suggests, representing an entropic, lackluster modern world.[70] Paper or literary

69. de Man, *The Rhetoric of Romanticism,* 80–81; Elbaz, *The Changing Nature of the Self: A Critical Study of the Autobiographic Discourse,* 1; Sontag, ed., *A Barthes Reader,* xxx; Thody, *Roland Barthes: A Conservative Estimate,* 3; Sontag, *A Barthes Reader,* xxxii.

70. Boyd, *Novels of Golding,* 204–5.

production has become jaded, mass manufactured, standardless. Words themselves seem to be "clipped like gold coins, adulterated and struck with a worn stamp" (*PM*, 60). Barclay is uncertain what his autobiography, *The Paper Men*, amounts to: "[T]he words are too weak, even mine; and God knows, by now they ought to be about as strong as most words can be" (*PM*, 60).

The Paper Men playfully alludes to several of Golding's earlier works and extends his trademark intertextuality and bricolage. As I have already suggested, Barclay resembles "Pincher" Martin and Sammy Mountjoy. On two occasions he refers to "rites of passage" (*PM*, 146, 147), and, finally, at the end of the book, his struggle to perceive that Tucker is about to shoot him resembles Lok in *The Inheritors* when he fails to interpret that he is being fired upon by the New People: "Rick is a hundred yards away across the river, flitting from tree to tree like playing Indians. I shall have an audience for my ritual. Now he is leaning against a tree and peering at me through some instrument or other. How the devil did Rick L. Tucker manage to get hold of a gu [*sic*]" (*PM*, 191).

In what seems to be a consequence of Barclay's alcoholism, fantastic and farcical visions of heaven and hell pervade the novel and establish an admixture of good and evil in what Kevin McCarron has called a "denial of distinctions." In an exaggerated postmodern skepticism, authority and grand narratives are in doubt, religious and literary authorities are questioned. The authority of religious supernaturalism is exploded by Barclay's drunken visions that are banal and farcical—we barely hesitate between natural and supernatural explanations. In Barclay's world, the miraculous is deflated. A miracle amounts to no more than a full, uncorked bottle of wine remaining untouched. In the hellish, depthless world of Barclay, Padre Pio's stigmata acts as a foil to Barclay's own parodic stigmata and supply of farcical dreams and ghostly visions. Here, Golding may be extending his general attack on religious authority. Like the statue of Psyche that he manages to damage, Barclay damages his own brain through drink and enters a jaded, all too easily explained fantastic world. More centrally, Barclay's self-generated hell, and his farcical and often cruel lifestyle, brings to mind the earlier novel *Pincher Martin* and its critique of English totalitarian "soldier-males."[71] In a close readapta-

71. Crompton argues that *The Paper Men,* like *Pincher Martin,* "makes use of a dramatic or phantasmagoric narrative mode." He continues: "[E]xtensive dislocation of the narrative, both in *Pincher Martin* and *The Paper Men,* could be regarded largely as the result of the pressure of the numinous upon the action." In both novels, "the confrontation with the supernatural breaks up the surface reality more comprehensively,

tion of themes in *Pincher Martin*, the "erotic" scholar, Johnny St John John, diagnoses Barclay as "'exoskeletal'" (*PM*, 144): "But you, my dear . . . have spent your life inventing a skeleton on the outside. Like crabs and lobsters. That's terrible, you see, because the worms get inside and, oh my aunt Jemima, they have the place to themselves'" (*PM*, 114). This image of worms under Barclay's carapace reminds us of the imagery of the Chinese box of maggots and metamorphosis in *Pincher Martin* that highlighted Christopher Martin's greedy, cruel totalitarian hardness. Later, courtesy of delirium tremens or what he calls at one point "delirious trimmings" (*PM*, 126), Barclay is subjected to a mock Pincheresque metamorphosis: "I got into a nursing home somehow. I'd had a vivid encounter with the red hot worms under my carapace and a nice female doctor got them out of me through various chinks that she demonstrated by showing me a live lobster from the fish market and then again sometimes I think I dreamed the whole thing" (*PM*, 118). Barclay's nightmare world continues on the island of Lipari with further disruptions in his perceptions when delirium tremens merge with volcanic tremors. A hell-like, Gothic, and apocalyptic gloom of black volcanic ash extends to the island's charnel houses, "dead" town center, inhabitants who move like "steam-driven" (*PM*, 124) mechanical dolls, and a preternaturally dark cathedral in which Barclay experiences the "vision" of a moving statue. It is unclear whether the statue is of Christ or Pluto, the god of the underworld. Again, like Christopher Martin, Barclay makes God in his own image—this time with the red eyes of an alcoholic.

We learn, of course, that Barclay's vision resulted from a "'leedle estrook'" (*PM*, 124), after which he continues to walk in a strange, often Gothic world of ghosts and gravestones. He suffers a topsy-turvy or "reverse" stigmata "for being a mother-fucking bastard as my best friend would say instead of getting them as a prize for being good" (*PM*, 159). Like an inverted Padre Pio, he has visions of Halliday, the "Devil," standing on top of a church in Rome. In his company, Barclay experiences a seemingly paradisial vision of musical, radiant youth who are "neither male nor female," and "creatures" singing in "a dark, calm sea" (*PM*, 161). It is unclear whether what Barclay sees is heaven or hell—or some admixture of both. He continues to be afflicted with dreams, madness, and

---

emphasizing the limits of probability and throwing the narrative open to larger and less finite possibilities. To some extent such confrontations are more easily integrated into looser genres—forms such as science fiction or the ghost story." Although Crompton finds the technique of verisimilitude to be dominant in Golding's writing, it is stretched "very thin" in both these novels (*View from the Spire*, 173, 175).

a Gothic sensibility. Reality is supplanted by the "indescribable, inexplicable, the isness" (*PM,* 176).

As in *Darkness Visible,* hell and the underworld are at the core of the fantastic in *The Paper Men.* Across the novel there are multiple, often casual references to the Devil and damnation. *The Paper Men* continues to explore the contemporary "darkness visible" or the underworld status of postmodern life and morality—and more narrowly its cultural productions. The price that Barclay and Tucker are willing to pay in their paper ambitions is to live in a self-made hell similar to that of "Pincher" Martin. Tucker enters into a pact to supply the Devil-like Halliday with Barclay's "life" or biography. The suggestion is that Tucker is prepared to sell his soul to be Barclay's official biographer: "'I'd give anything—*anything*!'" (*PM,* 45). Barclay reminds Tucker of the penalty for failing Halliday: "'If you haven't brought me to heel in seven years and achieved my authorized biography—incomplete, of course, as I am still to some extent on stream—there'll be wailing and gnashing of all those lovely teeth'" (*PM,* 144). Tucker, the Devil's agent, fruitlessly tries all the tricks in the book to get Barclay's signature, such as getting his wife, Mary Lou, to seduce him and by pretending to have saved his life at Weisswald.

In *The Paper Men,* postmodern uncertainty and the personal costs of living a depthless life are registered in the fantastic theme of madness. Like Matty in *Darkness Visible,* and Christopher in *Pincher Martin,* Barclay is psychically challenged: "Was I mad? Was Rick mad? There was an intensity at times about his stare, white showing all round the pupils, as if he were about to charge dangerously. A psychiatrist would find him interesting. . . . This was a mad house" (*PM,* 94–5). Barclay's drinking brings him into persistent bouts of delirium and fugue—a "'dipso-schizo'" world (*PM,* 116). He shares his madness with the obsessive, doglike Rick who ends up literally "barking." Between them they succeed in breaking the statue of Psyche that stands at Barclay's club, thus symbolizing their combined mental deterioration. This link is emphasized in the club secretary's comment, "'I simply don't know yet how much it'll cost to repair our Psyche,' and Barclay's response: 'Very aptly put, colonel, oh very apt'" (*PM,* 183). For Barclay the cost will be his own death at the hands of maddened Rick Tucker.

Again in its use of doubles and doubling, *The Paper Men* closely follows the representation of a schizoid postmodern uncertainty in *Darkness Visible.*[72] Barclay lives in a "dipso-schizo" world of sober reality and drunk-

72. Dick sees the novel as a failed replication of the dominant Golding motif of doubles (*William Golding* [1987], 137).

en unreality. Wherever he goes, he sees doubles of his ex-wife Liz. His split mind is replicated in the figure of Tucker who, reminiscent of Matty in *Darkness Visible,* has "two faces" that "would slide apart" (*PM,* 58) and a cleft chin that raises the question: "Was it a sign of a divided nature?" (*PM,* 84). Here, as in *Darkness Visible,* Golding suggests the Laingian "schizophrenia" that marks postmodern life. He rather playfully creates Barclay as a doppelgänger of himself, although, as Don Crompton insists, biographical correspondence occurs at only a superficial level. This notion of Barclay as a double for Golding would include *The Paper Men* as part of that "literature of duality" that Karl Miller sees as providing "a principled or accidental subversion of the author—of the kind of author who is deemed to create and control plot and character, to be separate from his characters, to be himself something of a character, and to hold, rather than administer or orchestrate, the opinions that go with a given work."[73] Again, this strategy is part of the short-circuiting that David Lodge diagnoses in postmodernist fiction.

The fantastic, then, functions both to reveal the self-made hells of the depthless literati, Barclay and Tucker, rather in the same way that it undermines Christopher Martin and Sammy Mountjoy, and also mirrors the deep epistemological uncertainties inherent in the postmodern condition. The carnivalesque, as we shall see, functions to expose what Golding views as the depthless nature of much contemporary literary and critical production by evoking the moral depravity and totalitarian personalities of Barclay and Tucker who cruelly disregard others, particularly their wives, and registers the marked relativity and "upside downness" of postmodernism, and its questioning of the status of language and literature.

Golding's attack on the English literature industry is problematical in that it presents itself in a rather crude or simplistic way. It offers a rather uncompromising view of depthless criticism and writing and suggests that in postmodern times there have been no advances in understanding literature through new theoretical approaches and that literature and, indeed, literary imagination have reached a kind of saturation point or entropy. In fact, I would argue that Golding does not really engage in serious analysis of the issues but, as Crompton has suggested, playfully sets "traps" for critics. We might suspect that his satire, which is narrow and crude, was delivered to raise the blood pressure of defensive literary critics. One imagines Golding sitting back and chuckling as critics take him seriously. We need to remain alert to the simplistic characterization that

73. K. Miller, *Doubles,* 99.

Golding effects and not get sucked in by this limited and tongue-in-cheek satire as if it corresponded in any realistic or mimetic way with the contemporary state of the English literature industry.

In *The Paper Men,* Golding presents Barclay and Tucker with their trousers down. He crudely portrays a depthless, entropic, and mutually destructive relationship between a popular creative writer and a literary critic that the novel's metafictional playfulness and, as I will discuss later, its reference to the "culture industry" and the fictional status of biography suggest take place in the postmodern era. They are both farcical yet highly destructive clowns. Golding presents us with a superficial literary world that Barclay, Tucker, Halliday, and others such as Johnny are a part of, which is a circus in the most derogatory sense. The carnivalesque circus imagery that dominates the novel is mostly noncelebratory. From the start, when Barclay's attempt to apprehend the "badger" ends with both him and Tucker pulling down each other's pajama trousers and looking suspiciously as though they were engaged in a homosexual act, "the spirit of farce" (*PM,* 11) dominates. The episode proves to Barclay his status as "nature's comic, her clown with a red nose, ginger hair and trousers always falling down at precisely the wrong moment. Yes, right from the cradle. The first time I shot over a horse's head my fall was broken by a pile of dung" (*PM,* 49). The clown imagery is repeated at various farcical moments in the novel such as when Mary Lou offers her body to Barclay and when he falls down a "cliff" at the Weisswald. "Wilf the clown" (*PM,* 133) describes being "saved" from tumbling into a harmless meadow rather than down a cliff as "one of those ordained moments of low comedy. . . . Once every ten years or so the life of the natural clown met with a proper, natural circus act" (*PM,* 135). Like Barclay, Tucker's trousers also keep falling down. At one point he is even dressed like a circus clown with his 1970s dyed Afro; white-flared, sequinned trousers; and open-chested shirt. Barclay considers his biography, *The Paper Men,* to be "a fair record of the various times the clown's trousers fell down" (*PM,* 189). He finds his stigmata to be "the real, theologically witty bit of his clowning" and awaits the final wound in the side to be provided like "a custard pie" (*PM,* 189). Of course, it will be Barclay's clown nemesis, Tucker, who will provide the "pie" in the shape of a discharge from Capstone Bower's hunting gun. In all, the topsy-turvy clown imagery presents the literary lives of Barclay and Tucker as amounting to little more than a shallow and fruitless farce. It also adds to the overall topsy-turvy status of the novel that complements its evocation of postmodern relativity and uncertainty.

As with the clowning theme, sexual outrageousness, sleaze, sadism, and exploitation undermine any artistic seriousness of the literary circles that Barclay and Tucker move in and are part of. It reflects much of Golding's previous portrayal of cruel totalitarian personalities. Literariness is persistently linked to lower body, transgressive activities, functions, and appetites. Barclay and Tucker are suspected of engaging in homosexual sex, and the often obscene and indecent Barclay is unfaithful to his wife in his affair with the sadistic Lucinda whose sexual appetites are "on the grey edge of the impermissible" or straight out of "the human farmyard" (*PM,* 51). Barclay's own sadism shows itself in his enjoyment of the dog-like submission of his wife and Tucker. Tucker arranges for his own wife to seduce the "ithyphallic" and sometimes pedophilic Barclay (*PM,* 49), and Halliday adds her to his collection of women.[74] Johnny St John John, an "erotic" scholar, entertains sadomasochistic homosexual appetites and as his name suggests—condom (johnny) and toilet (john)—is the most craven example of the novel's medley of literati who gather at the Random Club: "They—we—are an odd lot and connected with paper, from advertising and children's comics all the way through to pornography" (*PM,* 18). At this club, literature and art are cheapened in a depraved conversation among Johnny; his lover, Gabriel Clayton; Tucker; and Barclay about installing sculptures of "'mother-fucking'" and Johnny's powers of "'penetration'" (*PM,* 179). The club permits, as Johnny suggests, lower body behavior: "'Seduction . . . drag . . . bottomry . . . the occasional gang bang'" (*PM,* 180). In all, *The Paper Men* touches all areas of low, or base sexuality, particularly sex that has a cruel, sadistic, and misogynistic streak.

The cruelty and sadism, which we saw in Golding's earlier fiction as part of the totalitarian personality, are further advanced in the imagery and theme of people consuming or making a meal of one another. The aptly named Tucker (food) is presented as an underfed scavenger who is "making a professional meal" of Barclay (*PM,* 11). He consumes scraps of Barclay's papers and "juicy bits" of his life like scraps of food and ends up writing a contract for Barclay to sign on a menu. Like Tucker, Barclay, who is reduced to "eyes and appetite," consumes others (*PM,* 27). He eats English professors: "'I eat 'em for breakfast. Taste different, that's all'" (*PM,* 34). The consumptive nature of Barclay and Tucker closely reminds us of Christopher Martin's selfish and often cruel appetite. In a sense, Barclay gets what he deserves. He is a selfish, exoskeletal lobster that becomes food for others. Like "Pincher" Martin, he is eater and eaten.

74. The term *ithyphallic* is associated with the phallus carried in procession at carnivalesque festivals of Bacchus.

Scatological images of the dustbin and shit feature strongly in a network of references that reveals Barclay's rotten core and Tucker's willingness to go to any lengths for literary criticism. The action of their paper lives centers on the low ash can or dustbin from the very start of the novel. Tucker rummages through household detritus and mess to find critical gold: "scribbled, typed, printed, black-and-white and coloured—paper, paper, paper!" (*PM,* 16). Incriminating photographs, correspondence, evidence of "old shames" (*PM,* 16), and every "dirty piece of paper" (*PM,* 17) is up for grabs. The image of the literary critic and biographer descending to the world of dustbins—Tucker even has "OLE ASHCAN" (*PM,* 40) on his pullover at the expense of his University of Astrakhan—crudely attacks the critical enterprise as a "low," "dirty" business. Just as Tucker's behavior is critiqued in its proximity to dirt and filth, so is Barclay's self-centered life as a popular writer. He is a "'shit'" (*PM,* 18) who gets "filthy drunk" (*PM,* 27) and has stinking breath. He consumes hangover remedies that resemble "diarrhoea" or Mary Lou's vomit (*PM,* 39). Familiar with the stench of his own excretion, he copes better than Tucker does when they stray across human effluence used as fertilizer: "Some people can't stand heights. Others can't stand faeces" (*PM,* 82). Barclay seems to prefer the "primitive" sanitation on Lesbos to the cleanliness of men's rooms in good hotels. In fact, the majority of scatological references are deployed to undermine what Golding presents (tongue-in-cheek) as a postmodern English literature industry dominated by depthless writing and criticism that, like Barclay's journal, might as well be set down "on lavatory paper" (*PM,* 159).

In *The Paper Men,* Golding builds more crudely and playfully on his critique of the "culture industry" in *Darkness Visible.* The printed word is no longer superior to a variety of media such as photography, film, and television. The shallow writing of Barclay and vapid critical endeavors of Tucker blend with the trashy entertainments that the "culture industry" manufactures. Characters not only have become "paper men" but also live and act on the surface of late-capitalist multimedia. Barclay's wife, for example, becomes a perfect hostess as liquidly and depthlessly "as if she had switched channels" (*PM,* 14). There is play on the words *real* and *reel* that extends the concern with art and reality, and also represents the late-twentieth-century dominance of film: "I had an instant picture (reel) of myself" (*PM,* 159). Even Johnny gets caught up in nonliterary media. Thanks to being from the right school background, he lands the job of hosting a panel show, *I Spy.* The prominence of visual media is again in evidence at Liz's funeral when Barclay views the room of mourners "as on a screen" (*PM*, 188). At one point, Barclay discusses the further commodification of his novels into film, travel articles, and short stories as "exercises in how to cheat the public" (*PM*, 27). The frequent references to film and photography in the novel, as Kevin McCarron claims, reinforce "the suggestion that, in the late twentieth century, the author is dead in more ways than one."[75] Indeed, being an author no longer has the kind of mystique it once had: "There were authors enough to go round after all, authors by the thousand" (*PM*, 36). Barclay imagines being charged with "scrawling lies on paper into a shape that the weak-minded have taken as guide, comforter and friend, allegedly, often to their cost" (*PM*, 47). The idea of the writer giving a moral lead, as Don Crompton has suggested, is exploded by the character of Barclay. Now anyone can be a biographee, even "'multiple murderers'" and "'telly personalities'" (*PM*, 54). Pulp copies of such biographies can be mass-produced in the millions "without the subject's consent" (*PM*, 56). The depthless Tucker upholds the value of popular fiction, claiming that it is a "'common misconception'" that popular works are "'inferior'" (*PM*, 55). The fact that Tucker is caught up in a kind of biographical gold rush where he needs to "stake" his claim emphasizes the increased commodification of biography (*PM*, 58). Barclay, and again we sense Golding, despises biographers like Tucker who can be thought of as "pseudo-scholars queuing up in our dreadful explosion of reconstituted rubbish" (*PM*, 56). The satirical chaining of criticism to the economic market is further stressed in Barclay's reference to a "Shelley factory like the Boswell factory" that churns out everything connected with Shelley, even stuff he himself would not have published (*PM*, 59). In his earlier essay "Body and Soul," Golding denigrated both the "factory" approach to literature and the cultural depthlessness in the United States, particularly in terms of reproduction and simulacra (*HG*, 148–51).

To conclude, the fantastic theme of a Gothic, hell-like underworld that dominated *Darkness Visible* continues in *The Paper Men* and presents a dire and rather simplistic vision of an inferior postmodern English literature industry. This vision is arguably more a figment of Golding's imagination than a realistic representation of the industry as such. The carnivalesque exposes what Golding presents as a cruel, exploitative side to both the literary critical trade in "lives" or biographies and the self-obsessed, morally defunct world of popular writing. Unable to rise above the mire of the "culture industry," the selfish and often cruel behavior of Barclay and

75. McCarron, *William Golding*, 48.

and satirical purposes.[1] Nonsatirically, these modes complement a postmodern indeterminacy that is forged by a number of other aspects of the trilogy noted by previous critics. First, the trilogy is a "historiographic metafiction." Here, I am indebted to Linda Hutcheon's discussion of this form and Susana Onega's inclusion of the trilogy in a list of British examples of this type of literature. Second, as Kevin McCarron argues, a "coincidence of opposites" dominates the trilogy: sacred-profane, absolutism-democracy, upper class–lower class, art-reality, Augustanism-romanticism. Of course, though McCarron links this structure to fantasy, he does not produce a detailed analysis of the fantastic, its satirical and nonsatirical functions, or its relation to the carnivalesque. For McCarron, "fantasy" and "fantastic" are little more than synonyms for "coincidence." This lack in McCarron's study can be developed to offer new insights into the generation of postmodern indeterminacy, particularly in terms of Michel Foucault's *stultifera navis* or "Ship of Fools" and in viewing the trilogy's ludic pastiche of eighteenth-century literature as a "preromantic" debate. Also, Ovid's tale of Ceyx and Alcyone is among the many influences on the trilogy that, as McCarron notes, include Elizabeth Longford's *Wellington* (1969), Arnold van Gennep's *Rites of Passage* (1960), Patrick White's *Fringe of Leaves* (1976), and Conrad's *Heart of Darkness* (1902) and *Nigger of the "Narcissus"* (1897). S. J. Boyd suggests a parallel with Conrad's *Shadow Line* (1917).[2]

The strong or dominant status of "historiographic metafiction" that Hutcheon defines "in terms of its ability to contest the assumptions of the 'realist' novel and narrative history, to question the absolute knowability of the past, and to specify the ideological implications of historical representations, past and present" brings Golding's postmodernist turn to a kind of climax.[3] In *Darkness Visible,* Golding took a gloomy, apocalyptic angle of view toward postmodernity, postmodernism, and the "culture industry." Although this pessimism continued in *The Paper Men* in a crude presentation of depthless writing and criticism, we saw signs of a more lighthearted, playful, almost mischievous accommodation of postmodern indeterminacy. By *To the Ends of the Earth,* a more elaborately playful ques-

1. Page references in the text will refer to the 1992 edition of the trilogy, *To the Ends of the Earth,* rather than to the individual novels, *Rites of Passage, Close Quarters,* and *Fire Down Below.*

2. For a useful introduction to the "Ship of Fools," or *stultifera navis,* see Foucault, *Madness and Civilization: A History of Insanity in the Age of Reason,* 3–37; McCarron, *Coincidence of Opposites,* 75–77; Boyd, *Novels of Golding,* 160–61.

3. Hutcheon, "Historiographic Metafiction," 71.

tioning of epistemologies replaces the antagonistic and jaundiced approach of the previous novels. In the trilogy, Golding avoids bleakly diagnosing postmodern fragmentation and chaos. Rather, he revels in the ludic possibilities afforded by "historiographic metafiction" and shows a clean pair of heels to the more serious and anguished response to postmodern society and culture.

Historiographic metafiction most closely fulfills Hutcheon's "poetics of postmodernism": "Readers of historiographic metafiction will respond to historical material in such novels with a double awareness of its fictionality and its basis in real events, thus entering into one of postmodernism's definitively unresolved contradictions." It also puts Golding's "sea trilogy," as Onega contends, within a tradition of British historiographic metafiction that peaked in the 1980s with works such as John Fowles's *Maggot* (1986), Lawrence Durrell's *Avignon Quintet* (1974–1985), Graham Swift's *Waterland* (1983), Julian Barnes's *Flaubert's Parrot* (1984), Peter Ackroyd's *Hawksmoor* (1985), Rose Tremain's *Restoration* (1989), A. S. Byatt's *Possession: A Romance* (1990), Jeanette Winterson's *Passion* (1987), and Jim Crace's *Gift of Stones* (1988). Onega maintains that Golding, Fowles, Durrell, and Byatt belong to an older literary generation that "provides the link between modernism and postmodernism." Furthermore, and rather interestingly, she argues that "the eclosion [emergence] of British historiographic metafiction in the 1980s shows British novelists catching up with a world-wide phenomenon, which goes back not only to North American experimental 'fabulation' but also to Spanish-American 'magic-realism' and to Gabriel García Márquez and Jorge Luis Borges in particular"—a foreshadowing of the "metafictional and fantasy elements in the writings of novelists like Peter Ackroyd, Jeanette Winterson, John Fowles and Salman Rushdie."[4] Here, Onega fails to include Golding in this list.

Golding increasingly blends metafictional and fantasy elements in *Pincher Martin, Free Fall, The Spire, Darkness Visible, The Paper Men,* and the sea trilogy, although this fiction does not fall into the category of magic realism. The sea trilogy is perhaps Golding's most overt and systematic metafiction. It is a work befitting Robert Alter's definition of a self-conscious fiction in "which from beginning to end, through the style, the handling of narrative viewpoint, the names and words imposed on the characters, the patterning of the narration, the nature of the characters and what befalls them, there is a consistent effort to convey to us a sense of the

4. Ibid.; Onega, "British Historiographic Metafiction," 94–95, 101–2.

fictional world as an authorial construct set up against a background of literary tradition and convention." The postmodern status of the "historiographic metafiction," *To the Ends of the Earth,* with its ludic presentation of oppositions and nonresolution, is strengthened through a promiscuous, "consciously done," wild intertextuality that betokens postmodern literature, as Neil Cornwell suggests, and results in a playful or ludic pastiche of Augustan and romantic literature. Whereas this pastiche—or what Boyd calls "elaborate fake" and "stylistic forgery"—serves to illustrate topsy-turvy oppositions, it hardly amounts to productive parody. It provides a weakened or dead form of writing that Fredric Jameson likens to "speech in a dead language" that is "amputated of the satiric impulse." As such, it is part of a postmodern displacement of parody in preference for what Andrzej Gąsiorek identifies as a "depthless," "dehistoricized," "motiveless" form.[5]

Satirically, the carnivalesque is both lighthearted, Horatian, or celebratory and also serious, Juvenalian, or noncelebratory. Supported by a "residual" fantastic that disrupts various oppositions, not least that between upper and lower classes, its lighthearted form incorporates a comical, broadly scatological attack on the English class system. This means that, although Golding's perennial critique of the class system in that "we British are still so dunked from childhood" is apparent in the trilogy, the knives are blunted by the overall more optimistic and celebratory tone (*EE,* x). Golding also extends the broad attack upon religious authority that is inflected through much of his previous fiction, and is a central concern in *The Spire.* Here, the decrowning of the clergyman, Colley, has distant roots in *Free Fall*'s Father Watts-Watt. Yet, in an altogether more serious deployment, noncelebratory carnivalesque registers the violence that results from class conflict and also undermines a construction of Englishness in opposition to the atrocities carried out during the French Terror. This focus on atrocity is broadly related to Golding's earlier concerns about, and instantiation of, contemporary barbarity and the "totalitarian personality." However, Golding's writing has come a sobering distance from the more direct references to World War II atrocities. Though he maintains a strong interest or preoccupation with wartime violence and atrocity, as evidenced in the setting of the trilogy during a lull and then resurgence of the Napoleonic Wars with Britain, and frequent references

5. Alter, *Partial Magic,* xi; Cornwell, *Literary Fantastic,* 157; see Crompton, *View from the Spire,* 130; Boyd, *Novels of Golding,* 158; Jameson, *Postmodernism,* 17; Gąsiorek, *Post-War British Fiction,* 101.

to the French Revolution and Terror, the more comic tone and tireless contradictory or paradoxical blending of metafiction, historiography, intertextuality, and pastiche dispel much of the dark mood of Golding's earlier work.

Set in a period marked by revolution, *To the Ends of the Earth* is perfectly placed both to entertain class conflict in English society and to register indirectly the upheaval of postmodernism. However, since in England, unlike France and Germany, revolution arrived in literary ideas rather than social uprising, Golding's interrogation of the social injustice of the English class system is more limited to matters of style and taste rather than bloodshed. The ordered, social, prohierarchical world of Augustanism is set against the rebellious "lower" world of nonconformist, demotic romanticism with its championing of the outcast, and "common" or popular language: Talbot versus Colley.

The Augustan literature of Pope, Dryden, and Swift harks back to the "moderation, decorum, and urbanity" of the literature of Horace, Virgil, and Ovid during the reign of the Roman emperor Augustus. Romantic literature—Wordsworth, Coleridge, Blake, Byron, and so on—is often seen as beginning with the French Revolution in 1789 or the publication of Wordsworth and Coleridge's *Lyrical Ballads* (1798) and ending in the 1830s.[6] Between the two "periods" might be placed "preromanticism," as Marshall Brown argues—a kind of halfway house between old and new forms, extending from 1740 to 1798. As Brown indicates, romanticism developed and dynamicized themes of consciousness, time, space, formal variety, and the sublime explored in the earlier "preromantic" works of Gray, Thomson, Collins, and Cowper. Definitions of periods, however, always require cautious application and much hedging. In effect, literary periods can be as helpful and as useless as labels such as the 1960s, 1980s, and the like. What such periodization often brings about is a false comfort in having landmarks by which we navigate the complex world of literature. The oscillation, conflict, and even suspension between Augustanism and romanticism in *To the Ends of the Earth* suggest a kind of ongoing preromantic transition, since the trilogy is set in the early nineteenth century.

Thus, through the eighteenth century and into the nineteenth century, literary style appears quite divided as old and new forces diverge. Rather interestingly, whereas a mood of sanity and rationalism prevailed during the eighteenth century, several writers of the period had mental problems:

6. See M. H. Abrams, *A Glossary of Literary Terms*, 12, 113–14.

Collins, Smart, Cowper, Gray, Johnson, Boswell, Goldsmith, Sheridan, and Chatterton. In *To the Ends of the Earth,* Golding is able to utilize the Augustan-romantic antinomy as a means of extending his exploration of the limitations of rationality, especially in relation to contemporary, postmodern skepticism. Throughout his fiction, Golding has countered inflexible rationality and pointed to chaos and irrationality. This is signaled in his send-up of Augustanism or neoclassicism in his early poem "Mr. Pope" in which Pope's preference for a neatly landscaped, "chastely ordered" park with its "[t]rim rows of flowers" and trees standing "two by two" brings him to complain to God: "But one thing mars its loveliness / The stars are rather out of hand."[7]

This "mood of sanity" and rational order was the legacy of Augustans like Pope, but such thinking, such rational ordering, was already beginning to show fault lines in the middle of the eighteenth century. The darkness of consciousness, and consciousness of darkness, was beginning to play against Enlightenment ideas of rational progress. Perception was striving to move "beyond." It demanded more than reason: it desired. Augustanism's "urbane sublime"—a lofty, courteous style—promoted moderation, restraint, impersonality, detachment, and generalization. It presented itself as a kind of mood stabilizer—a control of passions, the irrational, and demons. Arguably, preromantic works such as Johnson's *History of Rasselas* (1759) can be seen as suspended, rather like *To the Ends of the Earth,* between opposites—particularly in terms of the choice of either radical or conventional lives.[8] There is a kind of double bind operating that mixes transcendence and nontranscendence just as the man attempting flight in *The History of Rasselas* plummets into the lake, and Talbot in the trilogy entertains radical, revolutionary ideas yet succumbs to worldly, "sensible" plans. The romantic dialectics of spirit versus matter, the eternal versus the temporal, attract Talbot but get stuck in his stiff Cartesian rationalism. He retracts from his taste of madness, disorder, and chaos and seeks the balance and social stability that goes hand in hand with his privileged status on the "dreadful ladder" of class.

Closely related to the debate surrounding sanity and insanity in *To the Ends of the Earth* is Golding's reference to the Ship of Fools. The Ship of Fools is central to Foucault's evocation of "insanity" in the Age of Reason when, he argues, madness was not tolerated as it had been in the Middle

7. William Golding, *Poems,* 26.

8. I am indebted here to McCarron's recognition that the trilogy owes something to the "choice of life" theme in *The History of Rasselas* (*Coincidence of Opposites,* 127).

Ages but subject to increasingly incarcerative responses. The Ship of Fools is an early, preasylum example of this silencing and "taming" of madness.[9] Golding uses the Ship of Fools motif partly to conduct his own Foucauldian debate on incarcerative practices of language and class, and to emphasize the opposition between fantastic romanticism and Augustan classicism that in contemporary terms gestures toward the vertiginous irresolution and uncertainty of the postmodern era. The key concern is to accentuate the liminality between rationality and irrationality, Augustanism and romanticism, sanity and insanity, reality and unreality, fact and fiction.

To the Ends of the Earth is a first-person narrative account of Edmund Talbot's adventures during a voyage to Australia where, through the nepotism of his godfather, he will assist the British colonial administration. It is set in the early nineteenth century, and portrays Talbot's maturation away from a rather stiff Augustan rationalism and classicism into an appreciation of more romantic, irrational forces at work in the world. In *Rites of Passage,* the first part of the trilogy, the death by shame of Colley, a young parvenu clergyman who succumbs to fellatio and buggery, and is subsequently victimized in the "badger bag" ceremony, undermines the religious authority invested in Colley, interrogates Talbot's gentlemanly manners, and exposes a seething pit of class bigotry and hypocrisy in the English class system. Finally, and centrally, Colley's demise reveals, quite starkly, an English appetite for cruelty or atrocity.[10] Golding gives the "provenance" of Colley's death by shame as a reference in Wilfred Scawen Blunt's *My Diaries* (1919–1920) that gave an account of the Duke of Wellington boarding a ship in order to lift the spirits of its shamed chaplain, Reverend Blunt, but failed and the man died.[11] Talbot's journey to

9. Foucault, *Madness and Civilization,* 36, 38.

10. Boyd notes that *Rites of Passage,* like *Lord of the Flies* and *The Pyramid* before it, reveals Golding's "deep bitterness" regarding the English class structure (*Novels of Golding,* 10). See also Dick, *William Golding* (1987), 117; Crompton, *View from the Spire,* 135–37, 139; and Dickson, *Modern Allegories,* 117.

11. Haffenden, "William Golding: An Interview," 9. Elizabeth Longford retells this death-by-shame incident: "After only three days at sea the unfortunate clergyman got 'abominably' drunk and rushed out of his cabin stark naked among soldiers and sailors, 'talking all sorts of bawdy and ribaldry and singing scraps of the most blackguard and indecent songs.' Such was his shame on afterwards hearing of these 'irregularities' that he shut himself up and refused to eat or speak. . . . Colonel Wesley's [Wellington] broad-minded and kindly attempts to 'reconcile Mr. Blunt to himself' were not successful. In ten days he forced himself to die of contrition" (*Wellington: The Years of the Sword,* 51).

the antipodes continues in *Close Quarters* and *Fire Down Below,* sequels that Boyd condemns as "soap-operatic" and marking a retrograde shift away from tragedy to the kind of comedy found in carrying-on films.[12]

In *Close Quarters,* Talbot suffers concussive madness and an exaggerated sensibility after he receives blows to the head during the near capsize of the ship and preparations to fight what is thought to be a French ship but turns out to be the friendly *Alcyone.* More and more like Colley, Talbot falls madly in love with the *Alcyone*'s Miss Chumley and grieves excessively on her departure. He is attended by Wheeler who, having been picked up by the *Alcyone* after being lost overboard, haunts him like some Morphean ghost. Golding seems to allude here to the tale of Ceyx and Alcyone in Ovid's *Metamorphoses* (11.410–748) or post-Ovidian works such as Chaucer's *Book of the Duchess* (1370), in which Morpheus appears to Alcyone as the ghost of Ceyx, her drowned husband.[13] In addition, this reference affords an ironic comparison between the reciprocal, perfect married love of Ceyx and Alcyone and the affair that we learn had taken place between Lady Somerset, the wife of the *Alcyone*'s captain, and the socially inferior Lieutenant Benét who is eventually swapped for the intolerable drunk, Deverel. Unfortunately, the newly arrived Mr. Benét's efforts to beat the doldrums by clearing weeds off the ship's bottom brings a further decline to the vessel's structural integrity when the keel is dislodged. In the generalized hysteria brought about by the threat of sinking, class divisions break down—the white line separating upper and lower classes is washed away—and Wheeler blows his head off in Colley's old cabin because he is unable to face drowning a second time.

Fire Down Below, which ends the sea trilogy, explores the aspirations and consequences of French revolutionary thought and practice alongside a cooler, commonsensical English outlook. Much of the drama surrounds Mr. Benét's efforts to repair the stricken mainmast with red-hot bolts. This provides the central image of "fire down below." Not only does it refer to the dangerous methods of the falsely named Mr. Benét, who hides the fact of his father's involvement in the French Revolution, but it also refers to the threat from "lower" orders, the transcendental mysticism of Mr. Prettiman and the general, heated passions and enthusiasms that threaten to engulf other passengers. While Talbot flirts with the liberatory sensibility promoted by Benét and Prettiman, he is too steeped in English class elitism to com-

12. Boyd, *Novels of Golding,* 178–79. This emphasis may itself owe something to Redpath's comment that an analysis of cinematic influence on Golding remains uncharted (see *Structural Reading,* 214).

13. See Larry D. Benson, ed., *The Riverside Chaucer,* 967.

mit himself to anything that might upset it. Talbot represents the English temperament for accommodating or playing with revolutionary thoughts and feelings while resisting them in practice. This is the same with class. Talbot appears to bring himself down to the level of the common sailor in his desire to climb into the fighting top of the ship, and does so only to advance his way in the world of politics: "'Suppose me—as may befall—to be a Member of Parliament. "Mr Speaker. To those of us who have actually climbed into the fighting top of a man of war at sea"'" (*EE,* 485).

The end of the trilogy culminates in Talbot's dream of Mr. Prettiman's joyful tribe on their quest in Australia for an Ideal City or Eldorado, when he decides that the price for such idealism is too high and chooses instead to throw himself into more worldly activity. It may be, as Boyd suggests, that in this service of mammon, Talbot, like the purser, Jones, evokes the monetary values espoused by Thatcherism in the 1980s.[14] Perhaps Golding wishes to attack this kind of monetarism by delivering a bogusly happy ending in which Talbot completes his fairy tale romance with Miss Chumley but cannot rise to the ideal, spiritual optimism of Prettiman. In Menippean style, Talbot's dream at the end of the novel interrogates notions of social utopia. It shows him "buried . . . all except my head" deep in a pragmatic, dull, worldly soil (*EE,* 752). Although the old Augustan, elitist, rationalist world that Talbot started out in has been inflected with a new romantic, irrationalist, revolutionary sensibility, he resists full membership. Yet his flirtation with this more radical sensibility is significant. Talbot shows that, in different political and cultural circumstances, the "civilized," commonsensical English might just as easily flirt with the kind of barbarity witnessed in the French Revolution. This last part of the trilogy also reflects the concerns about the "choice of life" found in Johnson's *History of Rasselas,* a text that shares preromantic, nonresolving oscillations or conflict between "high" Augustan rationality and the more plebeian romantic irrationality. But this indeterminacy is situated within a far broader metafictional concern that itself is amplified or complemented by the deployment of fantastic and carnivalesque modes.

Golding has a veritable armamentarium for making his trilogy, *To the Ends of the Earth,* highly metafictional and keeping its fictionality constantly at the end of the reader's nose, not least through theatrical imagery and metaphors.[15] The ship is presented as a "floating theatre" in which a

14. See Boyd, *Novels of Golding,* 185, 190, 198.

15. On *Rites of Passage* as metafiction, see Dick, *William Golding* (1987), 126–29; Gindin, *William Golding,* 74; Redpath, *Structural Reading,* 129; and McCarron, *William Golding,* 57.

number of performances take place, not least the central, partly farcical, partly tragic fall or decline of Colley (*EE*, 125). In addition to its overriding "theatrical presentation" (*EE*, 586), the ship also resembles to some degree Golding's earlier construction in *The Spire*. The damaged "mast" in the trilogy parallels the leaning "spire" in *The Spire* in an important sense. Apart from dramatizing the threat posed to "high" aspirations by "low," transgressive humanity in terms of the "fire down below" and pit, respectively, the "mast," like the "spire," also suggests the vulnerable status of the novelistic construction of meaning. This is suggested not just by this damaged, spirelike "mast" but also by the ailing structure of the whole ship that, as Mr. Gibbs notes, has a dangerous mix of seasoned and unseasoned wood. One does wonder, given the metafictional thrust of the trilogy, whether Golding is hinting here at his own admixture of older "seasoned" literature in terms of intertextual allusions and his pastiche of eighteenth-century forms with his own "unseasoned" fabrication and invention.

The trilogy is pervasively intertextual, of course, and littered with references to other writers and their works such as Homer, Shakespeare, Fielding, Coleridge, and Austen, to name but a few. But Golding's intertextuality also extends to his own fiction, as we saw above in terms of *The Spire*. In *Fire Down Below*, for example, Kevin McCarron finds similarities between Talbot's use and abuse of women and Mountjoy's behavior in *Free Fall*: "Talbot coldly observes the dying Zenobia Brocklebank, whom he has used in precisely the same way as Mountjoy uses Taffy, while his thoughts are solely on Miss Chumley. Significantly, an intertextual reference both emphasizes this connection with *Free Fall*, and further insists on the fictionality of *Fire Down Below*." McCarron finds more parallels between *Fire Down Below* and Golding's previous fiction such as the replication of the "bridge" image in *Free Fall* and paying only a "reasonable" price in *The Pyramid*.[16] But there are others. Alongside the parallel between the "spire" and "mast" structures, the *Alcyone*, "a halcyon" (*EE*, 726), recalls the kingfisher imagery toward the end of *The Spire*. In turn, this reference alludes to the Ovidian tale of Ceyx and Alcyone, in which the grieving Alcyone is reunited with her drowned husband, Ceyx, when both are metamorphosed into kingfishers. Mr. Talbot's burnt hair recalls Matty in *Darkness Visible*: "I swept off my hat. 'Mr Talbot—your hair!' 'An accident, ma'am, a trifle'" (*EE*, 729). Also, Talbot's description of the waves

16. McCarron, *Coincidence of Opposites*, 125–26.

as "organized in lines that might have been ruled they were so straight" reflects the fabricated sea of *Pincher Martin* (*EE*, 524). Finally, and in a way that bookends his whole oeuvre, the drama in the trilogy takes place on board a ship just as the island in *Lord of the Flies* was ship-shaped. All these links add to what McCarron rightly diagnoses to be a flagging up of the fictionality of the trilogy. This is extended by an overt focus on the layout or structure of the fiction.

Many of Talbot's entries in his journal are as "short as some of Mr Sterne's chapters" (*EE*, 63), and such shortness, combined with the problematization of chronology in Talbot's and Colley's accounts, the abrupt ending of *Close Quarters*, use of symbols to replace dates, inclusion of untranslated Greek, and reference to typographical features such as a line to indicate a missing day, increases the self-consciousness of the text. Self-consciousness is further increased by the persistent attention to the composition and selectivity of journal entries, and the impossible task of representing reality such as when Talbot complains, "I cannot get one tenth of the day down!" (*EE*, 28), and commentary about the choice of a happy, conventional ending to the trilogy. Golding constantly foregrounds the relationship between text and reality, as when Talbot finds Coleridge "mistaken" in his presentation of the superstition behind why sailors do not kill the albatross: "The only reason why they do not shoot seabirds is first because they are not allowed weapons and second because seabirds are not pleasant to eat" (*EE*, 76). The contrast here between a Coleridgean outlook and that of Talbot marks both the latter's Augustan obtuseness and his "textual" status. Ultimately, Talbot "exists" as a character referring to endless examples of textual production and the falsifying status of representations, not least historical ones. Even his conquest of Zenobia, for example, is self-consciously rendered in a parody of eighteenth-century erotic writing:

> My sword was in my hand and I boarded her! I attacked once more. . . . The bookshelf tilted. *Moll Flanders* lay open on the deck, *Gil Blas* fell on her and my aunt's parting gift to me, Hervey's *Meditations among the Tombs (MDCCLX) II vols London* covered them both. I struck them all aside and Zenobia's tops'ls too. I called on her to yield, yet she maintained a brave if useless resistance that fired me even more. I bent for the *main course.* We flamed against the ruins of the canvas basin and among the trampled pages of my little library. We flamed upright. Ah—she did yield at last to my conquering arms, was overcome, rendered up all the tender spoils of war! (*EE*, 75)

Again, Talbot meets sailors who had "moved out of books, out of the schoolroom and university into the broader scenes of daily life" (*EE*, 33), while Colley's Bible might have spoken of prostitutes but "did not include advice on how to recognize one by candlelight!" (*EE*, 61). Sometimes reality is presented like text or art, as with Colley's face being a "skimped and jagged line like the faces of peasants illustrated in medieval manuscripts" (*EE*, 58) or the sunrise and sunset at sea having "'that indefinable air of Painted Art'" (*EE*, 122). The blurring of art and reality continues in Talbot's objection to Brocklebank's heavily contrived representation of Nelson surrounded by his officers. Yet Brocklebank tells him: "'You are confusing art with actuality, sir'" (*EE*, 146). Brocklebank defends his right to exclude historical reality for the sake of salability. In his view, "'verisimilitude'" (*EE*, 148) is unpopular, as when Captain Anderson is indignant of the suggestion of portraying him in the thick of the action in a mere sloop. Ultimately, the nature and circumstance of Colley's death, like Nelson's, prove a matter of representation, in this case, between various written accounts. In so doing, much is missed: "His was a real life and a real death and no more to be fitted into a given book than a misshapen foot into a given boot" (*EE*, 227). Tellingly, Talbot informs Summers that "'Life is a formless business. . . . Literature is much amiss in forcing a form on it!'" (*EE*, 228). At several points, Talbot comments on the metaphorical and ambiguous nature of language: "What a language is ours, how diverse, how direct in indirection . . ." (*EE*, 261).

What is clear is that from the very title of the trilogy's lead novel, *Rites of Passage*, we are immersed in a ludic postmodern exploration of textuality. Golding plays on Talbot's journal and the voyage being one and the same. Ultimately, *To the Ends of the Earth* is concerned with issues surrounding the fabrication of a "sea-story" (*EE*, 238), and, indeed, Golding suggests that he would be happy for "the unnamed ship" at the heart of the trilogy to be called a *"Good Read"* (*EE*, xi–xii). This foregrounding of the ship as fictional construct is made within the text. At one point, Colley sees the bowsprit of the ship as a pen: "I could almost rejoice in that powerful circling which the point of the bow-sprit . . . ceaselessly described above the sharp line of the horizon!" (*EE*, 164). In a wonderfully subtle line early on, Golding plays on the creation of "Rites" (writes) of "Passage" (text) while at the same time preserving the sense of Talbot reporting on a reality "out there": "as I write these very words the pattern of our wooden world changes" (*EE*, 8). Following this, we find Talbot addressing his godfather: "[B]ehold me seated at my table-flap with this journal open before me. But what pages of trivia! Here are none of the interesting events, acute observations and the, dare I say, sparks of wit with which it is my first ambition to entertain your lordship! However, our passage is but begun" (*EE,* 16). Golding clearly plays on the double meaning of "passage" as both a journey and a text. This ludic concept of "passage" greatly enhances metafictional aspects of the trilogy. *Rites of Passage,* of course, alludes to van Gennep's account of various ritual passages or transitions, but also suggests rituals of text—a passage being a piece of text. Bernard Dick concludes that "the rites of passage the passengers are undergoing are of various kinds: tribal, social, linguistic, literary."[17]

The trilogy, rather like *The Paper Men,* advances the notion of the textual, papery, constructed nature of reality. Not only are there ample references to journals, papers, letters, books, bookishness, printing, and publishing, but in *Rites of Passage,* Talbot and Anderson appear like prototypes for Barclay and Tucker. Talbot is a textual addict, dependent on the *"furor scribendi"* (*EE,* 39) and with a future in governmental bureaucracy where "'offices are paved with paper'" (*EE,* 144). Similarly, Anderson rules over a ship "'ballasted with paper'" where every detail of the ship's "life" is charted: "'We record almost everything somewhere or another, from the midshipmen's logs right up to the ship's log kept by myself'" (*EE,* 144). Issues surrounding the doubtful status of autobiography and biography as a particularly postmodern concern in *The Paper Men* are extended in the trilogy. Talbot considers autobiography to be mere fabrication: "I have come to think that men commonly invent their autobiographies like everything else" (*EE,* 705). He finds truth "stranger than fiction" and considers that the "honest biographer, if such there be, will always reach a point where he would be happier if he could tone down the crude colours of a real life into the delicate tints of romance and legend!" (*EE,* 726). This difficulty of textual representations of "reality" is central to what can be described as the "battle of the manuscripts" in the trilogy.

The trilogy incorporates a discursive battle between versions of reality represented in Talbot's journal account of his voyage to the antipodes, Colley's manuscript letter that is embedded in this account, and entries that Captain Anderson makes in the ship's log. In the trilogy as a whole, separate versions of events compete for the status of being truth-bearing. These versions are part of a discursive battle or battle of the manuscripts that has no resolution. What is revealed by the "battle" is the difficulty of arriving at truth or, to redeploy McCarron, the coincidence of truths. The insertion of a variety of genres is a particularly Menippean strategy that

17. Dick, *William Golding* (1987), 129.

promotes a sense of the constructed and fallible status of "Truth." The reference to Talbot's journal being as "deadly as a loaded gun" (*EE,* 159)—quite possibly owing something to Emily Dickinson's poem "My Life Had Stood—a Loaded Gun" (1890)—seems to reveal Golding's awareness of wider academic commentary about the damaging impact of language on people's lives. Certainly, Talbot's bending of the truth in his letter to Colley's sister explaining the clergyman's unfortunate death is an attempt to limit the damaging effect of language. Yet this Marlowesque redemption of Colley from a Kurtzian bestiality also highlights the difficulty or nonresolution of truth in the trilogy, where the "deep" (*EE,* 34) or "liquid profundity" (*EE,* 168) become metaphors for unfathomable meanings. As the signal text of the trilogy, Philip Redpath argues that *Rites of Passage* "makes us realize how relative, multivalent, and obscure truth is." Similarly, S. J. Boyd writes: "The novel seems to mock the naive belief that a novel or a work of narrative historiography can be successful in telling the truth, the whole truth and nothing but the truth." The same may be said of its sequels. Kevin McCarron argues that in the last part of the trilogy, *Fire Down Below,* Golding slips in an anachronistic reference to Robert Hughes's *Fatal Shore,* published in 1987: "These fellows have found this shore in no way fatal to them!" (*EE,* 739). This "deliberate" reference, he maintains, "subverts the purposive historical authenticity of Talbot's writing and draws attention to the fictionality of the novel." McCarron later asserts that there are parallels to be found between Golding's trilogy and Edgar Allan Poe's *Narrative of Arthur Gordon Pym of Nantucket* (1838), both of which share "the journal form, the sea voyage, a deliberate blurring of fact and fiction."[18]

Textual self-consciousness and hermeneutical difficulty are further heightened in the letter from Lady Somerset giving permission for Talbot to correspond with Miss Chumley. Within it lies a smaller missive slipped inside by Miss Chumley that conveys her hope of meeting him again, and on the back of this missive are marks from writing that had lain under it while still wet and that poetically hint at Lady Somerset's eye for men. Talbot struggles to read these inadvertently preserved words with the help of a mirror: "The mind had to restore a whole word from one letter and a smudge, divine the sense with a passion rare in scholarship!" (*EE,* 420). Yet these marks are not the last. Talbot spies indentations that had been "pressed through a previous page by a lead or silver point, which

18. Redpath, *Structural Reading,* 71; Boyd, *Novels of Golding,* 158; McCarron, *William Golding,* 57; McCarron, *Coincidence of Opposites,* 134.

was why they became visible only when the paper was held at a certain angle" (*EE*, 423). Thus, Golding persists in highlighting the difficulty that can arise in interpreting texts and a certain playful quality to constructing meaning.

Throughout the trilogy, Golding parallels or juxtaposes issues of textuality and constructedness with "constructions" of class. In other words, he draws attention to the way that class is constructed through language or communication. At one level, he deploys class to exemplify the depthless state of constructed reality so radically exposed by postmodernist theories. Also, the relativization of class constructions serves the overriding postmodernist indeterminacy evoked in the trilogy. In his essay "Myth Today," Roland Barthes writes of the way that the bourgeoisie and the Right propagate their own set of norms and values through a wide variety of media or texts to the point that they converge as a naturalized, controlling myth. Such a controlling myth, Barthes maintains, functions "to empty reality," depoliticize it, and increase the chances of an "ex-nominated" bourgeoisie flourishing undisturbed or unchallenged.[19] It is a myth that defends, among other things, established social hierarchies.

In *To the Ends of the Earth,* Golding presents classes as social constructions and, indeed, fictions that maintain cruel and exploitative relations between individuals. By a process of reversal and debasement he shows the relativity of such distinctions. He also provides a class critique by interrogating the haughty world of Augustan manners and literature that is represented by Talbot and the dull, stuffy, embellished eighteenth-century style of his journal. Golding brings Augustanism into textual conflict with a "lower" romantic sensibility that focuses more on the "popular" feelings inspired by nonclassical reality.

Augustan elitism is also set against the historical tumult of the French Revolution and its guillotines. The social hierarchy is problematized: upper classes are exposed as having purportedly "lower-class" appetites; "superior" individuals like Talbot don "low" clothing; the lower classes parody the gentry; the constructed "white line" that separates the upper and lower classes and mirrors the "invisible line" in *The Pyramid* is erased in the "classless" hysteria that results from the possibility of the ship sinking. The sense of class as a "construction" that can be broken down is, of course, reminiscent of *The Pyramid.* As in *The Pyramid,* movement up and down the "dreadful ladder" is presented as a core feature of English life. The "pyramid" highlights that individuals are not naturally superior but

19. Barthes, *Mythologies,* 143, 138–41.

are constructed to be so. This constructedness of class is more directly interrogated by Golding in his linking of the theme of language translation with the idea of the "translation" of an individual from one class to another, which, as Colley exposes, is fiercely resisted in English life. Summers's comment bears out this point: "'In our country for all her greatness there is one thing she cannot do and that is translate a person wholly out of one class into another. Perfect translation from one language into another is impossible. Class is the British language'" (*EE*, 108). Golding suggests a rather Foucauldian sense of entrapment here. He elides the dominative practices of social exclusion with the exclusionary powers of English language itself. He appears particularly exercised about the way English language is bound up with class and acts as a kind of shibboleth to keep out "lower" orders. Throughout the trilogy, he draws attention to class differentiation in terms of how English is spoken. According to Talbot, Summers imitates "'to perfection the manners and speech of a somewhat higher station in life'" (*EE*, 44) than the one he was born to. Whereas Colley sees himself as having assimilated into the gentry class, Summers maps out telltale shortcomings that betray his lower-class origins, not least in terms of language: "'It appears in his physique, his speech and above all in what I can only call his habit of subordination'" (*EE*, 108).

The fantastic and carnivalesque modes play a central role in enhancing the relativity and uncertainty promoted through the "historiographic metafiction" at the heart of *To the Ends of the Earth.* These normally satiric modes work nonsatirically to reflect the deep skepticism and relativity of postmodernism expressed in *Darkness Visible* and *The Paper Men.* As I will discuss shortly, this topsy-turvy world, subject to disorientating seabound "ups" and "downs," brings with it a social reversal or inversion. What is "high" is brought "low" and vice versa; mystery, superstition, madness, and a Gothic mood unsettle rationality. This indetermination is closely welded to the oscillating presence of intertextual combat between Augustan and romantic styles of literature that invoke a conflict between rationality and irrationality. The difficulty or aporia surrounding the truth-telling ability of historiography—dramatized, not least, in the battle of the manuscripts—and the resultant hermeneutical dilemma find a complement in the relativity installed by fantastic and carnivalesque modes.

The fantastic and carnivalesque are vital to the blurring of distinctions and opposites, which leaves us, as McCarron suggests, with the kind of reading offered in *Darkness Visible:* a difficult one without resolution. The central "opposition" is between upper and lower classes. The fantastic and carnivalesque erode the dominating influences of such distinctions. They interrogate and symbolically dismantle the ground for such differentiation. They engage to blur the "white line" between the "lower" and "higher" social orders in conjunction with a debate throughout the trilogy foregrounding the "constructed" nature of English class and hence the reversibility of this structure—its vulnerability to deconstruction and erasure. Yet this function of the fantastic and carnivalesque has not been given sufficient attention, despite the strongly metafictional aspects of *To the Ends of the Earth* that highlight the ambiguities and limitations of language.

Throughout the trilogy, but especially in *Close Quarters,* Golding's use of "residual" fantastic motifs creates a background of uncertainty and irrationality.[20] He evokes a mood of nightmarish uncertainty that extends the disintegration of borders between rationality and irrationality, magnifying what McCarron sees as the novel's central theme of "the fallibility of reason."[21] The nature of reality is constantly questioned, and mysterious and disturbing aspects of life are shown to leak into Talbot's rationalist, Augustan universe. His grip on reality is weakened by concussion and the "magical effect" (*EE,* 395) of Wheeler's paregoric that brings "strange dreams" (*EE,* 11). Distinctions between reality and unreality are problematized even though natural explanations of strange happenings are foremost. Gothic imagery, the underworld, the double, and madness all advance the mood of uncertainty.

Perhaps most striking among Golding's deployment of fantastic motifs are those that we can place under the heading "Gothic." The ship is presented as a creaking, haunted, coffinlike vessel plagued by decay, ghosts, dwarfs, witches, corpses, and superstitions, not least in the case of Colley's cabin that is viewed as a cursed place. The references to Talbot's cabin as a "'little ease'" (*EE,* 244), the movement of the ship stretching him "on the rack" (*EE,* 24) or resembling "the pendulum" (*EE,* 397), the ghostlike purser who inhabits a dark world below deck where the lanterns perform a "strange dance" (*EE,* 372) and cast moving shadows, and the story of the decapitated gunner who carried on marching up and down the ship add to the Gothic mystery and grotesque strangeness of the trilogy. In a sense, the ship resembles the Gothic medieval cathedral in *The Spire*

20. Crompton maintains that the "dark places of the heart, the cellar, the cell and the pit, yawn just as hungrily as they had done in *Darkness Visible*" (*View from the Spire,* 24).

21. McCarron, *Coincidence of Opposites,* 134.

with its spirelike mast, but also with the Jocelinesque figure of Colley in his "black coat" (*EE*, 82) and the tyrant Captain Anderson as "grim as a gargoyle" (*EE*, 83). Equally Gothic, and again touching somewhat on the dark, Kafkaesque imagery of *ungeziefer* in *Pincher Martin* and *The Paper Men*, Golding describes Talbot moving "spiderlike" (*EE*, 255) and Benét removing his spyglass "as if he had extended another limb which until then had been folded in like the leg of an insect" (*EE*, 417). However, despite McCarron's observation that Talbot's cold indifference to women bears some resemblance to that shown by Mountjoy in *Free Fall*, these references barely extend Golding's earlier debate about the totalitarian personality.

In *Close Quarters*, Talbot learns more of the irrational side to life. Fantastic elements in this novel are more developed than in *Rites of Passage*, and consequently the mood of general uncertainty and relativity is intensified. Far more is made of the Gothicism of prisons, madness, torture, and darkness. Talbot's perceptions are disturbed after suffering a concussion, taking opium, and witnessing the uncanny reappearance of the "drowned" Wheeler. Talbot thinks he is hallucinating: "'Wheeler! You are a ghost. You were drowned, I said!'" (*EE*, 284). This uncertainty questions the status of Talbot's journal entries; reality is problematized. In terms of the fantastic, then, the ship becomes a kind of living thing, as its woodwork moves grotesquely: "There was a creeping and almost muscular movement!" (*EE*, 399). When a dragline is used to clean the bottom of the ship to increase her speed, it dislodges something nightmarish: "I saw with waking eyes . . . something like the crown of a head pushing up through the weed. Someone screamed by my shoulder, a horrible, male scream. The thing rose, a waggonload of weed festooned round and over it. It was a head or a fist or the forearm of something vast as Leviathan. It rolled in the weed with the ship, lifted, sank, lifted again" (*EE*, 457–48). It is uncertain what Talbot and the others see: "Its appearance cancelled the insecure 'facts' of the deep sea and seemed to illustrate instead the horribly unknown . . . the thing towered black and streaming above me. Then it slid sideways, showed a glimpse of weedy tar and timber massive as the king tree of a thythe barn, slid sideways and disappeared" (*EE*, 458). The mystery of the object deepens the irrationality versus rationality opposition in the novel. While Talbot is left "mesmerized by the apparition," Captain Anderson passes it off as "'flotsam'" (*EE*, 459), and Summers rightly thinks it to be part of the keel.

The fantastical and Gothic are woven into Colley's romantic view of the world. His letter journal betrays his deep sense of the "strangeness of the world" (*EE*, 169). He is strongly affected by the irrational and monsterish qualities of the universe. The sea becomes "not only the home and haunt of all sea creatures but the skin of a living thing, a creature vaster than Leviathan" (*EE*, 189). Colley's sensibility vibrates with this dark unknown or "*strangeness* of this life in this strange part of the world among strange people and in this strange construction of English oak which both transports and imprisons me!" (*EE*, 192). Again, Golding refers to the incarcerative nature of the ship.

As nightmarish as the released keel is for Talbot, it is nothing compared to the sight of Wheeler, afraid of drowning a second time, blowing his head off with the blunderbuss in Colley's old cabin: "Then as my mouth opened to dismiss him with a severe injunction against his haunting of my cabin . . . his head tilted and lifted. . . . He raised towards his lips a gold or glass goblet. Then his head exploded and disappeared after or with or before, for all I know, a flash of light" (*EE*, 462). Yet again, Talbot succumbs to a fainting fit. He is left with the sense of Colley's ghostly curse: "I could not but feel that the ghost of Colley was roaming the ship. Well—we were in mortal danger, and the mind plays tricks" (*EE*, 473). Talbotian rationalism is eroded or made topsy-turvy.

Across the trilogy, the many references to hell, the Devil, and damnation intensify the uncertain, Gothic mood. The whole crew, at different times, is caught up in damning others and finding the Devil in people and events. Imagery of hell and devils is widespread, not least in Talbot's frequent visitations to the dark bowels or "nether regions" (*EE*, 379) of the ship, where Jones, the purser, is referred to as "'The devil!'" (*EE*, 381). The plague of flies at the end of the trilogy extends this underworld focus in what has been seen by McCarron as a tongue-in-cheek reference to *Lord of the Flies:* "'The flies are the devil'" (*EE*, 711).[22]

Fantastic uncertainty is further amplified by the double motif that, as we saw in Chapter 6, is featured strongly in the postmodernist fictions *Darkness Visible* and *The Paper Men.* Talbot becomes Colley's double, moving into his cabin that is a "mirror image" of his own (*EE*, 354). Like Colley, he becomes "thin" and "haggard" (*EE*, 354), and is a convert to romantic, heightened sensibility. He grows tearful at Mrs. East's singing and finds himself brought into "halls, caverns, open spaces, new palaces of feeling" (*EE*, 338). In a more minor way, Colley experiences a "doubling" of Captain Anderson when he is knocked down by him and suffers a con-

22. McCarron has noted this and other references to earlier novels (see *Coincidence of Opposites*, 125–26).

cussion: "[F]or a moment it appeared that not one but two captains were staring down at me" (*EE*, 177). Of course, Colley is not the only passenger to suffer damage to his head, and beyond the uncertainty generated by the Gothic, underworld, and doubling, by far the most striking indeterminacy surrounds issues of sanity and insanity.

The ship Talbot sails in is in many ways a Ship of Fools that, as I indicated earlier, affords Golding an opportunity to foreground, in a Foucauldian way, the powerful and incarcerative status of class and, indeed, language. The Ship of Fools, which represents a silencing and incarceration of the mad, finds a parallel with the practices of social exclusion that are entertained on the vessel through constructions of class. It also amplifies the conflict between Augustan rationalism or sanity and romantic irrationalism or insanity; and hence, it adds further weight to our sense of postmodern indeterminacy in light of the trilogy's "historiographic metafiction," wild intertextuality, and pastiche of eighteenth-century literary forms. That the ship in the trilogy is rendered a kind of *narrenschiff* cannot be disputed. Madness abounds and destabilizes perceptions of reality, from Mr. Willis being "weak in his attic" (*EE*, 34) and Talbot's opiate-fed delirium and "tropical madness" (*EE*, 66) for Zenobia to the demented Martin and Mr. Prettiman who "patrols" the ship "in all his madness" (*EE*, 89), looking to dispel superstition by shooting an albatross. Captain Anderson is deemed "mad" (*EE*, 174), and Colley's "'reason is at stake'" (*EE*, 128) following his social fall as he succumbs to "melancholy leading on to madness" (*EE*, 181). *Rites of Passage* ends with Talbot's awareness of the strain on sanity that life on board has brought: "With lack of sleep and too much understanding I grow a little crazy, I think, like all men at sea who live too close to each other and too close thereby to all that is monstrous under the sun and moon" (*EE*, 239). References to madness are widely made across the trilogy. Captain Anderson diagnoses a Ship of Fools: "'I command silence and am answered by a gale, a positive hurricane of laughter, orders shouted, conversations—is this a ship, sir, or a bedlam?'" (*EE*, 278). When Talbot's ship meets up with the *Alcyone*, there is mad commotion: "It *was* bedlam, and I, with light and noise and news near enough as mad as the others!" (*EE*, 283). When Talbot informs Smiles that he considers Jones, the purser, to be a "'real madman'" for thinking that he could buy safety, Smiles suggests, like Anderson before him, that perhaps they are all on a Ship of Fools: "'There are ships, Mr Talbot, in which every man Jack is mad save one'" (*EE*, 402). Talbot believes sailors in general "must be mad" (*EE*, 402) to do the work they do. Concern that the ship might sink brings the laughter of "bedlam" (*EE*, 442) and an outbreak of "communal hysteria" (*EE*, 473).

But the theme of madness largely surrounds the "madman" Talbot (*EE*, 354). We are constantly reminded of his deranged perceptions as he struggles to decipher what is real and unreal: "I remember clearly telling myself that all this was not a dream nor a phantasy brought on by the wounding of my head" (*EE*, 302). His rational Augustanism begins to lose ground to an irrational, romantic, Gothic sensibility. He becomes vulnerable to what Miss Chumley calls "'the profounder human emotions'" (*EE*, 338). Despite Talbot's description of Byron as a "'non-sensical fellow'" (*EE*, 322), he yearns for Colley's romantic style of writing that he sees as the product of great suffering and loneliness. A more intense poetic feeling or sensibility has opened up for him since his head injury. In fact, he is testimony to the age-old link between madness and poetic exuberance, a link lost to the Augustans, but regenerated in romanticism. But his attempts at a more effusive style are farcical: "'The mists are golden.' 'That was almost poetical. How does your head, sir?'" (*EE*, 299). His high, lofty, distant, and impersonal Augustan Latin is simply not up to the task. Although he strives to achieve a more intimate, vernacular romantic lyric, he is thwarted "by the extreme rationality of my mind and coolness of my temperament!" (*EE*, 422). Talbot again suffers a relapse when begging Captain Somerset to let him continue his journey with Miss Chumley on the *Alcyone.* Plagued by delirium, Talbot questions the accuracy of his accounts of events. Uncertainty, not least of the truth of his journal, is magnified. He is treated as a madman and returned to his cabin, or rather Colley's, where he is administered a large dose of paregoric, which brings him to a "seventh heaven" (*EE*, 353). The centrality of opium in his induction into a romantic sensibility may allude to De Quincey's *Confessions of an English Opium-Eater* (1821).[23] When Talbot learns of the *Alcyone*'s departure, he becomes mad again, and this madness takes a jealous turn when he suspects Mr. Benét's love poem (in fact addressed to Lady Somerset, as we later learn from Mr. Gibbs) was written for Miss Chumley. Talbot's worsening mental state is mirrored by the ship's unsound structure.

The theme of madness provided so starkly in *Close Quarters* is not nearly as strong in *Fire Down Below,* but it is there all the same, as Mrs. Prettiman attests: "'Are all the young men in this ship stark, staring mad?'" (*EE*, 644). The madness theme is mostly employed in terms of the "madness"

23. On this idea, see Crompton, *View from the Spire,* 130.

of the sea and Talbot's afflicted sensibilities. This is particularly so when the ship faces the Gothic "monstrosities" (*EE,* 680) of ice that remind us of Shelley's *Frankenstein* (1818). Here, the wild threat of Nature "gone mad" (*EE,* 689) disturbs Talbot's Augustan realm as he becomes confused and delirious. Of course, throughout *Fire Down Below,* as with the rest of the trilogy, madness and uncertainty are couched in the suitably Gothic net of nightmare, ghosts, torture, and devilry. Fittingly for a novel that oscillates on the border between rationality and irrationality, it ends with Talbot's dream of being left behind while Mr. Prettiman searches for a pantisocratic community.

The fantastic functions primarily to enhance the pervasive mood of uncertainty and relativity, particularly in relation to the trilogy's status as "historiographic metafiction" and hence as a work that examines postmodern instabilities. Yet in its problematizing of distinctions and oppositions, it also serves the carnivalesque reversal and deconstruction of "constructed" social stratifications. Like the fantastic, the carnivalesque amplifies the sense of epistemological crisis but also functions separately to effect a critique of class stratification through a process of debasement and mocking of the upper classes and through a revelation of the cruelty of class distinctions in the violent carnivalesque attack on the "class-climber" Colley.

In *To the Ends of the Earth,* Golding's carnivalesque is far stronger and more pervasive than the fantastic and has attracted some attention from critics, albeit brief. Bernard Dick notes the "controlling metaphor" of inversion, the antipodal, and an Apollonian-Dionysian conflict. Nicola C. Dicken-Fuller argues that antipodean or "upside-down" symbolism dominates the sea trilogy and enhances the plots of each novel. S. J. Boyd's insights have perhaps been the most helpful in terms of accounting for the undermining of class through scatology. He rightly claims that although Golding's interest in class is as "obsessive" as Jane Austen's, *To the Ends of the Earth* mocks her "novelistic world by revealing those embarrassing areas of human life that Austen so signally ignores." In *Rites of Passage,* as indeed the rest of the trilogy, "the personages of Jane Austen's England are shown as their sweating selves and, worse, their vomiting and defecating selves as well." L. L. Dickson argues that these scatological elements "contribute to a satiric, almost Swiftian, effect of deflating particular characters."[24] But the brevity of reference to "topsy-turvydom" in

24. Dick, *William Golding* (1987), 116; Dicken-Fuller, *William Golding's Use of Symbolism,* 55, 59, 66; Boyd, *Novels of Golding,* 156; Dickson, *Modern Allegories,* 125.

Dick, Dicken-Fuller, or Boyd and Dickson's glib observation of satire in Golding do not do justice to the versatile and far-reaching functions of the carnivalesque to amplify nonsatirically (alongside the fantastic) the postmodern indeterminacy generated by "historiographic metafiction," satirize the English class system, and, finally, register the violence and abuse that such class distinctions and conflict generate.

In *To the Ends of the Earth,* we are treated to a full-blown topsy-turvydom, with copious lower body scatology, sexual transgression, and antipodal symbolism. The ship becomes a circus ring and marketplace, both of which are typical domains for a world turned upside down. The threat of carnival misrule, its inversions and promotion of relativity, is at the core of the trilogy and adds to a deep sense of uncertainty. From the outset, the story concerns Talbot's "passage to the other side of the world" (*EE,* 3) or journey "'from the top of the world to the bottom'" (*EE,* 244), where he expects to see "the moon stood on her head!" (*EE,* 171). As Boyd notes, it is a transition that undermines Talbot's easy certainties and rationality: "Once the equator is passed the world of the ship is turned gradually upside down." Miss Granham becomes less severe and even attractive to Talbot, the beautiful Zenobia Brocklebank physically deteriorates, the debonair Deverel is found to be pedophilic, Mr. Brocklebank searches for dignity, Captain Anderson softens, and Talbot doubles for Colley in his foolish love for Miss Chumley.[25] The crossing of the equator marks other inversions such as peace following war, the threat of the ship capsizing like "'a loaf turned upside down'" (*EE,* 50), and Talbot's shift from Augustan sanity to romantic madness. When Mrs. Prettiman shows surprise at Talbot's new passion for feelings above intellect, he suggests the reversal is appropriate to their circumstances: "'after all, the world is upside down, is it not? We hang from it by our feet!'" (*EE,* 647). Just as the ship is going "'downhill all the way to the Antipodes!'" (*EE,* 387), Talbot keeps his head down to prevent further concussive strikes to his head. This lowering of the head mimics the slow turning upside down of his upper-class mentality, although his conversion toward becoming a demotic romantic and "'common fellow'" (*EE,* 391) is never more than temporary. Across the trilogy, a vertiginous carnivalesque operates, inverting and disrupting familiar hierarchies and erstwhile stable perspectives. Much is played on the Bakhtinian "material bodily lower stratum" and the world below deck or, as the final part of the trilogy suggests, the world "down below"—the world of passions, low desires, and violence. Spatial

25. Boyd, *Novels of Golding,* 181–83.

topsy-turvydom is widespread as the ship hogs and sags in a chaotic, disorientating up-and-down movement that makes it appear "upside down" (*EE,* 398) or as if it had "stood on its head" (*EE,* 630) and has Talbot and Miss Granham falling "towards what was temporarily down" (*EE,* 411) and Bowles walking "uphill, then downhill" before falling into his seat "as the ship came up and hit him" (*EE,* 602).

Topsy-turvydom continues in cross-dressing, diverse sexualities, and a similar array of gender performatives to those found in *Free Fall* and *The Pyramid.* As in *The Pyramid,* the performative nature of gender also extends or complements the wider sense of "construction" in terms of class that dominates the trilogy. Talbot is brought to a "womanish state" (*EE,* 10) by mal de mer, sailors parody the effeminized Colley, Mr. Brocklebank secures his beaver with a lady's stocking and later wears "pink" (*EE,* 566), Talbot mistakes the cross-dressing Miss Granham for a sailor, and during her marriage to Mr. Prettiman, Talbot becomes "the lucky girl who gets the bouquet" (*EE,* 569). Even macho Captain Anderson tends his plants like a lady in an orangery and astonishes Talbot with an amiability "as if I were a lady come to visit him" (*EE,* 138). Like a "woman in a fishing boat" (*EE,* 167), Colley is passionate for the bronzed bodies of sailors. Finally, gender inversion is extended at the end of the trilogy when Mrs. Prettiman rides "astride" her horse while Mr. Prettiman rides "sidesaddle" (*EE,* 736). The problematization of gender advances the mood of uncertainty and provides what Peter Stallybrass calls "a concrete logic through which the subversion of deference and hierarchy could be rehearsed."[26] Yet how "subversive" it is remains doubtful because as in *The Pyramid, Darkness Visible,* and *The Paper Men,* Golding's instantiation of gender inversions and marginal sexualities equivocates between being liberative on the one hand and repressive on the other. This "polymorphous perverse" of gender positions in *To the Ends of the Earth,* alongside the diverse sexualities of prostitution, pedophilia, voyeurism, homoeroticism, and even frotting, may amount to a politics of inclusion.[27] It may reflect both Golding's apparent sympathy for so-called subordinate and marginalized groups, including homosexuals, and a postmodern decentering of notions of stable identity and sexuality. Sexual difference extends the general uncertainty of the novel, its "coincidence of opposites," and adds to Golding's declassification of epistemological domains and people themselves. However, although the wide reference to arguably marginal

26. Stallybrass, "'Drunk with the Cup,'" 54.
27. Dollimore, *Sexual Dissidence,* 205.

gender positions and sexualities may signal Golding's desire to disrupt dominant notions of identity or to engage in what Jonathan Dollimore calls "sexual dissidence," they are also employed satirically as repulsive, perverse, or deviant acts alongside widespread scatology to undermine notions of class superiority. Away from the carnivalesque function to advance indeterminacy, most strikingly through spatial topsy-turvydom and gender inversion, it is this other function of undermining of class hierarchy to which we now turn.

In many ways, the social hierarchy found on board forms an ideal setting for presenting, in a microcosmic way, class-ridden England. Golding has shown an awareness of the pettiness of naval class distinctions and hierarchy in his essay "A Touch of Insomnia," where he refers to his own experience of crossing the Atlantic on a liner: "Here the class system was axiomatic. You couldn't invade a plusher bar simply by readiness to pay more. Nor could you descend to a comfortable pub if you wanted to pay less. Where you were born, there you stayed" (*HG*, 135). Infected with an upper-class haughtiness, Talbot is acutely aware of his status and his connections with other powerful individuals. On a ship heavily demarcated along class lines, not least in terms of grading dining tables, toilets, speech, and clothing, he seeks out his equals and barely gives Colley the time of day. He looks out for the "better sort of officer if there be any" (*EE*, 8). Preoccupied with "rank" (*EE*, 34) or "orders" (*EE*, 57), the class-pickled Talbot is pleased to meet Mr. Summers: "It is not the captain, of course—but the next best thing. Come! We are beginning to move in society!" (*EE*, 39).

Throughout the trilogy we are alerted to the "infinitesimal gradations" of class (*EE*, 43). Talbot despises the common folk who attend Colley's religious service, as he does those who came to view his patron's Canalettos but really desired to see "how the nobility live" (*EE*, 60). It is Talbot's superior status that allows him to enter the quarterdeck uninvited, whereas Colley is not so lucky, finding himself humiliated by Captain Anderson. As Summers tells Talbot later, this happened "'because he could not humiliate *you*'" (*EE*, 115). Talbot is so steeped in notions of class superiority that it is only when Summers reminds him of "'*Noblesse oblige*'" (*EE*, 112), that he brings himself to visit the ailing Colley, and then only after his stinking cabin has been sanitized.

The parvenu Colley is accused of returning to his lower-class origins by crossing "the white line that separates the social orders" on board (*EE*, 235). In the front part of the ship, away from the gentrified aft, he succumbs to "low" desires. Thus, his "fall" is cast in "social terms" (*EE*, 89). Yet Golding shows that such low behavior is not the sole preserve of the common people. He reveals the same low-bound appetites for squalor among the upper classes. As we see with Brocklebank, who tries to pass off the prostitutes, Mrs. Brocklebank and Zenobia, as his wife and daughter, dirt gathers beneath the fingernails of the privileged classes as much as elsewhere.

Golding undermines class differences by presenting the universal nature of lower bodily functions and subjecting even the best or superior cabins to the seepage of fouled seawater. From the very beginning of *To the Ends of the Earth,* we are presented with a liturgy of anality and shit that emanates from all quarters of the ship and not just the crowded and "low" forecastle. Golding makes much of the ironic accommodation of the well-to-do passengers at the rear or backside of the vessel, and bowel actions, especially vomiting, as we have seen, have a lowering effect on the privileged passengers. In *Close Quarters,* it is "well-to-do" effluence as much as that from other passengers that circles the becalmed ships. In *Fire Down Below,* the haughty Talbot is as much part of a toilet world as those he might consider below him, like Summers, who had risen in rank by performing "'the naval operation known as "coming aft through the hawse-hole"'" (*EE,* 44). Talbot's sanitized, elevated status, which has been preserved by careful toileting, is increasingly challenged as he begins to stink like a common seaman and his private defecation is granted an audience. Talbot's class is besmirched by this intrusion of stink just as Brocklebank is lowered by being the trilogy's great producer of "'"*horrid smells*"'" (*EE,* 703). Equally, the diverse transgressive sexualities of the superior classes further undermine their status. Nearly all forms of sexual life are catered to here, as I noted earlier, such as Brocklebank's prostitutes, the "voyeurism" of Talbot's godfather who wants Talbot to "'Tell all'" (*EE,* 67) in his journal, the pedophilic desires of Deverel and, indeed, Talbot whom Benét accuses of preying on "'schoolgirls'" (*EE,* 628), oral sex practiced by Colley, the buggery of Colley by officers as well as common seamen, and even frotting: "We, so to speak, *rubbed* on each other" (*EE,* 507).

Golding cannot resist any opportunity to snipe at class. He attacks the sham politesse of the upper classes and uses Colley as a means of exposing the evil consequences of class-ridden English society. Colley acts as a kind of sacrificial victim caught in transition between the lower and upper classes. As René Girard has observed in his *Violence and the Sacred,* violent sacrifice lies at the heart of carnival festivals and rituals. Certainly, Greek Dionysianism and the Girardian focus on violence are more heavily stressed in Golding's carnivalesque than what Michael André Bernstein has viewed as the more "populist and idealizing optimism" of

Mikhail Bakhtin's presentation of carnival.[28] Colley, an "outsider" clergyman who obsequiously courts the "aristocratic" Talbot, pays a high price for investing in social face when he finds himself shamed by descent into what is deemed to be the squalid, sexually transgressive world of the lower classes. His descent reveals a good deal of barbarism lurking behind the notion of "civilized England" and the evil consequences of class division and conflict. As a dark, microcosmic presentation of England, the crowded, class-ridden ship is the site for violent carnivalesque behavior.

The ship in *To the Ends of the Earth* can be seen as a carnival square or even a Dionysian carnival float, or *carne navalis.*[29] A "spirit of farce" (*EE,* 223)—a theme replicated in *The Paper Men*—dominates the trilogy. A mood of carnival excess is apparent quite early on when Colley, walking like a "drunken crab" (*EE,* 13), vomits over Talbot and the "clownish" (*EE,* 18) lieutenant walks comically at an angle to the deck. As in *The Paper Men,* clowns and clownishness are featured strongly. When, for example, Talbot helps Miss Granham to keep her feet, he appears to "dance like a clown carrying a puppet" (*EE,* 411). Yet persistent undermining and turning upside down of seriousness or earnestness are most powerfully presented in attacks upon religion and its seagoing representative, Colley. Early on, Wheeler warns Talbot that wearing his greatcoat with its capes might lead to him being mistaken for a chaplain and hence a target for ridicule. Such ridicule is evoked early on in a service Colley conducts that is disrupted by the comical presence of the prostitute Miss Brocklebank dressed frivolously and wearing masklike makeup, "skylarking sailors" (*EE,* 59), and the "windmachine" Mr. Brocklebank who lets off "a resounding fart" (*EE,* 60). Later, when Colley visits the forecastle dressed in "ecclesiastical finery" (*EE,* 90), there are cheers and laughter "as if Colley were an acrobat or juggler" (*EE,* 92) or subject to "a mocking pantomime" (*EE,* 93). Talbot witnesses common sailors, dressed in Colley's clerical garments, perform an "exaggeratedly mincing parody of the female gait" (*EE,* 96). Talbot views this as a challenge from the lower classes to their social betters: "This play-acting was not directed only inwards towards the fo'castle. It was aimed *aft* at us!" (*EE,* 96). Talbot is ever sensitive to this "threat to social stability that might at any moment" easily arise out of "horseplay" (*EE,* 96). It is an awareness of the thin divide between carnival "fun" and violence, protest and revolution. Talbot's sensitivity to the possibility of carnival becoming a dangerous attack on social class and

28. Bernstein, *Bitter Carnival: Ressentiment and the Abject Hero,* 36.
29. Dick describes the ship as a "Dionysian theater" (*William Golding* [1987], 125).

stability is in keeping with legislative responses to carnival from the seventeenth to mid-nineteenth centuries that, as Allon White argues, set out "to eliminate carnival and popular festivity from European life." This can be seen as an attempt by privileged classes to dampen popular, subversive movements. It also marked the "pursuit of purity" that was a "fundamental aspect of bourgeois cultural identity"—a "purity" that is under attack in *To the Ends of the Earth.*[30]

A drunken and ecstatically joyful Colley finally emerges from the forecastle wearing "common" clothes (*EE*, 99). Stripped of his clerical garments, he has been inverted or "dethroned" (*EE*, 187).[31] With his head resting happily on Billy Rogers's chest, he makes his way to the bulwark and pisses against it. This "public micturition" (*EE*, 100) shocks Talbot and fellow travelers. We learn later that "clownish" (*EE*, 237) Colley had been decrowned or brought low by performing fellatio on his "king" (*EE*, 188), Billy Rogers—an act that leads to him being cruelly and violently mocked in a way that goes beyond a mere carnivalesque "'lark'" (*EE*, 69).

Whereas Colley is set up as the performer of religious rites such as birth, marriage, and death, his own various humiliations culminate in a pagan rite performed at the crossing of the equator. As "equatorial fool" (*EE*, 238), he is brought before a mock throne of King Neptune by Cumbershum and Deverel who are disguised in nightmarish "carnival mask[s]" (*EE*, 78) and thrown into the "'badger bag'" (*EE*, 69)—an awning full of befouled seawater. As the "excluded" (*EE*, 200) victim of the mob's "cruel sport" (*EE*, 204), he is subjected to the "rough music" or shivaree of "yelling and jeering and positively demonic laughter" (*EE*, 203) and suffers obscene questioning before being viciously gagged, smeared, or "'shampoo'd'" with the contents of the "bag" (*EE*, 204). This carnivalesque decrowning is greeted with a "storm of cheering and that terrible British sound which has ever daunted the foe; and then it came to me, was forced in upon my soul the awful truth—*I was the foe!*" (*EE*, 204). Here again, as in his earlier novels, Golding portrays how the English are quite capable of participating in the exclusionary practices toward abject outsiders that lie at the heart of noncelebratory carnivalesque. He reveals the violent, shit-bound reality underpinning the civilized gloss of English life. Like *Lord of the Flies, To the Ends of the Earth* presents English "childish savagery" (*EE*, 238). In the trilogy, Golding extends or revisits his earlier at-

30. White, "Hysteria," 160, 164.

31. As Boyd suggests, the inversion of Colley or his downfall is related in a "Pythonesque way" (*Novels of Golding*, 164).

tack on the construction of Englishness in opposition to Nazism at a different historical juncture. He undermines a construction of English national identity in opposition to French atrocities during the Terror by suggesting that given the right climate, such atrocities can erupt on English soil: "Yet now as I struggled each time to get out of the wallowing, slippery paunch, I heard what the poor victims of the French Terror must have heard in their last moments and oh!—it is crueller than death, it must be—it must be so, nothing, *nothing* that men can do to each other can be compared with that snarling, lustful, storming appetite" (*EE*, 204–5). Golding's reference to "childish savagery," use of ship imagery, and the links noted earlier between "flies" and the "devil" suggest an important continuity all the way through his writing, from *Lord of the Flies* to *To the Ends of the Earth,* in terms of attacking English notions of moral superiority, and also the low-bound appetites of the upper classes. In *To the Ends of the Earth,* as in *Lord of the Flies,* the upper classes are undermined both through their lower body needs and by their participation in exclusionary violence, although this is more ironically done in the trilogy in light of the fate of the privileged classes during the French Terror. They are willing spectators to the cruelty of the mob. Colley bemoans the fact that the "superior" classes failed to prevent "such an excess" directed against him and even encouraged it from the wings, as it were (*EE*, 204). Yet the attack on Colley is also a product of class divisions and conflict. As a social parvenu, he is a convenient target for the mob that wishes to vent its frustrations at the privileged classes on board, just as their continued ridicule and mocking are aimed "aft" in a gesture of class defiance.

The discharging of Prettiman's blunderbuss by Summers brings the "brutal sport" to a close, and the jesting of "the *people*" reverts to a "more jovial rather than bestial" form (*EE*, 205). However, Golding establishes quite clearly the ease with which English carnival practices like those elsewhere can turn nasty or vicious, or, as Anderson suggests, get "'out of hand'" (*EE*, 208). The threat of further violence hangs over the unfortunate clergyman who has been cast as the "archbishop" of the "lower" parts or "southern hemisphere" (*EE*, 84). Anderson and Summers warn him off from seeking repentance from the "people." They advise him that it may result in more conclusive violence. Indeed, apart from the "badger bag" abuse, it appears from the inquest following Colley's death that in addition to his indiscretion with Billy Rogers, Colley may have endured a gang rape in the forecastle: "'It is likely enough that the man, helplessly drunk, suffered a criminal assault by one, or God knows how many men, and the absolute humiliation of it killed him!'" (*EE*, 215). When Billy

Rogers is interrogated and accused of buggering Colley, the inquest is quickly folded up when he offers to name all the officers involved. Here we locate Golding's determination to implicate the gentlemanly officer class in rites of the "back passage"—sexual transgression that the upper classes might prefer to project on the lower classes when, in fact, the upper-class bugger is a well-known phenomenon going right back to at least the eighteenth century and prevalent in the nineteenth- and twentieth-century public schools. This play on "passage" and bodily orifices can be found elsewhere, for example, when Talbot believes Deverel knows about his lovemaking with Zenobia: "'For a moment I thought he might refer to the passage between me and Miss Zenny'" (*EE,* 78). In his treatment of Colley, Deverel considers Captain Anderson to have *"rode the man hard"* (*EE,* 105).

Carnivalesque aggression is not the sole preserve of the lower-class mob. We witness a certain brutality to Talbot's lovemaking with Zenobia, one of Brocklebank's "doxies" (*EE,* 105). There is an aggressiveness that belies his sense of class superiority, decorum, moral rectitude, and civility. In a juxtaposition of sexual dominance with masculinity and warfare—a feature of many of Golding's earlier novels—Talbot considers the gunnery a possible site for sex, bends for the *"main course"* in a manner reminiscent of earlier representations of male sexual consumption, and finally ejaculates at the same time that Prettiman's blunderbuss is fired by Summers. Following this Sternean farce, Talbot resembles Sammy Mountjoy or "Pincher" Martin in his cruel indifference and contempt for Zenobia: "I wished nothing so much as that she would vanish like a soap bubble or anything evanescent" (*EE,* 77).

In *To the Ends of the Earth,* Golding's preoccupation with masculine violence, especially homosexual and heterosexual sadism, is bound up with warfare. The buggery and violent, cruel mocking of Colley and Talbot's aggressive sexual consumption of Zenobia take place on an English warship during the Napoleonic Wars, and the ship's fighting credentials and weaponry are frequently referred to. Captain Anderson is despotic and tyrannical and heads a generalized propensity to macho acts of violence and cruelty. This "petty tyrant" (*EE,* 118) who is the originator or impetus for violence toward Colley stands with a "prayerbook clutched like a grenade" (*EE,* 224) at his funeral. War imagery adds to the sense of conflict in the wider world of politics, between Augustanism and romanticism, but also between classes. Although set in a historical period distant from his earlier preoccupation with World War II atrocity, Golding continues his attack upon English notions of moral superiority over its aggressors at a familiar wartime threshold. Lawrence Friedman observes that the setting of the sea trilogy around the "historical watershed" of the Napoleonic Wars rivals World War II as Golding's "usual demarcation between two worlds." He continues: "Perhaps because his own war triggered a critical shift in his consciousness, Golding situates his novels at moments of transition."[32] Furthermore, Talbot's concern that any peace following war could bring a chaotic "liberty" (*EE,* 55) may reflect Golding's own anxieties about the fragmented, libertarian postmodern society that seemed, in some way, the legacy of World War II.

Alongside the violent, carnivalesque treatment of Colley and Talbot's sexual consumption of Zenobia, a more diffuse record of public entertainment, foolery, public mocking, and carnivalesque behavior in the parody of a quadrille and the decrowning of "Lord" Talbot extends the overall attack on the English class system. Talbot's belief at the beginning of *Close Quarters* that he had "cured" himself of "a certain lofty demeanour" (*EE,* 243) is a little premature. He remains a class bigot who is complacent about the upper-class government of England and sees nothing wrong in his godfather's rotten borough. He chooses socially to "*cut* Zenobia Brocklebank since she has made a habit of parleying with the common seamen" (*EE,* 251). Mr. Askew attacks his haughty demeanor when Talbot, despite not being a peer, demands to be treated as a member of the elite or ruling classes. Such hauteur is reemphasized by his ingratitude when offered the small accommodation of the lieutenant's quarters following Wheeler's bloodbath suicide in Colley and Talbot's cabin. I suspect that he supports the kind of bigoted view that Brocklebank holds: "'It is fashionable to talk about the corruption and vice of high society. That is nothing to the corruption and vice of low society, sir! We should never forget that the vicious we have always with us . . . '" (*EE,* 456–57). Yet the threat of sinking due to the ship's increasingly sorry state breaks up the kind of hierarchy Talbot and Brocklebank sup on. Indeed, earlier in the novel, we find this kind of critique operating in the incident where the "high" Talbot bangs his head in the gunnery and receives applause for being a "common mock" (*EE,* 276). Such topsy-turvydom, of course, is placed within a wider context of carnival life spawned at the meeting of the two ships when a carnivalesque "fairground" (*EE,* 289), "bazaar," or "market" (*EE,* 298) mood ensues and a ball is planned. The threat of excessive carnivalesque behavior looms over preparations for the "'day of festivity'" (*EE,* 299). Miss Granham fears that the sailors might provide an unedifying en-

32. Friedman, *William Golding,* 141.

churned into froth and bubble by its passage into history. In this sense, Golding's interrogation of the "truth-telling" ability of history in his "historiographic metafiction"—and here we must include history of the Holocaust—may be seen as a corollary of the traumatization of epistemologies advanced partly by the new and darker level of atrocities spawned in the twentieth century, not least the Holocaust and mass bombing of civilian populations. Ultimately, Golding appears to be far more absorbed in producing "historiographic metafiction" and dismantling binary oppositions than revealing English propensities to atrocious violence or pillorying the upper classes. As in *Darkness Visible* and *The Paper Men,* the fantastic and carnivalesque in *To the Ends of the Earth* are central to a ludic postmodern reflection on epistemological uncertainties.

Despite John Bayley's insistence that Golding is not one of those "modish" writers "who continually dig us in the ribs to remind how roguishly they are exploiting the fictionality of fiction," he looks that way to me.[33] His trilogy, like *The Paper Men,* operates as a highly self-conscious text. He betrays a desire to languish in more pleasurable yet infinitely less significant subject matter. There is a sense that Golding wishes to escape, or at least mitigate, the horrific and disturbing subject matter of wartime violence and atrocity integral to his imagination by a more urbane and historically distanced focus on the status of language. Golding's comments on his use of "navalese" in the trilogy, or what Talbot calls "Tarpaulin," are especially revealing: "I learnt this language first of all from books and later from service in the Royal Navy during the Second World War. The language was one of my few pleasures during the experience and I immersed myself in it to the extent that by the end of the war professionals sometimes had difficulty in knowing what I was talking about" (*EE,* x). In *To the Ends of the Earth,* we can see Golding reenact his actual wartime strategy of escape, of immersion in the joy of a private language. It is as if Golding's focus on the status of language in the trilogy provides a similar insulation, this time from the memory of atrocity. We might say Golding has lightened up. He notes that "optimism . . . gained the upper hand" in the trilogy: "So Edmund Talbot or perhaps I myself found myself, himself or ourselves less and less inclined to portray life as a hopeless affair in the face of *this* enormity, *that* infinity and *those* tragic circumstances, particularly the ones which plagued poor Robert James Colley" (*EE,* xi). This optimism might be a relief to some, even to Golding. Yet his continued and darker use of noncelebratory carnivalesque to restate the potential

33. Bayley, "Seadogs and Englishmen," 30.

of the English to bloody their hands in excessive or atrocious violence and victimization opposes this optimism. This aspect, alongside the exposure of the low-bound appetites of the English upper classes, is as evident in Golding's final trilogy as it is in his first published novel, *Lord of the Flies.*

8

Conclusion

Socialist Subversions?
The Radical and Reactionary in Golding's Satire

As I have indicated on several occasions, I am indebted to previous critics for their limited references to historical context; acknowledgment of Dionysian violence, scatology, and topsy-turvy symbolism; brief advertisement of the fantastical and satirical aspects to Golding's fiction; discussions concerning his attack on class and exploration of the fictionality of fiction; and recognition of Greek, Latin, Christian, and secular influences. Yet these worthwhile strands of critical activity have lacked any comprehensive or focused appraisal as part of a whole. In other words, there has been no synthesis of available, though often underplayed, knowledge and insight to establish governing structures and functions to Golding's complex fictions. Significantly, there has been a general exclusion of "extraliterary" satire and the "subliterary" fantastic as not worthy of serious critical attention.

This book marks a radical departure from earlier Golding criticism. It begins to bridge the gap between the complexity of Golding's fiction and various critical readings of it that have not responded sufficiently to neighboring fields of study, inquiry, and analysis, but have run for the line with blinkers on. In an interview with John Haffenden, Golding insists, albeit rather pompously: "I've never read a criticism of my work which is half complicated enough."[1] Indeed, Golding constructs difficult, obfuscatory fictional labyrinths into which, one suspects, he rather gleefully watches critics disappear. His novels appear increasingly to offer a slippery, highly self-conscious literary performance against a background of source-hunting, overdetermining, and maybe superfluous criticism. Once he started noticing (as he could not fail to do) critical interest in his work, he inevitably attempted to keep several steps ahead of critics in the attitude of "Right, this will give them something to think about!" The analy-

1. Haffenden, "William Golding: An Interview," 9.

sis provided in this book gets to the hub of the difficult, interwoven, and diverse themes that Golding generates in his fiction by revealing the highly plastic fantastic and carnivalesque modes that lend themselves to pluriform and contradictory structures, not least in their ability to be both satirical and nonsatirical, celebratory and noncelebratory, and, in terms of the fantastic, to render qualitative analogues to those targets he attacks. These analogues include the Gothic deathliness of the class-ridden Stilbournians, or the shocking revelations of human evil through uncanny resolutions to fantastic hesitation, but also reflect or complement epistemological indeterminacy that is charted in both Golding's modernist and postmodernist self-consciousness and that, as I and others have suggested, may itself bear some relation to the upheavals of World War II and its aftermath. I consider that the synthesis and extension of previously separate but useful insights into Golding's use of the fantastic and carnivalesque reveal the engine house that generates the complexity and dizzying pluriformity of Golding's oeuvre. The fantastic and carnivalesque are by far the most crucial, dynamic, and plastic set of devices in his fiction. In a sense, the complexity of Golding's fiction is transcended by a closer understanding of the various operations of these modes.

The fantastic and carnivalesque are foundational to satirical and nonsatirical approaches that are broadly and respectively divided between Golding's early and late fiction. No previous study has analyzed or, indeed, acknowledged this central structure to his work. Nor have the related fantastic and carnivalesque modes and their functions or the interanimation that takes place in Golding's work between form and history been addressed properly and afforded the level of contextuality extended here. I directly link the various deployments of the fantastic and carnivalesque to historical, political, and social change in the late twentieth century. Prior to this study, a reading of the transition in Golding's fiction from a noncelebratory attack upon Englishness in relation to totalitarianism and class toward a more celebratory undermining of religious authority and the authority of the writer and critic, and, finally, a nonsatirical interrogation of postmodern indeterminacy, had not been achieved. However, this transition, which suggests a resolution of a grief response to World War II atrocity, is a halting one. Often, both satirical and nonsatirical functions are interwoven. Transition, if you like, is a matter of degree; Golding's later work is generally less satirical than his earlier work. Golding himself admitted to Haffenden that his earlier focus on human "malignancy" in the aftermath of World War II gave way or diminished as he got older: "But it is true that as one gets older and more objective, one loses some of the passionate, concentrated earnestness about the problem of a particular generation—my own generation."[2] We can also read here a decline in his appetite for radical or subversive politics.

My view that the development of Golding's fiction corresponds with historical change counters the notion of him as an individual literary genius producing universal fictions from under his skull without reference to his times or to other contemporary writing. In other words, social and political changes and literary "movements," or fashions that explore class, atrocity, and fictional representation, all shape Golding's novels. World War II and particularly the Jewish Holocaust greatly influenced his fiction of the 1950s. His more tentative, fabular representation of the Holocaust in the early 1950s (*Lord of the Flies* and *The Inheritors*) gives way to a stronger, more realistic historicizing of contemporary totalitarianisms in the late 1950s (*Pincher Martin* and *Free Fall*). All the novels in this period are concerned to interrogate English "immunity" to totalitarian behavior. This attack on English national identity that constructs itself in opposition to totalitarianism makes his fiction, like Orwell's, pretty unique, yet the general focus on atrocity and totalitarianism was shared by many European and several British writers. Golding's experimentalism in *Pincher Martin* and *Free Fall* also suggests a family resemblance with the self-conscious works of other postwar British writers that achieve a new level of postmodern skepticism after the 1960s. In the cold war chill, his novels of the 1960s (*The Spire* and *The Pyramid*) at first lost political edge, only to regain it in a rather contradictory fashion. *The Spire* marks an escape from contemporary life and an extension of aestheticism, although there is the suggestion that his attack on religious authority—a theme that occurs throughout his fiction in one form or another—may, as S. J. Boyd suggests, reflect the mood of Vatican II reform of previously rigid Catholic dogma. However, this link is rather tenuous. A more likely context is the similar reform movement in the Church of England. In more general terms, beyond the skepticism that led Golding to avoid signing up with any particular religious group, his interrogation of religious authority reflects a cooling of religious fervor in postwar Britain, evident in falling church attendance figures and increased secularization.

In *The Pyramid*, a more forthright attack upon the English class system appears to grow substantially from the kernel of "class war" lodged but underdeveloped in *The Spire*, and reflects the wider postwar appetite for "classlessness" and the writings against the class system by the "Move-

2. Ibid., 11.

ment" and "Angries" in the 1950s and 1960s. Yet, like much of this literature, *The Pyramid* often presents a comic collapse of serious concerns with the injustices of class. This deflation is all the more pronounced in Golding's later fiction, *To the Ends of the Earth.*

Golding's novelistic return in 1979 with *Darkness Visible* once again betrays a strong correspondence with historical and cultural changes. This melanoma of a novel grapples with the convulsive social upheavals in postwar Britain from the war to the 1970s, not least in terms of continuing atrocities and terrorism that, according to Golding, had been fueled by a chaotic permissiveness. The novel keeps company with a host of postmodernist fictions that reflect an unremitting assault on epistemologies in what is perceived to be an increasingly fragmentary, entropic, and depthless world. Unlike postmodernist texts that celebrate "surface" and new intensities of heterogeneity, *Darkness Visible* appears to react with Leavisite conservatism against the postmodern flood of multimedia culture, both installs and yet scorns new sexual liberties, and registers contemporary fears of nuclear apocalypse and calls for disarmament.

The Paper Men continues Golding's pessimistic grappling with postmodernism and reflects the increased prominence and challenge of new literary criticism in the 1970s and 1980s, particularly the Barthesian notion of the "death of the author" and the fictional status of biography. Like all Golding's novels, *The Paper Men* can be located in or on the edge of other literary camps or fashions such as those that lampoon university life or undermine the English literature industry—a fact that contradicts the often overexaggerated presentation of Golding as a literary loner who has little in common with other traditions.

To the Ends of the Earth further establishes him as a writer of his time whose creative designs are not entirely unique but reflect contemporary concerns and issues registered elsewhere. As a "historiographic metafiction," the "sea trilogy" joins a wide pool of writing that debates the "truth-telling" status of history. But it also marks a shift in Golding's initial prickly and contradictory response to postmodernism.

I have argued throughout this book that Golding deploys the fantastic and carnivalesque both satirically and nonsatirically. Before going on to discuss just how radical or reactionary Golding is in all this, I wish to give a summary of how various elements related to the fantastic and carnivalesque *work* in the novels, how they *differ* in the way they work from text to text, and what the ultimate significance of all this is for Golding's exploration of authority and authoritarianism in the aftermath of World War II. Because he uses a great diversity of fantastic and carnivalesque motifs to fulfil a number of functions, I want to argue that Golding is making some kind of reflexive commentary on the polysemic nature of these plastic forms and demonstrating the volatility between function and form.

Golding's versatile deployment of fantastic and carnivalesque modes—which find their base in Menippean satire—has revealed the flexible nature of these modes. A survey of these modes across the novels reveals "basic staples" that are used, bar the odd exception, throughout his work and also a great diversity in the constituency of these modes. Let us first list them. In the fantastic, for example, there are Gothic elements, particularly death, corpses, ghosts, nightmare, the grotesque, and darkness; dreams, visions, madness, doubling, the "other" or "outsider," and the underworld also loom large across his fiction, and appear in varying intensities. Outside of such "basic staples," Golding's fiction presents a wide spattering of other fantastic images and motifs, often along similarly Gothic lines, for example, vampirism, gargoyles, incarceration, dwarfs, rats, and the cellar. These elements are most prevalent in *Pincher Martin* and *Free Fall* where the theme of personal nightmare is particularly strong. Each of Golding's novels joins others in sharing various permutations of fantastic motifs, though few of them are exclusive to a particular novel and even then, with the exception of the "Beast" in *Lord of the Flies* and the "ogre" in *The Inheritors,* have a largely peripheral status: bats in *Pincher Martin,* rats in *Free Fall,* necrophilia in *The Pyramid,* and superstition in *To the Ends of the Earth.* The lack of strong differentiation between fantastic motifs used in any particular novel and those deployed elsewhere suggests their strong continuity and replication across his work. Or put another way, they achieve similar functions in different novels.

In terms of the carnivalesque, basic staples are found in general topsy-turvydom, conducted through a range of inversions, reversals, and decrownings; antinomian or potentially subversive behavior; transgressive sex such as rape; homosexuality, pedophilia, and sadism; consumption and the open mouth; the mob or crowd; festivity, transformative fire, oxymorons, foolery, and masquerade; and scatology and images to do with the lower body. More diversely, Golding refers to carnival sites such as the fair, market, tavern, village, or town square; swearing and obscenities; and shivaree and the mocking of cuckolds. Among the more interesting, though isolated, deployments of carnivalesque is the pig motif in *Lord of the Flies* that links childish savagery with anti-Semitic carnival practices and the *carne navalis* and "Ship of Fools" in *To the Ends of the Earth,* which emphasize the incarcerative nature of the English class system as well as adding their weight to the general topsy-turvydom. Again, the poverty of idiosyncratic deployment of carnivalesque motifs in individual novels follows that of fantastic motifs and further stresses the connectedness and interweaving of motifs across Golding's fiction. Significantly, when it comes to inclusiveness in terms of both "basic staples" and diversity of elements, *To the Ends of the Earth* appears to be something of a "catchall" work. Golding seems to pull out all the stops in terms of including most of the fantastic and carnivalesque motifs used throughout his work, even though fantastic hesitation itself is "residual" in the trilogy. Significantly, the trilogy combines all the major satirical and nonsatirical functions of the fantastic and carnivalesque, except in terms of attacking the English literature industry, and also neatly bookends Golding's oeuvre not just by repeating an attack on class and totalitarian behavior begun in his first novel, *Lord of the Flies,* but also by revisiting the theme of childish savagery.

A survey of major elements to Golding's fiction also identifies characteristics that display a significant shift between his early and later fiction. Golding's early fiction *(Lord of the Flies, The Inheritors, Pincher Martin, Free Fall)* is demonstrably different from the later fiction *(Darkness Visible, The Paper Men, To the Ends of the Earth)* in several ways, and these two fields are in some sense both separated and attached by the fiction of a middle phase to Golding's development *(The Spire, The Pyramid).* We can refer to each band as "early," "middle," or "late" fiction. Whereas the early novels are more dominantly fabular and tragic, the middle and later ones are more realistic and tragicomic. There is a distinctive lightening of tone between early and late fiction. There is a shift from noncelebratory to a more celebratory carnivalesque and from "durative" fantastic with shock breaking of hesitation to alternating "total" and "residual" fantastic forms that present greatly reduced shock breaking of much weaker hesitation. This shift corresponds to a perception of Golding's fiction as moving from a more satirical, pessimistic, and didactic early phase to a more optimistic, dialogical one in which there is a deflation of satire. The gloomier fiction of the early stage is certainly borne out by a number of aspects that, although revisited in later fictions, are more prominent here. These are satirical attacks on the construction of English national identity in opposition to totalitarian Nazism and communism and various fantastic and carnivalesque correlates or analogues: misogyny, totalitarian "soldier-male" behavior, metamorphosis, the *ungeziefer,* racism, the demonization of the Jewish "other" or "outsider," British imperialism, the Holocaust, sadism, the "open mouth" image of greed and consumption (particularly in terms of violent sexual exploitation and cannibalism), torture, executions, and decapitations. Although warfare is a staple of Golding's fiction generally, war and its related atrocities are more grimly and pessimistically treated in the early fiction, with the exception of *Darkness Visible* in the later phase.

In *Darkness Visible,* we locate a reflux of earlier concern with atrocity. This is reestablished, as it were, with references to other more contemporary atrocity concerns such as the Vietnam War and nuclear proliferation. Compared to the rather dour fantastic and carnivalesque focus in the early fiction, the later works deploy a more playful order of witches, ghosts, superstition, festivity, pantomimic mockery, and clowning. Interestingly, Golding's later presentation of totalitarian personalities in *Darkness Visible* and *The Paper Men* is more inclusive in terms of gender; he suggests more clearly than he did in *Free Fall* that women as well as men are attracted to authoritarianism. This has probably something to do with wider cultural changes in terms of the growing prominence of gender politics and feminism. Golding wanted to suggest that aggression, domination, and brutality are not simply attributable to masculinity or patriarchy and that feminist celebrations of women in opposition to men skew the truth that women also participate in this darker side.

Besides a more oblique attack upon class in *Lord of the Flies,* Golding's satire against the English class system is largely located in the middle and late phases of his work. In the middle phase, the attack on class in *The Pyramid* appears more in earnest than in *To the Ends of the Earth,* but again, compared to the early phase, is distinctly more lighthearted. A number of fantastic and carnivalesque characteristics peculiar to those works that wholly or in part attack class can be isolated. These are: the exclusion of the "other" or "outsider"; carnival mob or crowd; anal rape; carnival festivity and sites such as the square, fair, and market; and a mood of revolution or social subversion. These motifs and themes suggest the exclusionary nature of class hierarchy, domination, and exploitation of a "lower" class by a superior class—potently evoked in the image of anal rape—the gathering of "lower" classes in sites they typically control or, rather, are allowed to control (the market, fair, and square), and the threat that the gathered mob, crowd, or masses hold for social authorities in terms of riotous protest or revolution. As with class, Golding's other satirical attacks against religious authority—a minor feature in the early fiction, but most prominent in *The Spire,* and strongly featured in the later fiction—and against the English literature industry in *The Paper Men,* are all located in an increasingly celebratory, tragicomic, and playful literature. In terms of the attack on religious authority, most notably in *The Spire, Darkness Visible, The Paper Men,* and *To the Ends of the Earth,* cross-dressing and general mockery of religious figures or practice looms large. The effeminized status of cassocked clergy is particularly susceptible to cross-dressing gibes, as we saw in the treatment of Colley in *Rites of Passage.* Mockery of ecclesiastical offices, of course, pervades carnival practices down the centuries. In terms of Golding's attack on English literature, he deploys residual, farcical fantastic motifs and huge dollops of clownishness to interrogate the *author*ity of the writer and critic. In addition, and more seriously, he marks, albeit crudely, the exploitation and aggressiveness that can accompany a "paper" life through a redeployment of noncelebratory carnivalesque previously used to illustrate the "totalitarian personality." However, that said, and bearing in mind other earnest themes in *Darkness Visible* and *To the Ends of the Earth,* the later phase in Golding's work remains more celebratory, more tragicomic.

At the heart of this lighter phase of Golding's fiction is a pronounced development toward a ludic postmodern form of literature, which has both continuities and discontinuities with the earlier phase of modernist self-consciousness. Both the phase of modernist self-consciousness *(Pincher Martin, Free Fall, The Spire)* and postmodernist metafiction *(Darkness Visible, The Paper Men, To the Ends of the Earth)* share fantastic and carnivalesque features that are generally exclusive to or most pronounced in these phases and that intensify the mood of indeterminacy. Specifically, in both phases Golding deploys the following relativizing themes or motifs in a strong form: spatial topsy-turvydom, the relativity of mouth versus scatological anus, the underworld, theatricality of life, metamorphosis, madness, and variant mental disruptions such as dreams, visions, and hallucinations. However, in what appears to be a heightening and exaggeration of the early phase of self-consciousness and the questioning of epistemologies, Golding intensifies the theme of theatricality and several other relativizing themes located in his earlier fiction. Significant among these is a more formidable presentation of the theme of the double, the antipodes, opiate, and alcohol-induced delirium, ghosts, and transgressive sexualities, particularly gender inversion and cross-dressing. Golding also introduces into this later phase of overt farce the theme of the circus and clowns that magnifies a sense of playful abandon and carnivalesque relativity.

A closer examination of the deployment of fantastic and carnivalesque motifs reveals a quite stark and interwoven structure. There is a wavelike expansion and contraction in the range of fantastic and carnivalesque elements across the novels. What is noteworthy is that this expansion and contraction coincide with quite distinctive changes in theme or subject matter that occur between pairs or groups of novels: *Lord of the Flies* and *The Inheritors, Pincher Martin* and *Free Fall, The Spire* and *The Pyramid, Darkness Visible* and *The Paper Men,* and *To the Ends of the Earth,* which comprises *Rites of Passage, Close Quarters,* and *Fire Down Below* that for convenience, and because they are all of a piece, are dealt with together as a group not dissimilar to a "pair." As I indicated in the chapter headings, these pairs or groupings of novels are to a large degree thematically and respectively bound in terms of "literature of atrocity," "the totalitarian personality," "constructions of fiction and class," "postmodernity and postmodernism," and finally "historiographic metafiction." On examination, it appears that the fantastic and carnivalesque elements in *The Inheritors* closely match those in *Lord of the Flies*—its thematic partner—but are featured only minimally in the next pairing. In turn, *Pincher Martin* and *Free Fall* draw heavily on motifs used in the first novel of the previous pair, *Lord of the Flies,* but not the second, *The Inheritors.* This pattern has a kind of snowballing effect such that each subsequent pair of novels or group owes little to all the second novels of previous pairs but repeats many of the motifs of the first novels of each of them. Thus, finally, *To the Ends of the Earth* owes little to *The Paper Men, The Pyramid, Free Fall,* and *The Inheritors* (second novels in pairs) yet repeats many of the motifs of *Darkness Visible, The Spire, Pincher Martin,* and *Lord of the Flies* (first novels in pairs). I do not wish to suggest here that, from the start, Golding had a grand plan for structuring his fiction. Rather, I would suggest that this pattern developed out of Golding's acute awareness of or sensitivity to form and a need to differentiate between themes, and perhaps even owes something to his musicality.

Notably, whereas the second novels in any pair all share many of their motifs either moderately or strongly with the first novels of subsequent pairs, these subsequent pairs all have a surplus of motifs that bears little resemblance to previous second novels of any pair. For example, if we look at *Lord of the Flies* and *The Inheritors,* the latter shares a number of fantastic and carnivalesque motifs with the first novel of the second pair, *Pincher Martin:* from Gothic corpses, death, darkness, decapitation, execution, and the double to sadism, scatology, and images of consumption and the open mouth. *Pincher Martin* and *Free Fall,* however, deploy a host of motifs not found in *The Inheritors* such as ghosts, nightmare, torture, metamorphosis, underworld, madness, *ungeziefer,* antipodean imagery, pedophilia, shivaree, cuckolding, homosexuality, obscene language, theatricality, and foolery. Furthermore, many of these motifs that do not appear in *The Inheritors*—ghosts, nightmare, underworld, madness, homosexuality, and foolery—are to be found in *Lord of the Flies.* In effect, the first novel of any pair tends to have a strong signature of motifs shared by other first novels. Clear examples of this are found in the use of the fool or foolery, gargoyles, dwarfs, cellar, the antipodean, phallicism, anal rape, shivaree, cuckolding, billingsgate or swearing, theatricality, and the carnival square. This kind of signature is much weaker in the second novels of pairs that share only a few isolated and peripheral motifs such as vomiting and catascopia. In addition, some differentiation, albeit slight, also occurs in the deployment of motifs peculiar to, or that are featured more consistently in, the alternate first, third, and fifth pairs or groups. In *Lord of the Flies* and *The Inheritors,* there are the motifs of the "other" as beast or ogre, strange focalization, carnival pig, and decrowning. In *The Spire* and *The Pyramid,* there are the motifs of witches and a group of transgressive sexualities concerned with necrophilia, spanking, exposure, and incest. In *To the Ends of the Earth,* there are the images of the "Ship of Fools," *carne navalis,* and voyeurism. This kind of pattern or structuring of fantastic and carnivalesque elements is too consistent to be arbitrary. It appears that Golding used different ranges of motifs to separate different phases in his fictional development. At this level, then, I think that the fantastic and carnivalesque provide a kind of thematic punctuation.

Golding is undoubtedly a satirist in his general interrogation of the flawed nature of humanity; exposure of the destructive, exclusionary practices of the English class system; and instantiation of English totalitarianism, and in his attack upon religious authority and the authority of the writer and critic. Even when he is not being satirical as such, he employs satirical form to complement a presentation of modernist and postmodernist indeterminacy and to question epistemological authority in his increasingly metafictional novels. It is fair to say that the fantastic and carnivalesque combine and function satirically and nonsatirically in his novels to undermine all forms of authority and authoritarianism. In this sense, Golding is opposed to the exploitation, exclusionary practices, and injustice that attend everything "high," "superior," or "powerful" in all its guises, but especially in terms of "high" Englishness. Across his fiction, the authority of class and the barbarism of authoritarian regimes and behavior are persistently juxtaposed. However, Golding's broad critique of authority and authoritarianism becomes more lighthearted or, rather, less than decidedly pessimistic in his later novels.

Golding is an interesting test case, because at every turn it is difficult to argue one way or another about his micro- and macropolitical views. Making sense of his politics is a tricky business. The fragmented nature of his work intimates a progressive approach to social phenomena alongside a more traditional, reactionary response. There is, if you like, a strong sense in his fiction that he is struggling between deep-rooted traditional or conservative visions of social life and his left-wing insights. His overall political diversity and contradiction are emphasized in his approach to sexual identity, class, postmodernism, and the historical referent. It is to these four sites of contradiction that I now wish to turn my attention.

First, then, the topsy-turvydom of cross-dressing, gender inversion, and instantiation of marginal sexualities, particularly homosexual, pedophilic, and sadistic forms, occurs right across the novels and poses the question of just how radical a sexual dissident Golding really is. Certainly, he is ahead of his time in viewing gender as performative in *Free Fall, The Pyramid,* and *To the Ends of the Earth,* often in a way that complements issues of social construction and class. More radically, or beyond this, his representations of marginal sexualities throughout his work can be viewed as sexually dissident or disruptive of dominant notions of stable identity. Yet, he seems to mute such radicalism within a rather conservative and stereotypical presentation of both marginal sexualities and women. Strong, positive examples of the latter are not available in Golding's fiction. Contradictorily, the "soldier-male" thrust to his writing, which is highly critical of masculine barbarism, is combined with narrowly patriarchal representations of women and homosexuals. These groups are generally characterized in a negative and shallow manner that brings to mind popular, televized representations contemporary to Golding, along the lines of carry-on-type films and shows. Indeed, I suggest that Golding inflects his otherwise serious writing with rather narrow and fatuous representations of gender. He provides the kind of sexual dissidence that the sexually conservative can titillate themselves with and confirm their prejudices. In general, his novels gravitate conservatively toward the world of men—an approach that appears dated in light of more recent analyses of gender presentation.

In contrast to any claim that Golding is sexually dissident, he often merely invokes sexual diversity and topsy-turvydom either as a feature of his general theatrical theme, a satirical and hence condemnatory device, or as a means to bolster his portrayal of first modernist and then postmodernist uncertainty. Thus, we are unable to be categorical about what Golding achieves in his instantiation of gender inversions and marginal sexualities since his representations equivocate between being liberative on the one hand and repressive on the other. His claim that he extends homosexuals, for example, "every benefit" and counters homophobia is simply not true. Welding homosexual themes with pedophilia and sadism as part of satirical strategy in both his early and his later fiction, or as convenient fodder for his increasingly comical novels, is hardly being sexually dissident. Rather, it buys into homophobic constructions of homosexuality.

Second, although Golding appears to attack class, his universalizing notions of human hierarchy and psychologies within it can be seen as reinforcing the English class system rather than undermining it. He installs "class" at the same time that he attempts to subvert it. In addition, the fact that class issues are treated more comically in his later fiction suggests that Golding has little stomach for a more thoroughgoing critique. This is further confirmed in his promotion of middle-class dominance. Most of Golding's characters are middle class, and the few working-class characters are relegated to the equivalent of one-dimensional, walk-on parts. In *The Spire* and *To the Ends of the Earth,* the working-class role is narrowed to being a repository of fun, sexuality, and subversion, often of a violent sort. For example, in the sea trilogy, the working-class characters are like a baying pack of hounds dragging down the hindmost, Colley. The narrow appropriation and stereotyping of the working class are extended in Golding's presentation of them in a vision that propelled much of mid-twentieth-century socialism, that is, of the working-class, en masse, offering a salvific brake on capitalism and an antidote to the elite and pompous. In presenting the working class as a lumpen mass, Golding strips its individual members of their legitimate and diverse voices. Furthermore, there is something of the fairy tale about Golding's valorization of manual labor in his representations of working-class masons and sailors. There is not the ring of authenticity or sense that Golding had a great deal of contact with the working classes.

Third, Golding's use of postmodernist techniques is also contradictory because he seems to be opposed to such radical trends. He utilizes a whole spectrum of postmodernist techniques—cranked up from the earlier modernist self-consciousness to a new pitch of epistemological skepticism and representation of depthlessness—that can be seen as reinscribing what he seeks to oppose. In other words, his treatment of postmodernism involves him in unresolvable contradictions. In both *Darkness Visible* and *The Paper Men,* Golding takes a rather aggressive left-wing humanist stance toward the cultural threat posed by postmodernism and the rise of the "culture industry" and crudely critiques an English literature industry as having become a depthless phenomenon. Yet, he does this in the teeth of an extensive presentation and adoption of postmodernist tech-

intellectual trends such as those addressing the Holocaust and postmodernism. This anchoring of Golding in history and the history of ideas includes a more detailed understanding of his debt to a wide variety of literature, not least fantastic and carnivalesque writing, and advances the warrant for viewing him as a satirist. By demonstrating the richness of satirical content in Golding's work, the case is strengthened for investigating English literature that is not prima facie satirical. It has been my contention throughout that satire is far too important a subject of inquiry to limit to those candidates who more readily fit the label "satirist."

It is difficult to ascertain exactly what kind of left-winger Golding really was since it is patently difficult to do justice to or resolve the diverse politics that emerge in his fiction. At various points, Golding, with his background of left-wing nurturance and political engagement, does seem to be genuinely antipathetic to social injustice. This is revealed particularly strongly throughout his fiction in the horror he felt at the extermination of the Jews and violence toward outsiders and the weak generally, and in his anger about the damaging effects of class. Yet any radicalism is always dulled by reactionary and conservative aspects to his writing. One might be tempted to attach just one descriptive label to his political outlook, but doing so would not work. Golding evinces an array of radical and reactionary positions that causes us to think of him as several things all at once, most prominently as a non-Marxist socialist, left-wing humanist, conservative moralist, or sobered liberal humanist. Golding appears very much as a moderate left-wing writer who disdains both left and right political extremes, engages with politics and contemporary history in his fiction, yet at the same time is attracted to certain conservative values, particularly in relation to seeking universals of the human condition, his religious interpretations of the world (although generally laced with humanist skepticism), moral essentialism, and his elitist defense of literature as opposed to popular culture. Like Angus Wilson, we can see Golding in the middle-class liberal humanist tradition, although in a more jaded, postwar sense, expecting, as C. B. Cox puts it, "progress to come through education rather than political reform" and "concerned with the moral life of the individual, with ways in which he can develop a mature sense of values." Golding is more truly a liberal humanist turned pessimist, appalled by violent, radical, and coercive social change. Or, put another way, he both invokes liberal humanist values and tempers them in the light of twentieth-century barbarism. Cox asserts: "Since 1950, William Golding has emerged as the one new major English novelist who can describe human egotism and suffering with convincing realism but for who the individual life can still achieve meaning, and even heroism." Despite the view of Golding as a religious writer, he leans quite heavily toward a more humanistic skepticism, that is, to humanity having sole responsibility for changing material conditions, as Peter Faulkner indicates when he says that *Lord of the Flies* "suggests the existence of no power beyond humanity likely to help in solving the problems of human society; and relates these problems directly to the rejection of reason." Furthermore, in *Pincher Martin,* "the process by which Christopher Martin becomes Pincher the crab is seen in the terms of a humanistic morality. It is not his rejection of God that is emphasised, but his selfishness towards men." However, what marks Golding's "distance from humanism," Faulkner insists, is the fact that, rather than presenting an optimistic slant on humanity's ability to progress, he focuses on the "disease" of man.[4]

As a result of my approach in this book, we are able to characterize the historical and biographical shifts or developments in Golding's work more clearly. The early concern with World War II atrocity and trauma and totalitarianism gives way—rather like a grieving process—to a more playful, postmodern literature, although Golding is by no means entirely comfortable with postmodern indeterminacy and its ethical correlates. It is curious that in those works outlining Nazi actions and brutality, the references to totalitarianism are at their most oblique and allegorical. Here, Golding's radical unhousing of the fascist within by repeatedly pointing to the way everyday English people (as he depicts them), given the chance, will act in a totalitarian way is defused or muffled by universalism. The stronger historical instantiation of totalitarian behavior is made in a lurching progression to *Darkness Visible* against a recurrent tendency to escape contemporary history and engagement in favor of universalizing the human condition. In other words, Golding's apparent attack on English moral superiority suffers from a self-canceling aspect to his work. This ambivalence between the universal and the present is just part of Golding's widely contradictory viewpoint. If we are to attribute a label to Golding's overtly dialogized positions or approaches, then "subversive reactionary" rings true. We cannot resolve this puzzle. As Golding makes his historical attacks through the satirical and historicizing deployment of fantastic and carnivalesque modes, so too does he turn from history by using these versatile, fluid modes nonsatirically. These modes are per-

4. Cox, *The Free Spirit: A Study of Liberal Humanism in the Novels of George Eliot, Henry James, E. M. Forster, Virginia Woolf, Angus Wilson,* 6, 172; Faulkner, *Humanism in the English Novel,* 172, 177.

fectly suited to deliver the ambivalence and containment that the label "subversive reactionary" affords. These versatile forms, working on multiple levels of noncelebratory and more celebratory satire and nonsatire, allow Golding to twist and turn from any reductive criticism of his fiction and, in a paradoxical way, stand above the parapet and duck below it at the same time. They ensure that what Colin MacCabe calls "a battle of readings" rumbles on without an end in sight.[5] What I have tried to offer in this book is a clear-sighted, historicized, and politicized account of the nonresolution or nontotalization that arises out of Golding's novels and blocks any simple understanding of what they achieve.

Golding's novels have been a particularly tough testing ground for a politicized and historicized reading because they have been appropriated into the canon of English literature, widely read in schools, and subjected to a great deal of commentary and scholarship that has set a conservative tone. This book provides a sensitizing perspective for interrogating Golding's work and, indeed, other literature in a new way. The analysis of his complex and plastic use of the fantastic and carnivalesque to achieve multiple and sometimes coincidental functions promotes a strategy for reading his novels in a way that has hitherto slipped through the net of criticism. It also alerts us to the way Golding appears to have smuggled fantastical elements into mainstream fiction and the canon, giving us a fresh perspective of him as a partly transgressive writer. By mixing universal literature with more degenerate or devalued literary forms, and in combining the radical and reactionary, the satirical and nonsatirical, the tragic and comic, he attains a multivoiced and dialogical creativity. It is precisely the strength of taking a theoretically sensitive, synthetic, and historical approach that we can begin to register and, indeed, reconcile what might be seen as dialectical contradiction.

5. MacCabe, *James Joyce and the Revolution of the Word,* 26.

Bibliography

Abrams, M. H. *A Glossary of Literary Terms.* New York: Holt, Rinehart, and Winston, 1981.

Ackroyd, Peter. *Dickens.* London: Sinclair-Stevenson, 1990.

Adorno, Theodor W. *Negative Dialectics.* Trans. E. B. Ashton. London: Routledge, 1973.

Alter, Robert. *Partial Magic: The Novel as a Self-Conscious Genre.* Berkeley and Los Angeles: University of California Press, 1975.

Alvarez, A. *Beyond All This Fiddle.* London: Allen Lane, 1968.

———. "The New Poetry; or, Beyond the Gentility Principle." In *The New Poetry,* by A. Alvarez. Harmondsworth: Penguin, 1966.

Appleyard, Bryan. *The Pleasures of Peace: Art and Imagination in Post-War Britain.* London: Faber and Faber, 1989.

Arendt, Hannah. *The Origins of Totalitarianism.* London: Andre Deutsch, 1986.

Armitt, Lucie. *Theorising the Fantastic.* London: Arnold, 1996.

Armstrong, Nancy, and Leonard Tennenhouse, eds. *The Violence of Representation: Literature and the History of Violence.* London: Routledge, 1989.

Attridge, Derek, Geoff Bennington, and Robert Young, eds. *Post-Structuralism and the Question of History.* Cambridge: Cambridge University Press, 1987.

Babb, Howard S. *The Novels of William Golding.* Columbus: Ohio State University Press, 1970.

Baker, James R. *William Golding: A Critical Study.* New York: St. Martin's, 1965.

Bakhtin, Mikhail. *The Dialogic Imagination: Four Essays.* Ed. Michael Holquist. Trans. Caryl Emerson and Michael Holquist. Austin: University of Texas Press, 1981.

———. *Problems of Dostoevsky's Poetics.* Ed. and trans. Caryl Emerson. Minneapolis: University of Minnesota Press, 1984.

———. *Rabelais and His World.* Trans. Helene Iswolsky. Bloomington: Indiana University Press, 1984.

Bakhtin, Mikhail M., and P. N. Medvedev. *The Formal Method in Literary Scholarship: A Critical Introduction to Sociological Poetics.* Trans. Albert J. Wehrle. Baltimore: Johns Hopkins University Press, 1991.

Banville, John. "Introduction: George Steiner's Fiction." In *The Deeps of the Sea,* by George Steiner. London: Faber and Faber, 1996.

Barker, Paul. "The Way Up and the Way Down." *Times* (June 1, 1967): 7.

Barnes, Julian. *Flaubert's Parrot.* London: Picador, 1984.

Barth, John. "The Literature of Exhaustion." *Atlantic Monthly* (August 1967): 29–34.

Barthes, Roland. *Image Music Text.* Trans. Stephen Heath. London: Fontana, 1977.

———. *Mythologies.* Trans. Annette Lavers. London: Vintage, 1972.

———. *Roland Barthes by Roland Barthes.* Trans. Richard Howard. London: Macmillan, 1977.

———. *S/Z.* Trans. Richard Howard. New York: Hill and Wang, 1976.

Baudrillard, Jean. *Simulacra and Simulation.* Trans. Sheila Faria Glaser. Ann Arbor: University of Michigan Press, 1994.

Bauman, Zygmunt. *Life in Fragments: Essays in Postmodern Morality.* Oxford: Blackwell, 1995.

Bayley, John. "Seadogs and Englishmen." *Guardian* (March 17, 1989): 30.

Benjamin, Jessica, and Anson Rabinbach. Foreword to *Male Fantasies II, Male Bodies: Psychoanalyzing the White Terror,* by Klaus Theweleit. Cambridge: Polity Press, 1989.

Benjamin, Walter. *Illuminations.* Ed. Hannah Arendt. Trans. Harry Zohn. London: Fontana, 1992.

Benson, Larry D., ed. *The Riverside Chaucer.* 3d ed. Oxford: Oxford University Press, 1988.

Bergonzi, Bernard. *The Situation of the Novel.* London: Macmillan, 1970.

Bernstein, Michael André. *Bitter Carnival: Ressentiment and the Abject Hero.* Princeton: Princeton University Press, 1992.

Bertens, Hans. *The Idea of the Postmodern: A History.* London: Routledge, 1995.

Biles, Jack I. *Talk: Conversations with William Golding.* New York: Harcourt Brace Jovanovich, 1970.

Biles, Jack I., and Robert O. Evans, eds. *William Golding: Some Critical Considerations.* Lexington: University Press of Kentucky, 1978.

Blanchard, W. Scott. *Scholar's Bedlam: Menippean Satire in the Renaissance.* London and Toronto: Associated University Press, 1995.

Booker, M. Keith. *Techniques of Subversion in Modern Literature: Transgression, Abjection, and the Carnivalesque.* Gainsville: University of Florida Press, 1991.

Boyd, S. J. *The Novels of William Golding.* New York: Harvester, 1990.

Brake, Michael. *Comparative Youth Culture: The Sociology of Youth Cultures and Youth Subcultures in America, Britain, and Canada.* London: Routledge, 1985.

Briggs, Julia. *Night Visitors: The Rise and Fall of the English Ghost Story.* London: Faber and Faber, 1977.

Bristol, Michael D. *Big-Time Shakespeare.* London and New York: Routledge, 1996.

———. *Carnival and Theater: Plebeian Culture and the Structure of Authority in Renaissance England.* New York and London: Routledge, 1989.

Brooke-Rose, Christine. *A Rhetoric of the Unreal: Studies in Narrative and Structure, Especially of the Fantastic.* Cambridge: Cambridge University Press, 1983.

Brooks, Peter. *The Melodramatic Imagination: Balzac, Henry James, Melodrama, and the Mode of Excess.* New Haven: Yale University Press, 1976.

Bürger, Peter. *Theory of the Avant-Garde.* Trans. Michael Shaw. Manchester: Manchester University Press, 1984.

Burguière, André. "The Charivari and Religious Repression in France during the Ancien Regime." In *Family and Sexuality in French History,* ed. Robert Wheaton, Robert Hareven, and Tamara K. Hareven. Philadelphia: University of Pennsylvania Press, 1980.

Burke, Peter. *Popular Culture in Early Modern Europe.* London: Temple Smith, 1979.

Butler, Judith. *Gender Trouble: Feminism and the Subversion of Identity.* New York and London: Routledge, 1990.

Butler, Marilyn. *Romantics, Rebels, and Reactionaries: English Literature and Its Background, 1760–1830.* Oxford: Oxford University Press, 1982.

Butler, Rupert. *The Black Angels.* London: Hamlyn, 1978.

Cammarota, Richard S. "*The Spire:* A Symbolic Analysis." In *William Golding: Some Critical Considerations,* ed. Jack I. Biles and Robert O. Evans. Lexington: University Press of Kentucky, 1978.

Camus, Albert. *The Fall.* Trans. Justin O'Brien. London: Hamish Hamilton, 1957.

Carey, John, ed. *William Golding, the Man and His Books: A Tribute on His 75th Birthday.* London: Faber and Faber, 1986.

Cavaliero, Glen. *The Supernatural and English Fiction.* Oxford: Oxford University Press, 1995.

Chanady, Amaryll Beatrice. *Magical Realism and the Fantastic: Resolved versus Unresolved Antinomy.* New York and London: Garland, 1985.

Collins, Robert A., and Howard D. Pearce, eds. *The Scope of the Fantastic:*

Theory, Technique, Major Authors. Westport, Conn.: Greenwood, 1985.

Connery, Brian A., and Kirk Combe, eds. *Theorizing Satire: Essays in Literary Criticism.* New York: St. Martin's, 1995.

Cornwell, Neil. *The Literary Fantastic: From Gothic to Postmodernism.* New York: Harvester, 1990.

Cox, C. B. *The Free Spirit: A Study of Liberal Humanism in the Novels of George Eliot, Henry James, E. M. Forster, Virginia Woolf, Angus Wilson.* Oxford: Oxford University Press, 1963.

Coyle, Martin, Peter Garside, Martin Kelsall, and John Peck, eds. *Encyclopedia of Literature and Criticism.* London: Routledge, 1990.

Craig, David. *The Real Foundations: Literature and Social Change.* London: Chatto and Windus, 1973.

Crompton, Don. *A View from the Spire: William Golding's Later Novels.* Ed. and comp. Julia Briggs. Oxford: Blackwell, 1985.

Currie, Mark, ed. *Metafiction.* London and New York: Longman, 1995.

Danow, David K. *The Spirit of Carnival: Magic Realism and the Grotesque.* Lexington: University Press of Kentucky, 1995.

Darnton, Robert. *The Great Cat Massacre.* Harmondsworth: Penguin, 1985.

Davis, Natalie Zemon. *Society and Culture in Early Modern France: Eight Essays.* Oxford: Polity, 1987.

Dawson, Graham. *Soldier Heroes: British Adventure, Empire, and the Imagining of Masculinities.* London and New York: Routledge, 1994.

Debord, Guy. *Society of the Spectacle.* Detroit: Black and Red, 1970.

De Felice, Renzo. *Interpretations of Fascism.* Trans. Brenda Huff Everett. Cambridge: Harvard University Press, 1977.

de Man, Paul. *The Rhetoric of Romanticism.* New York: Columbia University Press, 1984.

Derrida, Jacques. *Of Grammatology.* Trans. Gayatri Chakravorty Spivak. Baltimore: Johns Hopkins University Press, 1976.

Des Pres, Terence. *The Survivor: An Anatomy of Life in the Death Camps.* Oxford: Oxford University Press, 1980.

Dick, Bernard F. *William Golding.* Boston: Twayne, 1967.

———. *William Golding.* Rev. ed. Boston: Twayne, 1987.

Dicken-Fuller, Nicola C. *William Golding's Use of Symbolism.* Lewes, England: Book Guild, 1990.

Dickson, L. L. "H. G. Wells Upside Down: Fantasy as Allegory in William Golding's *The Inheritors.*" In *The Scope of the Fantastic: Theory, Technique, Major Authors,* ed. Robert A. Collins and Howard D. Pearce. Westport, Conn.: Greenwood, 1985.

———. *The Modern Allegories of William Golding.* Tampa: University of South Florida Press, 1990.

Docker, John. *Postmodernism and Popular Culture.* Cambridge: Cambridge University Press, 1994.

Dollimore, Jonathan. "The Challenge of Sexuality." In *Society and Literature, 1945–1970,* ed. Alan Sinfield. New York: Holmes and Meier, 1983.

———. *Sexual Dissidence: Augustine to Wilde, Freud to Foucault.* Oxford: Clarendon Press, 1991.

Drew, Philip. "Second Reading." In *William Golding's "Lord of the Flies": A Source Book,* ed. William Nelson. New York: Odyssey, 1963.

Eagleton, Terry, "Awakening from Modernity." *Times Literary Supplement* (February 20, 1987): 194.

———. "Bakhtin, Schopenhauer, Kundera." In *Bakhtin and Cultural Theory,* ed. K. Hirschkop and D. Shepherd. Manchester: Manchester University Press, 1989.

———. *The Illusions of Postmodernism.* Oxford: Blackwell, 1996.

Eatwell, Roger. *Fascism: A History.* London: Vintage, 1996.

Eco, Umberto, V. V. Ivanov, and Monica Rector. *Carnival!* Berlin: Mouton, 1984.

Elbaz, R. *The Changing Nature of the Self: A Critical Study of the Autobiographic Discourse.* London: Croom Helm, 1988.

Eliot, T. S. *Collected Poems, 1909–1962.* London: Faber and Faber, 1974.

Emerson, Caryl. *The First Hundred Years of Mikhail Bakhtin.* Princeton: Princeton University Press, 1997.

———. "Irreverent Bakhtin and the Imperturbable Classics." *Arethusa* 26 (1993): 123–40.

Fairclough, Peter, ed. *Three Gothic Novels.* Harmondsworth: Penguin, 1968.

Faulkner, Peter. *Humanism in the English Novel.* London: Elek / Pemberton, 1976.

Feinberg, Leonard. *Introduction to Satire.* Ames: Iowa State University Press, 1967.

Feldman, Yael S. "Whose Story Is It Anyway? Ideology and Psychology in the Representation of the Shoah in Israel's Literature." In *Probing the Limits of Representation: Nazism and "the Final Solution,"* ed. Saul Friedlander. Cambridge: Harvard University Press, 1992.

Fiedler, Leslie. "The Class War in British Literature." In *The Collected Essays of Leslie Fiedler.* Vol. 1. New York: Stein and Day, 1971.

Foucault, Michel. *Madness and Civilization: A History of Insanity in the Age of Reason.* Trans. Richard Howard. London: Routledge, 1971.

Fowler, E. W. W. *Nazi Regalia.* Secaucus: Chartwell, 1992.

Freedman, Ralph. "The New Realism: The Fancy of William Golding." In *William Golding's "Lord of the Flies": A Source Book,* ed. William Nelson. New York: Odyssey, 1963.

Friedlander, Saul, ed. *Probing the Limits of Representation: Nazism and "the Final Solution."* Cambridge: Harvard University Press, 1992.

Friedman, Lawrence. *William Golding.* New York: Continuum, 1993.

Frye, Northrop. *Anatomy of Criticism.* Harmondsworth: Penguin, 1990.

Fuller, Roy. "The Writer in His Age." *London Magazine* (May 1957): 43–44.

Gąsiorek, Andrzej. *Post-War British Fiction: Realism and After.* London: Arnold, 1995.

Geertz, Clifford. *Local Knowledge: Further Essays in the Interpretation of Culture.* New York: Basic Books, 1983.

Gilman, Sander. *Franz Kafka: The Jewish Patient.* New York and London: Routledge, 1995.

———. *The Jew's Body.* New York and London: Routledge, 1991.

Gilroy, Paul. *There Ain't No Black in the Union Jack: The Cultural Politics of Race and Nation.* London: Hutchinson, 1987.

Gindin, James. *William Golding.* Basingstoke and London: Macmillan, 1988.

Girard, René. *Violence and the Sacred.* Trans. Patrick Gregory. Baltimore: Johns Hopkins University Press, 1977.

Goldhill, Simon. *The Poet's Voice: Essays on Poetics and Greek Literature.* Cambridge: Cambridge University Press, 1991.

Golding, William. "Crabbed Youth and Age." *Guardian* (November 20, 1975): 16.

———. *Darkness Visible.* London: Faber and Faber, 1980.

———. *The Double Tongue.* London: Faber and Faber, 1995.

———. *Free Fall.* London: Faber and Faber, 1961.

———. *The Hot Gates and Other Occasional Pieces.* London: Faber and Faber, 1970.

———. *The Inheritors.* London: Faber and Faber, 1961.

———. *Lord of the Flies.* London: Faber and Faber, 1958.

———. *A Moving Target.* London: Faber and Faber, 1982.

———. *The Paper Men.* London: Faber and Faber, 1985.

———. *Pincher Martin.* London: Faber and Faber, 1956.

———. *Poems.* London: Macmillan, 1934.

———. *The Pyramid.* London: Faber and Faber, 1969.

———. *The Spire.* London: Faber and Faber, 1965.

———. *To the Ends of the Earth: A Sea Trilogy.* London: Faber and Faber, 1992.

———. "War in Vietnam (Letter to the Editor with John Le Carré, Paul Scofield, C. P. Snow)." *Times* (May 23, 1967): 9.

———. "The Writer in His Age." *London Magazine* (May 1957): 45–46.

———. "Writers and the Closed Shop (with Sixty-two Other British Writers and Intellectuals)." *Times Literary Supplement* (April 25, 1975): 1.

Graff, Gerald. *Literature against Itself: Literary Ideas in Modern Society.* Chicago: University of Chicago Press, 1979.

Gregor, Ian, and Mark Kinkead-Weekes. "The Strange Case of Mr Golding and His Critics." In *William Golding's "Lord of the Flies": A Source Book,* ed. William Nelson. New York: Odyssey, 1963.

Gregor, James A. *Interpretations of Fascism.* Morristown: General Learning Press, 1974.

Gutleben, Christian. "English Academic Satire from the Middle Ages to Postmodernism: Distinguishing the Comic from the Satiric." In *Theorizing Satire: Essays in Literary Criticism,* ed. Brian A. Connery and Kirk Combe. New York: St. Martin's, 1995.

Haffenden, John. *Novelists in Interview.* London: Methuen, 1985.

———. "William Golding: An Interview." *Quarto* (November 1980): 9–12.

Halsey, A. H. *Change in British Society: From 1900 to the Present Day.* Oxford: Oxford University Press, 1995.

Hamilton, Paul. *Historicism.* London and New York: Routledge, 1996.

Hawkey, Andrew. Introduction to *Revolution and Reason and Other Essays by Oswald Mosley,* ed. Michael Quill. Lewiston, Maine: Edwin Mellen Press, 1997.

Hesse, Silke. "Fascism and the Hypertrophy of Male Adolescence." In *The Attractions of Fascism: Social Psychology and Aesthetics of the Triumph of the Right,* ed. John Milfull. New York and Oxford: Berg, 1990.

Hewison, Robert. *Culture and Consensus: England, Art, and Politics since 1940.* London: Methuen, 1995.

———. *In Anger: Culture in the Cold War, 1945–60.* London: Weidenfeld and Nicolson, 1981.

———. *Too Much: Art and Society in the Sixties, 1960–75.* London: Methuen, 1986.

Hirschkop, Ken, and David Shepherd, eds. *Bakhtin and Cultural Theory.* Manchester: Manchester University Press, 1989.

Hitler, Adolf. *Mein Kampf.* Trans. Ralph Manheim. London: Pimlico, 1992.

Hobsbawm, E. J. *Primitive Rebels: Studies in Archaic Forms of Social Movement in the 19th and 20th Centuries.* Manchester: Manchester University Press, 1959.

Hodson, Leighton. *William Golding*. Edinburgh: Oliver, 1969.
Hoggart, Richard. *The Uses of Literacy: Aspects of Working-Class Life with Special Reference to Publications and Entertainments.* Harmondsworth: Penguin, 1990.
Hollinger, Robert. *Postmodernism and the Social Sciences.* London: Sage, 1994.
Holquist, Michael. Prologue to *Rabelais and His World,* by Mikhail Bakhtin. Bloomington: Indiana University Press, 1984.
Holquist, Michael, and Katerina Clark. *Mikhail Bakhtin.* Cambridge: Harvard University Press, 1984.
Homer. *The Iliad.* Trans. Alexander Pope. London, 1821.
Horkheimer, Max, and Theodor W. Adorno. *Dialectic of Enlightenment.* Trans. John Cumming. London: Allen Lane, 1973.
Howard, Jacqueline. *Reading Gothic Fiction: A Bakhtinian Approach.* Oxford: Clarendon Press, 1994.
Hughes, Ted. "Baboons and Neanderthals: A Rereading of *The Inheritors.*" In *William Golding, the Man and His Books: A Tribute on His 75th Birthday,* ed. John Carey. London: Faber and Faber, 1986.
Hutcheon, Linda. "Historiographic Metafiction." In *Metafiction,* ed. Mark Currie. London and New York: Longman, 1995.
———. *Narcissistic Narrative: The Metafictional Paradox.* New York and London: Methuen, 1984.
———. *A Poetics of Postmodernism: History, Theory, Fiction.* New York and London: Routledge, 1988.
———. *A Theory of Parody: The Teachings of Twentieth-Century Art Forms.* New York: Methuen, 1985.
Hynes, Samuel. "Novels of a Religious Man." In *William Golding's "Lord of the Flies": A Source Book,* ed. William Nelson. New York: Odyssey, 1963.
Izenberg, Gerald N. "Text, Context, and Psychology in Intellectual History." In *Developments in Modern Historiography,* ed. Henry Kozicki. Basingstoke and London: Macmillan, 1993.
Jackson, Rosemary. *Fantasy: The Literature of Subversion.* London: Routledge, 1991.
Jameson, Fredric. *Postmodernism; or, The Cultural Logic of Late Capitalism.* London: Verso, 1991.
Jenkins, Alan. "The Cambridge Debate, Continued." *Times Literary Supplement* (January 30, 1981): 112.
Johnston, Arnold. *Of Earth and Darkness: The Novels of William Golding.* Columbia: University of Missouri Press, 1980.

Josipovici, Gabriel. *The World and the Book.* London: Macmillan, 1994.
Kaplan, Alice Yaeger. *Reproductions of Banality: Fascism, Literature, and French Intellectual Life.* Minneapolis: University of Minnesota Press, 1986.
Kermode, Frank, and William Golding. "The Meaning of It All." *Books and Bookmen* (October 1959): 9–10.
Kershner, R. B. *The Twentieth-Century Novel: An Introduction.* Boston: Bedford Books, 1997.
Kinkead-Weekes, Mark, and Ian Gregor. *William Golding: A Critical Study.* London: Faber and Faber, 1984.
Kozicki, Henry, ed. *Developments in Modern Historiography.* Basingstoke and London: Macmillan, 1993.
Kristeva, Julia. *Desire in Language: A Semiotic Approach to Literature and Art.* Trans. Thomas Gora, Alice Jardine, and Leon S. Roudiez. New York: Columbia University Press, 1980.
———. *Powers of Horror: An Essay on Abjection.* Trans. Leon S. Roudiez. New York: Columbia University Press, 1982.
Kundera, Milan. *The Unbearable Lightness of Being.* Trans. Michael Henry Heim. London: Faber and Faber, 1985.
LaCapra, Dominick. "Bakhtin, Marxism, and the Carnivalesque." In *Rethinking Intellectual History: Texts, Contexts, Language,* by Dominick LaCapra. Ithaca: Cornell University Press, 1983.
———. *Representing the Holocaust: History, Theory, Trauma.* Ithaca: Cornell University Press, 1994.
———. "Representing the Holocaust: Reflections on the Historian's Debate." In *Probing the Limits of Representation: Nazism and "the Final Solution,"* ed. Saul Friedlander. Cambridge: Harvard University Press, 1992.
Laing, R. D. *The Divided Self: A Study of Sanity and Madness.* Chicago: Tavistock, 1960.
Laing, Stuart. "Novels and the Novel." In *Society and Literature, 1945–1970,* ed. Alan Sinfield. New York: Holmes and Meier, 1983.
———. *Representations of Working-Class Life, 1957–1964.* Basingstoke: Macmillan, 1986.
Lang, Berel. "The Representations of Limits." In *Probing the Limits of Representation: Nazism and "the Final Solution,"* ed. Saul Friedlander. Cambridge: Harvard University Press, 1992.
Langer, Lawrence L. *Admitting the Holocaust: Collected Essays.* New York and Oxford: Oxford University Press, 1995.
———. *The Holocaust and the Literary Imagination.* New Haven: Yale University Press, 1975.

Leavis, F. R. *Two Cultures? The Significance of C. P. Snow.* London: Chatto and Windus, 1962.

Lemert, Charles. "The Uses of French Structuralisms in Sociology." In *Frontiers of Social Theory: The New Syntheses,* ed. George Ritzer. New York: Columbia University Press, 1990.

Le Roy Ladurie, Emmanuel. *Carnival in Romans: A People's Uprising at Romans, 1579–1580.* Trans. Mary Feeney. Harmondsworth: Penguin, 1981.

Lessing, Doris. *The Four-Gated City.* London: Panther, 1972.

Lipstadt, Deborah. *Denying the Holocaust: The Growing Assault on Truth and Memory.* New York: Plume, 1994.

Liu, Alan. "The Power of Formalism: The New Historicism." *ELH* 56 (1989): 721–71.

Lodge, David. *After Bakhtin: Essays on Fiction and Criticism.* London: Routledge, 1990.

———. *The Modes of Modern Writing: Metaphor, Metonymy, and the Typology of Modern Literature.* London: Arnold, 1977.

Longford, Elizabeth. *Wellington: The Years of the Sword.* London: Weidenfeld and Nicolson, 1969.

Losse, D. "Rabelaisian Paradox: Where the Fantastic and the Carnivalesque Intersect." *Romantic Review* 77 (1984): 322–29.

Lyotard, Jean-François. *The Differend: Phrases in Dispute.* Trans. George Van Den Abbeele. Minneapolis: University of Minnesota Press, 1988.

———. *Heidegger and "the Jews."* Trans. Andrew Michel and Mark Roberts. Minneapolis: University of Minnesota Press, 1990.

———. *The Postmodern Condition: A Report on Knowledge.* Trans. Geoff Bennington and Brian Massumi. Manchester: Manchester University Press, 1984.

MacCabe, Colin. *James Joyce and the Revolution of the Word.* London: Macmillan, 1978.

MacKenzie, John M. "The Imperial Pioneer and Hunter and the British Masculine Stereotype in Late Victorian and Edwardian Times." In *Manliness and Morality: Middle-Class Masculinity in Britain and America, 1800–1940,* ed. J. A. Mangan and James Walvin. Manchester: Manchester University Press, 1987.

Mackenzie, Suzie. "Return of the Natives." *Guardian Weekend* (November 16, 1996): 37–42.

Marcuse, Herbert. *One-Dimensional Man.* London: Sphere Books, 1968.

Marwick, Arthur. *Culture in Britain since 1945.* Oxford and Cambridge, Mass.: Blackwell, 1991.

Maslen, Elizabeth. *Doris Lessing.* Plymouth: Northcote, 1994.

McCarron, Kevin. *The Coincidence of Opposites: William Golding's Later Fiction.* Sheffield: Sheffield Academic Press, 1995.

———. *William Golding.* Plymouth: Northcote, 1994.

McEwan, Ian. *A Move Abroad; or, "Shall We Die?" and "The Ploughman's Lunch."* London: Pan Books / Picador, 1989.

———. "Schoolboys." In *William Golding, the Man and His Books: A Tribute on His 75th Birthday,* ed. John Carey. London: Faber and Faber, 1986.

McHale, Brian. *Postmodernist Fiction.* New York and London: Methuen, 1987.

McLendon, W. L. "Compatibility of the Fantastic and Allegory: Potocki's Saragossa Manuscript." In *The Scope of the Fantastic: Theory, Technique, Major Authors,* ed. Robert A. Collins and Howard D. Pearce. Westport, Conn.: Greenwood, 1985.

McLuhan, Marshall. *The Gutenberg Galaxy: The Making of Typographic Man.* Toronto: University of Toronto, 1962.

———. *Understanding Media.* London: Routledge and Kegan Paul, 1964.

Medcalf, Stephen. *William Golding.* Harlow: Longman, 1975.

Miller, Karl. *Doubles: Studies in Literary History.* Oxford: Oxford University Press, 1985.

Miller, Paul Allen, and Charles Platter. "Introduction." *Arethusa* 26 (1993): 117–22.

Milton, John. *Paradise Lost.* Ed. Alastair Fowler. London: Longman, 1971.

Morrison, Blake. *The Movement: English Poetry and Fiction of the 1950s.* Oxford: Oxford University Press, 1980.

Morson, Gary Saul, and Caryl Emerson. *Mikhail Bakhtin: Creation of a Prosaics.* Stanford: Stanford University Press, 1990.

Mosley, Nicholas. *Rules of the Game: Sir Oswald and Lady Cynthia Mosley, 1896–1933.* London: Secker and Warburg, 1982.

Moynahan, Brian. *The British Century: A Photographic History of the Last Hundred Years.* London: Weidenfeld and Nicolson, 1997.

Nash, Richard. "Satyrs and Satire in Augustan England." In *Theorizing Satire: Essays in Literary Criticism,* ed. Brian A. Connery and Kirk Combe. New York: St. Martin's, 1995.

Nelson, William, ed. *William Golding's "Lord of the Flies": A Source Book.* New York: Odyssey, 1963.

Scholes, Robert. *The Fabulators.* New York: Oxford University Press, 1967.
Scott, Joan Wallach. *Gender and the Politics of History.* New York: Columbia University Press, 1988.
Sedgwick, Eve Kosofsky. *Between Men: English Literature and Male Homosexual Desire.* New York: Columbia University Press, 1985.
Seidel, Michael. *Satiric Inheritance: Rabelais to Sterne.* Princeton: Princeton University Press, 1979.
Sharp, Buchanan. *In Contempt of All Authority: Rural Artisans and Riot in the West of England, 1586–1660.* Berkeley and Los Angeles: University of California Press, 1980.
Shreeve, James. *The Neandertal Enigma: Solving the Mystery of Modern Human Origins.* London: Viking, 1996.
Sibley, Gay. "*Satura* from Quintilian to Joe Bob Briggs: A New Look at an Old Word." In *Theorizing Satire: Essays in Literary Criticism,* ed. Brian A. Connery and Kirk Combe. New York: St. Martin's, 1995.
Siebers, Tobin. *The Romantic Fantastic.* Ithaca: Cornell University Press, 1984.
Sim, Stuart. *Jean-François Lyotard.* Hemel Hempstead, England: Prentice-Hall, Harvester Wheatsheaf, 1996.
Sinfield, Alan. *Cultural Politics: Queer Reading.* London: Routledge, 1994.
———. *Faultlines: Cultural Materialism and the Politics of Dissident Reading.* Oxford: Clarendon Press, 1992.
———. *Literature, Politics, and Culture in Postwar Britain.* Oxford: Blackwell, 1989.
———, ed. *Society and Literature, 1945–1970.* New York: Holmes and Meier, 1983.
Skidelsky, Robert. *Oswald Mosley.* London: Macmillan, 1981.
Sontag, Susan, ed. *A Barthes Reader.* London: Jonathon Cape, 1982.
Sorel, Georges. *Reflections on Violence.* Trans. T. E. Hulme. New York: B. W. Huebsch, 1914.
Stallybrass, Peter. "'Drunk with the Cup of Liberty': Robin Hood, the Carnivalesque, and the Rhetoric of Violence in Early Modern England." In *The Violence of Representation: Literature and the History of Violence,* ed. Nancy Armstrong and Leonard Tennenhouse. London: Routledge, 1989.
Stallybrass, Peter, and Allon White. *The Politics and Poetics of Transgression.* London: Methuen, 1986.
Steiner, George. *Language and Silence: Essays, 1958–1966.* London: Faber and Faber, 1967.

Storr, Anthony. "Intimations of Mystery." In *William Golding, the Man and His Books: A Tribute on His 75th Birthday*, ed. John Carey. London: Faber and Faber, 1986.

Subbarao, V. V. *William Golding: A Study.* London: Oriental University Press, 1987.

Taffrail [Henry Taprell Dorling]. *Pincher Martin, O.D.: A Story of the Inner Life of the Royal Navy.* Edinburgh: W. and R. Chambers, 1916.

Tallis, Raymond. *In Defence of Realism.* London: Arnold, 1988.

Theweleit, Klaus. *Male Fantasies I: Women, Floods, Bodies, History.* Trans. Stephen Conway in collaboration with Erica Carter and Chris Turner. Cambridge: Polity Press, 1987.

———. *Male Fantasies II, Male Bodies: Psychoanalyzing the White Terror.* Trans. Chris Turner and Erica Carter in collaboration with Stephen Conway. Cambridge: Polity Press, 1989.

Thody, Philip. *Roland Barthes: A Conservative Estimate.* London: Macmillan, 1977.

Thompson, E. P. "Rough Music: Le Charivari Anglais." *Annales, Economies, Societes, Civilisations* 27 (1972): 285–312.

Thurlow, Richard. *Fascism in Britain: A History, 1918–1985.* Oxford: Blackwell, 1987.

Tiger, Virginia. *William Golding: The Dark Fields of Discovery.* London: Calder, 1974.

Tilly, Charles. *Charivaris, Repertoires, and Politics.* Ann Arbor: University of Michigan Press, 1980.

Todorov, Tzvetan. *The Fantastic: A Structural Approach to a Literary Genre.* Trans. Richard Howard. Cleveland: Press of the Case Western Reserve University, 1973.

———. *Mikhail Bakhtin: The Dialogical Principle.* Trans. Wlad Godwich. Manchester: Manchester University Press, 1984.

Tully, James, ed. *Meaning and Context: Quentin Skinner and His Critics.* Oxford: Polity, 1988.

Tuohy, Frank. "Baptism by Fire." *Times Literary Supplement* (November 23, 1979): 41.

Varma, Devendra P. *The Gothic Flame.* New York: Russell, 1966.

Virgil. *The Aeneid.* Trans. C. Day Lewis. Oxford: Oxford University Press, 1966.

Wain, John. "The Writer in His Age." *London Magazine* (May 1957): 51–53.

Waugh, Patricia. *Metafiction: The Theory and Practice of Self-Conscious Fiction.* London: Routledge,1984.

Wayne, Don E. "New Historicism." In *Encyclopedia of Literature and Criticism,* ed. Martin Coyle, Peter Garside, Martin Kelsall, and John Peck. London: Routledge, 1990.

Webb, W. L. "Golding Goes Down the Sea Again." *Guardian* (October 11, 1980): 12.

———. "A Vision of England amid the Encircling Gloom." *Guardian* (October 3, 1979): 16.

Welsford, Enid. *The Fool: His Social and Literary History.* London: Faber and Faber, 1935.

White, Allon. *Carnival, Hysteria, and Writing: Collected Essays and Autobiography.* Oxford: Clarendon, 1993.

———. "Hysteria and the End of Carnival: Festivity and Bourgeois Neurosis." In *The Violence of Representation: Literature and the History of Violence,* ed. Nancy Armstrong and Leonard Tennenhouse. London: Routledge, 1989.

———. *The Uses of Obscurity: The Fiction of Early Modernism.* London: Routledge and Kegan Paul, 1981.

Whitley, John S. *Golding: "Lord of the Flies."* London: Arnold, 1970.

Whittaker, Ruth. *Doris Lessing.* London: Macmillan, 1988.

Widdowson, Peter. "Introduction: The Crisis in English Studies." In *Re-Reading English,* ed. Peter Widdowson. London and New York: Methuen, 1982.

Wiesel, Elie. *Night.* Trans. Stella Rodway. Glasgow: Fontana / Collins, 1972.

Wilkinson, Paul. *The New Fascists.* London: Pan Books, 1983.

Williams, Nigel. *William Golding's "Lord of the Flies."* Acting ed. London: Faber and Faber, 1996.

Williams, Raymond. *Britain in the Sixties: Communications.* Harmondsworth: Penguin, 1962.

———. *Writing in Society.* London: Verso, 1984.

Wilson, Angus. *Hemlock and After.* 1952. Reprint, London: Secker and Warburg, 1960.

———. *No Laughing Matter.* London: Secker and Warburg, 1967.

Wilson, Scott. *Cultural Materialism: Theory and Practice.* Oxford: Blackwell, 1995.

Ziółkowski, Theodore. *Disenchanted Images: A Literary Iconography.* Princeton: Princeton University Press, 1977.

Index